He couldn't think of anything he wanted more than for Jasmine to spend the rest of the night with him.

"Need to go?" he finally asked.

Jasmine hesitated. If he'd been in her situation, he would have, too.

Covering the few steps left between them, Royce let his body act on instinct. He reached out and cupped the cool skin of her upper arms. Then he rubbed up and down, aiming to warm her. But also to fulfill his own craving to simply touch her.

She stared up at him in the dark. Beneath his touch, she shivered, then she shook her head no.

"Then come back to bed."

That first touch of skin on skin exhilarated him. He rolled over her in the bed, covering her cool body with his warmth. Savoring the gasp of air that signaled her surrender.

* * *

A Family for the Billionaire
is part of Mills & Boon Desire's No. 1
bestselling

A FAMILY FOR
THE BILLIONAIRE

BY
DANI WADE

First Published in Great Britain 2017
By Mills & Boon, an imprint of HarperCollins*Publishers*
1 London Bridge Street, London, SE1 9GF

© 2017 Katherine Worsham

ISBN: 978-0-263-92834-1

51-0917

Our policy is to use papers that are natural, renewable and recyclable products and made from wood grown in sustainable forests. The logging and manufacturing processes conform to the legal environmental regulations of the country of origin.

Printed and bound in Spain
by CPI, Barcelona

Dani Wade astonished her local librarians as a teenager when she carried home ten books every week—and actually read them all. Now she writes her own characters, who clamor for attention in the midst of the chaos that is her life. Residing in the Southern United States with a husband, two kids, two dogs and one grumpy cat, she stays busy until she can closet herself away with her characters once more.

To all the sisters who have enriched
my travels and blessed my life—
LeaAnn, Sheridan, Tammy, Hannah, Nicole,
Kim, Kira, Andrea, Marilyn, Linda and LJ.

My journeys wouldn't have
been the same without you...

One

"I assume this meeting is being conducted with the utmost confidentiality?"

"Of course," Jasmine Harden said, though she had never before had to assure a potential client of that.

"Then I'll be honest."

She eyed Royce Brazier as he paced before her in his suit and tie. The floor-to-ceiling windows of his office overlooked the river and provided the perfect backdrop. Gorgeous—the man and the view. As he paused for a moment, she noticed just a hint of something on his neck, right above his collar in the back. Was that a tattoo?

Quickly Jasmine dropped her gaze. She knew exactly how easy it was to read her expression, so she turned her thoughts in more businesslike directions.

"Besides," he continued as he faced her once more, "if word got out, I'd know where it came from, wouldn't I?"

Okay, Royce was making it a lot easier to focus on business.

"My shipping fleet has done very well, but I'm interested in taking my business to a new level. To that end, I'm aiming to attract a certain family that I hope will contract extensive work from my fleet." A frown marred Royce's smooth forehead. She could almost see the thoughts as they took hold of him. "This family is very altruistic and so I want to do a fund-raising event that appeals to them."

"So this is all about a business deal?" Though she could understand the logic Royce was working with, the conclusion was still disappointing. The hot CEO apparently didn't have a heart…

"It's purely a business endeavor. As with other projects, I'll write the check, you do the work."

Wasn't that a nice attitude? Not. Though Jasmine regularly worked with high-profile businessmen in this city, she'd never had one approach her with a proposal this cold. "Why me?" she asked quietly.

"I did my research," he said, turning a direct stare on her that made her uncomfortably aware of things other than business. "You're well known in the circles I want to attract, your clients have a very high rate of satisfaction and we use some of the same vendors, the best vendors in the city of Savannah."

His praise should make her feel better, right?

"My assistant received some wonderful feedback on you. You were rated the highest of star-quality event planners in the region.

"I only work with the best of the best. That's how I can trust you to do the work."

Why did he have to be so handsome? A handsome automaton. That slight peek at a tattoo on his neck had led her to expect more. A huff of laughter escaped as she imagined him as a true robot in her overactive imagination.

"Is there a problem?" he asked, narrowing his eyes on her as if suspicious she was making fun of him.

"Nothing." At least she hadn't giggled. That would definitely be unprofessional. "Can you tell me what charity you have in mind?" she asked, trying to get back on track.

"I don't. Pick whatever you feel is appropriate."

Jasmine blinked. Everything about this meeting was completely out of the ordinary when it came to how she worked with her clients.

"I simply need an event that is noteworthy and appropriate," he continued. "They seem to be involved in quite a few causes. Oh, and I need it in less than two months."

Oh, my. "So you think I'm a miracle worker?"

This time he relented enough to offer a small smile. "I certainly hope so. Otherwise the event will be too late to have any impact on my bid. Can I count on you?"

She thought back over their conversation. No. No. And no. "Listen, I don't think I'm the right person for this job." Or quite frankly, for this boss. She had a feeling that working for him would be a minefield, and with her life in tumult already, she didn't need a difficult boss.

He stopped his pacing to stare. "Why not?"

You're too handsome, too business minded and too cavalier about this endeavor altogether.

Only she couldn't say any of that out loud. Questions rang in Jasmine's mind as she watched him, thinking hard. She'd heard plenty about Royce Brazier, but she'd never actually met him before today, despite her extensive work with Savannah's elite. One of the city's youngest billionaires—self-made through his dedication to his quickly growing shipping business—he attended only a few select events on the social scene. Considering his reputation as a hard-nosed, focused businessman and what she'd seen during this meeting, she had a feeling he only did that much to maintain his business contacts.

His presence was commanding, his look suave and professional. So suave she wanted to mess with his perfectly placed blond hair just for the heck of it. Jasmine was professional, too, but she often had the feeling she was herding cats—especially since the arrival of Rosie… and often feared that it showed.

"Look," she tried to explain, searching for words that Royce would understand. "I realize charity events are good ways of getting positive press and word of mouth, but my events are known for having heart."

"Good. Then you can give a heart to mine."

She was still unsure how to make him understand that this wasn't a good fit for her. To her relief, his phone rang.

"Yes, Matthew?" he asked over the speaker.

"I'm sorry to bother you, sir, but your lawyer just had the agreement you requested delivered."

"I need to take a quick look at this," Royce explained to Jasmine. "Excuse me a moment."

"No problem." A few minutes to herself might give her time to regroup.

Glancing around his office, Jasmine noticed right off that there were no personal touches. No novels or magazines. No photographs of his family…or even of him with friends. A framed photo of a large building graced a prominent spot on the wall.

Jasmine couldn't imagine being this impersonal. She knew a lot of people, cared about a lot of people, but her family was her core support. Few others got to see behind her public persona. After losing her parents when she was a teenager, she couldn't imagine the devastation she would feel if she lost any other members of her family.

She'd known Royce wanted an event planned—after all, that's what she did. But his complete lack of personal interest or passion was daunting. And though there were some charities that didn't require the benefactor to be very involved, it wasn't the way she wanted to work.

But how could she convince him that a more hands-on approach was needed?

"So what do you say?" The smooth smile on Royce's face as he returned to the room was so attractive it made her chest ache. She saw a lot of powerful, pretty men in her job, but Royce had to be the pinnacle. Frankly, she wasn't sure what to do with that, either.

"Should we start talking contracts?"

Jasmine nodded, willing her expression to remain neutral. "Yes, but I have a few requirements of my own."

Royce Brazier eyed the woman before him with concern itching at his brain, though he was too smart to let it show.

Jasmine didn't seem like the bargaining type. She appeared to be nothing like the cutthroat business people he dealt with on a daily basis. So why did he detect a hint of steel in those cornflower-blue eyes?

"A bit unusual for the event planner to start making demands, isn't it?"

She arched her brow in a challenging expression, but judging from the way she was tightly clasping her hands in her lap, he had a feeling it was false bravado.

"It's definitely not my normal MO," she said. "But a girl's got to have standards."

No apology—he liked that. "Name your price."

"Oh, it's not about price." She paused for a moment as she studied him. "It's about participation."

Royce was so caught up in her beauty that he wasn't getting all the cues. "I'm not following…"

"I'll happily take on your event—I already have some great ideas. And don't get me wrong. Being given a lot of freedom is an event planner's dream. But as I said, I have certain standards. This isn't about what's easiest for me…or you. A contract will require you to participate in each step of the process—"

"I guess we could touch base via phone." Though seeing her wouldn't be a hardship. Those blue eyes and her delicate bone structure were the first things to distract Royce from his business in a long, long time.

"You will participate by attending all the meetings that I deem necessary with vendors and representatives of the charity we support."

What? Hold on a minute. "Nice try, sweetheart. I have a business to run. And more than enough to do. That's why I'm hiring someone else to do this."

"I also have a business to run. And a reputation to protect. You need to be involved for this to work. So it's my way or no way."

Royce scrambled to figure out just what was going on here. "There's plenty of other event planners in this city."

Jasmine nodded graciously, but he again got the feeling there was steel behind the genteel smile. "And you're welcome to contact any of them, but they won't have the experience *I* have with your target audience." All too soon she was up and across the room, but she paused by the door. How could just the way she glanced back at him be so sexy? Especially as she proceeded to drop a bombshell. "I would like to remind you that I do know the Jeffersons personally, and I am a frequent guest at their parties."

Shock rocketed through him. How had she known?

"You *were* referring to the Jeffersons, weren't you? I do my homework, too."

As she strode out the door with a tempting flash of leg, Royce was impressed even though he knew he shouldn't be. *Sexy and smart.* It gave her too much of an advantage.

Two

"He knew exactly what he wanted," Jasmine told her sisters, "and he wasn't backing down."

"He's never come up against you before," Willow said with a grin. Jasmine's middle sister was a tenacious Southern woman, with the temper to match her copper-colored hair. Jasmine possessed a core of the same stuff but it only made a quiet appearance when necessary. She wouldn't scream and cry, but she didn't give up until every hope had been squashed flat by a steel-toed boot.

She might look like a lady, but she had more strength than most men. The tragedies in her life had demanded it. "Well, I believe I left him with some food for thought."

"So, you were wearing your blue dress?"

Jasmine frowned. Her sister's guess hit a little too close to home. "I didn't wear the dress to entice him. It's perfectly presentable."

Her sisters shared a grin. Jasmine tried to let it go.

After all, she knew more than most that a little cleavage helped smooth the path she traveled. She'd be a fool not to take advantage of her God-given assets—especially when they'd helped her put both of her little sisters through college—in a completely respectable manner.

"Well, maybe the dress helped a little…" she admitted in a low voice as Auntie stepped into the kitchen with Rosie. The sight of her adopted daughter, and being surrounded by the people who meant the most to her in the world, filled Jasmine's heart and pushed aside thoughts of today's tedious meeting.

She reached out for six-month-old Rosie. She was in her snuggly jammies, her skin lavender-scented from her bath. As she settled into Jasmine's lap, Jasmine breathed deep. "I love you, baby girl," she whispered against Rosie's curly black hair.

Then she smiled up at the older woman. "Thank you, Auntie."

"You're most welcome," Auntie said, bending to hug Jasmine and the baby together.

Jasmine would never have made it through the first six months of Rosie's life without Auntie. Technically, she wasn't their aunt. She'd been their mother's nanny when she'd been small. She'd returned to Savannah when their mother hadn't needed her anymore.

But when the girls' parents had died, leaving them with no family at a very young age, Auntie had brought them home to Savannah. Jasmine had been a young teen, but her sisters were even younger. Auntie had finished raising them in this house and never once complained. She was as close to a mother as she could get without being a blood relation.

Each of the girls loved her just the same.

Jasmine's baby sister, Ivy, joined them at the table

with a plate of oatmeal cookies Auntie had made while they were all at work that day. "I've seen Royce Brazier at some of the meetings of the transportation planning commission, since he owns one of the biggest shipping companies on the East Coast," she said, her bright blue eyes wide. "He's pretty hunky."

Jasmine could practically see every set of ears around the table perk up.

Ivy continued, "But I've heard he's all business, 24/7."

Jasmine agreed. "He made that very clear."

Willow pouted. "What's the fun in that?"

"Dealing with demands is a lot easier when they're pretty," Ivy said, with a grimace that still managed to look cute.

Jasmine threw her napkin across the table at her sister, making a sleepy Rosie giggle.

"The last thing I have time for right now is a man," Jasmine insisted.

Her cell phone gave a quiet chirp, which was the ringtone she used at home so she didn't accidentally wake the baby. She glanced at the screen. "He certainly is a workaholic," she mused as she handed Rosie over to her youngest sister. She hadn't expected to see Royce's name on the caller ID at this time of night—or at all, really. She'd assumed he would never go for her conditions. Which had made her sad, because she could have used the work. But she had her principles.

She needed to remember that.

"This is Jasmine," she answered, walking toward the door to the front parlor as her sisters mimed something and Auntie watched them indulgently.

"Brazier here."

She smiled. *I know.* "What can I do for you?"

"After careful consideration, I've decided to renegotiate our terms, if that's still possible."

Interesting. "May I ask why?"

"Well, you certainly have a lot to offer."

Was she just imagining his voice growing deeper?

He went on. "So I'll agree to your terms—within reason."

"Meaning?"

"I'll attend meetings with the charity and vendors and such, but I'm not decorating rooms or tying bows or stuffing bags. Understood?"

Good thing he couldn't see her smile. "Feel free to email me your demands and I'll consider them."

"You can't talk now?" he asked.

"Roy—Mr. Brazier. It's a little late. Almost nine o'clock." And Rosie would need to go to sleep soon.

"Is your husband impatient for you to get off the phone?"

Okay, no way had she imagined that change in tone. Choosing to ignore his question, because it was fun to keep him guessing, she countered, "Don't you have a family waiting for you to shut down?"

"No. A man with my schedule shouldn't have a family—it isn't fair to them."

She thought of the little girl in the other room—how sometimes it was hard to force herself out the door in the morning because being away from Rosie left her feeling incomplete. Of course, life hadn't afforded her the chance to stay home with Rosie—and there were plenty of family members in the house to keep her occupied until Mommy came home. "Commendable of you to realize that." Though most men usually didn't think that way.

"Simply practical—but you didn't answer my question."

And she didn't plan to... "Working 24/7 isn't good for anyone."

"You enjoy your beauty sleep?"

This conversation was definitely off the business track—her brain derailed into forbidden thoughts of him in her bed. "I'll watch for your email," she said, hoping she didn't sound too breathless.

She disconnected and returned to the other room. Her sisters were silent until she tried to pass, then they started in.

"Oh, Royce," Ivy said, gasping with an extra dash of drama. "I must, simply must, have your email."

"Is your wife waiting for you to get off the phone?" Willow teased.

"He asked first," Jasmine protested.

"Which just gave you permission to dig."

"It's a business deal." Why did she have a feeling she was trying to convince herself?

"It doesn't have to be," Auntie said as Jasmine lifted a sleeping Rosie into her arms.

Jasmine lowered her voice. "Not you, too, Auntie."

"Your mother would not want you to be alone."

The sisters froze at Auntie's words. She rarely butted into their personal lives; though she was free with her help and guidance, her one very short marriage hadn't qualified her to give advice to the lovelorn—according to her. So this was rare.

"I'm not," Jasmine insisted. "I have you, the girls, Rosie. What do I need a man for?"

"I love the little one, too, and all you girls," Auntie said. "But you keep yourself tucked away, protected. Your mother, despite everything she lost, still pushed forward and allowed love in. She would want that for all of you."

Jasmine studied her sisters, who looked at each other

slightly abashed. Theirs was a tight circle, and other than casual dates in high school and college, no man had ever infiltrated it. No man had even come home for dinner. And the sisters had always lived together, even through college.

They were their own island oasis. The thought of that changing sent a streak of unease through Jasmine.

As if reading her mind, Auntie nodded at her. "Keeping your circle small is not going to protect you from pain, Jasmine." She smiled sadly. "It's time, my sweets."

"For what?" Willow asked when no one else would.

Jasmine didn't want to know. Rosie was all the change she could handle in her safe little world. Her only challenges were in her career and she preferred to keep it that way. But when Auntie spoke in that all-knowing voice, things usually happened. Whether anyone wanted them to or not.

The older woman got up and crossed to the door. Jasmine could hear her progress up the stairs and eventually back down in the historic, but sturdy, home. Auntie came straight to Jasmine, leaving her with the feeling she'd been found by an unerringly accurate arrow.

Dropping into the chair next to her, Auntie held out a small jeweler's box. Willow and Ivy leaned across the table for a better look.

"Your mother wanted you girls to have this," Auntie said as she opened the box. "I found it with her things, packed away with a letter."

Inside lay a ring with a teardrop-shaped emerald stone surrounded by decorative gold filigree. They all gasped—Jasmine included. It was an involuntary reflex. The ring was gorgeous. Not only that, it seemed to have something…something special that Jasmine couldn't quite put her finger on.

"Wait!" Willow said. "I remember Mama wearing that—she said it was an heirloom or something…"

"Indeed," Auntie confirmed. "It was passed down to her from her mother, who received it from her mother, and so on."

Jasmine stared at the beautiful jewel, a sudden memory of it on her mother's hand filling her mind. Her mother had been dressed up. An anniversary dinner, maybe? She and their father hadn't ever gone to fancy parties and such. About as fancy as it got was her father's Christmas gathering for the professors at the university where he taught. But she remembered her mother letting her stroke one small finger over the emerald. What had she said?

Then Auntie spoke, "Legend has it—"

Willow squealed. Jasmine groaned. Auntie gave them both an indulgent smile. Willow was the resident myth and legend hunter. She'd truly followed in their father's footsteps, teaching history at the local community college. She loved tall tales, mysteries and spooky stories. She propped her chin on her palm, avidly awaiting Auntie's words.

Jasmine just shook her head.

"Legend has it," Auntie started again, "that this ring was given to the woman who founded your family line by the man she married."

"Here in Savannah?" Ivy asked.

"Oh, yes. He was a pirate, you see, and she was the beautiful but shy daughter of a prominent family here."

Jasmine had tried hard to forget that their family had once been wealthy and respected. Long before the scandal that had rocked their safe little world.

Auntie went on. "He didn't think he had any chance to catch her eye, so he simply admired her from afar. But on his travels, he came into possession of this ring. He was told by the old man he bought it from that the ring would bring the person who owned it true love."

"Ooh," Willow said, her grin growing bigger and bigger.

"Sure enough, he was able to win his woman's hand... and the ring has been passed down to every generation of your family ever since. Each has claimed its power is real."

Ever the skeptic, Jasmine couldn't help but add, "And look how that worked for them. Scandals, death. Our family has some of the worst luck ever."

When Ivy's hopeful expression fell, it made Jasmine feel like a big bully.

"It's said to bring its owner true love, not an easy life," Auntie gently admonished, ever the voice of wisdom. "Besides, if the scandal hadn't driven your grandparents out of Savannah, then your mother and father might never have met."

Jasmine didn't want to disrespect the memory of her parents, but... "A ring did not cause them to find each other—being in the same place at the same time did."

"Maybe so—"

"Don't be a realist, Jasmine," Willow complained. "Embrace the magic."

Ivy reached over to take the sleeping baby and snuggled her close. Rosie gave a shuddering sigh. "Is it really healthy to teach Rosie that there's no magic, no romance in the world?"

"She's only six months old," Jasmine protested. "Besides, I didn't say that—" Jasmine created magic every day with her events, or rather, the *feeling* of magic.

Willow added her two cents' worth, even though Jasmine considered her biased. "Yeah, Jasmine, haven't you ever heard of Cinderella? Rapunzel? Beauty? Wendy? Dorothy?"

"You want me to convince Rosie there's magic in the world by indulging this nonsense and snaring a man?"

"No—the man is just a bonus," Ivy said with a giggle.

"An uptight CEO?" Jasmine couldn't believe she was hearing this.

Ivy wasn't deterred. "The uptight CEO with thick hair, muscular build and a tight a—"

Willow gasped and covered the sleeping baby's ears. "Ivy!"

Ivy grimaced. "But yes—that is a bonus. You just need to sweeten him up a little."

"For Rosie?"

"Yes!" her sisters said in unison.

"She needs a man around," Ivy went on. "After all, we didn't have one. How can we possibly teach her anything about men?"

They all paused, silently weighing the loss of their father. The only man they could remember being part of their family...and that was a long, long time ago.

Auntie finally weighed in. "She's already going to hear enough reality when she gets older and learns what happened to her birth mother," she reminded Jasmine with a sad look.

"Or are you just afraid the ring will actually work?" Willow jumped in.

Was she? Jasmine secretly admitted that all the loss she'd suffered in her young life made her reluctant to let someone else in. Only dire circumstances had brought Rosie to her. Jasmine had adopted her as a newborn at the behest of the little girl's dying mother. A woman Jasmine had come to know at the City Sanctuary mission where she'd volunteered—and then lost when Rosie's mother succumbed to the cancer she'd never been able to afford to have treated properly.

"The ring is for all of you girls, but I think Jasmine has a unique opportunity here to prove her point…or ours." Auntie held out the ring box once more, smiling as if she understood Jasmine's dilemma all too well. "A little magic never hurt anyone," she said.

Somehow, Jasmine didn't believe that.

Three

So much for that businesslike attitude. Jasmine tapped her stiletto heel as she glanced at her watch once more. *He's twenty minutes late.*

She knew traffic hadn't held him up. The coffee shop she'd chosen for her brainstorming meeting with Royce was right near his office building. As she watched the boats on the river and the tourists wander by on the sidewalk, she struggled with her impatience.

Yes, something probably came up: a business call, papers to sign, something.

But why hadn't someone called? She'd sent the contract in plenty of time. Her racing thoughts were driving her crazy.

I'll wait ten more minutes.

Just sitting here was annoying her all the more, so she dumped her coffee and set off toward his office building.

The gorgeous architecture and sweet smell of pralines

from a riverside candy shop didn't calm her agitation as she walked over the stone pathways. Tension built up inside—a problem she'd never had with her clients. What was it about this guy? Usually she could just breathe and reroute her focus to where it needed to go in order to produce forward momentum toward their mutual goals.

Not today.

Days spent wondering what that tattoo was on his neck, whether his hair was mussed when he rolled out of bed in the morning or if he ever did anything but work had taken her to places she hadn't wanted to go. And the stupid ring wasn't helping.

She glanced down at the emerald she wasn't used to having on her right hand. So stupid. But if she backed down now, her sisters would never let her hear the end of it. So she'd prove to them that the legend wasn't real—and teach Rosie there were plenty of special things in life without magic.

Her phone started vibrating in her hand. Glancing down, Jasmine mumbled under her breath, "Well, it's about time."

"Hello, Mr. Brazier," she said.

His tone was as clipped as hers. "I need to postpone. Please come to my office in an hour." He was so short, she wondered if he even realized he was talking to an actual person.

"Excuse me?"

"Come here in an hour," he repeated.

Click.

An hour? Jasmine paused to scroll through the calendar on her phone. *Oh, my.* Since Royce had only allotted an hour for their meeting, Jasmine hadn't worried about the tight timeline she had for this morning. An hour would put her right smack in the middle of Auntie's doctor's appointment. Willow was in class. Ivy was at work. Which left…well, no one to watch Rosie. Except her.

He probably wasn't going to like how that went… But then again, he hadn't really given her much choice in the matter. It was time Mr. Brazier got his first lesson in seeing the person behind the business opportunity.

When Jasmine walked into the outer office a little over an hour later, Matthew's eyes widened. "Miss Harden, I'm so sorry." His eyes widened further—if that was even possible—as he glanced down. "I—"

"Just announce me, please, Matthew," she said with an overly sweet smile.

Her stomach fluttered from the nerves rushing through her in waves, but she reminded herself necessity took this out of her hands. Besides, he'd brought it on himself.

Jasmine went through the door while Royce continued to talk on the phone. His back was to her. Taking advantage of his distraction, she turned and smiled down at her surprise. Then she lifted Rosie from her stroller and turned to find Royce staring at her backside.

Jasmine should have been offended, but his distraction played to her advantage in this instance. When he finally realized where he was staring and looked up, the switch from lust to shock in his normally schooled expression was priceless.

"What's this?" he sputtered as he jumped to his feet.

Jasmine ignored Rosie's cooing, because breaking her businesslike facade wouldn't be to her advantage right now. "You told me to meet you here."

He frowned, proving himself to be heartless. No one could look at Rosie and refuse to smile. No way could he be human. "My office isn't a day care," he insisted.

"And my time is very tightly scheduled today," she

said with an arch of her brows. "I have commitments, just like you."

"I can't help that my earlier meeting ran over," he said defensively, straightening in his seat.

Jasmine took a deep breath, then blew it out slowly, pulling her chaotic thoughts from the last hour together. "Let me ask you a question," she began.

After Royce nodded, she continued. "Would you have called any of your fellow businessmen and given them commands about when to show up at your office?"

The surprise on his face only confirmed her suspicions.

"If I were one of your managers or the owner of one of your supply companies instead of an event planner, would you have had Matt contact me to reschedule instead of rudely cutting off our conversation earlier?"

"That's not why—"

"I made arrangements for a sitter as soon as this meeting was scheduled. I don't like to disrupt my daughter's schedule by carting her around to my business meetings. But by changing our scheduled time and refusing to discuss it with me or give me any options, I had no other choice...unless I wanted to be a no-show myself."

He didn't respond. His narrowed gaze still made her want to squirm, but she refused to back down.

"Now I'm very much looking forward to working with you, but my business is people. Is our phone conversation earlier how you conduct business? How you deal with your fellow business people and the community at large? Because it isn't how I conduct my business."

Lesson number one was over. The ball was in Royce's court now.

Rosie continued to coo, then snuggled against Jasmine as she settled into a chair with her child in her lap. This would never have worked if Rosie had a different temperament, but Jasmine happened to know that her daughter was one of the most easygoing babies in the world. She just hoped this was Royce's only lesson in seeing the people behind the business.

"If that's going to be a problem," she said, "then I release you from your contract right now."

He glanced back and forth between her and Rosie, as if he still couldn't catch the connection between his earlier behavior and having a baby in his office. But then he slowly shook his head. "No. I don't want to cancel our contract."

She wanted to ask why, but figured she'd pushed her luck enough for today.

"Maybe we should reschedule?" Royce said, staring down at them with a frown.

"Why?" Jasmine asked. "I'm here now. Your schedule appears to be free at the moment, which it hasn't been for the last two weeks. Let's talk."

When he hesitated, she prompted. "If we don't get started soon, we'll miss your window of opportunity. I can't work miracles in two months. And neither can the vendors I hire."

Royce's careful expression returned as he took his seat. "I've found most people have a price that will motivate them."

"And that's the difference between the two of us."

Surprise momentarily replaced his serious expression. "What do you mean by that?"

"Just that I prefer to endear myself to people," she said, keeping her tone even and calm, not accusing. "I find they're much more willing to work hard, which makes life easier and the results quicker, if I'm nice."

"As opposed to employing coercion?" His smirk reminded her of exactly how they'd gotten into this situation.

"Sometimes other tactics are necessary," she conceded, "but it definitely makes things messy and uncomfortable for everyone. Confrontation might be a necessity at times, but I don't like it."

They shared a look of mutual understanding. Royce agreed with a nod. "But it is interesting."

Interesting, indeed.

Royce studied the woman in front of him, carefully avoiding looking at the raven-haired child in her lap. The sight of the little girl in his office brought too many mixed emotions.

He'd never been so far off his game that he wasn't sure where to begin...until this moment. But he wasn't about to let Jasmine Harden know that. She was proving her point...he wasn't about to help her.

For a moment, he second-guessed his decision to continue with this conversation. Heck, this whole project. But it wasn't just her connection to the Jeffersons that kept him from calling a halt right now.

Deep down, as uncomfortable as this entire incident made him, his instincts told him a woman who was this passionate about people was perfect to create the event that would connect him to others who were just as passionate.

"So, what do you have for me?" he finally asked.

The twitch of her lips suggested she knew exactly how uncomfortable he was. She shifted the baby into the crook of her arm with the ease of an earth mother, despite her power suit, and started her pitch.

"I want to do a masquerade."

Masquerade? "Like a dance?"

A half smile formed on her elegant red lips. Why did they have to be shaped so perfectly? He'd promised himself he would keep his thoughts on business...not on the woman. And he'd succeeded until the minute he'd seen her in person again.

Then she'd had to insist on him seeing her as a person. This wasn't helping him with his perspective at all.

"Sort of. A masquerade includes dancing. The key focus is the anonymity. Each participant wears a mask, which lends itself to a mysterious atmosphere."

"Isn't the point for people to know me?" He had to admit, he wasn't an imaginative kind of guy. At least, not in this area. Give him a logistics problem with his shipping company and his brain went into overdrive. Fantasy? Not really.

"Oh, they will," she assured him. "There will be announcements throughout the evening of the money being raised so everyone will be aware of the sponsor. But for the *participants*, the atmosphere is key."

She reached into her oversize bag to pull out a tablet. Flipping the cover open, she deftly pulled up what she was looking for. "As you can see, this gives us a theme to work with—a theme our target audience will find very attractive."

Without missing a beat, she set the device upright on his desk and flipped through pictures on the screen of lavish decorations and food and costumes. The only thing Royce saw were dollar signs.

"This looks awfully expensive."

Jasmine raised her brows at him. "Is money a problem?"

How could she make him feel like a schoolboy with a single look? "It isn't unlimited," he insisted.

"I wouldn't think so, but you said you wanted to make an impression."

Royce studied the last photo. A woman in a fitted dress and feather mask was laughing up at a man in a black tux. The woman's dark hair reminded him of Jasmine's... No—she was an employee. An employee with a baby.

Totally off limits.

"Why can't we just do a dinner?" he asked.

Of course, she had to counter with, "Why would anyone want to come?"

He studied the picture, realizing how totally out of his element he was. Maybe she'd been right to get him more involved. He had no idea how to attract people to anything other than a business deal.

"The draw at a charitable event isn't even the charity," she said, "which is a shame, but true."

A shuffling sound had him looking up. The baby's chubby cheeks and pale round face surrounded by a halo of inky black hair made her look like a cherub. She stared at him with her eyelids at half mast, thumb firmly held between her lips. When had the cooing stopped?

Jasmine leaned over to reach into the back of the stroller. When she straightened, she held a bottle that the baby eagerly reached for. Royce couldn't help but notice that there wasn't a ring on Jasmine's ring finger. No wedding band? He should have been even more upset by this situation, given his own childhood. Instead, a relief he was ashamed of snaked through him.

The fact that she was available shouldn't matter to him.

Settling back into the chair, Jasmine cuddled the sleepy child against her chest. The juxtaposition of working woman and mother unsettled him. His own mother had never seemed that at ease. Royce had always felt like he hindered her work whenever he was around.

"People want to be entertained," Jasmine said. "You have to sell an experience in order to get people to show up and spend their money. Build something that intrigues them and they'll tell all their friends and soon you'll have people begging for tickets."

The brief flicker of her thick lashes as she looked down at the dozing child in her lap had him holding his breath until she looked back up. But then she narrowed her gaze on him, giving him the uncomfortable feeling that she saw more than he wanted her to. "The more people who talk about wanting to attend, the more likely the buzz will get back to the Jeffersons. The name connected to the event matches the name on the newest bid they received. Mission accomplished—or at least you'll have made progress."

Royce was far more comfortable talking strategy than entertainment. "I wondered how we would make that connection."

She seemed to pull the baby a touch closer in her arms. He didn't want to notice, didn't want to think about the child. Royce had never attended a business meeting that gave rise to this many emotions—unease, lust, surprise, irritation. How long until this meeting was over?

"Besides being the talk of the town?" she asked. Her smile turned as mysterious as the woman in the photograph. "I may have a few tricks up my sleeve. After all, we need to get the word out in certain circles...so I thought I would use a few exclusive invitations I receive to introduce you around, talk it up."

"You want me to make social appearances...with you?" As if social appearances weren't awkward enough for him.

She nodded. "Including at the Jeffersons' Sunday Salon."

"You get invited?" So, she hadn't been exaggerating when she'd claimed a connection.

"About every other month."

The Sunday Salon was a coveted invite that didn't come around that often for most people. The Jeffersons must adore Jasmine Harden, which told Royce he'd made the right choice of event planner—even if he didn't feel all that comfortable with it.

"All right," he said. "Tell me more."

He couldn't complain that Jasmine wasn't thorough. In ten minutes, he knew more than he really wanted to, but he had no doubt she was the best woman for the job. Before she finished he was convinced she would oversee every detail and nothing would be missed. She addressed every aspect of the planning, including quite a few things he never would have thought about.

"So what do you think?" she asked.

A lot of things he couldn't say at the moment—because they were completely unbusinesslike. Luckily she wasn't looking at him as she efficiently laid the baby down in the stroller. Was it terrible of him that he didn't know the child's name and was afraid to ask?

"Sounds good," he said, eager to be away from all the churning thoughts this meeting had raised. "Send the mock-up and budget projections to Matthew. Let me know when you need me for anything."

Her brows rose at his short tone, but she didn't question him. "I'll do that." She gathered her bag and tablet, then faced him once more. "When you look at the budget, remember that successful events involve getting all the details right, and that takes a lot of people."

"While logically I understand that—" and he truly

was getting on board with the concept "—I still have to look at the bottom line."

Jasmine stared at him a moment; he detected the barest hint of an eye roll before her thick lashes swooped down. "Let's put it this way—is the time and money worth it to gain the new contract?"

Her words registered, but instead of thinking about business, Royce found himself holding his breath, waiting to see if she would look back up and show him those intense blue eyes once more. Then the baby let out a big sigh and broke the spell.

As Jasmine leaned over to look into the stroller, he forcibly pulled himself back to reality—and the knowledge that this woman was off limits in more ways than one.

"Yes, it is," he said. "You may proceed."

"Okay—we will need to start with the charity."

"I've told you it doesn't matter to me. Pick whatever you want."

"I have. You'll be helping raise money for a new building for the City Sanctuary homeless mission."

Royce nodded even as he tuned her out—though it wasn't as easy as he would have liked. He didn't care about the details—didn't want to care. He also didn't want to care about her thick hair and expressive face or the curves highlighted by the black power suit she wore.

"Also, we need to pick a venue right away. What dates would work for viewing possible locations?"

Her sharpened tone caused Royce to snap back to attention. She hadn't been kidding about the participation thing. Her long stare reinforced her message.

"Check with Matthew. He'll know what's available."

Smartly she stood up and pointed the stroller toward the door.

Royce had the sudden conviction that he couldn't let her walk out the door without making himself clear, as well. "I realize my point of view isn't a popular one these days, but as the child of a hardworking single mother myself, I have a strong opinion about children in the workplace," he said.

Glancing back at him, she asked, "What's that?"

"My office isn't a day care but I do apologize for my rudeness on the phone."

She gifted him with a sexy smile that had no place in his office, as much as he wished it did. But then came the sass. "Remember that and we will work together just fine."

Before he could respond, she pushed the stroller out the door. He heard her tell Matthew goodbye with that same sweet tone—this time with no steel undercurrents. She was definitely infuriating and intriguing.

Thoroughly dangerous territory.

Four

He'd thought about not showing up at all.

Staring up at the austere lines of the museum Jasmine had chosen as a possible venue, he wished he had ditched their meeting. But standing her up again was not a good option. She'd taught him that much.

Besides, his mama would have considered it ungentlemanly to simply ditch her—even if memories of his mama were what made him not want to show up at the museum in the first place.

But he had to stand firm. Today, he would take back the reins because he would not hold his event in a building he could no longer set foot in—much less play host in for an evening.

He was still staring at the building when Jasmine pulled up beside him in a pristine compact sedan. After climbing out, she smiled at him.

"Well, look at you," she said, her voice as teasing as it

had been that first night on the phone when he'd called her. He didn't like to acknowledge the tingles of anticipation that hit him when he heard it—which were just as strong this morning as they had been then.

"I was a little unsure that you'd actually show up," she went on, "much less arrive early."

The tingle of anticipation grew, only this time it was for the challenge he knew was ahead of him. Still he struggled to keep any emotion from his expression.

"There's no point in going inside," he said, letting his tone match what he hoped was his deadpan expression.

Her frown as she shut the door and walked around the front of her car warned him that she was thinking hard about this turn of events. "May I ask why?"

"We aren't having my event here."

She glanced back over her shoulder at the building behind her, the multiple columns majestically holding up the austere gabled roof with its carved marble depiction of birds. When she turned to him, confusion reigned in those gorgeous blue eyes. "Again, may I ask why?"

"I don't want it here." And he didn't. No need for discussion about his troubled childhood or dead mother. "Personal reasons."

"Are they good enough reasons?" she asked, tossing her hair over her shoulder.

"It is when I'm signing the checks."

Her expression told him she wanted to be offended, even when she knew he was right. But she wasn't simply accepting his decree. "I thought you didn't want to be involved in the decisions?" she demanded.

This wasn't the same as dealing with any of his other business associates. When they slapped their hands to their hips, he never noticed the sway of their breasts. He shouldn't be noticing Jasmine's now, but somehow he couldn't help himself.

"And you said you wanted me to be involved in making the decisions," he reminded her. "Which is it?"

That little intake of air pushed her breasts out just a touch more. Heaven help him.

She nodded. He could tell she wanted further explanation. He wasn't giving it.

Finally she turned away, giving him a break from that penetrating gaze. "Let me go touch base with the manager," she said. "I need to stay on good terms here."

"Of course."

"Then we'll talk," she warned. Her heels clicked on the sidewalk as she strode away.

He waited until she went inside the museum before pulling out his phone. "Hey, Joseph," he said when his construction manager picked up. "How are things looking today?"

Joseph filled him in on the details of the kitchen installation at Royce's supersecret project, as well as other aspects of the restoration.

"Another day on track," Joseph confirmed.

"Good."

Royce hung up, a spur-of-the-moment idea buzzing in his brain. He had the lucky ability to run through all the immediate pros and cons of a decision in a relatively short amount of time. This had helped him jump on opportunities that other businesses spent months preparing for. Along with his intense drive, he'd used this to build his business to magnificent proportions at a very young age.

Today this ability would certainly come in handy.

He waited until Jasmine returned down the walk fifteen minutes later. His relief at finally being able to leave the site of one of his most traumatic childhood experiences was tempered with his desire to covertly take her in.

Jasmine seemed to enjoy ultrafeminine clothing. Even when she'd had the baby with her, she'd been wearing a women's business suit with a skirt and an undershirt with lace lining the deep V of the collar. Today, the bodice of her navy dress hugged curves that he normally wouldn't notice. But on her they made his mouth water. An inverted triangle cut out over her cleavage added to the effect. The flowing skirt that ended right below her knees revealed just enough of her legs to be tantalizing.

Was she trying to torture him?

"All done," she said as she approached. "What now?"

Oh, she was gonna love this. "I have an alternative. Let's go."

"Now?" Her frown was back.

"No time like the present. I'll drive."

But as they settled into the small space of his luxury sedan and the dark, sexy scent of her snuck up on him, he had to wonder whether he had made a wise choice.

Or was this self-sabotage?

Of all the things Jasmine had expected to do today, riding in the front seat of Royce's car was not one of them. The smooth, heavy scent of well-cared-for leather and a slight hint of aftershave teased her senses, making her notice things she wished she didn't.

This is business. This is business.

"Why don't you have a driver?" she asked, letting the first question that occurred to her pop out in an awkward attempt at conversation.

He glanced her way before returning his attention to the road. "That's a rather pretentious question, don't you think?"

"Actually it's simple curiosity that springs from experience," she corrected. "I've worked with a lot of Savannah's upper class. Most have their own drivers—at least, under certain circumstances."

The road was familiar to her from having lived in Savannah since she was fifteen years old. Though a lot of fine old houses could be found in the surrounding areas, she couldn't think of any in this particular direction. Where was he taking her?

She tempered her curiosity with more questions about his driverless state. If she had to be thrown off her game plan for the morning, at least she could work toward finding the human behind the robot. "You're the youngest billionaire in Savannah," she reminded him. "Heck, the entire South. Doesn't a driver come with that title?"

"That title came with a lot of hard work. Besides, I love to drive."

"So you're human?"

His locked-down tone surprised her. "More than you know."

Great. Her curiosity was growing like an overinflated balloon. Pretty soon she might explode from it—but that was better than drooling over his blond good looks.

"Why won't you share those personal reasons with me?"

She wasn't sure why she asked. Maybe to get herself away from her attraction to Royce. Maybe to dig deeper into the mysteries she had begun to see. If she hadn't been watching his face, she'd have missed the flicker of surprise that appeared on his expression before he shut back down.

"I told you, I don't want to talk about it."

He had, but that wouldn't stop her from trying. "Sometimes it helps."

"Not true."

Stubborn man. "Have you ever even tried?" She suspected not, considering that he seemed like the all-business-all-the-time type.

She could tell her question annoyed him by the way he tightened his hands on the steering wheel. "We're almost there," he said, instead of answering.

Fine.

Then Jasmine looked around, realizing exactly how far out of town they were. Uneasiness started to grow deep inside. "You realize that the farther we are from town, the less likely people are to attend the event, right?"

"Oh, they'll show up for this."

His confident tone didn't turn her into a believer— after all, she was the expert in this business.

The minute he turned down a particular driveway, her fears were confirmed. She'd only been down this driveway once. A very long time ago, and only by accident. Later when she'd started researching the place, she'd realized what it was. They could not have their event here.

"Royce, no." Her grip on the seat tightened as tension took hold of her. "We can't do this here. Do you know how long Keller House has been empty?"

"It was empty for over twenty years," he said. "The carriage house has been occupied for five years. It's currently the home of the caretaker."

Okay, so maybe she didn't know everything. "But the main house must be in need of hundreds of thousands of dollars of renovations."

"Four hundred thousand in renovations, to be exact," Royce said. She swore she could hear a smirk in his voice. "And that doesn't include the back gardens, which can't be started on until closer to spring."

She eyed him suspiciously as he pulled the car to a halt

before the front steps. He looked back with perfect calm, so she turned her attention to the house. The massive gray stone building seemed sad and silent from where she sat. "And how do you know that, Royce?"

He ignored her as he exited the vehicle. She stared up at the imposing edifice, waiting for him to come around to open her door. When he did, she got out and stood in the space between the door and the car to look him straight in the eye.

"I can't oversee renovations while I'm doing an event," she said. "And what owner in the middle of renovations would want an event here?"

"No, the renovations are my job. The event is yours," he said, enunciating clearly. "Just get out of the car."

I've gone from dealing with a difficult boss to biting off more than I can chew. Jasmine stepped away from the car and stood before the mammoth building. It was gorgeous, even in its rundown state. Ivy climbed up one corner. Though cracked in a few places, the gray stone still lent a majesty to the structure. Even the steps were made of it. She could imagine women walking up them in huge hoop skirts on their way to a ball here.

"I've always been curious about this place," she said. "My sister, who is a big history buff, says that the Kellers used to be the most prominent family in Savannah. Their house was detailed in many newspaper accounts and gossip columns throughout the years. But then the entire family was wiped out by smallpox."

"Shall we go inside?" he asked.

She met his gaze. "You're serious about this?"

"I am. We will hold the masquerade here."

She glanced between him and the house that hadn't been a home to anyone in a long time. He'd gone from uninvolved to highly involved more quickly than she could wrap her brain around. "So you are a bit of a philanthropist," she said.

"No. Real estate is a good investment."

But as he turned away she glimpsed something in his expression. Something he probably didn't want her to see. She had a feeling that like the building before her, he was hiding an awful lot behind that facade of his.

Five

Just a quick walk through to see the current state of renovations, let Jasmine take a quick peek and then they'd head back to the city. That was Royce's plan, and, by damn, he was sticking to it this time.

But it wasn't helping that he found her caution amusing as she stepped through the massive antique double doors. Clearly, she expected the inside of Keller House to be a disaster.

Granted, the exterior still needed work, but there was plenty of time to get to that. The exterior would be a years-long project, just as the inside had been. And the craggy, cracked surface had character that Royce kind of enjoyed.

The wonder on her face as she took in the already renovated foyer made his heart speed up. Royce quickly looked away. *No distractions. Focus.* He had a feeling her enthusiasm, in addition to being attractive, would be infectious.

But he was here for business.

As per his usual MO, he mentally identified what he needed to do. Then he started purposefully down the main hallway that cut the house virtually in half. The kitchen lay at the other end, which was where he hoped to find his construction crew hard at work.

"Wow! Is this staircase the original? Or a reproduction?"

Royce froze. "It's the original," he conceded, then moved a few more steps. Maybe if he kept moving, she would follow.

Her gorgeous blue eyes were roving up and down the magnificent two-story structure. "It's beautiful," she breathed. "Who did the renovations?"

He took a few more steps, even though she hadn't budged. "Jasmine, I don't have much time to get this done, so if we could move on—"

She nodded and moved to follow, though her gaze stayed glued to the refinished mahogany and blue tile patterns along the edges of the steps. He turned away and picked up speed. His brain started to produce a list of all the things he needed to discuss with the foreman.

"All these tiles…are they Italian?"

Royce heard the question but kept moving.

At first he thought he heard her following, but then the footsteps stopped and her voice sounded farther away. Royce paused, glancing over his shoulder. No Jasmine in sight. Then he realized what room she had disappeared into.

The ballroom. Of course that would interest her.

The urgent pull of business needled him to keep going. She could explore while he got things done. Problem solved. But there was also the worry that she would wander somewhere that she could get hurt. Not all the rooms were finished. Since they hadn't been expecting company, the dangerous areas weren't necessarily marked.

Then there was the question of her excitement and how he wanted to read it in her expression as she explored. He shouldn't care. The fact that he was even thinking about this meant he should keep going. Instead his steps took him back toward the open doorway.

The ballroom walls had been carefully stripped of ancient wallpaper to reveal intricate painted murals. They'd decided to clean and preserve them as is, rather than recreating them. Wear and tear showed in spots, but it was the kind of damage that one would find in an antique museum piece. It simply added to the charm. The crown molding surrounding the windows, murals and chandelier bases had been stripped and refinished in an off white. Eggshell, his mother had called it.

The elaborate crystal chandeliers had been refinished and rewired. The wood floor had been stripped of decades of dirt and grime and was waiting to be stained and protected with a thick coat of polyurethane. There was still a series of mirrors waiting to be hung.

The room was a showpiece in and of itself.

Jasmine twirled slowly in the center, taking in all the delights. She stopped as she came to face him. Some of his indecision must have come across as irritation in his expression, because her eyes widened for a moment.

Then a grin that could only be classified as cute spread across her face. "I can't help it," she said. "I need to see what I'm gonna have to work with."

"So you *do* approve?"

The expression he'd come to associate with her trying to figure out a way around him made a quick appearance. "Possibly." She turned away. The skirt of her dress swirled with her movements, giving him another glance at sculpted calves and pretty ankles. Didn't the woman ever wear pants?

"But I will need to see more before we know for sure."

Vixen. The minute the word crossed his mind, Royce had second thoughts. After all, he'd never thought about any of the other women he worked with, now or in the past, in such a way. It was surely inappropriate. But completely and totally true.

Jasmine knew exactly what she was doing—keeping him on his toes.

Resigning himself, he gestured for her to continue down the hall. "Everything else on this floor has been completed, except the kitchens." He hoped. "That's what I need to check on today."

As they made their way down the hall, he opened various doors. She got to explore. He got to maintain forward momentum. Win-win.

Only every peek into a room elicited the same excitement as a child opening presents on Christmas morning. The first gasps jumpstarted his heart, even though he tried to ignore them—and his physical reaction.

"Are these fixtures original?" she asked.

He nodded, warming to one of his favorite subjects outside of business. He and his mother had had two things in common—antiques and cooking. Their shared interests had strengthened their bond.

"All of the fixtures are original, unless they were broken beyond repair. Some of the back rooms had busted windows and weather damage, so we had to do some extensive replacements there. Everywhere else, I had what I could refinished. Some of the electrical components had to be updated. But the feel of the original should be maintained wherever possible—"

He noticed her watching him and felt a moment of unfamiliar self-consciousness. "In my opinion," he added. An opinion he had only shared with his contractor and his mother when she was still alive. Not only was it no one else's business, Royce had always found himself extremely protective of projects that he was full-on enthusiastic about.

Projects that sparked his creativity and drive, instead of the logical side of his brain. Only certain people who shared that drive were let in. He wasn't ready to let Jasmine in. These softening tendencies she inspired in him made keeping things strictly business with her an absolute must.

After what seemed like hours, they finally made it to the kitchen. Jasmine took herself off to pepper the workers with questions while Royce checked in with the foreman. He almost laughed at how short and to the point their discussion was, compared to the last hour with Jasmine. He had a feeling he would hole up in his office when he got back and communicate only by email. He'd used up his allotment of spoken words for the day.

It wasn't until they were on their way back out that Royce's relief was busted.

Jasmine's frequent glances warned him something was up. It didn't take her long to get to the point.

"One of the workers said your mother lived here."

Ah. Well, it wasn't like he'd told them to keep it a secret. "Yes. She lived in the carriage house for a few years before she died."

"I'm so sorry."

Royce just kept walking. He didn't want to get into how much he missed his mother, or how he hadn't felt he'd done everything he could for her before she died. There wasn't much point to those types of conversations.

"Was she interested in the renovations?"

Maybe they weren't done with this subject. "She definitely was. I bought the property for her, and she helped plan every facet of the renovations before she passed away. She was a history and museum buff."

"My sister loves history, too. She teaches it at the community college. She's the one who told me about this place."

The personal nature of the conversation set off alarms in his brain, but his sudden desire to talk to someone who understood the house and his love of it overrode his caution. "We discussed everything about the direction of the renovations. How much to save. How much to gut and start over on. She loved every minute of it."

He could almost feel Jasmine's warm gaze on his face. Then she said, "I bet she did. That must have been a wonderful thing for her."

He shrugged. "It was the least I could offer her. She was a single mother my entire life. She sacrificed more than any woman should. To make her comfortable and happy was a small gift in comparison."

He remembered watching Jasmine with her daughter, and how it had given rise to the uncomfortable memories of his own childhood. He'd told the truth. His mother had sacrificed a lot. So had he. Which had fostered his attitude on single mothers and the workplace.

As they walked back down the front steps, the burning question Royce had ignored for days finally surfaced. "Jasmine, do you regret being a single mother?"

She halted abruptly. The gorgeous, expressive face he'd been surreptitiously watching all morning shut down. He should have known—should have kept his mouth shut. Reason number two that he avoided social gatherings…he wasn't great at handling casual conversation.

Then her words hit him like bullets. "Never," she said. As she turned away, she added, "Without me, she'd have no one at all."

Jasmine sprinted around the corner of her regular event photographer's house, groaning when she saw Royce sitting in his car at the curb. She'd had her sister drop her off at the side of Dominic's, hoping she wouldn't have to explain how her morning had gone. The last thing she wanted to get into was why she'd needed a ride here instead of driving herself. Of course, the fact that she was fifteen minutes late and running in her heels probably raised eyebrows.

At least she'd texted Royce and Dominic to let them know she was running behind.

She took a few seconds to straighten her dress as Royce climbed out of his sleek car. The chaos of the morning made it a little harder to pull on her professional demeanor. She would blame that on the difficult circumstances rather than the effect every meeting with this man had on her.

Regardless, it didn't bode well for being in close proximity with Royce this morning.

Hopefully her smile wasn't strained enough to show the lack of sleep and worry. Rosie was teething again, so she hadn't slept well. Then Jasmine had worried about leaving her with Auntie when she knew her daughter would be more than a handful. And then…she'd gone out to find her car dead as a doornail.

Her frustration levels were maxed out.

She thought she'd masked her feelings pretty well, but Royce's double take as he approached her told her otherwise. For once, she prayed he'd stick to his strictly business MO. Even if she'd felt inclined to share her situation, his attitude about single mothers and the work-place gave her pause.

Instead, she tried to concentrate on the bright sunshine in hopes it would chase away her worries and gloom. Other than a brief good morning, she remained silent as they waited for Dominic to answer the bell. Unfortunately, the one day she wished Royce would stick to his robot impersonation, he had to deviate from the norm.

"Everything okay?" he asked.

This must be payback of some sort for her nosiness…

"Yes." She knew her tone would give away that she was lying.

"You seem upset."

Lord, why did she have to have such an expressive face? Why couldn't she just hide behind a stone facade? Of course, that was against her nature and normal method of dealing with clients. She liked being on friendly terms and being perceived as approachable. Which was why everything about her business interactions with Royce had felt wrong.

Fortunately Dominic opened the door of the house before she had to respond to Royce. The photographer's enthusiastic bear hug covered a lot of her strain and helped her regain her equilibrium. She'd worked with Dominic a lot over the last few years. His sheer size made clients think twice about hiring him—he looked more like a bouncer at a bar than an artist—until they saw his portfolio.

He had an ability to showcase emotion in an image that was sheer genius.

His handshake with Royce was firm but not a masculine attempt to dominate. He held the door open for them to enter the historic slate-gray and white Victorian cottage that served as his office, as well as the home that he shared with his partner, Greg.

"I'm so sorry that I was late," Jasmine said, taking a deep breath and noticing the intoxicating scent of baking cookies.

"No problem," Dominic said, always easygoing. In all the time she'd known him, she'd never seen him angry, even when dealing with some pretty demanding clients.

"Dang, Greg must be cooking," she teased. "I could gain weight just breathing." Greg was a baker who created incredible cookies and meringues in the industrial kitchen at the back of the house.

"We try," Dominic said with a wink before leading them into a nearby office. "He probably chose what to make the minute he knew you were coming over. A little sugar for our Sugar."

"He knows me well."

Just following Dominic deeper into the house helped Jasmine relax a little bit more. She'd never been the corporate office type. Her one venture into cubicle-land had convinced her it was the ninth circle of hell. Dominic's office echoed her own, though they were two totally different styles. His was comfortable, with masculine elements of leather, grommets, wrought iron. Hers was everything fluffy and feathery. But both were designed to be lived in, played in.

Which just made the work more fun.

"So, tell me a little about what you're aiming for," Dominic said, leading them to a round table in one corner.

"That would be Jasmine's department," Royce said as he held out a chair for her.

Royce might be all business, but his mama had obviously made sure he was a gentleman.

Dominic tossed Jasmine a brief glance, but she could

read a wealth of questions in the look. Like, what was this guy doing here if he wasn't doing the talking? But she didn't want to get into that right now.

"We're planning a masquerade event," she said.

The light in Dominic's eyes told her he was on board already.

"But we don't want just your traditional ball," she added. "We're also looking for other options for entertainment. I was thinking about that photo booth you set up for St. Anne's."

"A photo booth?" Royce asked, the doubt clear in his tone.

"Oh, it isn't your normal photo booth," Jasmine assured him.

Dominic eagerly reached for one of the large photo albums on the table. "Check it out."

He turned the pages slowly, giving them a chance to study the various options. "We created a background unique to the event and brought in props for the guests to use." He pointed to a group of people in a rowboat in front of a mural of a lake with a decorative bridge over it.

"I was thinking a mysterious castle," Jasmine offered.

The men batted ideas around for a minute. Against her hip, Jasmine felt her phone buzz. Since her family knew she didn't answer during meetings, she assumed it was a client and ignored it for the moment. When the buzzing started again after a few minutes, she stiffened, all her earlier tension returning.

Trying to brush it aside, she tossed out some more ideas. But the third buzz was her undoing. Slipping the phone from her pocket, she glanced at the screen. Two missed phone calls and a text from her sister Ivy.

911

She looked up to find both men watching her. Her smile was probably strained but she offered it anyway as she stood. "If you could excuse me just a moment, gentlemen?"

"Nothing wrong with that beautiful baby, I hope?" Dominic asked.

Seeing Royce's back straighten both unnerved her and ticked her off. "I certainly hope not," she said, unhappy with the quaver that had entered her voice.

But she wasn't backing down. She didn't know what his beef was with single mothers and families, but it wasn't her problem. There was no denying she wasn't a perfect mother. She had no delusions about that. The learning curve of the last six months had been steep. Still, she'd go above and beyond for Rosie and the rest of her family.

Family was the one thing that came before her clients, regardless of what they thought.

As she stepped back out to the porch, she prayed it was something like another stalled car or a burst water pipe. Things were replaceable. People weren't. Now that Rosie was a part of their lives, she simply couldn't imagine it any other way.

"Ivy?" she asked as her youngest sister answered the phone. "What's wrong?"

"I need you quick," Ivy said, her voice trembling and breathless. "I'm at Savannah General."

Jasmine's heart thudded in her ears, cutting off Ivy's voice. The hospital? So much for her day getting easier.

Six

Royce watched Jasmine disappear out the door with her phone and was surprised at his personal concern. Ordinarily, he would have been put out. He didn't have a problem with his employees dealing with life, as long as they did it on their own time. Normally he'd be formulating a few admonishing words after she'd kept him waiting this morning and then stepped out of a business meeting to handle what was obviously a personal call.

Instead, he sat here wondering what was wrong.

He turned back to find Dominic staring at the door with a frown on his face. The lines between his eyebrows said he was worried, too, but his expression turned more neutral when he caught Royce's look.

"Would you like to go over a few portfolios while we wait?" he asked, his voice calm even though he seemed to have other things on his mind.

Eager for a distraction, Royce gave a quick nod. Besides, they were here on business. He needed to focus.

Dominic was quick thinking and smart, which gave him a leg up in Royce's book. He pulled out examples of things he thought might work from the limited knowledge he had of their plans. Royce was impressed. He kept looking through one of the books while they discussed some photo booth ideas. Still, the whole time, his brain was ticking off the minutes that Jasmine had been gone.

What was going on? Did she need help?

As if his very thoughts had conjured her up, Royce turned the page to see a grouping of photos featuring Jasmine and her daughter. There was also another woman in the outdoor portraits, which seemed to have been taken at one of the local squares. The fountain behind them was familiar. The greenery provided a lush frame for the women.

"Oh, I'd forgotten which book those were in," Dominic said, surveying the spread with a smile.

Despite admonishing himself to focus on the meeting, Royce found himself tilting the album farther toward him so he could study the group of women more closely. Jasmine was her usual elegant self, her summer dress full and flowing with a fitted bodice. This was his first time seeing her hair down around her shoulders. The thick mass blanketed her pale skin in soft waves, the sunshine creating glossy highlights in the dark color.

Rosie looked to be newborn, but there was no mistaking those black curls. The other woman looked down at the baby with a smile. But upon closer inspection, Royce thought he detected a pervasive sadness in the woman's gaze that belied her indulgent expression as she watched the child.

Royce detected another subtle difference among the three. The third woman seemed sick. Her skin appeared a little gray, a little more aged than Jasmine's.

Though the three were grouped close together on a picnic blanket in dappled sunshine beneath the trees, the other woman seemed to be more of an observer than part of the group. Still, Dominic was definitely talented when it came to composing a shot.

"The resemblance is remarkable," Royce murmured. All that dark hair linked the women together. No male could penetrate their bond. Only it made him curious about Rosie's father and whether she looked like him at all…

No. He refused to entertain any thoughts like that. It was too personal…too tempting…

"I know," Dominic was saying. "Hard to believe they aren't even related, isn't it? You'd never know Jasmine wasn't Rosie's biological mother."

Royce's gaze snapped up to the other man. "What?"

Dominic's eyes widened. "Well…"

Without me, she'd have no one at all. Jasmine's words came back to him, haunting his mind.

"What do you mean, Dominic?" Royce forced himself to keep his voice nonchalant. He kept all urgency out of the question. Even though, suddenly, he wanted to know very, very badly.

"I'm not sure I should share Jasmine's personal business," Dominic said with a frown. "I spoke out of turn."

"I understand. I just wondered because Jasmine seemed so natural with her daughter. I knew she was a single mother," he added, sprinkling in the truth, "but I never would have guessed she hadn't given birth to her."

Dominic seemed to consider his words. "You've seen her with Rosie?"

"Sure. She brought her to the office the other day." Royce wasn't going to reveal any more details about that visit…details that would make him look bad.

"Oh, yeah. Rosie's such a good baby. Jasmine can pretty much take her wherever and the little one is perfectly content. And will charm anyone within smiling distance."

Which just resurrected images of the sleepy child grinning in Jasmine's arms. They'd looked so perfect together, which made it hard to believe that Jasmine wasn't the birth mother.

Royce tried to assimilate the new things he'd learned into the old image, but it wasn't working very well. An odd feeling started in his chest. And feelings weren't a normal occurrence when he conducted business. Yet he seemed to be having them more and more often around Jasmine Harden.

He needed to get a hold on that…later.

"Is this Rosie's mom?" he asked without thinking.

Dominic paused again, then shrugged. "Yeah. Jasmine met her at City Sanctuary mission. I'm not sure about the details, but I know Jasmine's family took her in early in her pregnancy. Something went wrong and she asked Jasmine to take Rosie if anything happened." He looked down at the smiling women in the picture. "She never even hesitated."

Royce wasn't surprised. Jasmine was strong. She ran a successful business and had a great reputation. He imagined she'd tackled motherhood with the same determination and grace.

He should be ashamed of thinking any differently. Except now he wanted the whole story.

"Dominic, will you call me a cab, please?" Jasmine's voice quavered as she asked the question.

Royce hadn't even realized Jasmine had reentered the office. He glanced up. Her expression was calm, but Royce could see the strain around her delicate mouth and eyes.

Dominic stood. "Sugar, what's wrong?"

Jasmine visibly pulled herself together. "I'm so sorry to cut this short, but Auntie is at the hospital. She fell."

As Dominic made the appropriate remarks, Royce stood. This type of thing was totally out of his realm of expertise.

He watched as Dominic slid an arm around Jasmine's shoulders, feeling completely lost in this situation. That's when he realized he didn't need to do that part. Dominic had taken care of the comfort side of things. Royce could go straight to the logistics of the situation—which was his area of expertise.

"Where's your car?" he asked, his tone now brooking no arguments.

She wouldn't look him straight in the eye, but mumbled, "It wouldn't start this morning. My sister Willow brought me."

No wonder she'd looked frazzled when she arrived.

"Let me cancel my next few appointments and we'll head over," Dominic said.

"Absolutely not," she countered, although her eyes were starting to look suspiciously glassy. "Just call me a cab."

As they argued with each other, Royce argued with himself. So she had no car. She needed to go to the hospital. A cab would take forever.

He didn't want to get involved in her personal life.

But she didn't have a car.

And he was an ass for even debating this with himself. Finally, he cut them both off with, "It looks like I'm your ride."

For the second time that day, Jasmine found herself riding in Royce's car. Sitting next to him reminded her of all the reasons she shouldn't be here.

The subtly spicy smell of him. The sight of his sure hands on the wheel. The overt luxury of the vehicle.

It was too intimate. Too much. There were too many reasons she should stay far away from personal situations with Mr. Business.

But what choice did she have?

Taking Dominic away from his other clients didn't seem fair, though he'd been more than willing to help her out as a friend. A cab would have taken a while. She needed to get to Auntie and Rosie as soon as possible. It was her job to take care of her fam—

"Who is Auntie?"

It took Jasmine a moment to register Royce's words because she'd completely blocked out any chance of his asking her a question about herself. Their few personal interactions so far had seemed as awkward for him as they had been for her. Maybe she'd been wrong.

"She's not really my aunt," Jasmine clarified. "She was my mother's nanny when she was little and my grandmother's best friend. We moved in with her after...anyway, all of us girls still live together now."

Royce nodded. She could see the movement out of the corner of her eye, even though she refused to look directly at him. His presence was overpowering in the small space, especially in her vulnerable state. It was simply too close for comfort.

"She must be older," Royce surmised. "A fall can be pretty serious in those circumstances."

Which was a fact Jasmine wasn't ready to confront. They'd be at the hospital soon enough, and she'd deal with it then. "She helps with Rosie when none of us girls are able to be home."

"I know one of your sisters is a college professor. What does the other one do?"

"She's an executive assistant at the McLemore firm."

"That's good. I'm glad you all are close and you have that kind of support. Rosie won't be alone when her mom's working."

Jasmine felt her body stiffen in defense, but something about the sad tone of his voice had her reconsidering. Before she could question it, he went on.

"Why didn't you tell me Rosie was adopted?"

The world swirled around Jasmine for a moment, disorienting her. This whole line of questioning was completely out of character for Royce. "I didn't realize you would care."

Why would he? Every encounter with her daughter, or even talking about her, seemed to bring a negative reaction from him.

As if he didn't realize the intent behind her answer, he mused, "You look so much alike. It never occurred to me."

Jasmine was getting more confused by the minute, but at least it kept her worry about Auntie at bay. It also loosened the hold she normally kept on her tongue in front of her clients. "I truly don't understand, Royce. What difference does it make? I'm her mother. I'm a damn good one. I would never deny her a home or neglect her to go out to earn a living."

"Why wouldn't you?"

The car came to an abrupt halt. At first, Jasmine thought she'd pushed too far. Then she realized he'd actually parked in a parking space. They'd arrived at the hospital more quickly than she'd expected.

Only as he was climbing out of the door did he answer. "My mom did."

As he softly shut the door, then walked around the car, Jasmine sat in stunned silence. Not only because Royce had admitted something so personal, but because it contradicted everything he'd told her about his mother at Keller House. He opened the door and helped her out as if he hadn't just dropped a bombshell of magnificent proportions on her. They walked into the hospital in silence.

What should she say?

He'd taken care of his mother before she died. She'd lived in the carriage house for years. Her son was Savannah's youngest, and most mysterious, billionaire. Had whatever happened to his mother colored how he saw women, how he saw Jasmine?

His earlier comment made the answer obvious.

Before she could get a handle on her reaction, they reached the waiting area where Ivy was sitting with Rosie. Thankfully, the baby was sleeping, though her pudgy cheeks were flushed with the slight fever Jasmine was learning to associate with her teething spells.

Jasmine leaned over to carefully hug her sister around the sleeping child. "What did the doctors say?" she asked as she crouched in front of the pair.

"We're still waiting on the X-rays to find out." Ivy worried her lower lip, making her look a lot older than her twenty-three years. "I'm sorry you had to come here. I just didn't know what to do."

"No. It's fine," Jasmine said. Though asking Ivy not to feel bad was like asking Jasmine not to worry. "The last thing I would have wanted was for you to be sitting here by yourself dealing with all of this. It's no problem at all."

"But your car—"

"Driving over here wasn't a big deal," Royce interjected. "We were about done, anyway."

Ivy glanced at him, her eyes growing wide with surprise.

"You had to get him to drive you?" she breathed. "I'm so sorry."

"Car trouble always hits at the worst possible moment." Royce tried to reassured her.

It didn't work too well. Jasmine spied a slight sheen of tears in her sister's eyes before she dropped her gaze and placed a kiss on Rosie's head. It still amazed her that her littlest sister handled difficult clients with such ease at work. Jasmine still saw her as the child in need of her protection and care. But in this situation, they were going to support each other through whatever challenges they faced.

"Is everybody okay?" Willow rushed up behind them.

Ivy stood as they all talked over each other, trying to share what they knew and offer comfort. Though Jasmine still felt a touch of panic over Auntie's condition, it was better with both of her sisters here. Out of the corner of her eye, she spied Royce standing to the side, watching them. His expression was carefully neutral. With a quick squeeze of her sisters' arms, she walked over to where he stood.

"Thank you so much for bringing me here. I didn't intend to disrupt your day."

A slight frown snuck across his face, but wasn't there long enough for Jasmine to figure out what it meant. Ivy appeared at her elbow with a blinking Rosie. Jasmine smiled at the little girl and got a crooked grin in return. Taking her into her arms, Jasmine hugged her close for a moment. Then she turned her focus back to Royce. She definitely noticed how his gaze had settled directly on her, avoiding Rosie completely.

Without thought, she softly asked, "Why would your mother leave you alone?"

For a brief second, she saw a flash of pain in his expression that was so intense it took Jasmine back to the days and weeks right after her parents had been killed in the car accident. But within the space of a blink, the emotion disappeared. Had she imagined it? When he dropped his gaze to Rosie, it made her wonder.

Then a nurse called from behind him, "King family?"

Recognizing Auntie's last name, she handed Rosie over to Willow and rushed to the edge of the waiting area. But the nurse wasn't very helpful, and Jasmine found herself returning with a clipboard in her hand.

"What did she say?" Willow demanded.

Jasmine shook her head, blinking so tears wouldn't well up in her eyes. "Just that they were waiting to take her to X-ray, and in the meantime they needed this paperwork filled out."

Seven

Royce shifted uncomfortably as he watched Jasmine blink before looking at her sisters. He remembered the many brave faces he'd put on with no one there to take notice except his mother. Turning away from the reminder, he took a seat across from Jasmine's sisters in the waiting room.

Jasmine settled into a chair and started on the paperwork. Her sisters studied him with varying degrees of interest.

"Is there a problem, ladies?" he finally asked.

"Why didn't Jasmine take a cab?" Willow asked.

"It would have taken too long."

"One of us could have picked her up," Willow said.

This felt a little like a what-are-your-intentions interrogation, not that he had any experience with those. Or with anything in this situation, really. Long-fallow instincts had kicked in when he'd seen Jasmine in need, overriding his usual laser focus on business.

"That would have taken even longer," he said, attempting to soften his clipped tone since they were just trying to look out for their sister. "Besides, my mother wouldn't have appreciated me leaving a lady high and dry."

The two women shared a look, one that should have made him very suspicious. But, like all good businessmen, Royce held his tongue. He knew better than to give them extra ammunition, especially when he wasn't sure what the bullet was actually made of in this instance.

Suddenly both women glanced down. Following their gaze, he took in how Rosie was snuggled up against Ivy. Her eyelids drooped. He could see the softening effect the little cutie had on Ivy and Willow, and even felt an echo deep inside himself. He hadn't dealt with so many emotions since his mother died.

Was it being in this place? The same hospital where they'd spent her last days? Or was it these women? Seeing their interactions, how they cared for each other, he found it fascinating. A little scary, too. Being the focus of their attention wasn't comfortable at all.

Like his mother, they seemed to be able to see past the front he presented to the world to the actual man beneath. He could almost feel the crack in his protective wall. He wasn't very comfortable with that.

Yet he couldn't bring himself to leave.

He reached out one hand to rub it gently against Rosie's chubby, flushed cheek. "She feels a little feverish."

"She's been teething," Ivy explained. "Which means she's often fussy and not sleeping well, poor thing."

"Poor Mama," Willow added, giving the little girl a loving look. "I don't think Jasmine's had a full night's sleep in days."

Which explained why Rosie was so tired today. But

Royce knew absolutely nothing about babies and teething, so he switched subjects. Anything to distract himself from the memories whirling through his mind. "So, what do you ladies do for a living?" he asked, even though Jasmine had already told him the answer.

Willow jumped in easily. "I teach history at the community college."

Royce nodded. "Any specialties?"

"American and local history. When you're descended from a pirate family, you can't help but immerse yourself in Savannah's colorful past."

"I'd imagine." Somehow he wasn't surprised to find Jasmine had some pirate blood in her. She certainly drove a hard bargain to get exactly what she wanted.

Ivy filled the pause. "I'm the executive assistant to Paxton McLemore."

That was interesting. "Intense guy to work for, isn't he?"

"At times, but I love it. Challenging but enjoyable."

Obviously they were a family of very smart women who were very good at standing on their own two feet, making their way in the world after losing their parents. He could relate. Impressive.

But, unlike him, they weren't focused only on making money. He thought over all the charitable causes for which Jasmine had coordinated events. The dossier his assistant had put together had been more than impressive.

As she rose and crossed the room to return the clipboard to a woman behind the desk, he couldn't help but think of all she'd dealt with at home while she'd been pulling off those events. Unlike Royce, she didn't go home, put up her feet and catch up on her rest after a hard day's work.

No, she worked just as hard at home. If not harder.

She kept her family together and fed. Took on the role of mother. And apparently offered hands-on help to the charity she'd chosen to support with his event.

Her life had turned out very differently from his.

The women across from him went suddenly silent. Royce followed their gaze to see Jasmine slowly approach from across the room. Before he knew it, her sisters were on their feet.

Royce watched the baby pass from sister to sister with a kind of bewilderment and an incredible calm. Until inevitably the baby was passed to him, and he found himself standing alone in the waiting room with the child snuggled carefully in the crook of his arm. He watched as the girls disappeared around a column and joined their sister.

He glanced down at the baby now in his arms. She was so small. Yet when she was awake and her eyes were open, that small body came alive with personality. Even at her young age.

As Jasmine turned back toward the hall, the child gave a shuddering breath, evoking sympathy for how miserable she must be at the moment. She probably wished she was home in her own bed instead of being carried around a noisy hospital waiting room.

Though he knew she couldn't have heard it from where she stood, Jasmine froze. Then she whipped her head around to survey her sisters. "Where's Rosie?"

As if passing the buck, both women pointed in his direction. Jasmine's eyes went wide with shock. But as she glanced down to see Rosie still sleeping, the tears that she'd held back earlier finally overflowed.

As the women before him sniffled and hugged each other, Royce moved closer to stand outside their circle with the baby nestled in his arms. For a brief moment, something akin to panic welled up in Royce's chest. A feeling he hadn't experienced since he'd first realized he was completely alone in the world. As if these people he barely knew had abandoned him.

Crazy.

A noise caught his attention. He glanced down, meeting wide dark eyes. The one difference between Rosie and Jasmine. The baby's eyes were dark and oddly wise. But beautiful. Compelling. Royce found himself as mesmerized as he'd been by his first glimpse of her mother's bright blue eyes.

Suddenly he realized that he was bouncing the baby slightly. It was a rhythm entirely seated in his bones, natural but unfamiliar. And he couldn't stop.

"King?" a nurse called from across the room. "The King family?" He looked up.

The women before him seemed completely oblivious. Stepping closer, he adopted a firm, no-nonsense tone. "Ladies, let's go see what the nurse has to say."

Immediately their tears stopped and they started across the room. "Purses," he reminded them.

They paused to rapidly scoop up all their stuff, then he ushered them across the carpeted floor to the staff member. She smiled, as if she were completely used to such a delay. He'd watched enough waiting room drama when his mother was sick to know she probably was.

Jasmine shifted impatiently as the nurse waited for all the sisters to gather around her. Then she said, "I wanted to assure you it's just a sprain..." She glanced around, meeting everyone's gaze. "It's a bad one, though. The doctor can explain more, if one of you would like to come back and speak with him."

"You, Jasmine," Willow said. "You'll remember more of the details than I will."

The nurse nodded, but Royce stepped forward. He kept his voice low, but firm. "Is there any possibility we could all go back with you? I realize the rooms are small, but the little one isn't going to do well without her mother."

The nurse took one look at Rosie and Royce could see her refusal melt on her tongue. "Poor baby. Is it a fever?"

"Just a low-grade one," Jasmine rushed in to answer. "From teething. She isn't sick."

"Oh, but that makes babies miserable, doesn't it?" The nurse cooed at Rosie for a few moments, gaining a gummy grin; Royce spotted just a hint of a tooth breaking the front skin. "Of course you need to be with your mama." Some semblance of a stern look returned to the nurse's face, but it lacked conviction. "But if it gets full in there, you'll have to wait across the hall."

"Not a problem," Royce said, eager to go now that he'd gotten his way.

The last thing he wanted was to split up the three women or find himself alone with the baby in his arms, which seemed to be drawing out all kinds of emotions he didn't want to handle.

Rosie was really good while they met with the doctor and received his instructions. After all of his experiences with his own mother, Royce knew that physical therapy wouldn't be easy for Auntie, but would be worth it for her to get fully back on her feet at her advanced age.

The half-jiggling, half-bouncing motion Royce's body had adopted worked wonders, but before long a little whimper erupted. A streak of panic burned through Royce, but he refused to let it show.

It almost slipped through when he found the women

watching him. Royce had an uncomfortable feeling they were finally evaluating his child-holding skills and finding him lacking.

"What?" he asked in a soft tone.

"Aren't you the guy Jasmine said didn't care about anything but business?" Ivy's blue eyes dropped to the baby in his arms.

He wasn't offended. "I'd say that would be an accurate description." Did he owe them an explanation? Did he even have one for why he was here right this moment?

As they stood around the tiny cubicle where Auntie lay in the hospital bed, Willow dug into the diaper bag she held. "Here," she said, holding out a ring-shaped toy. "Let's try this. Want me to take her?"

Royce took the toy but shook his head. "Actually, I want you to go get your car and pull it around to the entrance."

Willow glanced around. "But they haven't discharged Auntie yet."

"I'll help your sisters take care of that," Royce assured her. "You just bring the car around."

Willow nodded uncertainly, then kissed Auntie and went for the car.

Jasmine watched her go. "Why is she getting the car so early?"

"Because we're leaving," Royce assured her. "I want you to get Auntie dressed."

When she opened her mouth to question him, Royce simply shook his head. "Just do it."

Turning away, he went to find the nurse at her station. She watched him struggle with the now squirming baby; her teething ring was no longer keeping her occupied. "I know you have a lot going on around here," he said, "but we need to get this one home before we have a full-blown scene."

His only knowledge of babies was of them crying in restaurants and stores. He had no idea what would set Rosie off, but he'd use her to their advantage in getting Auntie released sooner.

The nurse cooed at Rosie, nodding her head. So at least he was right in one sense.

"I have my hands full with the ladies...all the ladies," he said with a smile. "Could you possibly help us out and get Ms. King released before things go downhill?"

Seeing the nurse snap into action, Royce had to wonder how much more he could accomplish in life if he had a baby as his wingman.

Less than twenty minutes later they were headed for the car. It was unprecedented in Royce's experience with hospitals, but he wasn't going to look a gift horse in the mouth. Willow was right up front, waiting for them.

The nurse who had wheeled Ms. King out got her settled into the front passenger seat with minimal effort while Jasmine supervised. Then Jasmine turned to look at him. She shook her head. "I can't believe you managed that." A gorgeous touch of pink lit up her pale cheeks. "And managed Rosie. That was incredible."

"Only to be thwarted by something as simple as a child's car seat," he replied as he nodded toward the contraption in the back seat.

Jasmine's eyes widened and she smiled. "Right. These things look way more complicated than they are. After all you've done, though, I think we'll overlook your shortcomings on that score," she said, taking the baby from him.

There was the sassy woman he'd come to know.

In two minutes, she had Rosie deftly strapped in and

content with her pacifier. Closing the door, Jasmine again gifted him with a smile. Maybe he was tired after the morning drama. Maybe he was still feeling the effects from holding the tiny, innocent child in his arms. Whatever it was, this smile snuck through his usual defenses and hit his heart with unerring accuracy.

"I still don't know how you managed it," Jasmine said. "I was so focused on Auntie and my sisters and taking care of them. But we are very, very grateful."

And that's when he stupidly ran off at the mouth before thinking. "I'm glad to know all of my experience came in handy. My mother had a very long stay at this hospital before she died here."

Eight

Jasmine sucked in a deep breath as she saw Royce slip through the coffee shop door. Her stomach churned, forcing her to leave her café au lait untouched. She had no idea how to act after their last encounter.

No idea how to return to business as usual.

The week he had been out of town since Auntie's fall should have helped give her some perspective. Frankly, it hadn't. Because her thoughts of Royce had turned very personal and she had no idea how to combat that. Except to only talk about business.

She could do that, right?

But his smile as he sat down wasn't business as usual. It sped her heart up a little…okay, more than a little. This wasn't right.

She glared at the green ring sparkling in the sunlight for a moment.

"Everything okay?" Royce asked as he sat down with his coffee.

"Sure," Jasmine said, consciously forcing herself to relax. "I appreciate you coming."

Reaching down, she pulled several small poster boards from her bag. "I've put together some visuals for you to see what the decorator is suggesting."

"I'm amazed you're only letting me view pictures, rather than insisting I attend an actual meeting with her."

Jasmine froze for a moment. Was he complaining because she'd excluded him? "Well, with you out of town, then her going out of town, I just thought this might be easier."

To her shock, his hand lightly covered one of hers. "It's okay, Jasmine. I'm just teasing you."

"Teasing me?" She almost swallowed her tongue, because teasing had never been on Royce's agenda.

"Yes," he said, drawing the word out. "After all, you've stuck to your stipulation that I attend every planning meeting pretty hard. I can't believe you're letting me slide on this one…"

Feeling like she'd stepped into an alternate reality, one that tempted her with the idea that Royce might actually be human after all, she grinned. "Well, everyone should get time off for good behavior."

His laugh rang out, startling her. The sound was oh, so sexy. Over his shoulder, she saw several patrons glance their way, most grinning in response to his amusement. Only one didn't seem amused, a rather dour, expensively dressed man at a choice table by the window overlooking the river.

Jasmine would rather focus on the man opening up right in front of her.

She pointed out the various options depicted in the photographs. The dark purple-and-black color scheme was her favorite, with highlights of white and bright red.

The elaborate table schemes included taper candles and crystals to mimic the chandeliers. Lots of rich fabric and sparkling highlights.

Event planning was her passion, so she could have gone on forever, but noticed the minute Royce's gaze started to glaze over. "Okay," she conceded, "I think I've tortured you enough."

"Honestly, give me the details of a ship's engine any day as opposed to decorating details. I only agreed to meet in the coffee shop so I'd have this to keep me awake." He lifted his coffee a few inches off the table. But it was the sheepish grin that got to her.

She'd never imagined seeing that expression on this driven businessman's face. Unfortunately, she liked it. Too much.

"So how are Ms. King and Rosie?"

"Oh, she'd just want you to call her Auntie."

He nodded, his expression remaining open in a way she wasn't quite used to or comfortable with.

"Physical therapy is going well, although she hates it." Royce shrugged. "Who wouldn't? It's torture."

"Even more so for her, because she thinks it's a burden to everyone that we're juggling her appointments with our jobs and Rosie's care. As if that matters to any of us girls."

"My mother was like that," Royce said, staring down into his cup. "She didn't ever want to tell me when she had a doctor's appointment or treatment—she felt it took me away from more important things."

When he looked up, his eyes were serious in the same way she'd seen at the hospital. "But she got over it after the one time she took a cab to the hospital for a chemo treatment. After that, she knew in no uncertain terms I would be there for every appointment, no matter what I had going on."

That had to have been a huge concession for such a driven man.

This led her to say what had been on her mind for over a week. "I really do appreciate all you did for us, for me, at the hospital. Especially knowing that there had to be a lot of bad memories associated with that place."

"It was nothing—"

"Don't."

When he finally looked at her, she reached out and cupped his hand where it lay on the table. "It wasn't nothing. No man in that frame of mind should have to hold a teething six-month-old for that long—it was a tremendous help to us. I won't let you dismiss that."

He glanced down at her hand over his. It wasn't until several moments later—moments of anticipation that caused Jasmine to shake inside—that he spoke.

"My mother, no matter how sick she was, always had a kind word for everyone she came across at that hospital. She would help in any way she could, sometimes even pushing herself past what she was capable of to help her fellow patients."

"And you were there to help her?"

"As much as possible." Still he wouldn't look up at her.

She couldn't resist pushing a little farther. "But I don't understand. You say she took care of you, you took care of her, but also that she abandoned you. What happened?"

"It wasn't because she didn't want me…" His husky voice trailed off. Beneath her palm, she felt his hand curl into a fist. Then she noticed the shadow across their table.

Glancing up, she found the stern man from the far table standing over them. He didn't look her way or acknowledge her. His gaze was trained tightly on Royce as he said in a gruff voice, "Getting involved with your employees never leads to anything good."

Then he turned and walked away.

"That was my father. Guess he didn't want to stick around and be introduced."

The bitterness in his own voice made Royce cringe.

Jasmine glanced over her shoulder to watch the man disappear out the door. "I'm confused," she murmured.

Join the club.

"He looked familiar," she said with a faraway tone in her voice.

Though he never talked about him, just this once Royce was happy to provide the basics. "He should. His name is John Nave."

He could see the light of recognition dawning in her sexy blue eyes. "That's right. *The* John Nave, from one of the oldest families in Savannah, and one of the richest."

"But I don't understand..." Jasmine said, her brow wrinkling in confusion. "He's your father?"

"My mother was his housekeeper." Royce hated saying it that way, because it sounded like he was defining his mother by her profession when she'd been so much more.

To her credit, Jasmine's expression didn't change. If anything, it turned a little stiff. "I'll be honest, I'm appalled he would say something like that to you, considering..."

She didn't know the half of it. "That's mild, for him. When he bothers to acknowledge me at all, he's usually pretty nasty."

"But isn't he married?"

"To one of the coldest women in the world," he murmured. "But that was a while after my mother had broken contact with him."

"How did your mother manage?" Jasmine whispered, her voice full of empathy.

"When she didn't get rid of me like he wanted, it took her a long time to find more work. But when she did, she worked her fingers to the bone, because the bastard made sure she couldn't get a judge in the county to award her child support."

Jasmine closed her eyes tightly, shaking her head. When she opened them, he noticed the glossy sheen of tears.

Were they for him? No one but his mother had ever shed a tear over the way he'd been treated.

"I'd like to say it surprises me," Jasmine said, "but I've seen it often enough at the mission. Dads who simply couldn't care less about a child out in the world with their DNA. Men who would have preferred for them to die than take on any obligation in their own lives."

Oh, how well he knew that type.

She leaned back, studying him. He wasn't sure when she'd stopped touching his hand, but he felt the loss of contact keenly. "I'm not really upset about me," he said, waving the thought away as if it were a particle of dust in the air. "It's more about my mom. What she was left to deal with."

"That's why she left you, isn't it?"

He glanced over her shoulder instead of looking into her eyes and seeing the knowledge there. He nodded. "She had to work a lot to keep us afloat."

"And you made it up to her."

Royce sat a little straighter. "I did. She loved that house. She used to work there when she first started." He could remember long stories she would tell about the few parties she'd helped serve at, then caring for the house until it was closed. "I wanted her to be in a place she loved, so I bought it for her."

Jasmine covered his hand with hers once more. "That's wonderful, Royce."

"It's what she deserved after all of her sacrifices for me. By damn, I was going to give it to her." He let a little smile slip out. "She was happy."

"She never fell in love again?" Jasmine asked. "Never wanted to have more children?"

"When would she have had the time? Nope. She loved me, but she wanted no more children to complicate her life. And I'll never have children, either."

Jasmine didn't draw up in shocked outrage the way he might have expected. She simply asked, "Why not?"

"I've made my choice. Business is a demanding mistress. I refuse to do both."

She pressed her lips together for a moment before letting herself speak. "It's a shame. You were good with Rosie."

"Raising a child is a lot different than holding one for thirty minutes."

She smiled, though there was a hint of sadness around the edges. "I'm learning that all too well. My mother died, too, when I was fifteen."

He'd gotten that impression but never asked the details.

"Both of my parents, actually. They were killed in an automobile accident." She absently ran her finger around the edge of her cup. "We came to live with Auntie. She took all three of us in when we had no other place to go. No other relatives. Not even distant ones."

"That's a big responsibility."

"Auntie said something to me then. Something I've never forgotten, even though I didn't fully embrace it at the time."

"What's that?"

"That children aren't everyone's cup of tea."

It made sense, especially to Royce.

Jasmine wasn't done, though. That sad smile returned as she added, "But some people should learn to be tea drinkers."

Nine

"I really don't see why we need to do this," Royce said as Jasmine approached over the cracked and broken sidewalk. "It's not necessary."

And here she thought she'd loosened him up a little. Especially after the surprisingly personal meeting at the coffee shop a few days ago. Of course, the way he'd conceded the design choices with a curt "You know better than I" should have reminded her he didn't want a say in everything.

"It's not necessary to educate yourself about the charity you are promoting with your big-ticket event?"

"I told you the charity was your choice."

She could just get right to the point, but why not enjoy teasing him for a minute? "What's the big deal? So you spend a few hours down here on a Saturday. What else are you gonna do? Work?"

They shared a look, his blue eyes narrowing as if he was contemplating retribution for her sarcasm.

"Just consider this part of your job," she said. "Trust me, I've been to dozens of these charity events. You're gonna get asked lots of questions about City Sanctuary mission. Do you want to appear ignorant?"

"I could refer them to you."

"And still appear ignorant. Especially to the Jeffersons."

He grimaced, probably because he knew she was right. "It should be enough that I'm donating money."

"Don't sulk, Scrooge. You just might enjoy yourself."

His eyes widened just a notch at her tone, but she ignored it and headed for the entrance. The parking area was hidden from view of the building by a tall retaining wall that supported the elevated ground the original church had been built upon. Excitement filled her as they made their way to the break in the wall for the stairs leading to the lawn. There she caught the first glimpse of the ancient stone chapel. Though the additions made to the compound over the years didn't entirely match the architecture of the original building, which had stood since just a few decades after Savannah was founded, they didn't detract from the atmosphere, either.

Jasmine followed the gravel path with ease, having developed a familiarity with the place after years of volunteering here. She greeted the regulars as they passed.

She'd always felt safe here. The mission's destitute clients had never scared her. She'd experienced more fear among Savannah's elite, to be honest.

Everyone she greeted along the way to the entrance followed the same pattern: a smile and hello for her, then a quick suspicious glance at the man behind her. Strangers to the mission were often regarded that way, at first, but this was probably enhanced because she'd never been here with a man. Usually she was alone; only occasionally did she visit with her sisters.

They entered through the main registration lobby, where Jasmine paused. "This is the area where most public traffic comes in," she said. "Overnight guests are assigned their spaces, and those who need other services are directed to the areas or personnel they need."

She waved to the couple who usually handled the front lobby on Saturdays, then led Royce to the first large hallway. "The building was originally a church, and has been added to over the years. This makes it a little confusing for newcomers." She gestured to the left. "There are offices down here. A couple of classrooms where we hold seminars or tutoring. And there's a closet at the far end where we store used clothing to hand out."

After giving him a minute to process, she turned right. "The main dining area is at the back. I'll take you there in a little while. It was the most recent area to be updated, because part of it collapsed during the last hurricane that came through. A tree fell on it, so we had to do some structural repairs."

They stepped through a set of double doors into a gymnasium with a scuffed but decent floor. Royce, who had been silent the whole time, took in the group of children playing basketball. "This looks nice."

"It is—we use it for some after-school programs and there's actually a men's basketball group that meets here. Anyone in the building is allowed to participate." She nodded toward the far corner. "But here's the problem. This room has to serve double duty."

"Are those beds?"

"Foldaway cots. We have a women's dorm in the back, which has a leaking roof. The old chapel serves to shelter small family units when necessary. This is the men's dorm. So every night we have to pull the beds out onto the floor and every morning they are stripped and put away."

"That's a lot of work," he murmured.

"It is." She took a deep breath, almost afraid to share her hopes for the fund-raising event. "The neighbors here were an elderly couple and they gifted their land to the mission upon their deaths. But there aren't any funds to build on it." She met his solemn gaze. "A fully functioning building with single-purpose sleeping quarters would make a big difference in this part of Savannah."

"Miss Harden! Watch this!"

Jasmine glanced over as one of her little tagalongs, Oliver, jumped toward the basketball net. At five, he wasn't tall enough to make headway, but he had enough enthusiasm to make his jump impressive. "Great job!" she yelled back.

He dribbled the ball over to them, showing off his skills. "Look what I learned to do." He grabbed the ball up and rolled it across his outstretched arms and along the back of his neck.

Jasmine laughed. "Well, that's pretty cool. But how is it gonna help you play basketball?"

"Mr. Mike said it will help me learn dex—um, dexter—"

"Dexterity?" Royce offered.

"That was it."

"I see," Jasmine said. "You are well on your way to being a professional ball player, in my opinion."

The little boy stopped moving and gave her a cheeky grin. "Didn't you say you don't know anything about basketball?"

She brushed her knuckles against his cheek. "That's

true. But I know determination when I see it, and you have tons of that, my sweet."

He giggled, then dribbled the ball back toward the court. She smiled after him. "He's such a cutie. His mama named him Oliver after a cocky, sneaky cat in a cartoon. I have a feeling he's gonna live up to the name."

Instead of a chuckle, Royce said, "My mother named me after my father's car."

She swiveled to face him. "What?"

"My father's Rolls Royce. He told her the only thing he'd ever loved was his car. Guess it was some kind of dig to remind him that a kid deserved love, too. Didn't work so well."

"Or maybe it was to remind her that she got the better end of that deal."

"What do you mean?"

"Cars don't give an awful lot of love in return, Royce."

As they turned back toward the main building, Jasmine spouted facts about the various aspects of the homeless mission's programs. Royce wasn't tracking. Her words from the gym kept ringing in his ears. He couldn't help but wonder—were they true?

"Jasmine, *ma fleur*. So wonderful to see you."

Royce forced himself to tune in as they were approached by a man in khaki pants and a polo shirt. Jasmine introduced him as Francis Staten, the director of the mission.

"So wonderful to meet you," Francis said with a firm handshake that matched his calm, competent expression. "We are so grateful for what you are doing for us."

Royce was having none of that. "You know I can't take the credit. Jasmine is the one who brought the need to my attention."

Francis smiled. "And *you* must know that with her running your event, it will be very successful."

"That's my sincere belief, also," Royce agreed.

Francis gave an appreciative chuckle. "Before she combusts from that blush, shall I show you around?"

Jasmine smiled in a sheepish way. "Well, we've already looked over the gym, front offices and lobby."

"Excitement got the better of you, huh?" Francis asked as they headed farther down the hallway toward the back of the building. "I've never had a more enthusiastic volunteer than Jasmine here. She was such a sad girl when she first came to us, and she has become the mission's biggest asset."

"All of our volunteers are," Jasmine insisted.

That blush sure was cute.

As they crossed through a large double doorway into a spacious banquet room, Francis explained, "This is our main dining area, with industrial kitchens on the other side of those serving tables. The kitchens were refurbished by a major pledge drive. We serve hundreds of meals per day. The kitchen updates made it so much easier to keep the food fresh, hot and plentiful."

The long room was broken up by rows of tables and chairs. Only about a third of them were occupied at this time on a Saturday. "We'll start serving lunch soon," Francis said.

A lady sitting at the first table with a group of her friends called out to Jasmine and waved. With a smile, Jasmine excused herself to go over to them. Royce and Francis watched as she hugged each woman in the small group.

"She's incredible," Francis said. "A young woman who lives her beliefs, rather than simply talking about them."

He glanced over at Royce, lowering his voice a touch. "Have you met Rosie?"

Royce nodded. His stomach flipped as he imagined Rosie in this environment. Her birth mother had been a frequent guest here, so Rosie would have grown up with no stable, secure home base. "She's a beautiful little girl," he murmured. "It's hard to tell she was adopted."

"Indeed," Francis agreed. "Jasmine had known Rosie's mother for several years. One thing you learn very quickly here—you can't force your own beliefs or preferences on those who aren't as fortunate. You can only offer them whatever you have. Some are on the streets because life has given them no other choices. Some are there because it is safer or more comfortable for them than the places they left behind."

"Was she very young?" Royce asked.

"Twenty-six when she died."

Royce couldn't bring himself to ask the obvious question.

"She confided in Jasmine one night. She wanted so badly to have the child, but knew her health wasn't all it should be. It took her a lot of courage to go to the doctor. By then, the cancer was too far advanced for treatment, even if they could have done anything while she was pregnant. When Jasmine offered to take her in, she agreed with great reluctance. She'd been on the streets so long, but she knew she had to overcome her fears for her baby to live."

"So she lived with Jasmine's family before the birth?"

"And after," Francis confirmed. "Her health declined rapidly. But she was smart enough to make sure Rosie wouldn't end up on the streets. They'd barely finished the adoption process before she died."

Jasmine glanced their way. Her smile here had a different, softer quality. Instead of the take-charge woman he'd butted heads with, in this environment, her leadership abilities seemed to be subdued under a layer of compassion.

Francis cleared his throat, reengaging Royce's attention. "All that to say, Jasmine has volunteered here for years, but she's also changed her entire life to take care of someone in need. There's no doubt she loves Rosie. Her entire family loves her. But it was, and is, a huge sacrifice in one so young."

"Why are you telling me this?" Royce asked. After all, this was technically a business meeting.

Francis studied him for a long moment, a slight smile on his face. "Call it intuition or the prompting of the Spirit, but something tells me you need to know. Even if Jasmine is just your event planner."

Why did that last statement sound more like a question to Royce? And why was he trying to fool himself into thinking he wasn't interested?

"What about the children here?" Royce asked, eager to change the subject. He thought back to the boys in the gym. He hadn't failed to notice the worn lettering on their clothes and thinness of the soles on their shoes—and remembered the years that his own clothes had looked the same. "Is there anything special they need?"

"Right now, just the usual things that they always need. We have families who fund scholarships for some of our regulars in the after-school programs for disadvantaged families. Those scholarships and donors are coordinated by the Jefferson family from Savannah."

The Jeffersons. Instead of filing that detail away to use to his own advantage, Royce felt gratitude wash over him. They were doing so much for these kids. How much of a difference would it have made to him, to his mother, if he'd had the opportunity to participate in an after-school program like they offered here?

"We do have some other special programs we would love funding for, but I don't want to appear greedy."

Royce waved away his words. "It's not greedy when I asked. I'll have my assistant contact you for more information, okay?"

Francis nodded. "Thank you again."

"It's my pleasure." And Royce had a feeling he was going to have to admit to Jasmine that he'd changed his point of view. He wanted to be more involved in this charity event now. That had probably been her whole point in bringing him here: educating him for far more than just being able to talk knowledgably about his event's charity.

She'd done a thorough job of it, too.

Sure enough, they'd barely made it to the sidewalk in front of the cars when she paused and said, "Not as bad as you thought, was it?"

He turned to face her where she leaned against the moss-covered retaining wall. "You enjoy being right, don't you."

"Only with you." She grinned, her sassy joy drawing him out of his shell and into the sheer life she exuded. He found he was beginning to like her energy and enthusiasm—very much.

He shook his head, knowing he was going crazy. But for once, he didn't care about losing control. "You're incredible, you know?"

"Not really."

Royce leaned in close, propping one hand against the wall next to her glossy black hair. He swallowed hard against the emotions welling up despite himself. "To prove to my father that my life was worth something, I pursued wealth that would far surpass his."

For the first time, he let himself reach over and touch her thick hair. "To prove that life was still worth living after your parents died, you dedicated yourself to your family and taking care of others."

He stepped closer, bringing their bodies together even though he knew he shouldn't. "In the eyes of most people, that's incredible. Especially me."

Then Royce let his logical brain take a hike and brought his lips down on hers. Her taste was just as exotic as her name. Royce's craving shifted into overdrive.

If he'd thought it would just be a quick peck, he was mistaken. Instead, his body pressed closer. His mouth opened over hers. Her lips left a slightly sweet taste on his tongue, but it was the heat inside that he sought.

The catch of her breath sent a streak of sensation through him. He wanted to explore all the ways he could make her react. All the hidden places on her body that would make her gasp and moan. But for now, he focused on the heat of her mouth and the sexiness of her response.

After long, exquisite moments, Royce forced himself to pull back. To regain control. To think about Jasmine instead of his own sorry self.

Which meant he couldn't bring himself to look into those gorgeous blue eyes to see exactly how he'd ruined everything.

Ten

How in the world was she supposed to act after that kiss?

As Jasmine waited for Royce outside the nondescript building that housed one of the hottest restaurants in Savannah, she tried to shut her brain down. But the question wouldn't go away.

Not even in the face of her curiosity about the restaurant. She'd never been to After Hours before today. Word in elite circles was that it was incredible, but Jasmine had never been able to afford to eat here. And, to her knowledge, they didn't cater events, so she'd let it slide off her radar.

But Royce had insisted he knew exactly what he wanted done with the food for the charity event, and After Hours was it. Since she didn't have to pry or coax the opinion from him, she'd let him lead.

"Are you ready?"

Jasmine jumped. Tightening her control, she forced

herself to take a deep breath before turning toward Royce. "I'm not sure," she admitted.

Instead of leering, Royce faced her with a benign grin. He could have approached the situation any number of ways, considering how she'd sprinted for her car after he'd kissed her on Saturday, but he didn't appear to be messing with her.

Though there was something suspicious…

"What's so funny?" she demanded, hiding her embarrassment behind a sassy attitude.

"You," he admitted. "Seeing you off kilter is honestly a little fun."

She studied him a little closer, but still didn't see any signs of sexual innuendo. That was a relief, but she still had the urge to call him a brat. Even if Auntie would say it was unladylike.

Instead she let him lead her inside with a light grip on her elbow. Being on his territory was fun, but not nearly as comfortable as being the one in control. His confident stride and barely there grin said he definitely knew it.

The closed restaurant was dark, though sunshine tried to peek in around the drawn blinds. The hushed emptiness was disconcerting, though as much as she hated to admit it, the darkness evoked a sense of intimacy.

This meeting didn't have the same strictly business feel that their previous ones had started out with, even if they had all ended up being out of the ordinary. Especially the last one—that kiss had changed everything for her.

Though she'd never admit it, even under threat of torture.

One of the tall silver doors at the back of the room swung open, revealing a tall, lanky guy in a white chef's coat. "Royce!"

"Marco." Royce stepped forward to shake the other

man's hand with more enthusiasm than Jasmine had seen from him before. "Good to see you, buddy."

"I wouldn't miss this for the world."

"Marco, this is my event planner, Jasmine Harden."

The chef turned his smile in her direction. "Welcome to After Hours."

"Thank you for having us," she murmured, leaving out how she'd always wanted to see the inside of this place. Now didn't seem the time to fawn over something that was so far outside her middle-class budget. Instead, she tried to keep her demeanor as professional as possible.

"Why don't y'all come back into the kitchen first?" Marco asked.

Jasmine followed him, her heeled boots clicking against the Italian tile floor.

"Royce mentioned that you were unfamiliar with our restaurant," Marco said over his shoulder. "We serve fresh, local, organic food whenever possible. The focus here is a modern Mediterranean cuisine, though we can add some Latin influence, since I know Royce likes things spicy."

"Royce Brazier?" Jasmine asked, thinking of the by-the-book businessman she constantly butted heads with. "Are you sure?"

Marco simply laughed, even though Jasmine was only half teasing. And she was pretty sure she could make out the hint of a blush stealing over Royce's fair cheeks, despite the darkness.

Not wanting to embarrass him further, or draw out any discussion over how "spicy" he might like things, Jasmine said, "I wasn't aware After Hours catered." They'd never been on her list before today.

Marco grinned. "That's because we don't."

Jasmine looked between the two men. "I'm not sure I understand."

"We don't actually cater here, but I told Royce I would help him out for this event."

Jasmine was already shaking her head. "That's not a good idea." The last thing she wanted was an inexperienced staff working her star event.

"Don't worry," Royce said. "Marco did plenty of catering during school and early in his career."

"And I'm strictly a food man these days. So I've already partnered with Geraldine's to handle the catering service and staffing. You've heard of her?" Marco asked.

"Yes. I've worked with her on several occasions." Knowing that the logistics were taken care of helped calm Jasmine's panic.

Royce nodded as if that settled everything. "Well," he said, "let's show Jasmine what we had in mind."

Jasmine glanced over at him in surprise. That conspiratorial look was back again. For good reason.

When it came to food, Royce showed that he had a few surprises up his sleeve over the next half an hour. Instead of sitting back and only asking a few questions, as he had throughout most of their other meetings, the catering discussion brought out a passion in Royce she'd never seen before...or rather, only seen once before.

She'd more than seen it when he'd pressed his lips against hers.

She watched in unabashed awe as they tossed around menu ideas involving lobster, truffles and exotic spices. Royce certainly knew gourmet food. Jasmine had very little to add except for a few tips and tricks she'd learned throughout all the events she'd executed over the last five years.

Before long, Marco was shooing them to a table in

the main room so he could assemble some sample plates for them. Jasmine grinned at Royce as they were seated. "He doesn't have to do this. I have a feeling anything that comes out of that kitchen is gonna be incredible."

Royce shook his head. "I never turn down the chance to taste anything Marco wants to make for me."

"You seem to know each other well."

"Since we were kids. We grew up not far from each other."

Jasmine wasn't sure if she wanted to broach the subject of his childhood. To change the conversation from business to personal. Instead, she glanced around the elegantly stark room now that the lights had been turned up some.

"Is he the one who taught you so much about food?"

Royce only hesitated a moment before he said, "I learned to cook really young, because my mom was gone at all hours."

So much for avoiding the personal.

"She would also bring home leftovers from different events where she served. That's how I developed a taste for food that was far out of our budget."

"I can sympathize." Jasmine rarely sampled anything that could be labeled *cuisine*, except at her events. They were more of a down home food family.

Royce grinned. "I'll have to cook for you sometime."

Seriously? The guy could cook?

He must have read the thoughts on her face. "Let me guess. You thought I was only the order-in type."

"Instead of?"

"The mess-up-the-dishes-and-have-to-run-the-dishwasher type." He relaxed back into his chair. "I spend all day out. Believe it or not, cooking is very relaxing."

"Well…I wouldn't know," she admitted.

This time he was the one to look shocked. "You don't cook? I thought every good Southern girl cooked."

"I prefer to eat the fruits of someone else's labors, in this instance."

"Then this is perfect for you," Marco said as he approached across the room.

He deftly placed a couple of long, hand-glazed platters on the table, each filled with gorgeous little colorful morsels that smelled as good as they looked.

"Oh, my."

Royce glanced up at his friend. "I think she's sold without a single bite."

"Just wait until she tastes it," Marco said with a grin, then strode back toward the kitchen.

Jasmine surveyed the bounty. "I don't know what to try first."

"There's an art to it."

She raised a brow at him. This was the first time the tables had been turned—a nonbusiness situation where Royce gave *her* advice.

"Trust me?"

He waited for her nod before lifting a tiny lettuce leaf cradling what appeared to be a meat and vegetable mixture off one of the trays. "Start here."

Before she could lift a hand to take it from him, he'd brought the bite to her lips. Jasmine felt her smile disappear as she blinked. She could do this. She would remain professional.

Even though this felt far from professional.

She let her lips open. Just as she took the food into her mouth she glanced up and met the delicious heat of his stare. Their proximity reminded her of his kiss, his lips over hers. Talk about delicious.

Sudden flavor burst over her tongue. Cool, crisp lettuce.

Spicy meat with an undertone of shrimp. A sweet drizzle that she couldn't quite identify. As she moaned, she could see a reflection of her own experience in his eyes. His grin said he knew exactly what she was tasting. He picked up a matching hors d'oeuvre and slid it between his lips.

"Just the right amount of sweet to balance the spice," he said after he swallowed. Lifting a wineglass from the tray, he washed the morsel down.

Jasmine did the same. Her inspection of the trays revealed several options for her next bite, but Royce knew exactly what he wanted her to have. Taste after taste, he walked her through the platters. Spicy butter glazed lobster skewers, meatballs spiced up with chorizo, jerk chicken mini-pizzas...her taste buds were in heaven.

"You were right," she admitted about halfway through.

Royce gave her the most suggestive look she'd ever seen on his face. "About what?"

"The food."

He feigned shock. "I did something right?"

"This time you did, smart aleck. This food will be the talk of the town for months after the event."

"Marco will be thrilled to hear it."

"But you won't."

He shrugged, sobering a little. "I really couldn't care one way or another. But if I can help him even a little with this, then I'll count it as a plus."

"That's a great thing to do."

He shrugged again, then searched the platter with renewed enthusiasm and chose another morsel. Jasmine thought she heard the buzz of a phone but couldn't bring herself to care as she helped herself to a hyped-up version of teriyaki steak that ravished her taste buds.

A good fifteen minutes later, Jasmine heard the phone buzzing again. This time it was accompanied by Royce's grimace. He pulled his cell phone from his pocket and read the texts. "It's Matthew."

For the first time, Jasmine wished that he would ignore his phone. For the first time, her reasons were personal.

The telltale buzz filled the space between them. Matthew wasn't giving up. "I have to go," Royce said.

For the first time, the regret in Royce's voice matched Jasmine's feelings.

"Too bad," she said, not caring that her voice had gone husky. "I was having fun."

His gaze met hers, bringing a return of the electric atmosphere from earlier. "Me, too."

"Isn't your business ever fun?" Deep down, she knew she was past the point of being strictly professional.

"I'm good at it," he finally answered. "But no. Business has never been fun...until now."

"So the ring is working!"

"No," Jasmine insisted, frowning at her youngest sister. "That is not what I said at all."

"Close enough."

Why had she even broached this topic? Jasmine should have known better. Her sisters—both of them—had a tendency to take a notion and run with it. Auntie presided over the scene from her recliner in the corner of the breakfast nook. The mischievous look on her face meant there would be no help coming from that direction.

"I don't know why I tell y'all anything," Jasmine complained. "It's just—" But the word *business* wouldn't move past the constriction in her throat. She crossed the kitchen to stir the big pot of soup on the stove. Willow had chosen the perfect dinner for a rainy Saturday.

Though the chatter continued behind her, Willow appeared at her side. "Are you okay?"

While confident and decisive, Willow was also very sensitive to others. No one was more willing to lend a helping hand when she saw someone who needed it.

Jasmine lowered her voice. "I just can't forget how he talked about learning to cook because his mother was never home. And about being named after his father's car."

She absently stirred the soup, watching chunks of veggies appear and disappear beneath the liquid surface. The lack of sunlight in the room left the green jewel in her ring lackluster; Jasmine still had the feeling the jewelry was mocking her.

"I don't know what this is, but Ivy's right—it's not just business anymore."

Ring or no ring.

Willow gave a tiny squeal that she quickly silenced under Jasmine's glare.

"What about him? What does he think?" Willow asked, echoing Jasmine's own questions.

She didn't want to admit that Mr. Business was turning out to be someone completely unexpected. Jasmine could never have guessed that the stern CEO she'd met in his office that first day would be able to melt her with such a hot kiss. But hadn't that tattoo on his neck hinted at hidden depths? A tattoo she had yet to see in its entirety, now that she thought about it.

"From your silence, I gather Royce is showing signs of moving in a different direction, too," Willow filled in for her.

"Surprisingly," Jasmine mused. "I think so."

"So why not just go with it?"

Jasmine gave the soup a final stir, then peeked into the oven at the cornbread sizzling in a cast-iron skillet. It was a simple delaying tactic, since they all knew cooking wasn't in her skill set.

"It's not that easy." She glanced over her shoulder to check on Rosie, who was cooing at Auntie and Ivy from her bouncy seat. "Even leaving aside the fact that he's my boss...of sorts. How can I get involved? Royce definitely isn't the family type. I have Rosie..."

"She's six months old," Ivy said from right behind them.

Jasmine jumped. "How'd you move that quick?"

Ivy had a baby face, but her grin made her look even younger. "I have my ways." She shook her head, making her blond curls dance. "And I wasn't about to miss what all the whispering was about, now, was I?"

She linked her arm with Jasmine's and adopted the expression of a captive audience. "Now's the perfect time for you to live a little. Rosie isn't old enough to notice at this age. Later, you'll need to be more careful because she'll realize when Mommy is gone or bringing someone to visit."

"I don't know." Everything about this change in their attitudes toward each other had Jasmine off kilter. She and Royce had sparred from the moment they met. But now, something different was emerging. Something she wasn't sure she was ready to face.

Willow nodded in agreement with Ivy, but Jasmine didn't want to concede that her baby sister was right. She searched for a reply that didn't make her look like a scaredy-cat. From across the room, Jasmine's ringtone filled the air.

"Sweetheart," Auntie called. "It's that nice young man from the hospital."

Jasmine shared a look with Willow. The temptation to ignore the call was strong. Jasmine wasn't ready for the test she could sense was coming around the corner.

"Why don't you answer it?" Ivy teased. "After all, it's just business."

"Brat."

Willow was less about talk than action. She simply herded Jasmine in the direction of her phone. Jasmine removed her apron as she went. She caught the call right before it switched to voice mail. As she answered, she was acutely aware of her audience.

"Hello?"

"Jasmine?"

Even his voice sounded different. The cadence a little slower. The tone a touch deeper. How was that possible? "Yes?"

"Since our tasting session was cut short, I thought I'd make it up to you by cooking dinner for you."

That was more like Royce—straight to the point. It was the nature of his point she couldn't quite grasp.

She could feel the eyes of everyone in the room staring at her. Even Rosie seemed to be watching, still and waiting for her answer to an unknown question. Jasmine hesitated. Going to Royce's penthouse was definitely not business. She glanced back and forth between Willow's encouraging expression and Ivy's excited one. Jasmine forced herself to turn away, to lay the burden of other people's expectations aside for once.

Even as she paced a few steps and opened her mouth to answer, she wasn't sure what to say. Was she ready for this? Probably not.

But then she thought over everything she'd been through in the last year. Learning Rosie's mother was pregnant, that she would probably die. Bringing her to live here. Taking care of her family while learning to be a mother for the first time. All while holding down a crazy job.

What the hell—it was time to live for once.

Eleven

Royce knew he was in trouble the minute Jasmine walked out of the elevator into the foyer in one of those feminine, flowy dresses she wore. Only this one seemed to have a little more oomph—a little extra cleavage, a slit up one side. Or was his overheated brain imagining that?

He felt like someone had flipped a switch inside him, jumpstarted an electrical pulse that shot through him whenever Jasmine was near. It was like the exhilaration of implementing a successful business plan—only a hundred times harder and sharper.

He didn't want to fight it anymore. Didn't want to fight her.

Make love, not war. Wasn't that a phrase from days past? His mother used to say it. Not that it had gotten her far. Her inability to go to war against his father had turned her life into endless days of drudgery—until Royce had stepped in to change that.

Royce opened the door to his penthouse to allow Jasmine inside. Her heels clicked on the glossy black tile. She breathed deep. "Something smells incredible," she said. Her slight smile intrigued him.

Was she nervous?

When she swallowed, it confirmed his suspicions, though he had to look hard to notice. "You weren't kidding that you could cook," she said.

"I just need to finish a few last-minute things. You aren't averse to any particular seafood, are you?"

She shook her head, bringing his attention to the thick dark hair swinging around her shoulders.

"That's good, or else this would be a complete disaster," he said with a laugh that seemed to break the unexpected tension between them. "I'm finishing up some shrimp scampi. The sides and salad are ready. But I wimped out on the dessert."

"Not you," Jasmine mocked in her sassy way.

"I'm not a pastry chef. I figured since we didn't make it to dessert the other day, I'd go by Marco's and pick up a praline cheesecake."

The O of her mouth was encouraging—and sexy as hell. "Sounds awesome," she said. "But I'm surprised you would admit you can't cook everything."

"I realized a long time ago that there was no point in pretending to be something I'm not."

Her delectable body went still for mere seconds, but Royce caught it. He should have expected a question to follow.

"Was it a problem? Early on?"

He waved her farther into the living area as thoughts swirled through his mind. He watched her take in the comfortably luxurious space. Royce had never wanted to live in a showplace. A few designers had tried to convince him otherwise, but eventually he'd found someone who understood his preferences. The magnificent space was in one of Savannah's formerly dilapidated shipping warehouses, now refurbished for people who could afford the best—although his "best" meant an awesome sound system, overstuffed leather furniture and a magnificent view. Not high-priced works of art and anemic, uncomfortable chairs.

Jasmine seemed to agree. "Wow," she breathed as she approached the wall of windows looking out toward downtown and the river.

The architect had pushed out the walls so the floor extended all the way to the stone arches that used to frame an old balcony for ship watching. The arches were now fitted with glass panes for an extended view from inside the unusual room.

"This is an incredible blend of old and new," she said. "I'm very impressed."

"It's relaxing when I finally make it home at night."

The black mirrored tile from the foyer gave way to glossy wood floors in the living areas. Royce walked over to the bar in the far corner. "Having you here gives me a chance to use the bar. I hardly ever have company."

He fixed the martini she requested while she strolled along the long wall of windows, skirted the corner bar and continued along the shorter wall. "Incredible."

"Thank you."

"And thank you for inviting me here." This time her look was more straightforward, promising.

Royce felt his insides heat up. "Well, thanks to you, I'm learning to mix business with pleasure."

She lifted the martini glass in salute. "Me, too."

If he let this go much farther, dinner would be burned beyond recognition. "I'd better finish up the food."

As he turned away, he heard her footsteps behind him. "Mind if I join you?"

He paused, giving her a chance to catch up. "Please feel free."

As they walked down a short corridor and into his designer kitchen, he had to chuckle.

"What's so funny?" she asked.

"I just realized." He paused, then let a long, slow breath ease out, surprised he was admitting this. "I just realized that, besides my mother and the cleaning lady, you are the first person to ever join me in my kitchen."

"Wow. Really?"

He watched as her blue gaze roamed over the mahogany cabinets with their black hardware, the cream ceramic appliances and the black tile on the walls. She made a beeline for the stools on the other side of the kitchen island. The large room was designed for social gatherings, but Royce had never used it as such.

"Yes," he murmured. "Really."

But what was even odder was how comfortable he felt with her in his space, if comfortable was even the word to describe the electrical connection that continued to surprise him.

But it wasn't the only thing that surprised him. He was also bemused by how completely at ease they were with each other. They ended up eating at the island in the kitchen, seated across from each other on stools. Her eyes sparkled just as much as her wineglass under the lights. Their conversation flowed naturally from the upcoming masquerade to other events they'd attended.

After exclaiming over the food with genuine enthusiasm, Jasmine took her wineglass and wandered back down the hallway to the living room. Night had taken full hold. The mature trees below and the climbing ivy overflowing the outer walls onto the windowsills gave the impression of being protected by nature as they looked onto the lights spread out before them. Savannah was a city of hard brick and lush greenery. "It really is beautiful, Royce." She half turned toward him. "I can't believe your mother loved the manor house more."

"She did enjoy the view here, but I think Keller House made her think of a time when she was happier, when life had possibilities."

Jasmine was nice enough to add, "But in the end, she was left with the knowledge that she had raised a fully capable young man who would take care of himself and her."

He glanced down into his glass, feeling a familiar mixture of sadness and pride. "She didn't have to worry anymore."

Suddenly he felt a brush of warmth on his arm. Through his dress shirt, he could feel the outline of Jasmine's hand. He couldn't count the number of times recently he had dreamed of how soft her skin would be against his. How those perfectly manicured nails would feel against his back. Or how the curves of her body would feel pressed against his.

She was offering comfort. He needed to remind himself of that.

Then she stepped closer. Any effort at restraint became exponentially harder. He allowed himself a glance, only to find her gaze locked on him. And it wasn't overflowing with sympathy. With just one look they both knew exactly where this was headed. "Will you stay the night?" he finally asked.

"Do you really need to ask?"

That amused him. "Sweetheart, with you I never assume anything."

Her smile was a concession to everything they'd been through so far. "Then let me make myself plain. Assume all you want."

Royce may have been cautious about getting to a more intimate stage, but when the time came, Jasmine found he was as focused in the bedroom as he was in the board-room.

One minute they were facing each other, then he took a few purposeful steps to bring her within reach. She barely had time to blink before Royce's hand was in her hair and his mouth once more covered hers. The heat that she remembered from their first kiss was there, this time underpinned by a purpose that made her insides melt.

He tasted spicy, which ramped up the temperature in-side her. There was nothing tentative about his kiss. In-stead, he conquered her with smooth glides and strong pulls. There was nothing more for her to do than enjoy.

When he pulled back, she was tempted to beg him not to stop, but she clamped her teeth over her lower lip to keep the words inside. Her body was anxious, aching for the race to be finished. But Jasmine wanted to savor the ride. She glanced up to find his gaze glued to the deep V of her neckline—a design she'd deliberately chosen with him in mind.

Then her own gaze dropped and she glimpsed the edges of his neck tattoo above the open collar of his but-ton-down shirt. Curious, she let her fingers trail over the skin of his neck to push the material aside.

To her surprise, the elegant tendrils she'd often glimpsed above his collar gave way to a solid shield, an old-world symbol emblazoned with a brilliantly colored dragon. It stood for strength. Protection. Not what she'd expected, but somehow very fitting for the man she was coming to know.

Her smile gave him all the permission he needed. His palms slid from the back of her neck down over her collarbones, leaving warm trails that quickly faded. When he finally reached her breasts, she gasped. Her nipples tightened in a quick rush, eager for attention.

He simply held them, each mound a handful. The heat from his hands soaked into her skin through the layers of her clothing. She couldn't stop her back from arching just a little. Then his thumbs began a dedicated exploration that made her wish her clothes would just disappear.

She had no recollection of ever needing someone to see her, touch her, this badly. It was scary—just as much as it was exhilarating.

After long, long moments of exquisite torture, his devilish hands moved down—tracing her generous curves. His touch wasn't simple. No. It was magic. The pressure and heat imprinted the feel of him on her skin.

How could a seemingly innocent touch make her knees go weak? Cause her bones to melt until she leaned forward, her hands braced on his shoulders as he knelt before her?

He eased off one of her high-heeled pumps. His thumbs traced the line of her foot before he squeezed hard into the arch, surprising a gasp from her. Maintaining the pressure, he slid his fingers along the silky surface of her thigh-highs. Too soon, he reached underneath her skirt to find the tops of her stockings and roll them down her legs.

Who knew being undressed could be such a sensual dance?

By the time both legs were bare, Jasmine's entire body throbbed. Royce looked up at her from his crouching position. "Take your dress off for me."

She knew where every tie was, every clasp. But she kept her movements slow, taking her time, building anticipation. It was worth ignoring her own need to see his eyes widen as she revealed a pale pink, lace-edged slip over matching bra and panties. When the dress finally puddled at her feet, he gripped her silk-covered hips and buried his face against her.

She thought she heard him suck in a deep breath. His hands tightened for a moment. Her tummy quivered beneath his cheek. Her throat went dry while she grew slick between her thighs.

Royce stood, only pulling his hands away at the very last minute. That small concession told her more than anything that he wanted her as much as she wanted him. Then he circled around her to take in the view from every angle. To her surprise, he turned her to face the window. That's when she realized their reflections stared back as if from an antique mirror. Hazy. Shimmery.

"This," he said, running a finger along one bra strap, then the lace that edged the top curve of one breast, "is very sexy." He pulled the straps down off her shoulders. Then he hooked his fingers in the material of her slip and slowly eased it down over her curves. "But it isn't what I'm most interested in seeing."

She had only a moment to catch the reflection of herself in the bra and panties before he picked her up and carried her down a longer hallway to the back of the penthouse.

With a quick sweep of her gaze, she took in the dim bedroom with dark furniture and smoky walls before Royce arranged her on the comforter on her knees, facing him as he stood beside the bed. The soft moonlight from the bedroom windows revealed his outline, but the details of his expression were now lost to her. Once more he traced the edges of the clothes she had left before slipping his hands beneath the silk of her panties to cup her rear.

His touch was firm, with just enough concession to her softness. Pulling her close, he rubbed his fully clothed body against her. The fact that he was covered while she was practically naked left her feeling decadent. The pressure of his erection excited her. Her body went wet in anticipation.

Again, that firm grip guided her down until she lay on the bed. His mouth devoured hers, teeth nipping her lips, tongue delving inside to stroke against hers.

She lost herself in the sensations.

Then, somehow, his mouth was sucking at her naked breast, pulling cries from her straining lungs. He worked one nipple, then the other until they were tight and hard. Electrical pulses streaked through her. She lifted her pelvis against him, more than ready for some relief from the driving urges inside her body.

Deftly, Royce rose to his knees. His dress shirt was gone in seconds. He opened his pants to reveal the very thing she needed in this moment. He put on protection quickly, efficiently. Then, with a snap of his wrist, he broke through her panties. All barriers were gone. Finally his body covered hers.

She could feel the rub of his suit pants against the insides of her thighs as his body searched for her opening. His fingers spread her wide, coating her with her own moisture to ease the way. Then they teased her, drawing out her cries of desperation.

Not soon enough, he entered her. She struggled for a moment to accommodate him. The pressure was exquisite. One lift of her hips and he slid inside.

There was no more waiting, no more savoring. They were both too desperate.

She clutched at his ribs as he pistoned into her, demanding her response. Indulging his own. Her cries mingled with his groans in the darkness.

All too soon, she needed more. Needed his utmost. She dug her nails into his buttocks, urging him to give her everything.

Then the exquisite pressure burst. The world turned white in a shower of stars. But the best part of it all was knowing that he followed her.

Twelve

Royce woke to movement on the other side of the bed. He opened his eyes. Though there weren't any lights on, he could see Jasmine walk around the end of the bed and out the door to the hallway. It was 1:30 a.m.

The normal debate he'd expect to have with himself never occurred. He simply acknowledged that he had no desire for Jasmine to leave. Getting up, he took a few seconds to pull on a pair of boxers—more for her comfort than his. Then he followed her to the living room.

He located her in one corner near the window by the light of her phone. She seemed to be reading from the screen. As he got closer, he could see that she'd pulled on her slip. Just the thought of that silky material over her naked skin sent him spinning.

Now he knew how someone could become addicted after just one hit.

"Everything okay?" he asked softly, hoping not to scare her.

She only jumped a little. Then she shook her head. "Yeah. I was just checking in."

The silence hung between them for a minute, but for Royce it wasn't the usual awkwardness that came with this situation. Though he could honestly say he'd never been in this situation before. He'd never fallen asleep next to any of the few women he'd bothered to let distract him enough from work to get to sex. Now he couldn't think of anything he wanted more than for Jasmine to spend the rest of the night.

That should have had him freaking out, but he wasn't going to analyze why it didn't.

"Need to go?" he finally asked.

Jasmine hesitated. If he'd been in her situation, he would have, too. Honestly, there was no way she could possibly imagine him wanting her to stay. After all, look at his past behavior.

Covering the few steps left between them, Royce let his body act on instinct. He reached out and cupped the cool skin of her upper arms. Then he rubbed up and down, aiming to warm her. But also to fulfill his own craving to simply touch her.

She stared up at him in the dark. Beneath his touch she shivered, then she shook her head.

For him, the answer was simple. "Then come back to bed."

When they got back to the bed, that first touch of skin on skin exhilarated him. He rolled over her, covering her cool body with his warmth. Savoring the gasp of air that signaled her surrender.

Royce moaned against her neck, opening his mouth to feel her pulse against his tongue. Her taste was unique, almost floral, but sweet, too. His body responded by hardening, and he reached for her. *Holy smokes*.

"You are like a gourmet meal for me alone."

Jasmine arched against him. He breathed her in, nipping her ear and burying his hands in her hair. This time he savored her touch, too. The feel of her palms grazing down his sides. The light scrape of her nails across his ass. The softness of her lips beneath his.

Her legs slid apart, making a home for him between them. He rubbed himself against her most sensitive spot, wanting to shout because she was so wet for him.

Lifting himself a little, he regretted the space he had to create, if only for a moment. Quickly he covered himself with a condom, then worked his way inside of her. So tight. Incredibly hot. There was no way he could wait.

He was overcome with an instinct to imprint her with his scent, his touch, in case she ever thought she could walk away. Where the possessive urges came from, he had no idea. They were unique to Jasmine. He couldn't resist.

As he gave his first long, slow thrust, he rubbed his body up hers. Never had full body contact felt so good. He felt her slick skin, alert nipples, harsh breath. Most of all, the clasp of her around him.

He anchored his hands in her hair. Then he started to thrust in earnest. The strain in his thighs, the twist of his hips, didn't seem to be enough. Her nimble legs encircled his hips, urging him to thrust harder. Faster.

He attuned his senses to her body's responses. Not just her breath and the lift of her hips, but the subtle clutch of her muscles around his hardness. He nurtured every hint of ecstasy until she called his name in the darkness. They worked together until Royce thought his heart would explode. But he couldn't let go until she did.

Shifting his angle, he ground against the soft cushion of her mound with his pelvis. Her breath caught. Her neck arched. Her hold on him tightened. Then there was the extra force that threw her over the edge.

Her incredible cries filled his ears as her body clamped down hard and milked him dry. There was no denying the demand for him to join her.

Now or ever again.

"I haven't seen you in three days," Royce pointed out. With some men, the reminder would have been a whine. With him, it was a simple logical statement. Until he got to the question. "Are you trying to tell me something?"

In this instance, the complications were all on Jasmine's side. Not Royce's. Most men would have been trying to find ways to keep a woman at arm's length. Not this time.

Much to her surprise.

She wanted to sigh as she glanced over the planner on the desk before her. She wished it wasn't overflowing with Willow's classes, Ivy's job and blocks of time that she really needed a sitter for Rosie. Facts were facts. She should have known life would interfere with the blissful two weeks she'd spent exploring the incredibly sensual side of Royce Brazier—but she couldn't keep business and her personal life separate forever.

She'd never been good at juggling.

But *business* wasn't even the right word. What she and Royce were doing in the luxurious bedroom of his penthouse had nothing to do with business. Still, she was doing her best to keep him and her family far away from each other. Royce had made it clear he wasn't in the market for a family. She was a single woman with a small child. The last thing she wanted was for him to think she was daddy hunting.

For a man like him, the title of *daddy* would never be an option.

"I just can't get away tonight." The planner clearly showed that Willow had a night class to teach. And Ivy had called to say she would probably be working late that night. Auntie was recovering nicely, but her abilities and stamina with a small child were limited. This left Jasmine between a rock and...well, a very lonely, needy place.

Royce hesitated for only a moment. "Would your family object to me dropping by?"

"Why would you?"

Silence greeted her unexpected question, but only for a moment. Just long enough for her to feel mortified.

"Believe it or not, Jasmine," Royce said, without any of the angry heat she would have expected, "I do enjoy more about you than just the sex."

Jasmine almost choked.

"And they have met me before," he reminded her.

Not as a potential suitor. At least, in her eyes. This visit just might confirm what her family was expecting...except Jasmine knew her liaison with Royce could never live up to the romantic fantasy they would build in their minds.

When she finally answered, her voice sounded small. "It just didn't occur to me you would want to come by."

"Jasmine." His voice deepened, almost a reflection of the turmoil rumbling around inside of her. "I'm finding, to my surprise, that I'll take you any way I can get you."

Royce always was one to tell the truth, whether the other person wanted to hear it or not. The sheer enormity of his confession shut her up quick. They agreed on a time for him to drop by.

The bewilderment and need in his voice were still

eliciting tremors later that evening as she waited for him to arrive. Mostly because they echoed her own feelings.

She found her attachment to Royce too close for comfort. Her craving for him only grew each time they were together. She wanted to bounce ideas off him at odd times. She even wished she could spar with him on occasion. Talking to him. Cooking with him. Making love with him. He never failed to stimulate her in some way—in all the ways that mattered.

But he wasn't a family man—had no desire to ever be one. So her need for him to be more than he could offer scared her more than anything.

Her hands still shook as she opened the door that evening. It should have been a scene from a romantic movie—a handsome man on her doorstep with blooming trees filling the background behind him as the sun set. Instead, it could have been the boogeyman at her door, if her feelings of trepidation were to be believed.

"Hey," she greeted him, her voice hushed.

"Hey, yourself." He matched his tone to hers as he glanced behind her. "Are we having a secret liaison on your doorstep or is there something I need to know?"

That would have been funny if she hadn't actually been keeping her family in the dark as much as possible since that night two weeks ago. Still, she tried for an amused grin, ignoring her nerves.

"No. Auntie and Rosie fell asleep."

Letting him in, she gestured toward the entrance to the family room, where Auntie could be seen lying propped up with lots of pillows on the couch. Rosie reclined against her, pacifier in place, blanket snuggled close. There was a cartoon on the TV turned to a low volume.

"They were watching television together. But Rosie

seems to have caught Auntie's tendency to take cat naps now that she's having to rest her leg so much."

Royce studied the sleeping pair, though Jasmine couldn't read his expression. "She looks peaceful."

She assumed he meant Rosie. "She's a good baby. I'm very, very lucky."

He turned back. "So am I, hopefully."

Jasmine raised an eyebrow. "Trust me. There's not enough time for sex."

Royce quickly smothered a laugh. "I guessed that much. But is a proper hello too much to ask for?"

Jasmine's cheeks burned. Shame on her for accusing him of only having sex on the brain.

Leading the way to the kitchen at the back of the house, she busied herself putting coffee on to perk. Anything to give her blush a chance to subside. She'd learned that Royce was an avid coffee drinker. Caffeine didn't seem to faze him. He drank it at all hours of the day—not that he slept much, anyway.

Only after the task had distracted her from her embarrassment did she cross the room and kiss him. It was a little more than a peck, but not much more before she pulled back. "How was your day?"

Dang it. Though she'd asked him that before, in this setting it took on a different connotation. More of a "How was your day, dear?" connotation.

"The Jeffersons have received my proposal." He grimaced, staring off into space for a moment. That tiny frown between his brows when he focused on something was unexpectedly sexy. "I hope they find everything in order."

"How can they not, with all the hard work you and your assistant put into this? And the masquerade will be fabulous. You're definitely gonna be noticed."

Even though she doubted he needed one, she gave him a hug. Her entire family were huggers. It served as greeting, comfort, reassurance, encouragement, celebration—like a language all its own. She and Ivy had talked at length about the difficulties of being a hugger in a business setting. It was a hard habit to shut off.

Finally, she leaned back to look at him. "Besides, I got good news today."

"What's that?" His voice had gone husky, warning her he was losing interest in business and moving on to far more interesting topics.

She couldn't help but smile. As much as she knew she shouldn't—she loved the effect she had on him. "I received an invite to the Sunday Salon yesterday. We attend on the fifteenth."

"Yes, ma'am. I'll be there with bells on, as my mama used to say." She couldn't help but notice that, even though the words were right, his eyes were trained on her lips.

"That would make a memorable fashion statement," she murmured, just before his lips found hers.

They'd just reached the gasping-and-fumbling-with-clothes stage when Jasmine heard a whimper from the other room. She stiffened.

Pulling back, Royce straightened his tie, then took a deep breath. "I'll just fix myself a cup of coffee," he said.

Leaving him to fend for himself, Jasmine rushed to the living room where Auntie was still snoring softly and Rosie was rubbing her eyes.

After picking the baby up and soothing her with a soft swaying motion for a moment, Jasmine headed back to the kitchen, not wanting to disturb the older woman's rest. Auntie hadn't slept well since her fall. Simply finding a comfortable way to sit or lie down could be a challenge on the bad days.

As soon as she stepped into the kitchen, Jasmine ran into another problem. Rosie stiffened a moment when she noticed the unidentified male in the room. But it didn't bother her for long.

Jasmine was in the process of saying, "You remember Mr. Royce, don't you?" when the little girl threw her whole body forward in a swan dive. Right in Royce's direction. The move was so unexpected that Jasmine wasn't able to get a good grasp. Rosie would have slipped from her arms if Royce hadn't stepped forward and caught Rosie.

Jasmine didn't know if it had been instinct for him, but it saved her daughter from what could have been a nasty tumble to the tile floor.

As soon as she'd caught her breath, Jasmine exclaimed, "Oh, goodness. I don't know how that happened." Her panicked mind replayed the child's jump for Royce over and over.

"No problem," he said, sounding far calmer than she felt. He immediately righted the baby and positioned her in his arms as if it were something he did on a daily basis.

All Jasmine could do was blink and breathe.

Rosie, the little stinker, ignored the drama she'd caused her mama and immediately began to babble at her captive audience. Royce's colorful tie seemed to fascinate her. And Jasmine could swear the baby was actually flirting as she glanced up at Royce's face and bestowed a big, gummy grin on him.

It might have been funny if it was anyone but Royce. The man who wanted nothing to do with family.

"Here. I'll take her," Jasmine offered with a step forward.

"It's fine," he assured her.

Unsure what else to do, she waved toward the table. "Have a seat."

As he settled them in at the dining room table, Jasmine brought his forgotten coffee from the counter. She stood next to them for a moment, fascinated and embarrassed by her daughter's animated behavior—and Royce's ability to take it all in stride. When had this happened?

Before she could get a handle on the scene before her, Jasmine was mortified to hear her sister Ivy say from behind her, "Well, isn't this the perfect picture of domesticity?"

Thirteen

This was not how Royce had planned to spend his evening. Very few men would complain about being surrounded by a roomful of beautiful Southern women, being served delicious home cooking—and Royce wasn't going to be the one to start.

He'd simply planned to spend it with Jasmine. Alone. Preferably naked.

It took considerable self-control not to watch her every move with a hungry gaze, though baby Rosie's attachment to him had dampened his ardor significantly, as had the avid speculation on the other women's faces. He wasn't sure what was up with the little squirt, but she'd apparently decided Royce was her one and only adult tonight. She wasn't having it any other way. Any time Jasmine or her sisters tried to hold Rosie or move her away from him, big tears flooded her little eyes and rolled down her cheeks.

Much to his chagrin, Royce was a sucker for it.

Her high chair had been set beside him with Jasmine on the other side. The setup felt unreal to him, as if his brain couldn't comprehend what he'd gotten himself into. But he also had no desire to hightail it for the front door—an odd development, to say the least.

Normally, he would have been the first one to hit the road.

As they ate, Rosie alternated between her baby food and sippy cup, and playing with the emerald ring on Jasmine's right hand.

"You wear that ring a lot," he said. "Where's it from?"

The table went strangely silent, as if he'd asked something completely inappropriate—or something they didn't really want to answer.

"It's an heirloom piece we recently found in an old jewelry box," Auntie finally said.

Royce could swear the women around him slumped just a little.

"The girls' family line goes all the way back to the origins of Savannah. Their ancestor was a pirate who turned respectable and married the daughter of one of the founding families."

Royce grinned at Jasmine over Rosie's head. "Respectable, huh? So that's where you learned to fit in with the elite crowd so well."

"It's in the genes," she confirmed, putting on a fake bravado.

"It's actually quite fascinating," Willow said before launching into a monologue about Savannah's origins.

"History nerd," Jasmine mumbled out of the side of her mouth.

Royce quickly smothered his laugh when Willow glared. "I would hope so," she declared. "Otherwise I'd suck at teaching it."

"That makes perfect sense," Royce said. "I'm sure someone who loves history makes it much more interesting for her students."

That seemed to mollify Willow—that and sticking her tongue out at her sister.

Royce felt himself relaxing even more. Dinner around the family table was an experience he'd never had. When he and his mother had eaten together, usually on Sundays, they'd sat next to each other in front of the television, eating off of TV trays. He hadn't expected to enjoy this when he'd sat down tonight.

Just then, a soft weight rested against his arm. He glanced down into the two soft brown eyes in Rosie's tiny round face. She blinked slowly, then rubbed her head against his arm.

"Um…" Royce glanced around the table, something akin to panic building in his core.

Willow giggled first, then Ivy. Auntie simply smiled.

Jasmine rolled her eyes, shaking her head at her daughter. "You big flirt."

"She is a woman, after all," Auntie said.

Royce glanced back down. The baby grinned, showing the first of her teeth in her otherwise empty gums. The panic disintegrated. A feeling he didn't recognize settled in its place. Something similar to how he felt when lying exhausted in Jasmine's arms. Almost like…peace.

"How about a change of subject?" Jasmine asked. "After all, I'm not sure how comfortable I am thinking about my six-month-old as a woman. Too early." She turned to Royce. "Shall we talk about the Jeffersons' soirée?"

"Oh, you get to go to that?" Ivy asked. "I loved the times I was allowed to go as Jasmine's guest."

Willow frowned. "Not me. Too many people and I had no idea what to talk about. I much prefer smaller groups."

"Which is why I'm going to the masquerade and you aren't," Ivy said.

"Have fun." Obviously Willow was not the social butterfly type.

Jasmine explained, "Willow is more of an introvert than the rest of us."

"My students are about as big of a group as I can handle," Willow said. "And even that exhausts me sometimes."

"I can sympathize, Willow," Royce said. "I'm a homebody myself. Comfortable only in my private spaces or the office. I don't often attend social events, but when I do, I try to think of these things as business meetings—just with more people present and a more fluid agenda."

"I hate to burst your bubble, but not this time," Jasmine said.

Royce glanced at her over the baby hugging his arm. "What do you mean?"

Her blue eyes were slightly somber. "The Jeffersons don't do business at these things. It's very socially oriented. That's why they are picky about the guest list."

"All of these social events are covers for getting business done. You may not see it, but it's there," Royce insisted. He'd been to enough of them to know, even if such parties weren't his preferred venue. "Otherwise, they'd be a big waste of time."

She was already shaking her head. "Not this time. While there are usually a lot of business people there, it isn't discussed directly. Remember my little talk about building connections, not just business deals? They're just as important. Trust me."

"Sure." *We'll see.* Jasmine was a smart woman. A

whole lot more people smart than he was. But Royce knew business…and he was determined to advance his at every opportunity—no matter what she thought she knew.

Royce would trust his instincts. Every time.

Jasmine smoothed out the collar of her dress, then the skirt. It felt weird to be heading to a public event with Royce. They'd spent plenty of time together in private—delectable time. And, yes, they'd occasionally talked business or gone over progress for the masquerade, but this was different. Something they had never addressed.

Attending the Jeffersons' Sunday Salon with Royce put her on a path that left her with no distinct sense of how to act. Was this business? Was it a date? Would she look into his eyes and see the heat that often exploded between them without warning?

How should she react? Naturally? Or keep it under wraps? All the questions had her twisting her hands together in her lap.

Suddenly Royce pulled his car over and put it in park. Jasmine's stomach flip-flopped. But she swallowed against the tightening in her throat and asked, "Is something wrong?"

"You tell me. *Is* something wrong, Jasmine?"

"How did you know?" As if her stiffness this morning wasn't a clear sign. She'd been hoping he would ignore it.

"You're not at all your normal happy, mischievous self today."

She glanced over at him, realizing that was probably the first time she'd looked directly at him since they'd gotten into the car. No wonder he'd asked. Royce wasn't stupid.

"Sorry."

"Just tell me what it is and we'll figure it out."

He was right. Even though this was the last thing she wanted to talk about, what was the point of prolonging the torture that she'd been enduring for over a month? "I'm just not sure…" She swallowed, trying to loosen up her throat. This was something she'd never had to say to a client. "I'm not sure how you want me to act while we are here…out in public."

His grip tightened on the steering wheel as he nodded slowly. "I see what you mean."

"I know you hired me as your event planner. Attending this party was part of our business agreement. I'm just—"

Without warning, he leaned across the console to cup her face with his palms. The press of his lips to hers was so familiar now, almost as necessary as breathing. The fear, the uncertainty sparked by that revelation, was something she spent a lot of energy ignoring every day.

She opened her eyes to meet his, just inches away.

"I should have known this would be a problem," he murmured.

Her heart sank.

"I have no idea where this is going between us," Royce said.

This was it…he was going to dump her because she'd asked how he wanted her to behave in public.

He rubbed his thumb against her cheek. "But it's time we just accept that it's there and deal with it. Don't you agree?"

"Wait. What?"

"Surprised?" He granted her his rare grin. "Me, too."

As if he couldn't stop himself, he kissed her again. His touch was tinged with a gentleness that had tears burning behind her eyes.

"Listen," he said. "We don't have to be all over each

other. We don't have to ignore what's happening between us, either."

Jasmine took a deep breath, searching his expression. "You don't care if people talk?"

"My mom and I learned a long time ago that talk can't hurt you if you don't let it. You and I started on this path with business as the sole purpose, but we left that behind a while back."

She sat stunned while he pulled back out onto the road. She'd been working hard to convince herself that her time with Royce was limited and would eventually end. That he could never accept Rosie or Jasmine's commitment to her family. All to keep herself from getting too involved.

He'd been so accepting of Rosie the other night. Jasmine hadn't tested it further, but seeing her daughter cuddle up to Royce's arm had done something to her. Made her wonder, for the brief moment she'd allowed herself to, whether this might actually be a possibility. Could this be another sign that what was happening between them might actually work? For real?

Silence reigned until they pulled into the long drive to the Jeffersons' palatial home. They lined up behind the considerable number of cars already parked out front.

It wasn't until Royce came around to help her out that he spoke. And he was so relaxed, it was as if there hadn't been a long silence between them. "So, you just be your beautiful, smart self, and I promise not to accost you when everyone is looking. Okay?"

"What about when they aren't?"

Again he reached out to her cheek, smoothing the pad of his thumb across it as if testing the texture of her skin. She heard the telltale note in his voice that always signaled his arousal as he said, "I'm sorry. I can't make any promises about that."

For the first time since she'd woken up that morning, Jasmine laid her worry aside and smiled. "I guess I'll have to live with that."

It was different, entering the stately house on Royce's arm. She'd been there over a dozen times before, and the Jeffersons had never made her feel anything but welcome. They did the same this time. Still, her smile was a little bigger, her confidence a little higher and her mood a whole lot brighter. Royce stiffened as they went in, but she chalked it up to adrenaline. She doubted Royce ever really felt nerves. But something had to power him through all those business negotiations and decisions.

"Royce Brazier, this is Don and Marilyn Jefferson, our hosts," she said, automatically attempting to put everyone at ease.

The man she'd respected for a long time shook Royce's hand without hesitation. "Welcome to our home. I believe we've met once or twice before, but always on more formal occasions," Don Jefferson said with his slow Southern drawl.

Jasmine was grateful to see Royce meet his gaze and shake his hand without any of the macho posturing she'd had to endure in some Savannah circles. "I believe so, sir. Thank you for having me."

"Always a pleasure. We're glad to see you, but would welcome anyone Miss Jasmine cared to bring with her."

"It was gracious of her to include me in her invite, sir," Royce said, with a smile in her direction that lingered just a little longer than normal.

Jasmine warmed from the inside out, despite the sleeveless summer dress she wore.

"This is my wife, Marilyn. Please, call me Don. Now Jasmine, why don't you show Royce where the food is?

Make yourself at home. We can talk after a while," Mr. Jefferson said.

Fifteen minutes of mingling, with Royce's hand at the small of her back and a mimosa or two, helped Jasmine get a handle on how to behave. She let Royce lead, but introduced him to a few couples he hadn't met before. Most were familiar with his meteoric rise in Savannah's shipping industry but were gracious enough not to grill him on his presence at today's party.

"So, what are you working on now?" Evette Pierce asked Jasmine. She'd been to several of Jasmine's events, and they'd worked together on a charity event last spring.

"It's gonna be so much fun." Jasmine knew she was gushing, but she couldn't hold her excitement in. "We're working on a masquerade night in late May. You'll love it."

"Sounds fascinating."

"It will be. And the proceeds will go to build a dormitory for the mission."

Evette raised her wineglass. "A cause very close to you, I know. You can count on me being there."

As they moved away, Royce leaned closer to whisper, "I thought this wasn't the place to discuss business?"

"She asked," Jasmine said with a shrug. "Besides, it wasn't really business. I was just passing her information about something fun I think she would enjoy."

"Po-*tay*-toes, pot-*ah*-toes."

She simply grinned. "Told you. Everything has a social spin."

"And you are the smarty-pants I should trust to know what she's doing?"

"Every time."

Royce grinned down at her. Movement in the doorway behind him caused her to glance over his shoulder. Don and Marilyn were greeting a man in the foyer. Suddenly Don looked toward her, a frown on his face as his gaze met hers. Only as the other man faced her did she realize who it was. And why Don looked so unhappy.

The man who had just arrived was Royce's father.

Fourteen

"I do want to apologize for the mix-up," Don said as he led Royce down an ornately paneled hallway into an office.

"What mix-up?" Royce asked.

Don let the heavily carved door close then studied Royce for a moment. He had a feeling this wasn't going to be a very comfortable conversation. And he could think of only one subject that would warrant this type of formality from his host.

"Of having your father here without any warning."

Bingo.

Don stepped into the room, gesturing Royce toward a chair while he took the one behind the large desk. "Not all of our guests are as courteous as Jasmine about letting us know who they are bringing with them."

Royce felt the unease that had been simmering since he'd first caught sight of his father rise a little higher. Not for himself, but— "I don't like the idea of him having access to Jasmine." Especially without him there to run interference.

Don offered an approving look. "We agree. Marilyn will be watching over her until you return. I assure you, she's quite capable of handling men of his ilk." He grinned. "Jasmine can, too, though she's often polite to a fault."

He studied Royce for a minute more before he asked, "Does he know about the two of you?"

"What?"

"That your relationship has become personal as well as professional?"

Royce wasn't sure he wanted to address that issue yet. Something had been bothering him since this conversation started.

"How did you know he was my father?" Royce asked. "That's not something I advertise."

"I don't blame you. He's not the kind of man I'd want to claim as a relation, either."

Royce met the other man's gaze in surprise. It wasn't often he had conversations with people who would admit to disliking his father as much as he did.

Don explained. "I'm a very thorough man. I know a lot about you, Royce. I've kept you on my radar for a while. With your meteoric rise on Savannah's business scene, it was inevitable we would do business with each other at some point. When your proposal came in, we had you investigated."

"Why?" But there was something Royce wanted to know more. "Actually, right now, I just want to know if my father has ever tried to do business with you."

Don nodded slowly. "He has attempted to work with us in the past. And, yes, I did investigate him just as thoroughly. But I didn't find the connection at that time."

He smiled at Royce. "I didn't need to investigate to see your relationship with Jasmine. It's all in her face, though she tries to hide it."

Royce could see it, too, every time she looked at him. He was deeply worried his own feelings showed just as clearly, and he wasn't ready for that.

Don leaned back in his chair, causing it to creak. "As to why we investigate the personal backgrounds of potential business associates, I like to know who we're working with. Not just what you're capable of in a business arena, but who you are as a person. Unusual, but that's just how my wife and I like running our company. It works for us."

Royce wasn't sure how he felt about that. He could understand the concern, but the idea that his personal life had been scrutinized wasn't something he was comfortable acknowledging.

"Of course, we don't usually share that knowledge with our employees or contractors," Don said, "but in this instance, I felt it was particularly important."

"Again, why?"

"Well, I doubt this will make you feel any better about my snooping, but we happen to have taken a special interest in Jasmine Harden."

Royce wasn't above digging for his own information. This he wanted to hear. "My event planner?"

Don cocked his head to one side. "Is that all she is?"

"You tell me. You're the one hunting for info."

"Touché. You've just never been known to date much. She's never dated any of her clients."

This was getting more bizarre by the minute, but the fact that Don was concerned about Jasmine oddly reassured Royce. "I guess the real question is—is there a problem with anything you found out?" He might as well know if his history was about to stand in the way of his future.

"You've done very well for yourself—and in the best way possible. The only complaint I could find out about your company, or you for that matter, is that it isn't very child friendly."

"It's a business." *Not a day care.* But, for once, he kept that part to himself.

"I get that," Don conceded. "And a better understanding of a healthy work environment and happy employees will come to you with more life experience—but it's not a concern for us when it comes to doing business with you."

The proposal.

Don continued, "I'll be honest. I was skeptical at first. You see, we believe business should have a soul."

Royce shot his host a questioning look. The phrase sounded vaguely familiar. Royce wondered if it was something he'd read on Don's company website.

Luckily, Don was willing to enlighten him. "We believe that all of our business efforts should be done with our fellow man in mind wherever possible—helping take care of those who can't, keeping the environment stable and as unharmed by our work as possible, providing safe working conditions—and by extension, creating better living conditions for those who can't afford to do that for themselves."

Okay, this sounded familiar. The Jeffersons' company was known for its environmental stewardship and humanitarian working policies, in addition to its philanthropic efforts.

"When you first applied," Don continued, "I didn't believe this was a philosophy you readily embraced, despite your own efforts to make your shipping company as environmentally friendly as possible. Don't get me wrong—you've accomplished incredible things at a very young age."

Don grinned at Royce. "I can say that from my very advanced age and not sound Scroogy.

"Then I found out about your work with Jasmine. I know you have a charity event you are planning together. One we are much looking forward to, by the way. Sounds exciting."

Royce relaxed—a little. "Isn't anything Jasmine plans exciting?"

"Just about…" Don smiled. "She's an incredibly talented woman."

That was an understatement. Royce had learned more about the hidden depths of Jasmine Harden than he'd ever dreamed he would. She was smart, sexy, bold yet gracious, tenacious and amusing. And the first woman he'd ever wanted to stick around for longer than a night.

"My concern might sound a little old-fashioned. But I would never presume to insist that you marry her or stay with her. That's not anybody's place," Don conceded.

Royce acknowledged the sentiment with a nod.

"But she doesn't have a father present, and Marilyn and I are friends of hers, so I do feel a bit of a responsibility to request that you treat her decently. That's all any of us can expect."

"It's what any woman deserves," Royce said tightly, thinking of the man in the other room.

Don's nod was slow, almost contemplative. But Royce sensed it had nothing to do with studying him to get more inside information. Instead, the wisdom in Don's mature gaze told Royce he had more than an inkling about the hardships and poverty he'd suffered as a child…and why.

"I agree," Don finally said. "I'm glad to know we're on the same page."

* * *

Jasmine realized she was in for it when Marilyn smiled her way and asked, "So, Royce Brazier, huh?"

The older woman nodded sagely when Jasmine didn't answer right away. Instead she snagged them each a pretty mimosa off a passing waiter's tray. Jasmine sipped, grateful to have something to occupy her.

Under normal circumstances, she had no problem talking with Marilyn. They could cover a wide range of subjects without running out of steam. This time, she tried to act cool, but the blood rushed to her cheeks, anyway. She'd never discussed Royce like this outside of her family—and at home she was mainly deflecting her sisters' teasing.

His father standing across the room made her even more uncomfortable. She twisted the emerald ring round and round her finger until Marilyn laid a hand over hers. Jasmine met the older woman's understanding gaze.

"How did you know?" she asked.

Marilyn's expression showed delight that she'd guessed correctly. "I have a feeling about people. He isn't the first male client you've brought to our little get-togethers, but he's the first one you've looked at like that. Or who has looked at you the same way."

Suddenly Jasmine's mouth felt like a desert. She took a quick sip of the fizzy drink. "Like what?" she asked, almost afraid of the answer. So far, there'd been no one to see her with Royce except her sisters. And they were biased.

"Like he discovered a diamond in the midst of his sandbox. I remember." She leaned her head a little closer to confide, "Don looked at me that way, too."

"Really?"

Marilyn raised her glass. "I was his secretary," she said, then took a drink.

"No," Jasmine breathed. Somehow, she'd never thought to ask how Marilyn and Don had met. She'd just assumed Marilyn came from an upper-class family that wasn't from around here.

"Oh, yes, sweetheart. I married way above my class, which ended up being the scandal of the year. No one would mention it now, but they weren't afraid to criticize then. To Don's face, no less."

"I can't imagine." Jasmine felt privileged Marilyn was actually bringing up something this personal. "That must have been incredibly difficult."

"Don wasn't as powerful then—but he also wasn't as diplomatic. Or patient." Her smile was gracious, knowing. "People aren't quick to learn, you know. And Don doesn't enjoy repeating himself."

Jasmine doubted Royce would jeopardize his client relations to defend her like that, though she knew he wouldn't allow others to be disrespectful. She had no idea where his happy medium would be between the two stances—and had no desire to find out.

As if on cue, Royce's father appeared beside Marilyn. He wasn't as tall as his son, but their bearing was the same. Straight spine. Squared shoulders. Royce always looked as if he were bracing himself against whatever the world dared throw at him. His biological father looked like he knew what was coming and was prepared to take the hit. The gray creeping into his sandy hair reinforced the impression.

John Nave greeted them both but his eyes were trained on Jasmine. She shivered. Therein lay a key difference between the two men. Royce might be focused on his business, but his expression was still open. His father's was cold and closed down tight, not letting even a glimpse of emotion through. It was as if he evaluated her solely on what she was capable of providing him—and didn't care one bit about her as a person.

She'd never done business with Royce's father. And she hoped she never did.

One look at Marilyn and she knew her friend was aware of who he was—and possibly the story behind his connection to Royce. But Marilyn's smile as she turned to him was perfectly polite and diplomatic. "Mr. Nave, I'm surprised to see you here."

"These little get-togethers are good for business," he said, not bothering to look in Marilyn's direction. "Right, sweetheart?"

Shock shot through Jasmine. "Excuse me?"

"I said—"

"I heard what you said." Jasmine tightened the hand at her side into a fist, hoping it would help steady her... and her voice. "My name is Jasmine."

As if he didn't already know that. He nodded slowly, continuing to study her.

Jasmine glanced at her friend, who had let a frown break through her polite mask. Before she could say anything, John spoke again.

"There are also a lot of different kinds of distractions at these parties. Which are you?"

Okay, this was a bit much. She'd dealt with the public since she was a teenager and wasn't about to be walked all over—no matter who he was. She gifted them both with the sweetest smile she could muster. "I think distraction is good for you every now and again."

His eyebrow shot up, vaguely reminiscent of Royce when he was being obnoxious. "Not if you want to achieve success."

"Depends on the type of success you're aiming for," she countered.

"Very well put," Don said, as he and Royce joined them. Jasmine had been so focused on John that she hadn't noticed their approach. "I couldn't agree with you more, sweet Jasmine."

The endearment sounded so much nicer like that.

Don gave her a direct smile and an encouraging look. . "I've always maintained that your intelligence is way above average—just like my dear Marilyn's."

Don stepped through the middle of their little gathering to gift his wife with a kiss. Jasmine was relieved to have a break from John's stare, though her tension was still through the roof.

"Darling, the caterer was looking for you," Don said. "Shall we?"

Marilyn nodded, smiling her goodbyes as Don settled her hand in the crook of his arm and led her away. Jasmine couldn't help but notice Marilyn didn't glance toward John. She was probably afraid she'd stick her tongue out at him.

Jasmine wanted to flip him the bird.

After the Jeffersons left them, Jasmine noticed that John had turned his stare toward his son. "I'm disappointed in you, Royce."

Heaven forbid we should make polite, pleasant conversation...

Royce wasn't daunted, though. He cocked his head to the side, looking down at the older man. "I'm not sure why you're bothering to think of me at all."

"As my only progeny, you'd be surprised how often you come to mind. Though I'm disappointed after our last meeting."

"Why?"

John shifted his gaze to Jasmine for only a moment. She could feel her thunderous emotions start to play out in her expression.

"I see you didn't take my advice."

"This is beginning to feel a little surreal," Royce said with a quick look around. "This conversation makes no sense whatsoever. Since when have I ever listened to anything you've said to me, on the rare occasions when you've said anything? Why would I start now?"

John shrugged, not seeming the least offended. "I've always hoped my genes would prevail."

"I believe the better genes did. My mother's."

Hear, hear.

"You can go so much farther, even farther than me, if you remain unattached. I mean, she's pretty," John said with a lazy gesture in Jasmine's direction. "And I'm not saying they aren't fun to play with…"

"Wow." Jasmine was amazed at the scene playing out in front of her…with her as the object of attention. Or, rather, derision. And she was done being a passive bystander. "Royce, let me say I agree with you. The better genes do prevail in you."

His father turned his hard gaze her way once more, but she wasn't backing down.

"It's a good thing your opinion doesn't count. At least, not for long."

Royce stepped forward, crowding into John's space. "Actually, her opinion counts for a whole lot more than yours—and it always will."

Fifteen

Anger pushed Royce to drive mindlessly. He sped out of the Jeffersons' long drive with a little more acceleration than was necessary. But the squeal of the tires on the asphalt gave him a brief moment of satisfaction.

He remained silent, teeth clenched, because if he spoke, the rage of years past might spew out on someone who didn't deserve it. So he locked himself down tight, his fists clenched around the wheel. His gaze was narrowed, focused solely on the road before him.

Only when they got to the parking garage of his building and he opened her car door did he tune in Jasmine. Her stillness. Her silence.

I'm not the only one involved.

He'd forgotten. It had been years since he'd had to worry about a woman's feelings, a woman's reactions. He remembered how his mother had internalized everything, taking the burden of whatever they'd endured onto herself as if she simply deserved it.

Jasmine certainly hadn't taken anything his father had dished out passively, though she'd maintained her ladylike demeanor better than his father had deserved. Now she sat looking up at him from the passenger seat, but she made no move to exit. Her posture was almost expectant, but his mind wasn't in a place to comprehend what she was waiting for.

"Something wrong?" he asked.

"I've been wondering if it was safe to ask you that."

As if realizing he was losing patience, she got out of the car but lagged behind as he strode toward the elevator.

"What?" He winced when his voice echoed off the brick and concrete walls of the garage, and he heard just how impatient he sounded.

"Do you really want me here?" she asked.

Her confusion and the lost note in her voice were finally breaking through his self-absorption. He softened his tone. "Unless you don't want to be here. I can't stop you from leaving, Jasmine."

"You already have."

Royce glanced around in confusion. "What?"

"My car isn't here," she pointed out, exaggerating her enunciation, probably hoping he'd catch on.

That's when he remembered picking her up at her house. He squeezed his eyes closed and cursed under his breath. How had he let that man get so far under his skin? *Jasmine.*

Royce opened his eyes and looked at her expression, which was now slightly amused. Though he could still detect some concern lingering around the edges.

This was why he'd gotten so upset. So angry.

Royce had become immune to his father's reprimands and insults throughout the years, though his conversations with his father were few and far between.

Just the way he liked it.

So this anger wasn't about him. More than anything, Royce didn't want Jasmine hurt by his father. He didn't even want her touched by anything his father said or did.

Now he understood why his mom hadn't fought very hard. It wasn't like she'd had a lot of options. Certainly no lawyer in town had been willing to let her set foot in their firm.

Officially, it had always been her word against his father's. Those close to the situation had known the truth. But his mother simply hadn't wanted to be in the same room with the man who could treat her so disrespectfully after she'd served her purpose. The man who would threaten her and her son so he didn't have to part with the paltry sum it would have taken to lift their lives above poverty level.

Better to cut that person from her life than to allow him to destroy her, piece by piece, over years of contact.

That hadn't been an option for Royce, if he wanted to be any kind of businessman in Savannah. But he'd done his best to ignore John over the years. John seemed to prefer it that way, too. Now it seemed his father had taken some kind of interest in him.

Royce refused to let that dictate anything about who he was or his actions.

Reaching out, he took Jasmine's hand in his. But he just stood there. He didn't rush upstairs. Instead, he let his eyes close once more and let the early summer breeze carry her scent to him. When he opened his eyes and his gaze found her face, he took in how she was patiently waiting. He offered a sheepish smile.

"Would you like to come up for a while?"

"Only if that's where you want me."

Silly woman. "I can't think of anything I want more right now."

"Me, either."

That's when he noticed the slight strain in her smile, the tightness around her eyes. Their encounter with his father had affected her almost as much as it had him.

But he waited until much later, when he held her tight against him in his bed, to ask, "What did he say to you before I showed up?"

The delicious lassitude that fitted her perfectly to his side drained away. He felt her body stiffen, though she didn't retreat from him. "Honestly, I'm doing my best to forget. Let's just say, your dad is very much a sexist pig."

"First of all, he isn't my dad. He's the sperm donor."

His tone was light, and sure enough, she laughed. Unfortunately, the sentiment came straight from his heart.

"Second of all, it amazes me how he knew anyone willing to bring him. As you can tell, he isn't the most personable of people. But money talks."

"It must, because I can't imagine how that man ever got married." A shiver shook her body.

Royce hugged her closer. "I agree. Although, from the rumors I've heard, she's just as cold."

"Then why bother? I don't understand."

Neither did Royce. "It's marriage as a business merger. They're the perfect example."

"An example of what not to do," Jasmine murmured.

"I guess it works for them." He shrugged. "I'd rather be alone than endure something that emotionless."

She patted his chest. "That's because you actually have a heart...and human emotions."

"I know a few people who wouldn't agree with you," he said with a chuckle.

"*I* might not have agreed with me a month ago."

"And I wouldn't blame you for your assessment."

She snuggled closer. Her breath was warm across his skin. She was silent for so long that he began to wonder if she'd fallen asleep. Then she whispered, "So why be that way?"

It's safe. There was no way he was offering that explanation. Not even to Jasmine. Instead, he said, "It's what I know."

"What do I wear to the ball? Cinderella's eternal question shared by women everywhere."

Jasmine glared at her little sister as she walked past, her arms overflowing with formal dresses. Ivy's words made Jasmine even more stressed. The store owner helped Ivy arrange her potential choices on a rack before she headed down the hall to a dressing room. Jasmine's arms were still empty.

They'd been looking at dresses for the masquerade for over half an hour already at a small local boutique where Jasmine usually bought her formal clothing. Ivy was attending the masquerade with her. She loved parties. Willow was more than happy to help pick out everyone's attire, then stay home with Auntie and Rosie.

The three of them had done this on quite a few occasions. Many times Ivy had assisted Jasmine at her events so she had an extra pair of hands. This time, her little sister was coming because what Jasmine and Royce had put together was totally cool.

But Jasmine had never had a problem finding a dress. Today was the exception, apparently.

She knew what the problem was, but she didn't want to acknowledge it. What difference did it make what dress she wore? After all, Royce had seen her naked on more than one occasion. But her stupid feminine psyche seemed stuck on finding *the perfect* dress. The dress that would wow Royce, make him proud to have her standing next to him.

At least, she assumed that's what she would be doing… when she wasn't conferring with caterers and waitstaff and Dominic, among others. Royce hadn't actually spelled that part out yet.

But she wasn't going to live with the same angst she'd had before their visit to the Jeffersons' Sunday Salon. They'd gone out to dinner a few times since then. She'd felt safe assuming they'd present themselves as a couple, of sorts. By now she knew Royce wasn't the type of man who needed her on his arm the entire time. But when they were together, she knew he wouldn't ignore her.

Still, she hoped she got to have at least one dance with him…

"So, what's the problem?" Willow asked.

"I just can't find what I'm looking for." Jasmine glanced once more across the rows and rows of silky fabrics and sequins.

"What *are* you looking for?" Willow asked, the confusion in her voice echoing Jasmine's own conflicted emotions.

"I haven't figured that out, either."

Luckily, Willow didn't lose patience quickly. "At least we know where the problem is."

Jasmine tried to explain. "I don't want it to be too sexy, because I'm also there in a professional capacity. But I also don't want it to be too businesslike, because…"

"Royce won't find that sexy?"

It took her a minute to admit it. "Well, yes."

"Where are these nerves still coming from? Y'all are great together."

And Jasmine knew that was true. In every single way

except one: Rosie. After seeing Royce with his father, she knew better than anyone why he limited his time around children. A conviction that deep wasn't going to disappear overnight. She felt like she had to protect at least part of her heart, when what she really wanted was to jump in with both feet and leave her worries in the dust.

"I really enjoy being with Royce," she began.

Ivy stuck her head out of her dressing room. "Of course you do."

"But I just don't know that it can ever be something permanent."

Willow seemed to get this, although Ivy rolled her eyes. "Don't you trust Royce?" Ivy asked.

"In just about every way."

Willow peeked at her solemnly over the stack of dresses she'd started loading into her arms. "Then what is it that's holding you back?"

"Rosie."

"Why?" Ivy asked again.

"Babies are a big responsibility."

Ivy shrugged. "He seems to do fine whenever he's with her."

"But the occasional cuddle here and there isn't the same as living with a child. Royce has…issues."

"This is true," Willow confirmed.

Ivy, however, wasn't convinced. "What kind of issues?"

Jasmine forced herself back to her task, listlessly sifting through the racks. She wasn't sharing Royce's secrets. They were his to share, not hers. Willow reached over her to pick up dresses she'd overlooked.

After an uninspired search, they wandered toward the dressing rooms with just a few items. "Did the Jeffersons give you flack because you're dating your client?" Willow asked.

"Nope. Which surprised me a little. I wasn't sure how they'd feel." Jasmine glanced over at Willow and lowered her voice a little, even though they were the only ones there at the moment. "Turns out Marilyn used to be Don's secretary."

Willow's green eyes went wide. "Wow. Never would have guessed that one. Every time I've met them, she just seems to…fit."

"I know. From admin assistant to billionaire wife. She has always seemed the perfect person to be at Don's side."

Ivy called from her dressing room. "Ooh, maybe I should join the trend…"

Jasmine was standing in the hallway not far from Ivy's curtained alcove. "It isn't as easy as you think."

"Why not?"

Jasmine couldn't tell if Ivy was being serious or just giving her older sister a hard time, which she liked to do on occasion.

"What if it ends?" Jasmine finally asked. "You're in the position of needing a new job then. If just one of you decides it isn't working, it can get messy. How do you act in front of people?" Jasmine was up close and personal with that particular situation, which was made even trickier because her business was dependent on appearances. "How much do you tell? How much do you keep to yourself? It's just very complicated."

"True. Still…"

Willow leaned closer but didn't bother to lower her voice. "Have you seen Ivy's boss? He's dreamy. He might actually be worth the risk."

"Well, if Ivy thinks it's worth it, *she* can have this ring." It was just complicating Jasmine's life. Though she'd never admit it to her sisters, the ring had indeed done its job. She couldn't deny that she wanted Royce forever…but a big part of her still doubted she would actually have him that long.

"Maybe the night of the masquerade," Ivy said, "especially if I wear this—"

She came out of the dressing room in a formal green dress. It faithfully followed her curves. Jewel chips formed flowers across the bodice and down one hip. The fit was gorgeous on Ivy's petite yet rounded figure. The color perfectly complemented her dark blond hair.

"Wow, Ivy," Jasmine breathed. "That's beautiful."

"Considering he's never seen me in anything but a business suit, I certainly hope *my* boss thinks so…"

Sixteen

Jasmine hung her dress in the alcove off the ballroom of Keller House, once again amazed at its brilliant blue color. The off-the-shoulder style and intricate beading were perfect. A fitted bodice flowed into a layered, full skirt that showcased her shape. Thank goodness the owner of the shop had stepped in and found an answer to her dress conundrum.

If only everything else were that easy.

The next two days certainly wouldn't be. She was at Keller House today to oversee the final setup. Most of tomorrow would be spent in preparation for the masquerade tomorrow night, and then there would be the event itself. Sunday she was hoping for a lazy sleep in, but as little as poor Rosie had seen of her this week, she wasn't holding her breath that the munchkin would cooperate.

She could at least have a lazy Sunday at home, though. She made her way through the finished hallways to the incredible kitchen Royce had had installed. It was up and running, the catering staff currently finding a home for everything. She could see Geraldine laying out her plan and giving instructions on how to execute it. Having worked with the woman before, Jasmine didn't think there would be any problems there. Geraldine was as thorough and organized as Jasmine.

It would all work. The food was one area Jasmine didn't have to worry a lot about, but she couldn't stop herself from going over her checklist.

"Dominic, are you bumming samples?" Jasmine teased when she found the photographer in the kitchen.

He grinned. "Busted."

"We can always use an independent taste test," Geraldine said.

"Then you are a more generous woman than me." Jasmine smiled. "Of course, I know exactly how much he likes the sweet stuff. Doesn't Greg keep you in good supply at home?"

"Don't give away my secrets," Dominic said in a mock whisper.

"Okay…I'll distract you with a video, instead."

"Miss Rosie?" he asked.

"You bet."

Jasmine pulled out her phone and cued up the video Ivy had sent her from the night before. She'd been in the other room on the phone, confirming the catering list. Her sisters hadn't wanted to yell and distract Rosie, so they'd videoed it while they could. Thank goodness for modern digital technology.

Dominic gasped when Rosie started to show off her new crawling skills. "She's been rocking for a couple of weeks now…" Jasmine explained.

"And she just took off?"

Jasmine nodded. The excited conversation attracted the attention of the caterer and the kitchen staff, who converged on the phone to see Jasmine's daughter's new and exciting prowess.

Dominic shook his head, eyeing Jasmine with a mischievous look over the crowd. "Oh, you are in trouble now, girl."

"For what?" Royce asked as he entered the room. His business voice was one she rarely heard anymore—the no-nonsense, almost stern tone he used to command and commandeer. She and the entire kitchen staff jumped.

Dominic ignored them. "Check out this video of Rosie, Royce."

Jasmine suddenly felt like a kid caught with her hand in the cookie jar. The phrase *not a day care* roamed round and round in her brain. Not only had she been discussing her daughter in detail during work hours, but she'd distracted the staff with the video, also.

She was disrupting their productivity and focus...

Surprisingly, Royce did look at the video...actually, he frowned. To Jasmine's shock, he then swiped a finger across the phone and started the video over again.

Finally, he said, "She crawled? Even though she's so little?"

Royce's gaze met hers, and she could see her own feelings mirrored in his eyes. Awe, excitement and a touch of fear.

Dominic said, "Cool, isn't it?"

"She's actually crawling right on time," Jasmine said, unable to quell her need to chatter. "Seven months. The doctors had worried about issues with her motor skills after..." Jasmine swallowed hard, trying to push back the memories of Rosie's mother struggling with drugs early in her pregnancy to ease the pain of her cancer. But the moment she'd known Rosie was there, she'd never touched anything her doctor didn't approve. "But she's a little trouper."

Royce shook his head slowly back and forth. "I'd be afraid of stepping on her or losing her."

Jasmine and Dominic shared a smile. "Well, it's not like I'm suddenly giving her free rein in the neighborhood or the keys to the car," Jasmine teased.

Dominic nodded in her direction. "Trust me, it's time to invest in some baby gates. She'll be into everything, as curious as she is."

"How do you know?" Royce asked.

Dominic puffed his chest out. "Proud, loving uncle to five nieces and nephews."

"Five?" Royce's surprise amused Jasmine.

"That's right," Dominic confirmed. "Five. And this little cutie is gonna be a handful. I guarantee it."

"I'd rather you didn't," Jasmine warned.

Despite her concern, Jasmine felt the glow of maternal pride. It was still fairly new, though less tentative than when Rosie had been a newborn. It had taken a while to give herself permission to feel it, to embrace it. Even though she'd legally been Rosie's mother from day one, it had taken time for her to grow into the role. She'd shared the daily responsibilities with Rosie's biological mother until she hadn't been able to help anymore. Her health had gone downhill rapidly after Rosie's birth. Her death had thrown Jasmine headlong into the reality of being responsible for such a small being's life.

Dominic winked. "Oh, before you know it, she'll be standing beside you at events like this in her own ball gowns."

Jasmine was shaking her head before he even finished, the words causing a distant panic to mix in with her pride.

"Let's get through the challenges of potty training first… for now, back to work."

More than anything, she didn't want to push her luck with Royce. He'd been pretty understanding about this whole thing, had even participated in the conversation, but she was holding up progress here. Any minute he might remember that.

With a quick wave and a chorus of goodbyes from the kitchen staff, Jasmine headed back down the hallway to check out the formal living area where they were setting up carnival-type booths. Albeit for a very fancy carnival, that was for sure. Royce suddenly appeared at her side. For several moments, Jasmine maintained their silence.

She could tell Royce wanted to ask her something. She was simply afraid of what it was.

"Why weren't you there?" he finally asked.

"Where?"

"Watching Rosie crawl."

Jasmine froze, feeling as if someone had just punched the air from her lungs. She took a deep, extra-heavy breath, then said, "I was in the other room, confirming the menu with Marco."

She could feel her body stiffening, bracing herself for his derision.

"I'm sorry," he said simply.

What? "No *I told you so*?" Even though she kept her tone mild, Jasmine knew the words weren't. But frankly, she was tired of playing a guessing game. Now was as good a time as any to figure out where Royce stood on the subject of her and her child.

Even if it might burst her romantic bubble.

To her surprise, Royce reached out to rub his thumb across her left cheekbone. "My mother would say you've given me a wonderful gift."

His soft tone, his happy expression, reduced her question to a whisper. "What's that?"

"Helping me to see that women do whatever is necessary...which isn't always the same as what they want."

For a moment, Jasmine held her breath, afraid she might cry.

"What is it?" Royce finally asked.

"Your words are a gift to me, too."

Later that evening, everyone but Jasmine had finally left the restored mansion. She could almost feel the emptiness as she made one last check of the areas of the second floor that would be open to the public at tomorrow's masquerade.

In midafternoon, Royce had finally left to take care of some things at his office. Dominic had finalized the process for photographs and finished setting up the incredible photo booth. The backdrop was a doctored photograph of the house itself, looking mysterious draped in gray fog under a full moon struggling to be seen. Guests would sit in an elegant open carriage polished to a fine shine. Even Jasmine couldn't wait to have her picture taken.

She'd made the last touches to the flower arrangements on the side tables and in the seating areas. The ice sculpture would be delivered tomorrow, along with the centerpieces for the dining tables.

On her way back to the ballroom, Jasmine checked the long parlor along the front of the house where the carnival booths were set up. The whole length of the house had been beautifully restored, lovingly repainted with gold leaf accents. The chandeliers were original crystal period pieces and the long parlor had vintage wallpaper that Royce's contractor had ordered from overseas. But there was only one place in the house that caused Jasmine to hold her breath when she stepped in: the ballroom.

It was hard to believe people had homes with literal ballrooms in them anymore. But Royce's made Jasmine feel like a princess whenever she walked over the threshold. One entire side featured a series of large mirrors hanging in gilded frames. The rest of the walls had panels of hand-painted murals of lords and ladies from centuries past. Jasmine had only seen them in a horrible, degraded state. The experts Royce had brought in had restored them to their former glory as closely as possible.

Jasmine walked across the refinished floors, the click of her heels echoing. She went directly to the far wall where there was a hidden door in one of the panels. With a simple push, it allowed entrance to an alcove, but getting the right spot without knowing it beforehand was almost impossible. The room might once have been a ladies' sitting room, a place for women to catch their breath on elegant chaises, fix their hair and check makeup in the mirror of the old-fashioned vanity, or simply stare out the window over the back gardens.

Jasmine had a sudden itch to see her dress in the ballroom mirrors before tomorrow night's crowd cluttered the view. After stripping to her underwear, she took the gown carefully down off the hanger and stepped into it.

Only half of the chandeliers were on in the ballroom, giving it an even more magical feel. Jasmine had kept her heels on, so only the barest hint of the bottom edge of her dress touched the floor. Once, twice, she absently twirled before the mirrors.

The lights sparkled off the bodice and the tiny jewels adorning the edges of each layer of the skirt. Definitely princess material. She couldn't quite bring herself to pretend she was dancing, but the skirt flared out elegantly as she turned around and around in a circle. On one twirl, she spotted a shape in the doorway. Her heart jumped, throat closing for a moment until Royce stepped out into the soft light. Her pause was involuntary. It was as if everything stilled, waiting for him to lead the dance they'd come to share.

Royce walked slowly toward her, the look in his eyes nowhere close to businesslike. He was wearing his everyday suit, not a tux, but he pulled off a princely demeanor, anyway.

Feeling the pressure to fill the silence, she said, "Your mother would love what you've accomplished here. This house is magnificent."

He kept his solemn expression as he moved closer to her. "She'd appreciate it far more than my business accomplishments. I'm sure you would agree."

"Actually, Royce, I'm a businesswoman myself. While I love what you've done with the place in your mother's honor, I realize you couldn't create something this incredible without being successful in your professional life."

"She didn't approve of my work in many ways, didn't want me to follow my father's path."

Which he'd done wholeheartedly…until now. "But you haven't really, have you? You aren't your father."

He nodded slowly, as if he were thinking over his answer. "Maybe not."

Finally he stood before her, studying her with dramatic effect before stepping close to take her into his arms. But before he moved, he used one crooked finger to lift her chin so she could meet his look.

"Jasmine, I'll be so proud to have you by my side tomorrow."

Then he started to dance her around the room. There was no music, just the rhythm created by his body. Several times Jasmine caught the surreal sight of them in one of the mirrors. An elegant man and lady moving in time with each other. The fabric of her brilliant blue dress swirled and brushed over the legs of his pants.

But it was the look in his eyes that held her enthralled.

She'd been through so many changes this year. She'd lost a friend. She'd gained a child. She'd embarked on a journey as a mother. But, for the first time in a long time, her doubts were quiet and she was completely happy.

Maybe he will *accept all of me.*

Seventeen

Royce couldn't quite believe the woman in his arms was his. Soft. Sweet, with just enough spice. And he had no doubt that she was giving herself to him fully in this moment.

Was it possible to feel humbled and powerful at the same time?

He'd certainly never had the heady experience before, but he wasn't going to waste it. With the expert skill he'd never thought he'd need, he waltzed Jasmine in a full circle around the room, coming to rest near the alcove door. Knowing the house had been cleared of workers, he didn't bother leading her to a more secluded spot.

Privacy wasn't as important as their hunger for each other.

He thanked the universe for the opportunity and crowded her against the wall with his body. Her eyes widened. Her breasts plumped above the edge of her dress. Her skin was pale against the deep blue. Royce wanted to explore every inch, but for tonight, he would taste her right here.

His lips stroked over hers. He savored the mewling from her throat as their tongues entwined. She tasted of surrender, though he knew her strength; she had tested him with it more than once. And would again in the future.

But, for tonight, she was his.

She wasn't a passive princess. Her deft fingers unbuttoned his jacket then slid inside to spread warmth to his ribs through his thin dress shirt. Her touch sent a surge of need rushing through him. His hips pressed closer. She gasped.

He had to taste more of her.

Bending low, he placed his mouth right below her ear. One of the most tempting things Jasmine did to him every day was wear her hair up. It was gorgeous down, and it was pure pleasure burying his hands in its thickness. But when it was pulled up into a twist, a bun or, hell, even a ponytail, he couldn't resist the length of her neck and the sensitive skin he knew was there.

She clutched at him once more as his mouth covered the pulse point below her ear. Her breath hitched as he suckled lightly. The tension invading her body drove his own need higher. The fact that he knew how to make this woman ache with pleasure brought him the most satisfaction of anything he'd experienced thus far in life.

It was addictive. Necessary.

Slowly, he let himself meander the familiar but exciting path down her straining muscles. Her skin was smooth. Her body was responsive on every level. He lapped at the hollow at the base of her throat, savoring the rapid beat of her pulse. Her cries filled his ears. He knew without a doubt that she was ready for him.

But he wasn't taking things any further without sampling the top curve of her breasts, slightly salty from her day of work. He pulled her closer and lifted her higher with his hands at her waist. The tender flesh plumped beneath his lips. He couldn't stop working her until he nuzzled one tight nipple. Her textures and flavors amazed him.

He drew on her carefully, knowing how sensitive she was here. Her cries grew loud enough to echo off the walls. Strange how satisfying that was to hear. Royce played for long moments, feeling her fists clench and pull at his shirt.

Now. He needed her now.

With more haste than finesse, he scrambled beneath the layers at the front of her dress until his hands found skin. Then he followed the trembling muscles of her thighs to her damp underwear. Quickly he stripped it from her.

Mine. Mine.

He readied himself, practically tearing open his fly and fitting on a condom. He lifted one of her legs, making a place for himself between them. The moment that he slid inside, her head fell back against the wall. He captured her open mouth as he forged into her. The thrust and retreat was exquisite. His hips drove hard as she gasped out his name.

The feelings were too intense to last long. In a flash, they were both consumed. He gave one last thrust and her body clamped down on his with a demand of her own. And he obeyed without protest.

In the throbbing, heated aftermath, Royce knew a part of himself was now forever tied to this woman. For the first time, he could admit that he had no desire to fight the pull.

* * *

Jasmine's heart thrilled at the sight of hundreds of masked attendees in line to enter the mansion. The dark tuxes and formal gowns befit the setting, taking her back to a bygone era when this house was a mecca for Savannah society. The masks ranged from plain and simple to elegant affairs adorned with sparkles and feathers. They lent just the right touch of mystery, even when Jasmine knew who the wearer was.

Excitement filled the air as guests made their way inside. The chatter of each group transformed into oohs and aahs as they discovered all the wonderful entertainments available in the various rooms.

After most of the guests had arrived, Jasmine turned to the next person in line, only to discover Francis Staten. His long hair had had a slight trim and he sported a smooth new tux. She smiled. "Well, don't you look spiffy?"

His grin was a little shame-faced. "I was just gonna dust off the old suit, but Royce had this delivered. I feel almost guilty wearing it."

"Don't." After years of seeing him in his khakis at the mission, she completely understood. Still… "Let him do this for you. Represent the mission tonight, in the midst of these people, with pride in all you do every day."

Jasmine knew how much more confident and comfortable she was among Savannah's elite when she dressed the part.

"I don't want people to think—"

"No, Francis. No one will think you are using the mission's money to buy yourself a suit. If they do, they won't understand what we're trying to do there, anyway. Just enjoy yourself, have a glass of champagne and talk us up."

"At least I'm comfortable giving speeches. Unlike wearing this bow tie."

He pulled at his collar as he walked away, but Jasmine was glad to see him join a conversation almost immediately. She didn't want him to feel alone all evening. Royce paused for a few moments to greet Francis, then made his way back to Jasmine's side.

His black tux and matching half mask set off his blond hair. Jasmine could have watched him walk toward her all day. He was so incredibly sexy…and all hers.

"Everything is going very well," he said, as he bent to kiss her.

"Thank you," she murmured against his lips.

He pulled back a fraction. "For what?"

"Francis's tux," she said, nodding in the other man's direction.

Royce glanced over his shoulder before turning back to her. "I figured it would help him feel more comfortable here. If he had the money for one, that's certainly not what he would spend it on."

"How did you know that?" Because Royce was exactly right.

His dark gaze was intense behind the mask. "I know a few things about people, you know. Even if I've never put them to good use in social situations before."

"Well, thank you for seeing that."

"Thank you for taking me to the mission so I could see it."

Before Jasmine had a chance to savor his words, the Jeffersons appeared before them. "Jasmine," Don said, "you have gone above and beyond this time. This masquerade is incredible."

Marilyn Jefferson's eyes sparkled behind her purple

feathered mask. "And this house! I didn't even realize it was being renovated."

"For several years now," Royce said. "In honor of my mother. She loved this place."

"I'm sure," Marilyn said with a soft smile. "I just hate that she didn't see it like this. In the glory you've worked so hard to achieve."

Jasmine explained, "She lived in the carriage house for a few years as the renovations began."

"The final version that I executed is almost identical to the plans she drew up herself," Royce said.

"Congratulations, Royce," Don said. "Tonight will be a smashing success, I know. For you and the mission. On Monday, let's make an appointment. To talk."

Jasmine knew Royce wanted to smile big, but he kept it under wraps pretty well. Still, she could feel the jolt of excitement that ran through his body. "I will set that up. Thank you, sir."

After the Jeffersons had walked away, Jasmine kissed Royce hard and long, not caring who watched. "Congratulations," she finally murmured.

The evening was as successful as Don Jefferson had predicted. Preliminary counts said they had earned more than enough money to pay for a nice, large building with sleeping quarters on the mission's campus and some additional upgrades, as well.

It wasn't until after the big announcements late in the evening that Jasmine even realized Royce's father was there.

She recognized that analytical gaze easily, despite the plain black mask he sported. Just the feel of him looking in her direction made her stomach clench and bile back up in her throat. Yet, for the next half hour, she saw him everywhere she looked, no matter what she was doing.

Finally she was able to break away from her hostessing duties and find Royce. To warn him. But she arrived only seconds before his father did.

Royce glared at the man over her shoulder. "You're not welcome here."

Jasmine turned to find John completely unmoved by Royce's anger.

"I bought a ticket," he said with a shrug.

"And I'll happily refund your money."

John cocked his head to the side, studying Royce as if to figure out exactly what he needed to say to get through to the man before him. "If word got around that you threw me out, that might hurt donations."

"We don't need any more." Royce's expression was undeniably proud. "But if we did, I'd make it up out of my own pocket."

"That's not good business, Royce. You know that." John shook his head as if Royce were behaving childishly. "You cannot let your emotions rule over money."

"Tonight's not about business," Jasmine insisted.

But the look John turned her way reminded her she wasn't speaking for herself. "You sure?"

Suddenly she remembered Don Jefferson's invitation to set up an appointment with Royce. The real reason he had started this venture so long ago. But before she could respond, Ivy appeared at her elbow. "Jasmine, the catering lady has a question. She's looking for you."

"Right," John said, "Go on back to work now."

Royce stepped firmly between her and his father, brushing a brief kiss over her brow. "Go ahead," he murmured. "Don't worry. I'll handle dear old Dad."

Eighteen

So Jasmine left, but forty-five minutes later, she realized that Royce was nowhere to be found. Oh, the party was in full swing without him, but that didn't defuse the worry that settled in her gut.

She knew he wasn't in the front parlor, because she'd just been through there. Everything was running smoothly and the vendors had given her very positive feedback. But there'd been no sign of Royce.

Next, she checked the ballroom as best as she could. Between the dancers and those milling around listening to the small orchestra, it was a little too crowded for an accurate reading. But she didn't see him. The kitchen and dining rooms were also a bust.

Though he could have stepped outside to cool off, that didn't feel right. Besides, Jasmine wasn't familiar enough with the grounds to trust herself to go looking around in the dark.

Instead, she climbed the back stairs. Several rooms at

the front of the second floor had been opened for guests to tour, including a grand sitting room and a couple of bedrooms. There were other completed rooms on this floor that weren't open for viewing. One she knew to be an office that Royce had set up with equipment in case he needed to be reached or do something while he was out here—which he often had been during the last month or so.

As she reached the top of the stairs, muffled voices reached her. Alert that there was someone in the office, she approached the closed door with trepidation. Why would Royce have brought his father up here? Or was it just someone else he'd wanted to talk to?

She didn't want to interrupt business. But the thought that he would be taking a business meeting in the middle of their event was upsetting.

At first she thought the door was closed, but as she reached it, she realized it was cracked. The voices filtered through enough that she recognized Royce…and his father. She should have just turned away, gone back downstairs and left Royce to handle it. Instead, she reached out and pushed the door back an inch, allowing her to see a small sliver of the scene inside.

John Nave flicked a silver lighter, then used it to light a thin cigar. He puffed a few times, causing the tip to glow red. "I, more than anyone, know how disruptive women can be," he finally said.

Royce turned to him. The lamp nearby allowed Jasmine to read the surprise on his face. Unconcerned, his father blew out a stream of cigar smoke. "Yes, your mother wasn't the first. But she was the only one I made the mistake of getting pregnant."

"I wouldn't consider myself a mistake."

John paused in that way he had, as if he considered

every word before speaking it. "I did, at the time. But I've checked in through the years. You've turned out well. Still, I felt it was best if I married after that."

Royce scoffed. "I wouldn't call what you have a marriage. More like a business arrangement."

"I call it the best of both worlds. I handle the business. She handles the house and our image. And takes the edge off when I really need it. What more could I want?"

Jasmine waited for Royce to say *love*, but he remained silent.

"You've made a terrible misstep, son. I've seen the way you look at her. You're going soft. Besides, that woman has a baby, for Christ's sake. One that's not even hers."

"How did you find that out?" Royce stalked closer to stand over John's chair. "Never mind. I'm sure I can guess. A better question is, why do you care?"

"Because *you* should," John insisted, gaining his feet to meet Royce head-on. "You should care that her middle-class family is going to suck your focus away from your business. Why would you let someone like that stand in the way of achieving all that you can?"

Royce's voice hardened. "I have never let anything stand in the way of my success. I'm not about to start now."

John extended his hand to shake Royce's. "Good. I'm glad to hear that."

Jasmine's last look showed Royce and his father standing close to each other, hands clasped, the picture of power and business acumen.

There was no place in that picture for family or all the tender, passionate emotions Royce inspired inside her. Emotions he obviously didn't return. Had he been pretending all along?

Turning, Jasmine fled back along the hall and down the staircase, holding her quiet sobs inside and lifting her skirt just enough to keep her from tripping and breaking a bone.

She rushed along the hall behind the kitchen, her only thought that she needed out before she broke down completely. Then she ran smack into someone tall and solid.

"Sugar, what's the matter?" Dominic asked.

Just hearing his voice brought reality back in a rush. Jasmine clutched at the front of his jacket, dragging in deep breaths in an attempt to get herself under control. Unfortunately, that just made the darkened hall whirl around her. "I feel dizzy."

"Come here."

Dominic clutched her to his solid chest as he led her to a small storage room where he pulled out one of the folding chairs they were using for seating in the dining room and settled her into it. Then he opened one for himself and sat next to her.

"Now, tell me what's wrong."

Jasmine shook her head, unable to put into words the pain she felt. "I trusted him."

"Who?" Dominic asked, laying his large hand against the bare skin of her upper back. His heat calmed her, centered her focus on that one spot. Oddly enough, it made her realize that the rest of her body was chilled, inside and out.

"Royce. I thought..." Why had she thought that she would be enough to make the leopard change his spots? "I thought maybe he might be different."

"Was he ugly to you? Did he hurt you?"

"No." *He simply chose business over me.* "I just overheard something I shouldn't have."

"Maybe you didn't hear enough."

She hadn't wanted to hear more. She shook her head. "I don't know if I can do this."

Dominic's hand flexed against her, drawing her focus away from the pain in her heart. "You can," he said. "Tonight is your crowning glory, and it's almost over. Ivy and I will help you finish what you need to, I promise."

Jasmine just hoped that would be enough.

Royce concentrated hard on the feel of John's hand against his, letting the sounds of the party in the house disappear. He'd never touched his father before. He'd never wanted to be this close to him.

Just as he'd expected, the grip was firmer than it needed to be—a competition to see who could outman the other. It wasn't the recognition and respect Royce had exchanged with men like Don Jefferson. Men who were high achievers in their businesses, but who were also intent on contributing to the greater good in their families, their communities and the world.

Royce tightened his hold before stepping in, mere inches away from his father. He had to admit the slight advantage he had in height made him feel superior, even though it was a petty sentiment that shouldn't have a place here. Then again, his father preferred for this meeting to be about strength, and probably his own superiority to his son. Apparently, he'd come here to school Royce in how he should live.

But he had no lessons Royce needed to learn.

He found himself leaning close to his father's face, looking him dead in the eye and acknowledging the biological link between the two of them. Then he grinned, because he didn't have to base his life and decisions on that biology. Or, rather, he'd prefer his maternal biology to any genes this man had passed on to him.

"That's right," he said, his voice low but clear. "I've

never let anything stand in the way of achieving my goals…only my goals have changed."

John's eyes widened as Royce's grip turned punishing. After a few seconds, Royce turned away. But he wasn't done proving his point. "Success isn't defined by money, *Father*, despite this belief system that you've built your life upon. I've seen many examples in the business community of men who care just as much about their fellow man as they do about themselves."

"And they're poorer because of it," John insisted.

"How much money do you really need to live, John? After all, you can only drive one Rolls Royce at a time."

The other man's gaze flared at Royce's words.

"I'd rather have one or two fewer cars and build a dormitory for homeless men at the City Sanctuary mission. I'd rather make a little less money on a shipping contract and know that people are getting life-saving supplies that they need. After all, I only require one place to live."

He gestured around the luxury office he'd built here at Keller House. "All of this is simply surplus."

Royce returned to his post behind the large mahogany desk but didn't sit down. Instead, he faced his father— businessman to businessman. "But most important, John, I'd rather have the love of a good woman and a family as my legacy than the money to build a huge mausoleum for all the people who couldn't give a rat's ass about visiting my grave after I'm gone. That's *my* definition of success."

"You're wrong."

"Am I? Because tonight I have my money, my woman and a child with the sweetest smile in the world. A child who deserves a chance to achieve her own success, no matter who contributed to her biological makeup. What do you have besides your money, a wife who couldn't care less about you and a big, empty house?"

Royce braced his hands on the desktop, staring the other man down. "Now, while this little family reunion has been very enlightening, in the future, you will not contact me. If you see me in public, you will walk the other way. If you see my future wife, future child, employees or anyone associated with me, you will keep on walking. If you don't, I will make sure you regret it. Because I don't need you in my life."

It was almost amusing to see his father draw his body straighter, even though he was facing defeat. "I doubt you can do that."

"Oh, I can. You see, I know what you value the most, *Father*. And while I'm sure you had plenty of cronies to help you disavow me and leave my mother poverty-stricken while she raised your child, this is a new day. A new culture. And news of the steps you took to ruin that woman and your biological child won't go over nearly as well in today's business climate—especially coming straight from that child himself. Who is now a very successful man in his own right."

Royce smiled, though he knew it wasn't a pleasant expression. "So I will warn you again—you keep your mouth shut. That is, if you want me to do the same."

Nineteen

Jasmine kept herself busy. Since she knew she would need to leave sooner rather than later, she quietly made preparations to disappear once the midnight unveiling had happened. For the first time ever, she had no plans to stay at her event until the last guest had left and the last plate was packed.

Ivy seemed to have disappeared while Jasmine was upstairs, and she wasn't answering her phone, so Jasmine went to the point person in each area to make sure they were covered. Plans had been made to close the party at 2:00 a.m. Every staff member knew what was expected of them. A cleaning crew would be here tomorrow.

She'd hoped her sister would stay behind as her eyes and ears, but she'd make do as best she could. Who knew how long she'd be able to hold all these emotions inside? And the last thing she wanted was to make small talk with Royce while wondering if he was simply humoring her to get her into bed.

There was nothing she wanted more than to get out of this dress and be home with her family. That was the difference between her and Royce. They were her comfort, her sustenance. Royce would have to settle for sleeping with cold hard cash if his success meant so much to him.

Jasmine's hypervigilance allowed her to spot him when he came down the stairs. John wasn't with him. Luckily, Royce paused with some guests, so she headed in the opposite direction. It wasn't like she didn't have plenty to do.

The waiters started to circulate throughout the ballroom with fresh trays of champagne while staff informed guests throughout the house that it was almost time for the midnight unveiling. Jasmine had been so looking forward to this part of the night. That romantic moment when masks were discarded, when the true person behind the mask was revealed.

Even though she and Royce recognized each other behind their masks, she'd still looked forward to meeting his gaze in that moment.

Now the last thing she wanted was to look at Royce without the protection of her mask hiding her expression.

She saw his sandy-blond head as he entered the ballroom. Even from this distance, she knew he was looking for her. And she couldn't handle it. She simply couldn't.

As she backed slowly away, her hand made contact with the wall behind her. That's when she realized the panel where she stood was actually the door to the private ladies' alcove. She hadn't revealed the existence of the little room to the guests. Jasmine took a quick look around to see if anyone was watching, but they'd all turned their attention to the MC preparing the crowd for the pinnacle of the evening. So she opened the door and slipped inside.

Only seconds after she'd quietly closed the door, her phone vibrated. It was her sister.

"Ivy, where are you?" she whispered frantically.

It wasn't as if there was anyone in the room to hear her, but she couldn't help it. Her rapidly beating heart felt as if it was calling out across the room. What if Royce found her here?

She wasn't sure she could face him.

"I'm so sorry, Jasmine," her sister said from the other end of the line. "I left."

"You what?"

"I left...with someone."

Even though Jasmine should have been questioning her sister or concerned for her safety, she could only respond with panic over her absence. "I need your help. Right now."

"I'm on my way to Paxton's apartment."

"What?" Oh, that was a bad idea. A very bad idea.

"I just...I want this, Jasmine."

"Please don't. I'm telling you, Ivy. This is not a good choice." Jasmine knew that for certain. Now more than ever.

"But it's my choice," Ivy said softly. "And I'm going to make it."

"Ivy!" Jasmine cried, but her sister had already hung up. "Damn it."

Why wouldn't her little sister listen to her? She was getting her own heart broken over a client right now. She knew just how dangerous those working relationships could be.

But Ivy, as the youngest, had been trying to prove she wasn't a child for a while now. This act of rebellion might end up costing her more than her job.

As the sounds of a trumpet heralded the coming of

midnight in the ballroom, Jasmine quickly gathered her purse and keys, a plan forming in her mind. She'd slip from the room while everyone was distracted and make her way to her car. She could send Ivy back to Keller House for the rest of her stuff tomorrow.

Right now, she just needed out.

Away from the fairy tale she'd thought was happening and home to the day-to-day drudgery and chaos that was her life. She'd find magic again, someday, but she'd learned her lesson. Never date a client. Never get so close you think you're seeing behind the facade, only to learn the facade had been the reality all along.

Time to go.

Desperate to get away, Jasmine jerked the door open, only to find herself face-to-face with the one man she never wanted to see again. Well, maybe he wasn't the only one. She'd be happy never to see his father again, either.

"Jasmine, where have you been?" Royce's hard business tone scraped over her nerves.

"I could ask you the same thing," she choked out.

"What are you talking about?" He frowned. "I've been looking everywhere for you."

"Why?" A small spark of her normal sassiness finally made an appearance. "Are you unhappy with my service in some way?"

"What?"

She shook her head, grief overwhelming that tiny spark.

"Jasmine, what is it?"

The words simply wouldn't come. She had no idea whether to lay into him, scream and cry, or simply skulk away from the humiliation of knowing he'd lied to her. Granted, he hadn't turned into some kind of super-involved family guy. If anything, at times he'd seemed lost.

But he hadn't retreated, hadn't rejected Rosie completely. And he'd made love to Jasmine with a passion she'd never experienced before and hadn't been strictly business outside of the bedroom. Memories of him holding Rosie at the hospital, helping them get Auntie taken care of, talking about his mother's death…he'd opened himself up to her and her family.

Had the confrontation with his father washed all of that away?

I have never let anything stand in the way of my success. I'm not about to start now. No. She wasn't strong enough to find out.

Around them the crowd erupted in applause. The lights dimmed for a moment, then the orchestra struck up a lively tune. But Jasmine and Royce remained frozen in their silent battle. Without permission, Royce reached up to touch the mask she'd had made to match her dress. His other hand found the ties at the back of her head.

He was so close, his touch so intimate, that she was transported back to the night before, when he'd shown her in no uncertain terms just how much he enjoyed her. Only now, their encounter felt dirty, tainted by motives she could only guess at.

It wasn't until the strings came loose and Royce pulled the mask away that Jasmine felt the tears spill onto her cheeks. Royce's eyes widened and what looked like panic washed over his expression. But all Jasmine could feel was the humiliation of knowing she was crying over a man who would walk away from her whenever business demanded.

So she walked away first and didn't look back.

Royce looked down at the paper Matthew had handed him and cursed. Jasmine's final invoice.

She hadn't wasted any time. It had only been three days since the masquerade. Three days in which she wouldn't return his phone calls or text messages. He'd even gone by the house once. Auntie had answered the door, holding Rosie, only to tell him that Jasmine wasn't home. From her worried expression, he assumed she was telling him the truth.

But she'd also refused to tell him anything else.

He'd learned nothing about what had upset Jasmine that night, though he suspected it had something to do with his father's visit. As far as he could tell, they hadn't spoken to each other alone. She could have overheard something, but what?

Royce was an astute businessman, but when it came to women, especially upset women, he was more than a little lost. He'd have given anything to have his mother there so he could ask her advice. Did he confront Jasmine? Leave her to stew for a while? What?

"I just don't understand, Matthew," he said, more as a way to express his frustration than anything.

"I know. She was perfect for you." As soon as the words left his mouth, Matthew must have realized what he'd said, because his assistant's eyes went wide and worried.

"You're right. She is."

Matthew started to shake his head and back away. He was probably wondering where the heck his real boss had gone.

Royce was beyond caring about keeping things professional. He ran a rough hand through his hair, no longer worried what it would look like afterward—or who might see it messed up. He was no longer the consummate professional. Jasmine had stripped the superficial facade away. "But I can't fix what's wrong until I know what it is."

Matthew studied him for a moment, then cautiously offered, "Obviously you aren't trying hard enough."

"What? I've texted, called, gone by the house."

"Come on," Matthew admonished, the tension in his body easing up some. "Where's the guy who beat out every shipping company in Savannah to get Jefferson's contract? I'm pretty sure you stepped out of your comfort zone to accomplish that."

Boy, had he. "But this is a woman."

"No different...except you might need a little more finesse. Use some of those personal negotiating techniques Jasmine taught you."

"A little more finesse, huh?"

Royce thought about that the rest of the day. Jasmine's techniques had really just been about seeing people for who they were, treating them with respect as human beings. She'd drilled that into him, but he still needed a little more work in that area.

Starting now.

Even though it was about an hour before he normally left the office, Royce headed for the door. "Take the rest of the day off, Matthew."

He had to smile at his assistant's gasp. Those words hadn't been uttered in Royce Brazier's office, well, ever.

So why was Royce grinning as he got into his car?

Today was a Thursday. Jasmine always volunteered at the mission on Thursday evenings. She had for the entire two months he'd known her. Why not use that knowledge to his advantage?

As he drove toward the mission, he experienced an unfamiliar sensation of freedom. So this was what playing hooky felt like.

Of course, it didn't hurt that he had some business to

discuss with Francis Staten. Royce hadn't changed his stripes *entirely*.

He walked into the mission's large dining area just as the line was forming for dinner service. Sure enough, Jasmine stood behind the steam tables. Their eyes met across the room. He could read the jolt in her body, even from this distance.

The pull to go to her was strong. He wanted to be near her, beside her. But he had to make things right first.

So he crossed the room to find Francis, instead. The director stood with several visitors, chatting before the meal. He greeted Royce with a smile and a warm handshake. "So good to see you here."

"Thank you," Royce replied. "I wonder if you would spare me a few moments of your time."

"Absolutely." Francis said his goodbyes to the others, then gestured for Royce to follow him out of the room. "I hope this isn't bad news."

Royce was quick to reassure him. "Definitely not." But he waited until they reached Francis's office before filling him in.

"Everything has been tallied and totaled, and we had some very generous donors at the masquerade," Royce said.

"That's good," Francis said with a smile. "And I can't remember ever enjoying an evening so much. What you and Jasmine put together was pure magic."

"Yes, it was, wasn't it?" He and Jasmine were magic together, too, if only he could get her to see that.

"Now, why do the two of you both turn so solemn when I say that?" Francis's gaze was a little too astute.

And here Royce had thought he was going to be able to stick to business, at least for this part of the evening. "Just a little misunderstanding that I'm hoping to clear up."

"I hope so, too. Jasmine deserves to be happy. And so do you, young man."

"Happiness never factored into the equation for me before," Royce said with a sigh. The happiness he'd found with Jasmine would leave a hole in his life if they weren't together. *Please let me be able to fix this.*

"What about now?"

Now, Royce was determined to make Jasmine the happiest woman on earth. If he had to give up every dime to do it.

But instead of saying that, Royce simply smiled and returned to the original subject. "The truth is, we made far more than our goal at the masquerade."

"Oh?"

"It will mean you'll have more to work with when you build the men's sleeping quarters. But I have an idea I would like to propose."

Francis beamed at Royce as he explained his plan. The money he gave wasn't going into this man's pocket, yet it still made Francis happy because it meant he could help more people every day. That humbled Royce.

"There isn't enough to cover all I'm suggesting, but I'm willing to donate the additional funds myself," he said, waving away Francis's protests. "But I have a confession to make."

Francis was all ears.

"I'm going to need your help."

Thirty minutes later, Francis was more than on board.

Twenty

Jasmine watched the men approach, her mouth dry and her heart pounding. Her hands shook as she tried to maneuver the hot pan of food into the empty slot on the steam table.

They sure looked chummy.

Not that she wanted Francis to be angry at Royce. She'd deliberately told no one except her sisters about the break because the responsibility was hers. Royce had told her, warned her in many different ways, that he wasn't built for family or forever. She'd chosen to listen to her heart, instead. And she'd paid the price.

Now, part of her felt violated that he was here, in her space, her territory. Not that she owned the mission. The feeling was ridiculous. But it was there, nonetheless.

She also needed to face the fact that she might be seeing a lot of Royce during the upcoming construction. Or maybe not. Certainly if he returned to his normal way of conducting business, it wouldn't be a problem.

He'd just put someone in charge and go on his way.

But she never would have imagined him coming to the mission of his own accord, so anything was possible. And something in his expression told her that he was going to choose a hands-off approach.

"Jasmine," Francis started, "Royce brought delightful news today."

Her smile felt unnatural, like hard plastic. But it was better than crying.

In contrast, Francis looked ecstatic. "We're not getting just one new dormitory, but two."

Shock rippled through her. "Excuse me?"

"Royce himself is donating the cost of a new women's dorm—in full. We will be able to provide better accommodations and turn the original housing into small private rooms so families can stay together while they're with us."

"Um…" Speechless didn't begin to touch it. This was a dream she and Francis had discussed for several years but they'd figured it was forever out of reach.

"And he wants you to work with him on it."

Whoa. What? "I do events, not buildings."

"But you know more than anyone what these women need," Francis pointed out. "You could offer great insight into planning and utilization of the space to meet those needs."

Why wasn't Royce saying anything?

"You two talk about it. Then come see me." Francis laid a hand on Jasmine's arm and gave her the same comforting smile he'd been offering since she first walked through the door at fifteen. "Just consider it."

Jasmine forced herself to tell the woman working next to her that she needed to take a break. Then she stripped off her gloves and headed out the back door to the small lawn where Francis maintained his beloved rose bushes. Royce could follow if he wanted.

Her thoughts whirled ninety to nothing. When she couldn't stand the chaos anymore, she turned on him. "Seriously? What is this? Some kind of ploy?"

"Actually, it's an apology."

Surprise left Jasmine speechless for a moment. There'd been way too much that left her speechless today. She crossed her arms under her breasts and summoned the firm tone she used when the boys in the afterschool programs decided to act the fool. "Explain."

"It's an apology from me to Francis…and to you. And a decision my father will hate—so it's a win-win."

She raised a brow, completely uninterested in talking about John Nave.

Royce stepped closer. Jasmine was glad she had her arms crossed in front of her. It lessened the temptation to reach out and touch him. "It's an apology for acting out of greed."

Jasmine found herself holding her breath as he met and held her gaze. "I started all of this in an effort to make money, Jasmine. Now, on the other side of it, I realize how wrong that is. You were right. I wish I could say I did the masquerade in an effort to help people, to help the mission. But I honestly didn't care about the mission's needs."

His next step brought him just inches from her. "But I was right about one thing."

"What's that?" she whispered, then cleared her throat.

"You were the heart of all we did together."

She couldn't push him away when he leaned down to kiss her, but she couldn't pull him closer, either. The conflict inside of her refused to die.

And he refused to move away. "Now, tell me what happened, Jasmine."

This time she was silent because she wasn't sure what to say, not because of sheer stubbornness.

"I'm used to the sexy, strong woman who set me straight in her own sweet and sassy way. This silence is scary."

"Well, it's easier to be sassy when there's nothing big at stake."

"Is there something big at stake now?"

Jasmine turned away. She just couldn't bear to face his intent gaze. "Just leave it alone, Royce."

"I didn't get where I am by walking away."

That sparked her temper. "I'm not a business deal." Her voice rose as she tossed the words back over her shoulder.

"And I'm not a robot. Next to losing my mother, nothing has impacted me like losing you."

She wanted to believe that, but she couldn't ignore what she'd heard. "Then why would you do it?"

"Jasmine, I'm afraid I need more to go on."

"I overheard you with your father, Royce!" Jasmine whirled around to confront him. "How could you shake that man's hand and say 'I have never let anything stand in the way of my success. I'm not about to start now'?"

"Because I needed to speak in a language he understood."

The confusion on his face frustrated her. She groaned, then stomped away. How could he dismiss this so easily?

"I'm going to guess from your reaction that you didn't stick around for anything further?"

This time she faced him from the safe, much more comfortable distance of a few feet. "What more could be said after that?"

"How about—I'll do whatever I can to achieve success…but my definition of success has changed?"

His answer was so unexpected, she almost couldn't get her question out. "To what?" she whispered.

"Jasmine, you've taught me so much over the last couple of months," he said, shaking his head as if he still couldn't believe it. "Not just you, but Don and Marilyn, Dominic, your family. The problem with immersing yourself in business is that, after a while, that's all you see."

And that described the Royce she'd met that first day.

He went on, "My mother tried to warn me, but I refused to listen. I just knew that I had to prove myself, and my father's measuring stick was money."

"But you had your mother."

"I did," Royce conceded. "And I took care of her as best as I knew how. But emotionally…emotionally, Jasmine, I'm not nearly as savvy as I am at business." He stepped carefully into her personal space. "Actually, I'm in desperate need of someone to teach me what I need to know."

"Teach you?"

He nodded, but it was the look in his eyes that took her breath away. "I think it's time I conquered a new arena."

"What's that?"

"Love. Family."

Was this really happening? Jasmine was almost afraid to believe.

"Would you and Auntie and Rosie and your sisters be willing to take on a workaholic CEO and teach me how to be…human?"

Yes, this might actually be happening. "I think your mother would have liked that."

"I know she would."

With the gentlest of touches, Royce cupped his hands around Jasmine's face. As his lips touched hers, she again felt the magic of connecting with him.

After long minutes, he murmured against her lips. "I need you, Jasmine. Please help me become the man I should be. A husband. A father."

Was it possible for your heart to explode, simply from emotion? But Jasmine couldn't give in to the mushiness too fast. "On one condition."

"What's that?"

Jasmine dragged in a deep breath before she said, "That whatever we do…we do it together."

"That's a deal I'll never turn down."

* * * * *

*If you liked this story
pick up these other novels from
Dani Wade!*

HIS BY DESIGN
A BRIDE'S TANGLED VOWS
THE BLACKSTONE HEIR
THE RENEGADE RETURNS

Available now from Mills & Boon Desire!

And don't miss the next
BILLIONAIRES AND BABIES *story,*
BILLIONAIRE BOSS, HOLIDAY BABY
by Janice Maynard.
Available October 2017!

*If you're on Twitter, tell us what you think
of Mills & Boon Desire!*

"What? Did you forget to frisk me before I leave the building?"

"Don't tempt me, Sally," Kirk said.

"Don't be so pompous. You've lied to me from the moment you met me. Why not try being honest for a change?"

"You want honest? I'll give you honest. You caught my eye the second you arrived in the bar that night. I didn't recognize you immediately but I couldn't take my eyes off you."

She snorted. "I may be naive, but don't expect me to believe that. There were any number of women far more beautiful than me in the bar that night."

"And yet I only had eyes for you."

The look she gave him was skeptical. "A little clichéd, wouldn't you say?"

"Stop trying to put up walls between us." Kirk stepped forward and took her by the arm. "You're still carrying my baby," he said. "I have a duty to care for...my child."

He wasn't holding her firmly, but he wasn't letting go, either. It drove home the fact that the life she thought she'd had was not her own.

* * *

Little Secrets: The Baby Merger
is part of the Little Secrets series:
Untamed passion, unexpected pregnancy...

LITTLE SECRETS:
THE BABY MERGER

BY
YVONNE LINDSAY

First Published in Great Britain 2017
By Mills & Boon, an imprint of HarperCollins*Publishers*
1 London Bridge Street, London, SE1 9GF

© 2017 Dolce Vita Trust

ISBN: 978-0-263-92834-1

51-0917

Our policy is to use papers that are natural, renewable and recyclable products and made from wood grown in sustainable forests. The logging and manufacturing processes conform to the legal environmental regulations of the country of origin.

Printed and bound in Spain
by CPI, Barcelona

A typical Piscean, *USA TODAY* bestselling author
Yvonne Lindsay has always preferred her imagination
to the real world. Married to her blind-date hero and
with two adult children, she spends her days crafting the
stories of her heart, and in her spare time she can be
found with her nose in a book reliving the power of love,
or knitting socks and daydreaming. Contact her via her
website, www.yvonnelindsay.com.

This one is dedicated to my family,
each of whom hold a piece of my heart
in their hands and whose love and
support keep me going every day.

One

A flash of pale gold hair near the entrance caught Kirk's attention in the dimness of the bar. A woman came through the door, a tall, well-built man close behind her. She turned and said something, and the muscle looked like he was going to object, but then she spoke again—gesturing vaguely across the room—and he nodded and disappeared outside. Interesting, Kirk thought. Clearly the guy was an employee of some kind, perhaps a body-guard, and he'd obviously been dismissed.

Kirk took a sip of his beer and watched the woman move through the area, searching for someone. There was an unconscious sensuality to the way she moved. Dressed down in a pair of slim-fitting trousers topped by a long-sleeved, loose tunic, she seemed to be trying to hide her tempting mix of curves and slenderness, but he saw enough to pique his interest. Most women hated it when they had well-rounded hips and a decent butt, and judging by the way she'd dressed to conceal, she was one of those women who wasn't a fan of her shape and form. But he was. In fact, he really liked her shape and form.

Who was she meeting here? A partner, he wondered, feeling a small prick of envy as his eyes skimmed her from head to foot. The weariness that had driven him here tonight in search of better company than employee files and financial forecasts slid away in increments as his eyes appreciatively roamed her body.

He knew the instant she saw the person she was looking for. Her features lit up, and she raised a hand in greeting, moving more quickly now toward her target. Kirk scanned ahead of her, feeling himself relax when he saw the couple who reached out to greet her affectionately. Not a partner, then, he thought with a smile and took a sip of the malty craft beer he'd ordered earlier.

He noticed one of her friends pass her a martini and pondered on the fact that they'd already ordered her drink for her. Obviously she was a reliable type, both punctual and predictable. Too bad those were not the traits of someone who might be interested in a short, intense fling, which was all he was in the market for. He had his life plan very firmly set out in front of him, and while his company's merger with Harrison Information Technology here in Bellevue, Washington, would definitely fast-track things, a committed relationship was still not in the cards for a long time. When he was ready, he'd tackle that step the way he did everything else, with a lot of research and dedication to getting it right the first time. Kirk Tanner did not make mistakes—and he definitely wasn't looking for love.

Kirk turned his attention away from the woman, but something about her kept tickling at the back of his mind. Something familiar that he couldn't quite place.

He looked across the room and studied her more closely, noting again the swath of pale gold hair that fell over her shoulders and just past her shoulder blades. Even from here he could see the kinks in her hair that told him she'd recently had it tied up in a tight ponytail. His fingers clenched around his glass, suddenly itching to push through the length of it, to see if it felt as silky soft as it looked.

As if she sensed his regard, the woman turned and glanced past him before returning her attention to her friends. This gave him the most direct view so far of her face—and yes, there was definitely something familiar about her. He'd certainly have remembered if he'd met her before but perhaps he'd seen her photograph somewhere.

Kirk searched his eidetic memory. Ah, yes, now he had it—Sally Harrison, the only child of Orson Harrison, the chairman of Harrison Information Technology. The very firm his own company was officially merging with at 3:00 p.m. tomorrow. The idea of a merger with Sally Harrison held distinct appeal, even though he knew she should be strictly off-limits.

Her personnel file had intrigued him, although the head shot attached to it had hardly done her justice. He scoured his memory for more details. Since high school she'd interned in every department of the head office of HIT. In fact, she probably knew more about how each sector of the company ran than her father did, and that was saying something. She'd graduated from MIT with a PhD in social and engineering systems. And yet, despite her experience and education and the fact she was the chairman's daughter, she'd apparently never aspired to anything higher than a mediocre middle-management position.

Granted, her department was a high performer and

several of her staff had been promoted, but why hadn't she moved ahead, too? Was she being very deliberately kept in place by her father or other senior staff? Was there something not noted in her file that made her un-qualified or ill-suited for a more prominent position in the company?

And—the more compelling question—did she per-haps have sour grapes about her lack of advancement?

Her knowledge about the firm made her a prime can-didate for the investigation her father had asked him to undertake as part of his staff evaluation during the merger.

Under the guise of seeing where staff cutbacks needed to be made, he was also tasked with investigating who could most likely be responsible for what could be unwit-ting or deliberate leaks to HIT's largest business rival. Orson suspected that the rival company, DuBecTec, was accumulating data to undermine his company with a view toward making a hostile takeover bid in the next few months. He had instructed Kirk to look at everyone on the payroll very thoroughly. Everyone including the very appealing Ms. Sally Harrison.

Kirk took another sip of his beer and watched her across the room. She'd barely sipped her drink yet but swirled the toothpick in her martini around and around. Just then, as he was watching, she removed the tooth-pick from her drink and, using her teeth and her tongue, drew the cocktail onion off the tip and crunched down. His entire body clenched on a surge of desire so intense he almost groaned out loud.

Sally Harrison was a very interesting subject indeed, he decided as he willed his body back under control. And before he left the bar tonight, he would definitely find a way to get to know her better.

* * *

Company merger. For the best.

Even though she was going through the motions, saying all the right things as her friends excitedly told her about their recent honeymoon, Sally couldn't stop thinking about her father's shocking announcement over dinner tonight. If she hadn't heard it straight from the horse's mouth, she would have struggled to believe it. She *still* struggled to believe it. And the fact that her father hadn't shared a moment of what had to have been an extensive forerunner to the merger with her raked across her emotions.

It was a harsh reminder that if she was the kind of person who actually stood *with* her father, versus sheltering behind him, she'd have been a part of the discussions. Not only that, if she'd been the kind of person she ought to be, confident and charismatic instead of shy and intense, this entire merger might not even have been necessary.

Her whole body trembled with a sense of failure. Oh, sure, logically she knew that her dad wouldn't have entered into this planned merger if it wasn't the best thing for Harrison IT and its thousand or so staff worldwide. And it wasn't as though he needed her input. As chairman of HIT, he held the reins very firmly in both hands, as he always had. But, until now, HIT had been the family firm, and darn it, she was his family. Or at least she was the last time she'd looked.

Of course, now the company would be rebranded— Harrison Tanner Tech. Clearly things were about to change on more than one level.

She could have predicted her father's response when she'd questioned the secrecy surrounding the merger.

"Nothing you need to worry about," he'd said, brushing her off in his usual brusque but loving way.

And she wasn't worried—not about the company, anyway. But she did have questions that he'd been very evasive about answering. Like, why this *particular* other company? What did it bring to HIT that the firm didn't have already? Why *this* man, whoever he was, who was being appointed vice president effective tomorrow? And why did her dad want her to be there during the video link when he and the new vice president of the newly branded Harrison Tanner Tech would make the merger announcement simultaneously to the whole staff? She couldn't think of anything she'd rather do less. Aside from the fact that she hated being in the public arena, how on earth would she look her colleagues in the eye afterward and possibly have to face their accusations that she'd known about this merger all along? Or worse, have to admit that she hadn't. Just the thought of it made her stomach flip uneasily.

Her father had always told her he worked hard so she didn't have to. She knew he worked hard. Too hard, if the recent tired and gray cast to his craggy features was anything to go by. It was another prod that she hadn't pulled her weight. Hadn't been the support he deserved and maybe even needed. Not that he'd ever say as much. He'd protected her all her life, which hadn't abated as she'd reached adulthood. To her shame, she'd let him.

Thing was, she *wanted* to work hard. She wanted to be a valued member of HIT and to be involved in the decision making. She wished she could shed the anxiety that led to her always hovering in the shadows and allowing others to run with her ideas and get the glory that came with those successes. Okay, so not every idea was wildly successful, but her phobia of speaking in groups had held her back, and she knew others had been promoted over her because of it. Her personality flaws meant she wasn't perceived to be as dynamic and forward thinking as people in upper management were expected to be.

When her crippling fear had surfaced after the death of her mom, and when years of therapy appeared to make no headway, her father had always reassured her that she was simply a late bloomer and she only needed time to come into her own. But she was twenty-eight now, and she still hadn't overcome her insecurities. She knew that was a continual, if quiet, disappointment to her father. While he'd never said as much, she knew he'd always hoped that she could overcome her phobia and stand at his side at HIT, and she'd wanted that, too. She'd thought he was still giving her time. She hadn't realized he'd given up on her. Not until today.

This latest development was the last straw. Her father had always included her in his planning for the firm, even implemented an idea or two of hers from time to time, but this he'd done completely without her.

The shock continued to reverberate through her. The writing was on the wall. She'd been left in the dark on this major decision—and in the dark was where she'd stay going forward unless she did something about it. She couldn't make excuses for herself anymore. She was a big girl now. It was past time that she stretched to her full potential. If she didn't, she'd be overlooked for the rest of her life, and she knew for sure that she didn't want that. Things had to change. She had to change. Now.

Gilda and Ron were still laughing and talking, sharing reminiscences as well as exchanging those little touches and private looks that close couples did all the time. It was sweet, but it compounded the sense of exclusion she felt at the same time. In her personal life as well as in the workplace, the people around her seemed to move forward easily, effortlessly, while she struggled with every step. She was happy for the others, truly—she was just sad for herself.

When they both looked at their watches and said they needed to be on their way, she didn't object. Instead she waved them off with a smile and stayed to finish her barely touched drink.

She should go home to her apartment, get an early night—prepare for the big announcement tomorrow. Should? It felt like all her life Sally had done what *should* be done. Like she'd spent her life striving to please others. But what about her? Change had to start from a point in time—why couldn't that change start now? Why couldn't she be bold? Accept new challenges?

"Ma'am? The gentleman over there asked me to bring you this."

A waitress put another Gibson on the table in front of her. Sally blinked in surprise before looking up at the girl.

"Gentleman?"

"Over there." The waitress gestured. "He's really hot."

"Are you sure it was for me?" she asked.

"He was quite specific. Did you want me to take it back?"

Did she? The frightened mouse inside her quivered and said, *oh, yes.* But wasn't that what she would have done normally? In fact, since she'd dismissed her personal security, wouldn't she normally have left with Gilda and Ron and shared a cab so she wouldn't be left on her own like this? Open to new experiences? Meeting new people? Flirting with a man?

Sally turned her head and met the gaze of the man in question. She'd noticed him before and rejected him as being way out of her league. *Hot* didn't even begin to describe him. He wore confidence as easily as he wore his dark suit and crisp, pale business shirt, top button undone. Sally felt every cell in her body jump to visceral attention as his eyes met hers. He nodded toward her, raised his glass in a silent toast, then smiled. The kind of smile that sizzled to the ends of her toes.

Be bold, a little voice whispered in the back of her mind. She turned her attention to the waitress and gave the girl a smile.

"Ma'am?"

"Leave it. Thank you. And please pass on my thanks."

"Oh, you can do that yourself. He's coming over."

Coming over? Sally's fight-or-flight reflexes asserted themselves in full screaming glory, shrieking, *take flight!* like a Klaxon blaring in the background.

"May I join you?" the man said smoothly, his hand hovering over the back of the chair Gilda had recently vacated.

"Certainly." Her pulse fluttered at her throat, but she managed to sound reasonably calm. She lifted her glass and tipped it toward him in a brief toast. "Thank you for the drink."

"You're welcome. You don't see many people drinking a Gibson these days. An old-fashioned drink for an old-fashioned girl?"

His voice was rich and deep and stroked her nerves like plush velvet on bare skin. And he certainly wasn't hard on the eyes, either. He filled his suit with broad shoulders, and the fine cotton of his shirt stretched across a chest that looked as though it had the kinds of peaks and valleys of toned muscle that a woman like her appreciated but oh so rarely got to indulge in. His face was slightly angular, his nose a straight blade, and his eyes—whatever color they were, something light, but it was hard to tell in here—looked directly at her. No shrinking violet, then. Not like her. His lips were gently curved. He didn't have the look of a man who smiled easily, and yet his smile didn't look fake. In fact, he actually looked genuinely amused but not in a superior way.

Not quite sure how to react, she looked down at her drink and forced a smile. "Something like that."

Sally looked up again in time to see him grin outright in response. Seeing his smile was like receiving an electric shock straight to her girlie parts. Wow. Shouldn't a man need a license to wield that much sex appeal?

"I'm Kirk, and you are?" He offered her his hand and quirked an eyebrow at her.

Sally's insides turned to molten liquid. Normally, she wouldn't give in to a drink and a slick delivery like the one he'd just pitched, but what the hell. She was fed up with being the good girl. The one who always did what was expected. The one who always deferred to others and never put herself forward or chased after what she wanted. If she wanted to make a stand in anything in her life, she was going to have to do things head-on rather than work quietly and happily in the background. Hadn't she just decided tonight to take charge of her life and her decisions? For once, she was going to do exactly what she wanted and damn the consequences.

She put out her hand to accept his. "I'm Sally. Next round is on me."

"Good to meet you, although I have to warn you, I don't usually let women buy me drinks."

Sally felt that old familiar clench in her gut when faced with conflict. The kind of thing that made her clam up, afraid to speak up for herself. It was one of her major failings—another thing she hid behind. But she'd told herself she wouldn't hide tonight. She pasted a stiff smile on her lips. Pushed herself to respond.

"Oh, really? Why is that?"

"I'm kind of old-fashioned, too."

She couldn't stifle the groan that escaped her. Despite being head of a leading IT corporation, her dad was also the epitome of old-fashioned. The very last thing Sally needed in her life was another man like that.

"But," he continued, still smiling, "in your case I might be prepared to make an exception."

Taken aback, she blurted, "In my case? Why?"

"Because I don't think you're just buying me a drink just so you can take advantage of my body."

She couldn't help it. She laughed out loud. Not a pretty, dainty little titter—a full-blown belly laugh.

"Does that happen often?" she asked.

"Now and again," he admitted.

"Trust me, you're quite safe with me," she reassured him.

"Really?"

Was it her imagination, or did he sound a little disappointed?

"Well, perhaps we should wait and see," she answered with a smile of her own and reached for her martini.

Two

How had it gone from a few drinks and dancing to this? Sally asked herself as they entered his apartment. Kirk threw his jacket over the back of a bland beige sofa. She got only the vaguest impression of his place—a generic replica of so many serviced apartments used by traveling business people with stock-standard wall decorations and furnishings. The only visible sign of human occupation was the dining table piled high with archive boxes and files.

That was all she noticed before his hands were lifting her hair from her nape and his lips pressed just there. She shivered at the contact. Kirk let her hair drop again and took her hand to lead her through to his bedroom. He turned to face her, and she trembled at the naked hunger reflected in his eyes.

Be bold, Sally reminded herself. *You wanted this. Take charge. Take what you want.*

She reached for his tie, pulling it loose, sliding it out from under his collar and letting it drop to the floor. Then she attacked his buttons, amazed that her fingers still had any dexterity at all given how her body all but vibrated with the fierceness of her longing for this man. A piece of her urged her to slow down, to take care, to reconsider, but she relegated that unwelcome advice to the very back of her mind. This was what she wanted, and she would darn well take it, and him, and revel in the process.

Kirk didn't remain passive. His large, warm hands stroked her through the fabric of her tunic, which, beneath his touch, felt like the sexiest thing she'd ever worn. She sighed out loud when she pushed his shirt free of his body and skimmed her hands over the breadth of his muscled shoulders, following the contours of his chest. While they'd danced, she'd been able to tell he was in shape, but, wow, this guy was *really* in shape. For a second she felt uncomfortable, ashamed of her own inadequacies—her small breasts, her wide hips, her heavy bottom. But then Kirk bent his head and nuzzled at the curve of her neck, and the sensation of his hot breath and his lips against her skin consigned all rational thought to obscurity.

For now everything was about his touch. She was vaguely aware of Kirk reaching for the zipper at the back of her tunic and sliding it down, then deftly removing her trousers, and felt again that prickle of insecurity as he eased the garment off her body, exposing her pretty lace bra and her all too practical full briefs.

She stifled a giggle. "Sorry, I wasn't quite expecting this outcome when I dressed for today."

"Never apologize," he ordered. His voice was deep and held a tiny tremor, which gave her an immense boost of confidence. "You're beautiful. Perfect, in fact. And, for the record, I happen to find white cotton incredibly sexy."

She looked at his face—studying it to see if he was serious or if he was simply saying what he thought she needed to hear—but there was an honesty there in his features that sent a new thrill through her. She bracketed his cheeks with her hands and pulled his face down to hers, kissing him with all that she had in her. With just a few well-chosen words, he'd made her feel valued, whether he knew it or not.

She couldn't pinpoint the exact moment he unhooked her bra, but she would remember forever the first time his hands cupped her breasts. His touch was reverent but firm. His fingers, when they caressed her nipples, teasing but gentle. Unable to help herself, Sally arched her back, pressing herself against his palms, eager to feel more. She was no shrinking virgin, but she'd never experienced this kind of responsiveness before in her life. Right now she was lost in sensation and anticipation of his next move.

When he lowered his mouth to capture one taut nipple, she keened softly in response. Her legs felt like jelly, as if they could barely support her, and at her core her body had developed a deep, drawing ache of need.

"Perfect," he whispered against her wet and sensitive bud, sending another shiver through her body that had nothing to do with cold and everything to do with an inferno of heat and desire.

Kirk's hands were at her hips a moment later, easing her panties down over her thighs. She stepped out of them, for the first time in her adult life unembarrassed by her nakedness.

"It seems you have me at a slight disadvantage here," she said with a teasing smile.

"I'm all for equal opportunity." He smiled in return

and spread his hands wide so she could reach for his belt buckle.

She wasn't sure how he did it, but he managed to make shedding his shoes, socks, trousers and boxer briefs incredibly sexy. Or maybe it was just that she was so looking forward to seeing him naked, to having the opportunity to investigate every curve of muscle and every shadow beneath it, that every new inch of bared skin aroused her even more.

His skin peppered with goose bumps as she trailed her hand from his chest to his lower abdomen. His erection was full and heavy, jutting proudly from his body without apology or shame.

"You do that to me," he said as she eyed him.

Again he made her feel as though she was the strong, desirable one here. The one with all the authority and control. Without a second thought, she wrapped her fingers around his length, stroking him and marveling at the contradiction in impressions—of the heated satin softness of his skin and the steel-like hardness beneath it.

Somehow they maneuvered onto the bed. Again an exercise in elegance rather than the convoluted tangle of limbs she'd always experienced in the past. Sally had never known such synchronicity before. Exploring his body, listening to and watching his reactions as she did so, became the most natural thing in the world. Despite the sense of urgency that had gripped her at the bar, right now she wanted to take all the time in the world. Kirk, too, seemed content to go along for the ride, to allow her the time to find out exactly what wrung the greatest reactions from him, how to take him to the edge of madness and how to bring him slowly down again.

And then it was his turn. His hands were firm and sure as they stroked her, his fingers nimble and sweet as they tweaked and tugged and probed until she was shaking from head to foot. Wanting to demand he give her the release her body trembled for, yet wanting him to prolong this torturous pleasure at the same time. And all the while he murmured how beautiful she was. How perfect. It was the most empowering experience of her life.

When he finally sheathed himself and entered her body, it was sheer perfection. Her hips rose to greet him, and as he filled her she knew she'd never known anything quite this exquisite and might never know anything to match it again. Tonight was a gift. Something to be cherished. All of it—especially the way he made her feel so incredibly wanted when he groaned and gripped her hips as he sank fully within her.

"Don't. Move," he implored her as she tightened her inner muscles around him.

"What? Like this?" She tightened again and tilted her hips so he nestled just that little bit deeper.

"Exactly *not* like that."

She did it again, savoring the power his words had given her. Savoring, too, each and every sensation that rippled through her body at how deliciously he filled her. He growled, a deep, guttural resignation to her demands and began to withdraw. Then he surged against her. This time it was Sally who groaned in surrender. Her hands tightened on his shoulders, her short, practical nails embedded in his skin. She met him thrust for thrust, her tension coiling tighter and tighter, until she lost all sense of what was happening and felt her entire being let go in a maelstrom of pleasure so mind-blowing, so breathtaking she knew nothing in her life would ever be the same again.

As she lay there, heart still hammering a frantic beat, her nerve endings still tingling with the climax that had wrung her body out, she thought it such a shame that this was to be only a one-night stand. A woman could get used to this kind of lovemaking. But not a woman like her, she reminded herself sternly. She had a career path to follow. A life to build and a point to prove, to herself if to no one else. Throwing herself into another doomed attempt at building a satisfying relationship would only distract her from her goals. She had to take this rendez-vous for what it was—a beautiful anomaly—and then thank the nice man for the lovely ending to the night before getting dressed and going home.

She couldn't quite bring herself to do it. To pull away and leave the welcoming warmth of his embrace, to end the age-old connection of their bodies. Kirk murmured something in her ear and rolled to one side, bringing her with him until she was half sprawled over his body. Oh, but he was magnificent, she though as she studied his upper torso. How lucky was she to have met him to-night? She lowered her head on his chest and listened to his heart rate as it changed from racing fast to a slower, more even beat. His breathing, too, changed, and his fin-gers stopped playing with her hair.

He was asleep. Five more minutes and it was time to go. Gently she extracted herself from his arms and tiptoed around the bedroom gathering up her things. A quick trip to the bathroom to tidy up and get dressed and she was out of here. No sticking around for embarrass-ment in the cold light of morning. No recriminations or awkwardness over breakfast.

She let herself out of the apartment and slipped her phone from her bag. She'd just opened an app to order a cab when her phone—put on silent when she'd gone out to meet her friends—lit up with an incoming call. She recognized the name on the screen immediately. Marilyn had been her father's PA since before she was born and had become a mother figure to Sally after her own mother's death. But it was late, after midnight. What on earth was Marilyn doing calling her now?

"Hello?" Sally answered as the elevator doors opened onto the lobby.

"Where are you?" Marilyn asked sharply. "I've been trying to call you for the past two hours."

There was a note to the older woman's voice that Sally had never heard her use before. She identified it immediately as fear and felt her stomach drop.

"What's wrong?" she asked, getting straight to the point.

"It's your father. He came back into his office tonight, and security found him while they were on their rounds. He's had a heart attack and he's at the hospital now. It's bad, Sally, really bad."

A whimper escaped her as she took a mental note of the details of which hospital he was at.

"Where are you?" Marilyn asked. "I'll send Benton with the car."

"No, it's okay. I'm not far from the hospital. I've got a cab coming already. Are you there now?"

"Of course," the PA answered. A note of vulnerability crept into her voice. "But they won't tell me anything because I'm not next of kin."

"I'll be there as soon as I can. I promise."

Waiting for the cab was the longest five minutes of her life, and as it pulled away from the curb, Sally wondered how life could turn on the dime like that. How, in one moment, everything could be perfect and exciting and new, and in the next all could be torn away.

She should never have left her father after dinner tonight, especially on the eve of something as big as tomorrow's merger announcement. But how was she to know he'd go back into the office and, of all things, have a heart attack? And why had the security guards called Marilyn instead of her? Surely she, as his daughter, should have been listed on the company register as his immediate next of kin? But then, he'd always sheltered and protected her, hadn't he?

She remembered how drawn he'd looked tonight. How she'd dismissed it so easily as nothing out of the ordinary. She hadn't even asked if he was feeling ill. Guilt assailed her. He hadn't wanted to worry her about the merger, so why would he worry her about not feeling well? Suddenly her decision to be bold and chase after her own pleasure without thinking of the consequences tonight seemed horribly pathetic and selfish. If she'd simply gone home after her friends had left the bar, she'd have gotten the call and been at the hospital hours ago. What if she arrived too late? She didn't know what she'd do if she lost her dad. He was her rock, her mainstay, her shelter.

"Hold on, Daddy," she whispered. "Please, hold on."

Always an early riser, Kirk woke as sunlight began to filter through the blinds, his body satiated like it had never been before. He took a moment to appreciate the feeling and decided he could definitely go for another round of that. He reached across his sheets for Sally's warm, recumbent form beside him and came up with empty space. When had she pulled away from him? It wasn't like him to sleep so deeply that he couldn't remember his bed partner leaving, but then again he'd all but lost consciousness after the force of passion they'd shared.

Maybe she was in the bathroom. He looked across the bed to where light should have gleamed around the bathroom door frame, but there was only darkness. He sat up and cast his gaze around the room looking for her clothes. They were gone, as was she.

It shouldn't have mattered—after all, he knew he'd see her again at the office, even if she wasn't aware of that little detail just yet. But there was something almost shameful in the way she'd slipped out of his room without saying goodbye. As if she was embarrassed by what they'd done or wanted to pretend it hadn't happened.

Well, maybe it hadn't been as good for her as it was for him. He shook his head and told himself not to be so ridiculous. He knew she'd been there with him, every step of the way. Sometimes leading, sometimes allowing herself to be led. In fact, just thinking about her reactions—the sweet sounds she'd made, the responsiveness of her body beneath his touch—brought his desire immediately to full, aching life again.

Kirk groaned and pushed back the covers, remembering he hadn't rid himself of the condom he'd miraculously had the presence of mind to slip on last night. The groan rapidly turned into a string of wild curses when he realized the condom wasn't intact. He went to the bathroom and took care of what was left of it.

Now wide awake, several scenarios ran through his head. Of course, she could be on the Pill. Goodness only knew he hadn't stopped to ask. He'd barely stopped to put on protection himself, for all the good it had done. Either way, he had to tell her, and soon. He wondered how that would go. It's not like he could wait for her dad to introduce them at the office and shake her hand and say, "Hi, about last night…the condom broke."

He heard his cell phone ringing from the sitting room and walked, naked, to retrieve it from his suit jacket. He recognized the number as Orson Harrison's private line and answered immediately, surprised to hear a woman's voice, though she quickly introduced herself as Marilyn, Orson's assistant, and explained the medical emergency from the night before. His blood ran cold as he heard the news.

"Assemble the board as quickly as you can," he instructed Harrison's PA. "I'll be there in twenty minutes."

Three

Kirk's head was still reeling. At the emergency board meeting, everyone had been shocked to hear the news of Orson's heart attack, but all had agreed that the company could show no weakness, especially when Orson's confidential report on his reasoning behind the merger had been presented to them. Therefore, they'd appointed Kirk interim chairman.

The new responsibility was a heavy weight on him, along with worry for Orson Harrison's health. And on top of all that, he still had to tell Sally about the possibility she might be pregnant. He closed his eyes for a brief moment. He'd been such a fool to allow desire to cloud his judgment. It was the kind of impulsive emotion and need-driven behavior he'd always sworn he'd never indulge in. And now look where it had landed him.

He was investigating her, just as he was investigating every staff member here—he never should have allowed sex to muddy the waters.

He had no doubt she wouldn't be happy to hear his news. Who would be, especially while her father's life hung in the balance? So far the hospital had released very little information—only that Orson was in critical condition. Even Marilyn, who'd known Orson for almost thirty years, had been trying on the phone all morning, and remained unable to get past the gatekeeper of patient details at the hospital. To be honest, Kirk had been surprised to see the woman at her desk this morning and he'd expressed as much. She'd curtly informed him that someone had to hold the place together in Orson's absence and had been ill-pleased when she'd been informed of his appointment as interim chairman.

Kirk flicked a glance at his watch. Perhaps she'd gotten ahold of Sally again by now. He hit the interoffice button to connect with the prickly PA.

"Any updates regarding Mr. Harrison?" he asked.

"No, sir." The woman's voice was clipped.

She'd made it quite clear that she wasn't happy about him using Orson's office—interim appointment or not. She was even less impressed when he'd ignored her protests and taken up residence. It made sense to him to stand at the helm right now, when he was supposed to be steering this particular ship. It would help the staff to see someone visibly taking charge. Well, the staff except for Marilyn.

"Thank you, Marilyn," Kirk replied, keeping his voice civil. "And Ms. Harrison? Has there been any communication with her yet?"

"I believe she's in the building but I haven't spoken to her myself, yet."

Kirk looked at his watch. Two thirty. They were going forward with the planned announcement of the merger—it was, after all, the only thing that would explain why

Kirk had taken temporary leadership—and the video link announcement was scheduled to commence at three sharp. Did Sally still plan to be there? He knew her father had wanted her by his side, but in light of recent events, he wouldn't blame her for skipping out. Coming into the office at all couldn't have been an easy decision to make with her father so desperately ill.

"Could you get a message to her and ask her to come to my office as soon as possible? I want to brief her before the video link."

"Certainly, sir."

Again there was that brief hesitation and slight distaste to her tone as she said the word *sir*. He'd already asked her to call him by his first name, but it seemed his request had been ignored. That, however, wasn't important to him right now. He had a far greater concern on his hands. Like, how the hell did he tell Sally about the condom?

It was only a few minutes before he heard women's voices outside the office door. The double doors began to swing open, and he heard Marilyn's voice call out in caution.

"Oh, but there's someone—"

And there she was. Sally Harrison appeared in the doorway, her head still turned to Marilyn, a reassuring smile on her face. A smile that froze then faded into an expression of shock when she saw him rise from behind her father's desk.

"K-Kirk?" she stammered.

Her face paled, highlighting the dark shadows of exhaustion and worry beneath her eyes that even makeup couldn't disguise. Kirk moved swiftly to her side, aware of Orson's PA coming up behind Sally. He gently guided Sally into a chair.

"A glass of water for Ms. Harrison, please, Marilyn," Kirk instructed the PA, who raced to do his bidding.

She was back in a moment, and Kirk took the glass from her before pressing it into Sally's shaking hand.

"Mr. Tanner, it's really too much to expect her to attend the video link," Marilyn began defensively. "She shouldn't have to—"

"It's entirely up to Ms. Harrison. Marilyn, perhaps you could get something for her to eat. I bet you haven't had anything today, have you?" he asked, looking at Sally directly.

Sally shook her head. "No. I couldn't bear to think about food."

She tried to take a sip of the water. Her hand was shaking so much Kirk wrapped his fingers around hers to steady her and keep her from spilling. She flinched at his touch, a reaction he was sure Marilyn hadn't missed.

"You need to eat something," he said. He turned to the PA. "Could you get a bowl of fruit from the executive kitchen for Ms. Harrison and perhaps some yogurt, as well?"

"Is that what *you* want, Sally?" Marilyn asked, moving to Sally's other side. "Perhaps you'd rather I stayed here with you while Mr. Tanner got you something to eat."

Kirk bit back a retort. He wasn't about to enter into a battle of wills with Marilyn here and now. And given the time constraints that now faced them, he wouldn't be able to have the discussion with Sally that they really needed to have. He studied her from the top of her golden head to her sensibly clad feet. Even in a demure pale blue suit and with her hair scraped back into a ponytail that gave him a headache just looking at how tightly it was bound, she still affected him.

Could she already be pregnant with his child? The thought came like a sucker punch straight to his gut.

"Good idea," he said, making a decision to leave their discussion until they could be guaranteed more privacy and uninterrupted time.

Of greater importance was letting Sally come to terms with his presence here—and the fact that he'd kept it from her last night. Once the shock wore off, he had no doubt matters between them would be less than cordial, especially once she discovered that he'd known exactly who she was all along.

Sally looked from him to Marilyn. "It-it's okay, Marilyn. You know what I like. Perhaps you could get it for me? I really am feeling quite weak."

"Of course you are," Marilyn said in a more placatory tone and patted Sally on the shoulder. "You've always had a delicate constitution. I'll be back in a moment."

Marilyn closed the door behind her with a sharp click, leaving Kirk in no doubt that even though Orson's PA had left the room to do his bidding, she certainly wasn't happy about it.

"Have another sip of water," he urged Sally.

He was relieved to see a little color coming back into her face.

"How is your dad doing?" he asked, determined to distract her until Marilyn's return.

She drew in another deep breath. "He's in an induced coma and they say he's stable—whatever that means. It's hard to see it as anything positive when he looks so awful and is totally nonresponsive." Her voice shook, but she kept going. "They're hoping to operate tomorrow. A quadruple bypass, apparently."

Kirk pressed a hand on her shoulder. "I know your dad. He's strong, he'll come through."

She looked up at him and he saw a flash of anger in her blue eyes.

"Just how well do you know my dad?"

Kirk felt a swell of discomfort, with just a tinge of rueful amusement. Trust Orson's daughter to cut straight to the chase. "I've known him most of my life, to be honest."

"And how is it I've never met you before last night?"

There was still a slight tremor to her voice, but he could see her getting stronger by the minute.

"Our parents were friends until my father died. After that my mom and I moved away. I was a kid at the time. There was no reason for you to know me before last night."

He kept it deliberately brief. There wasn't time for detail now.

"And now you're back." She fell silent a moment before flicking him another heated look. "You knew all along who I was, didn't you?"

Kirk clenched his jaw and nodded. He'd never been the kind of person who lived on regret, but right now, if he could have turned back the clock and done last night over again, he absolutely would have. Or would he? He doubted she'd have come home with him if she'd known he'd soon be her boss. Would he have missed the chance to lose himself in her arms the way he had? Never have known the perfect passion they'd experienced together? *Never had the broken condom*, the snarky voice in the back of his mind sharply reminded him. Okay, so he'd have skipped that part.

"I see." Sally swallowed another sip of water before speaking again. "She called you Mr. Tanner. That would be the Tanner in Harrison Tanner Tech? The new vice president?"

He nodded.

She pressed her lips together before speaking. "It seems you had me at a disadvantage right from the start. Which asks the question why you'd do something like that. Did it give you a kick to sleep with the chairman's oblivious daughter? Never mind—don't bother answering that."

Sally waved her hand as if to negate the words she'd just uttered.

"Look, can we talk about that later, over dinner?"

"I do not want to go out to dinner with you. In fact, I don't even want to be in the same room as you."

Her cheeks had flushed pink with fury. At least that was better than the waxen image she'd presented to him only a few moments ago.

Marilyn returned to the office and set a small tray on Sally's lap.

"There you are, my dear. Goodness knows, with your father so ill, the last thing we need is you collapsing, too. I've been telling your father for years now that he needs to slow down, but do you think he listens to me?" As if suddenly aware of the leaden atmosphere between Kirk and Sally, Marilyn straightened and gave Kirk a pointed glare. "Is there anything else...sir?"

"No, thank you, Marilyn. That will be all for now," Kirk replied. He flicked a quick look at his watch. "Eat up," he instructed Sally. "We have fifteen minutes."

"I don't feel like eat—"

"Please, Sally, at least try. It'll boost your blood sugar for now and hopefully tide you through the next few hours," Kirk said. "Whether you like it or not, we have to work together, today in particular. The last thing I want—and, as Marilyn already pointed out, the very last thing Harrison Tanner Tech needs—is you collapsing live on camera, especially during the merger announcement and even more so when news of your father's heart attack becomes public knowledge."

They locked gazes for what felt like a full minute before Sally acceded to his request and began to spoon up mouthfuls of the fruit.

"I still don't want to go out for dinner with you," she muttered between bites.

"We need to talk about last night, and we don't have time now."

"I don't particularly wish to discuss last night. In fact, I'd rather forget it ever happened."

Her words were cutting. Her anger and distrust right now felt like a palpable presence in the room. Such a contrast to the sweet openness she had shown him last night. And the tension between them was only going to get worse when she heard what he had to tell her. There was a knock at the door, and one of the communications team popped his head in.

"Ten minutes, Mr. Tanner! We need you miked and sound checked now."

"And me, too," Sally interjected in a shaking voice.

"Are you sure, Ms. Harrison?"

It wasn't Kirk's imagination—she paled again. But in true Harrison spirit, she placed her bowl on the desk in front of her and rose to her feet. She straightened her jacket and smoothed her hands over her rounded hips. Yes, there was still a tremor there.

"Absolutely certain. Let's get this over with," she said tightly.

"You don't have to speak. In fact, you don't have to do anything at all. I can handle the announcement."

"Really? Do you think that's a good idea given that people will be expecting to see my father? A man they know and *trust*—" she paused for emphasis "—and instead they're getting you?"

There was enough scorn in her voice to curdle milk.

"They can trust me," he said simply. "And so can you."

"You'll excuse me if I find that hard to believe."

Sally wished she hadn't eaten a thing. Right now she felt sick to her stomach. How dare Kirk have hidden his identity from her like that? What kind of a jerk was he? Was this some form of one-upmanship, lording his conquest over her before he'd even started here—making sure she knew exactly who was the top dog? And what if he tried to hold their one-night stand over her?

Sally stiffened her spine and looked him straight in the eyes. "In my father's absence, I would prefer to make the announcement regarding the merger. You can fill in the details afterward. It's what Dad would want."

The sick sensation in her stomach intensified at the thought of being the figurehead for making the company-wide statement. But she could do this. She had to do this, to save face if nothing else. Kirk looked at her for a few seconds then shrugged and reached across the desk to grab a sheaf of papers. He held them out to her.

"Here's the statement your father prepared yesterday. If you're sure you can handle it, I have no objection to you making the announcement and then I'll field any questions from the floor. After the Q and A from the video feed closes, we'll repeat the same again for the press announcement."

"Why will you be answering questions? Why not Silas Rogers, the CEO, or any of our other senior management?"

"Sally, your father and I have been working together

in the lead-up to this for several months now. No one else can give the answers I can. I'm the one who can carry out the plans your father and I made—that's why I've been appointed interim chairman. The board gave their approval at the meeting that was called this morning."

This morning. While she'd been at the hospital, out of her mind with worry over her father's condition. Her mind latched onto one part of what he'd said and yanked her out of her brief reverie.

"Several months?" Sally couldn't stop the outburst. "But I didn't hear about it until yesterday!"

"It was your father's decision to keep everything under wraps for as long as possible. Obviously he'd hoped to do the announcement with me today, present a united front and all that, but since he can't, we'll do the next best thing. Are you okay with that?"

Okay with it? No, she wasn't okay with it—any of it. But her dad had thought of everything, hadn't he? And none of it, except for a rushed dinner together last night, had included her.

"Sally?"

"Let me read the statement."

Sally scanned the double-spaced pages, hearing her father's voice in the back of her mind with every word she read. It wasn't right. He should be here to do this. This company was his pride and joy, built on his hard work, and he respected each and every one of his employees so very highly. Somehow she had to remember that in what she was about to do. Somehow she had to put aside her phobia and be the kind of person her father should have been able to rely on.

With every thought, she could feel her anxiety levels wind up several notches. *Be bold*, she told herself. *You can do this.* She drew in another deep breath then stood up and met Kirk's gaze.

"Right, let's go."

"Are you sure? You'll be okay?"

Blue-green eyes bored into hers, and she felt as though he could see through her bravado and her best intentions and all the way to the quivering jelly inside. He knew. Somehow, probably through her father, he knew about her glossophobia—the debilitating terror she experienced when faced with public speaking. Shame trickled down her spine, but she refused to back down.

"I'll be fine," she said, forcing a calm into her voice that she was far from feeling. "It's a video link, isn't it? Just us and a camera, right?"

"Look, Sally, you don't have to—"

She shook her head. "No, trust me, I really do."

He might not understand it, but this had become vital to her now. A method of proof that she was worthy. A way to show her father, when he was well enough to hear about it, that she had what it took and could be relied upon to step up.

Kirk gave her a small nod of acceptance. "Fine. Remember I'll be right beside you."

She'd been afraid he'd say that. But as they walked out of her dad's office and down the carpeted corridor toward the main conference room, she felt an unexpected sense of comfort in his nearness. She tried to push the sensation away. She didn't want to rely on this man. A man she knew intimately and yet not at all. *Don't think about last night! Don't think about the taste of him, the feel of him, the pleasure he gave you.*

She needn't have worried. Last night was the last thing on her mind as they entered the conference room and she was immediately confronted by the single lens of a

camera pointing straight toward her. And beyond it was
a bank of television screens on the large wall of the conference room—each screen filled with faces of the staff
assembled at each of their offices. All of them staring
straight at her.

Four

Kirk felt the shift in Sally's bearing the second they entered the conference room. He cast her a glance. She looked like she was on the verge of turning tail and running back down the corridor. She'd already come to a complete halt beside him, her eyes riveted on the live screens on the other side of the room, and he could see tiny beads of perspiration forming at her hairline and on her upper lip. And, dammit, she was trembling from head to foot.

"Sally?" he asked gently.

She swallowed and flicked her eyes in his direction. "I can do this," she said with all the grimness of a French aristocrat on her way to the guillotine.

Sally walked woodenly toward the podium set up in front of the camera. The sheaf of papers he'd given her earlier was clutched in one fist, and she made an effort to smooth them out as she placed them on the platform in front of her.

He had to give it to her. She wasn't backing down, even though she was obviously terrified. He wished she'd just give in and hand the papers back over to him. Making her go through this was akin to punching a puppy, and the idea made him sick to the stomach. Probably about as sick as she was feeling right now.

The camera operator gestured to Kirk to take the other seat and Kirk hastened to Sally's side. As he settled beside her, he could feel tension coming off her in waves. She'd grown even paler than when they'd arrived.

"Sally?" he asked again.

"Five minutes until we go live!" someone said from across the room. "Someone get mikes on them, please."

Kirk reached across and curved his hand around one of hers. "Let me do this. I've had time to prepare. You haven't."

He held his breath, waiting for her reply, but they were distracted by two sound technicians fitting them each with a lapel mike and doing a quick sound check.

"One minute, people."

Kirk squeezed her hand. "Sally, it's your call. No one expects this of you. Least of all your father—and especially given the circumstances."

"Don't you see," she whispered without looking at him. "That's exactly why I need to do it."

"Ten, nine, eight…"

"You only have to be here, Sally. That's more than enough given what you've been through."

"Live in three…" The technician silently counted down the last two numbers with his fingers.

Kirk waited for Sally to speak, but silence filled the air. Sally was looking past the winking red eye of the camera to the screens across the room, to the people of Harrison IT. Then, infinitesimally, she moved and slid the papers over to him. Taking it as his cue, Kirk pasted a smile on his face and introduced himself before he launched into the welcome Orson had prepared for his staff, together with a brief explanation that a medical event had precluded Orson from participating in the announcement.

Sally stood rigidly beside him throughout the explanation of the merger and the question-and-answer session that followed. The moment he signed off and the red light on the camera extinguished, Sally ripped off her microphone and headed for the door. He eventually caught up with her down the hallway.

"Leave me alone!" she cried as he reached for her hand and tugged her around to face him.

Kirk was horrified to see tears streaking her face.

"Sally, it's all right. You did great."

"Great? You call sitting there like a barrel of dead fish *great*? I couldn't even introduce you, which, in all honesty, was the very least I should have done given you are a total stranger to most of those people."

Distraction was what she needed right now.

"Dead fish? For the record, you look nothing like a barrel of anything, let alone dead fish."

She shook her head in frustration, but he was glad to see the tears had mostly stopped.

"Don't be so literal."

"I can't help it." He shrugged. "When I look at you, the last thing I picture is cold fish of any kind."

He lowered his voice deliberately and delighted in the flush of color that filled her cheeks, chasing away the lines of strain that had been so evident only seconds before.

"You're impossible," she muttered.

"Tell me how impossible over dinner after the press conference."

"No."

"Sally, we need to talk. About last night. About now."

He could see she wanted to argue the point with him, but he spied one of their media liaison staff coming down the corridor toward them. He was expected at the press conference right away.

"Please. Just dinner. Nothing else," he pressed.

He willed her to acquiesce to his suggestion. Not only did he need to talk to her about the broken condom, but he found himself wanting to get to know her better away from the confines of the office. He didn't realize he was holding his breath until she gave a sharp nod.

"Not dinner. But, yes, we can talk. I'm heading back to the hospital for a few hours first. I'll meet you later in my office. You can say what you have to say there."

It wasn't quite the acceptance he'd aimed for, but for now it would do. He watched her walk away and head to the elevators.

"Mr. Tanner, they're waiting for you downstairs in conference room three."

He reluctantly dragged his attention back to the job at hand. Unfortunately for him, Sally would have to wait.

It was late, and most of the staff had already headed home. The media session had run well over time, and afterward he'd been called into an impromptu meeting with the CEO and several others. The board might have agreed to appoint him interim chairman, but the executives still wanted to make it clear that they were the ones in charge. But he'd handled it knowing he had Orson's full support at his back, and that of the board of directors, too.

Now, he had a far more important task at hand. Kirk

loosened his tie and slid it out from beneath his collar as he approached Sally's office. He bunched the silk strip into his pocket and raised a hand to tap at her door. No response. He reached for the knob, turned it and let himself in.

The instant he saw her, motionless, with her head pillowed on her arms on the top of her desk, he felt a moment of sheer panic, but then reason overcame the reaction and he noted the steady breathing that made her shoulders rise and fall a little. She'd removed her jacket before sitting at her desk, and the sheer fabric of her blouse revealed a creamy lace camisole beneath it.

Desire hit him hard and deep, and his fingers curled into his palms, itching to relieve her of her blouse and to slide his hands over the enticement that was her lingerie. He doubted it was quite as silky soft as her skin, but wouldn't it be fun to find out?

No, he shouldn't go there again. Wouldn't. Whatever it was about Sally Harrison that drew him so strongly, he had to rein it back. Somehow. It would be a challenge when everything about her triggered his basest primal instincts, but—he reminded himself—didn't he thrive on challenges and defeating obstacles? He forced himself to ignore the sensations that sparked through his body and focused instead on the reality of the woman sleeping so soundly that she hadn't heard him knock or enter her office.

She had to be exhausted. She'd been through a hell of a lot in the past twenty-four hours. Any regular person would have struggled with the onslaught of emotions, let alone someone forced to be part of a video conference who suffered a phobia like hers. Orson had forewarned him that Sally experienced acute anxiety when it came to public speaking. He'd had no idea how severe it was or the toll it obviously took. Having seen her like that today went a long way toward explaining why she'd remained in a safe middle-management role at HIT rather than scaling the corporate ladder to be at her father's side.

He'd never before seen such despair on a person's face at the thought of talking in public and, he realized, he'd never before seen such bravery as she'd exhibited in pushing herself to try. Perhaps if she hadn't been so emotionally wrung out, she'd have been in a stronger position to attempt to conquer her demons today. But she hadn't and, from their conversation in the hall, he knew she saw that as a failure.

He made an involuntary sound of sympathy, and she shifted a little on the desk before starting awake and sitting upright in her chair.

"What time is it?" she demanded defensively, her voice thick with exhaustion. "How long have you been waiting?"

There was a faint crease on her cheek where she'd rested her face on the cuff of her sleeve. Oddly, it endeared her to him even more. This was a woman who needed a lot of protecting—he felt it to the soles of his feet. She was the antithesis of the kind of women he usually dated, and yet she'd somehow inveigled her way into a nook inside him that pulled on every impulse.

"Not long," he answered. "And it's late. I'm sorry, I got held up. How was your dad?"

"As well as can be expected. He's still stable and continues to be monitored, and they're confident he'll come through the surgery well tomorrow."

As well as can be expected. It was an awful phrase, he thought, remembering hearing the exact same words from the medical team who had looked after his mother after the first of the strokes that stole her from him.

Sally pushed up from her desk and stood to face Kirk. "But you didn't come here to talk about him, did you? What did you want to say to me?"

"I was hoping we could discuss it over dinner. I don't know about you, but I'm starving after today."

"I thought we were going to talk here," she hedged.

"Can't we kill two birds with one stone?"

"Look—" she sighed "—is this really necessary? There's no need to spend an hour making small talk over a meal before we get to the point. We're both adults, so surely we can continue to act as such. I'm quite happy to forget last night ever happened."

Kirk ignored the sting that came with her words. He couldn't forget last night even if he wanted to—especially not now. "And, as adults, we should be able to enjoy a meal together. Really, I could do with a decent bite to eat, and I'm sure you could, too."

She looked at him and for a moment he thought she'd refuse, but then she huffed out a breath of impatience.

"Fine. I'll let my security know I'm leaving with you."

Ah, that explained the muscle who'd accompanied her to the bar last night. "You have security with you whenever you're out?"

"One of the examples of Dad's overprotectiveness. When I was little and HIT was beginning to boom, there was a threat to kidnap me. Ever since he's insisted on me having a bodyguard. Trust me, it's not as glamorous as it sounds."

"It's hardly overprotective," Kirk commented as he helped Sally into her suit jacket. "Your father clearly takes your welfare seriously."

He felt a pang of regret as she buttoned up the front of her jacket, hiding the tempting glimpses of lace visible through her blouse.

"He likes to know I'm safe."

"I protect what's mine, too," Kirk replied firmly.

Sally raised her eyebrow. "Isn't that a little primitive?"

"Perhaps I should rephrase that. Like your father, I take my responsibilities *very* seriously."

"Well, considering you're standing in for my father at the moment, I guess I should find that heartening."

Kirk smiled. "I will always do my best by the company—for your dad's sake, if nothing else. You can be assured of that. He has my utmost respect."

"You say you've known him most of your life, and yet I had no idea he even knew you. No idea at all." For a second she looked upset, but then she pulled herself together. "Let me call Benton and then we can go."

He could see it really bothered her that her father hadn't shared anything about the merger until the ink was drying on the paperwork. But was that because she was disturbed her father had made those decisions without consulting her, or because she had something to hide? Kirk couldn't be absolutely sure either way.

She made the call, and in the next few minutes they were riding the elevator to the basement parking. Kirk led the way to his car—a late-model European SUV.

"You must be relieved for your dad. That he's stable, I mean."

"I'll be relieved when I know he's getting better again." She looked away, but he couldn't mistake the grief that crossed her face. "He was so gray when I left him this afternoon. So vulnerable. I've never seen him like that. Not even when Mom died. And he still has a major surgery to get through."

"Your father has more strength and determination than any man I've ever met, and he'll be receiving excellent care at the hospital. He'll come through this, Sally."

The words seemed to be what she needed to hear to pull herself together again. She looked up and gave him a weak smile. For a second he caught a glimpse of the woman he'd danced with last night, but then she was gone again. Kirk waited for Sally to settle in the passenger seat and buckle her seat belt before he closed her door and went around to the other side. She was still pale, but she appeared completely composed and in control. Not quite the woman he'd met last night, but not the woman caught in the grip of the anxiety attack from this afternoon, either.

He pulled out of the parking garage and headed down the road.

"Any preference for dinner?"

"Something fast and hot."

"Chinese okay, then?"

"Perfect."

A few blocks down, he pulled into the parking lot for a chain restaurant he knew always had good food.

"Looks like this is us."

He rushed around to her door and helped her from the car and they were seated immediately.

"A drink?" he asked Sally when the waiter came to bring their menus.

"Just water, thank you."

Probably a good idea for both of them, he thought, and gave his request for the same to the waiter. "Do you mind if I order for us?"

Sally shook her head, and he turned to the waiter and requested appetizers to be brought out to their table as soon as possible and ordered a couple of main entrées to share, as well.

Her lips pulled into a brief smile. "You really are hungry, aren't you?"

Sally slipped out of her jacket and put it on the seat

beside her. He looked at her across the table, noting again the imprint of her lacy camisole beneath her blouse. "You could say that," he replied with a wry grin.

Oh, yes, he was hungry for a lot of things, but only one of his desires would be satisfied by this meal tonight. To distract himself, he also shrugged off his jacket and undid the cuffs on his shirt and began to fold them back. He looked up and saw Sally's gaze riveted on his hands. Even in the dim light of the restaurant, he saw the rose pink stain that crept over her cheeks and her throat. Was she remembering exactly what parts of her body his hands had touched last night? Did she have any idea of how much he wanted to touch her again?

As if she sensed his gaze, she shook her head slightly and stared off into the distance, watching the other diners. Then, with a visible squaring of her shoulders, she returned her attention to him.

"Okay, so what was so important that you couldn't tell me at work?"

Kirk shifted in his chair. "It's about last night—" He paused, searching for the right words.

Sally felt her cheeks flush again. Did they really need to hash this all out? She'd much rather they just moved on.

"We covered this already," she interrupted. "Yes, it's awkward that we're working under the same umbrella after spending last night together. It happened, but it won't happen again. I'm sure we can be grown-up about it all and put it very firmly in the past. It doesn't have to affect our working relationship, such as it will be, and I'd prefer we just forget about it entirely."

She ran out of breath. Kirk eyed her from across the table.

"Are you quite finished?"

"Finished?"

"Your commendable little speech."

"Oh, that. Yes, I'm done."

"Great. I'd like to agree with you. However, we have a problem."

Sally looked at him in confusion. Did he think he couldn't work with her? She knew he'd mentioned redundancies in his announcement today. Surely he didn't mean to dismiss her from her job? Could he even do that? Was that what this dinner was about? Cold fingers of fear squeezed her throat shut.

"A problem?" she repeated.

"The condom broke."

Five

Of all the things he could have said, that was the last she'd expected. Sally felt the tension inside her coil up a few more notches. *The condom broke?* It kind of put her fear of redundancy in the shade, didn't it? She became aware that Kirk was watching her intently, waiting for her reaction. She forced herself into some semblance of composure. He'd seen her at her absolute worst already today—she couldn't afford to appear that weak to him again.

"Is that all?" She smiled tightly. "For a second there, I thought you were about to give me notice that you were terminating my job."

"You thought I was going to terminate you? Hell, no. But seriously, Sally—the condom. You have to let me know if—"

"You really have nothing to worry about," she interrupted him. She didn't want to hear him verbalize the words that were on the tip of his tongue. Didn't want to believe that pregnancy was a possibility, even though children were something she'd always desperately wanted. But not until it was the right time and, more importantly, with the right man. Certainly not with a man who would hide his identity and sleep with her while knowing exactly who she was.

"I'm on the Pill," she continued. "We're fine. Absolutely, totally and utterly fine."

"If you're sure?"

"One hundred and ten percent. Actually, no—just one hundred percent. One hundred and ten doesn't exist, really, does it? Percent meaning per hundred, right? So how can you have one hundred and ten hundredths?"

Darn, she was rambling. Nerves, combined with a healthy dose of anger, often did that to her in one-on-one conversation with people she didn't know well. It was a shame her phobia about public speaking didn't extend to rendering her mute in a situation like this, too. Kirk gave her a gentle half smile that made her stomach do a dizzy little flip, and beneath the lace cups of her bra she felt her breasts grow heavy and her nipples harden. Her body's helpless reaction to him served to stoke the fire of anger that simmered deep inside. He'd used her, she reminded himself.

"Okay then," he said with a gentle nod. "We're good. But if anything did happen, you'd let me know, right?"

"Of course," she answered blithely.

To her relief, the appetizers arrived and she helped herself to a lettuce wrap. She wasn't in the mood for small talk, and thankfully, now that Kirk had obviously gotten the business of the broken condom off his chest, he was far more invested in alleviating his hunger than indulging in idle chatter.

It didn't take long, though, before he steered conversation to work matters. It took a while to warm up to the discussion, and he seemed far more interested in asking questions than answering them, but overall she was surprised to find that Kirk agreed with and supported most of the principles she was passionate about for the company—especially her pet project of steering the head office at HIT, or HTT as it was now, toward more sustainable energy technologies and policies.

She wasn't certain if it was his skillful questioning or the energy burst she'd received from eating her first proper meal in twenty-four hours, but she found herself becoming quite animated as she delved deeper into her vision for the company.

"We could be leaders in this area if we do it right," she said passionately. "And with the correct systems set in place, we could take that platform to our clients, as well."

"Do it," Kirk said concisely.

"Do it?"

"Yeah. Draw up the proposal for me. I can already see how it would benefit us, but I'm not the only person you have to sell the idea to, right?"

This idea had been her baby from the outset, and she'd had a bit of pushback from a few of the senior managers when she'd floated it before. But getting the green light from Kirk was exciting, even if he was a low-down, deceitful piece of—

"I'll get onto it as soon as I can," she said. "I have most of the data assembled already."

"I look forward to seeing it," Kirk said. "Now, I think we've covered everything and it's probably time we headed home. You have an early start tomorrow, right?"

And just like that she hit the ground again. Her dad's surgery. How on earth could she have forgotten?

"Sally, don't feel bad. It's okay to escape now and then. Orson will come through this. You have to believe it."

Tears pricked her eyes, and she dragged her napkin to her lips in an attempt to hide their sudden quivering. After everything the last day had delivered, his unexpected compassion was just about her undoing. She blinked fiercely and put the napkin back down again.

"Thank you," she said. "Now, if you'll excuse me, I need to get a cab."

"No, I'll see you home. It's the least I can do."

She accepted his offer because she was absolutely too worn-out now to protest. She gave him her address and he smiled.

"Isn't that just a few blocks from the office?"

"It is. I like the building and it's close to Downtown Park when I need a blast of fresh air."

When they arrived at her apartment building, he rode the elevator with her to her floor.

"I'll be okay from here," she said as the elevator doors swooshed open.

"Let me see you to your door. It's what your guy— Benton?" he asked and waited for her nod before continuing "—would do, isn't it?"

She shrugged and walked down the hallway, hyperconscious of his presence beside her. Her hand shook as she attempted to put the key in the lock, and she almost groaned out loud at the clichéd moment when she dropped her keys and Kirk bent to retrieve them for her.

"Here, let me," he said.

Kirk suffered no such issues with his coordination, and he handed the keys back to her the moment the door was open. She looked up at him, all too aware of his strong presence beside her. Even though weariness tugged at every muscle in her body, she still felt that la-

tent buzz of consciousness triggered by his nearness—
and with it the tension that coiled tighter inside her with
every moment they stood together. Suddenly all she could
think about was the scent of him, the heat of his body,
the sounds he'd made as she'd explored the expanse of
his skin with her fingertips, her lips, her tongue.

She made a small sound and tried to cover it with a
cough.

"You okay?" Kirk asked.

"I'm fine, thank you. And thanks for dinner, too."

"No problem."

Silence stretched out between them, and it seemed
inevitable when Kirk lifted a hand to gently caress her
face. The moment his fingers touched her skin, she was
suffused with fire. *No*, she told herself frantically. She
wasn't going down that road again. Not with him. She
pulled back, and Kirk's hand fell to his side.

"Good night," she said as firmly as she could and
stepped through the doorway.

"Good night, Sally. Sweet dreams."

She closed the door and leaned back against it, trying
to will her racing heart back under control. One more
second and she'd have asked him to stay. She squeezed
her eyes shut tight, but it was no use. The image of him
remained burned on her retinas.

Sally opened her eyes and went to her bathroom, stripping off her suit and throwing it in a hamper ready to
send to the dry cleaner. She took a short, hot shower,
wrapped herself up in her robe and went to her bedroom.
Perched on her bed, she opened her handbag, pulling
out the blister pack of contraceptives she carried everywhere with her.

She studied the pack, then flipped it over to check the
days. Her chest tightened with anxiety the moment she

realized that somewhere along the line she'd gotten out of sync. Probably around the time a couple of weeks ago when she'd traveled to the small European kingdom of Sylvain for the christening of the baby of her best friend from college. With the time zone changes and the busyness of travel and jet lag and then getting back to work, she'd slipped up. Normally, it wouldn't have been a problem—it wasn't as if she was wildly sexually active. But it certainly was a problem now.

She couldn't be pregnant. She simply couldn't. The chances were so slim as to be nearly nonexistent, weren't they? But the evidence of her inconsistency stared straight at her from the palm of her hand.

Sweet dreams, he'd said. How could she dream sweet dreams when every moment had just become a waking nightmare?

It had been four weeks since her father's surgery, and despite a minor post-op infection in a graft site on his leg, everything had gone well. He was home now, with a team of nurses stationed around the clock to ensure his convalescence continued to go smoothly. Sally bore his daily grumbles with good humor—especially when, as each bland meal at home was served to him, he called her to complain about the lack of salt and other condiments he'd grown used to.

She was too relieved he was still alive and getting well again to begrudge him his complaints. He still had a way to go with his recovery, despite how well he was doing, but it was ironic that each day he seemed to have more energy, while each day she had less.

She chalked it up to the hours she was working. After all, what with juggling expanding the proposal for sustainable strategies she'd discussed with Kirk the night before her father's operation and daily visits to her father on top of her usual duties here at the office, it was no wonder she was feeling more tired than usual.

She was no longer worried about the broken condom or the mix-up with her Pill. She knew people who'd tried for years to get pregnant. The odds of her having conceived after just that one encounter with Kirk…? No, she wasn't even going to think about that again. For her own peace of mind, a couple of weeks ago she'd taken a home test and it had showed negative—to her overwhelming relief. She was just tired. That was all. Things would settle down after the presentation, she told herself.

It had become vital to her to make her presentation better than her best effort. She had no room for error on this. There were plenty of people in the office who were on the fence about the whole concept of energy technology and sustainability in the workplace. All it would take was a slipup from her and a damning comment from the chief executive officer, Silas Rogers—who she knew already disagreed with her on principle—and no matter how much support she had from Kirk, the concept would be dead in the water.

It had been interesting these past couple of weeks, watching people react to Kirk being installed as interim chairman in her father's absence. There was a fair amount of wariness interspersed with the obvious suck-ups who wanted to ensure that their jobs would remain secure in the merger transition that would take place over the next twelve months. And maybe that was another reason she wanted to make this presentation flawless. If it went ahead, she'd be project manager, and her own position and those of her team would be secure, too. And maybe, just maybe, she'd be able to prove to herself and to her father that she had what it took.

Another week later and Sally was finally satisfied she had everything in place. She'd booked the conference room on the executive floor, she'd gone through her PowerPoint, tested transmitting it to her team's portable devices and rehearsed her part of the presentation until she could recite everything forward, backward and in Swahili. Okay, so maybe not in Swahili, but she knew her stuff and so did her team.

For all that they were an information technology company, there were several diehards among the senior management who still preferred a paper handout to reading a handheld screen. After today she hoped to change that. She was so excited about seeing her team put forward the full development of their ideas. It could mean such wonderful things for Harrison Tanner Tech long-term that she hadn't even had time to feel anxious about talking in front of a group. Granted, it wouldn't be a huge crowd and she knew every person who would be there, but that hadn't stopped her phobia from taking over before. This time, though, felt different. She felt as though she could really do this, and her veins fizzed with anticipation as opposed to the dread she usually felt.

Sally had taken extra care with her appearance that morning, choosing a dress she knew flattered her. Her hair was pulled back into its customary ponytail, and her makeup was perfectly understated. Kirk would be at the presentation. She felt a flush of color steal into her cheeks. She had barely seen him since the night they'd had dinner together, although they had spoken on the telephone. He'd said it was to check for updates on her father's recovery, but she had a suspicion that it had more to do with his concerns about their failed contraception. Her notion was backed up when the calls stopped after she'd told him about the home test result.

She knew Kirk had been in and out of meetings and had spent some time back in California, finalizing things for his move to Seattle. It had filtered through the grapevine—not without a few remarks, both envious and full of admiration—that he'd bought a lakefront property here in Bellevue. She'd been relieved that their paths hadn't had to cross.

A chime at her door told her that Benton was there to take her to work. As soon as she arrived in the HTT building, she went straight to the main conference room on the senior management floor. It was time to slay her demons. The last time she'd been here—for the video feed announcing the merger—she'd made a complete idiot of herself in front of Kirk, not to mention all the staff. She'd heard one or two comments, hastily hushed, as she'd gone by in the office. While some people knew she held her position here in her father's firm purely on merit, there were a handful, including the CEO, who made their thoughts on nepotism perfectly clear.

She had so much to prove today. Normally, such a realization would have been daunting, but right now she felt completely in control. Sally looked around the room and silently approved the layout that she'd requested together with the screen that had been set up in readiness. She did a quick run-through with her tablet. Everything was working perfectly. She had this.

Over the next thirty minutes, the chairs slowly filled up as senior managers made their way into the room. There was a hum of activity when Kirk arrived, and Sally found herself holding her breath in anticipation as he walked toward her to say hello.

Her nostrils flared slightly as he neared, the delicious scent of him sending a tingle through her body. A tingle she instantly did her best to quash.

"Good morning," she said, pulling together all the smoothness she could muster. "I hope your trip back to California was successful."

"It was, thank you." His eyes raked over her and her heart rate picked up a notch or two. "And you've been okay?"

"Just fine," she replied with a smile fixed to her face. "Tanner, good to see you back."

Kirk turned to acknowledge Silas Rogers, who she knew couldn't wait to see her fail. He'd never liked her, and she could see that despite the congenial look pasted on the man's face, he resented Kirk's presence here, too. After all, he would have been the natural fill-in for her father during his illness and recovery had it not been for the board's appointment of Kirk.

Sally cast a glance at one of her team and gave them her signal to commence. She'd decided to keep her speaking role strictly limited to explaining the concept she wanted to see the company adopt in their head office and how it could be expanded over the next five years through all their branches. As soon as her second in charge, Nick, was finished with his spiel, she was ready to whirl into action.

A tricky little wave of nausea surged through her. Sally reached for her water glass and took a sip then breathed in deeply. Nick was beginning to wind up his introduction, and all eyes would soon be turning to her. Her armpits prickled with perspiration, and another wave of nausea swelled. Again she took a small sip of water then focused on her breathing. The sick feeling subsided. She let a sense of relief flow through her. She could do this.

"...and without further ado, here's our team leader, Sally Harrison, to fill you in on why we're all so excited about what this proposal will do for HTT now and in the future. Sally?"

She rose to her feet, tablet in hand, and started her spiel. If she kept her eyes fixed between the projector screen and her tablet, she could even pretend there were no other people in the room.

The first few minutes of her presentation went extremely well, as she explained why it was important for HTT to evaluate the energy technologies available to them, and the next stage started brilliantly as she showed how going paperless in the office was one small step on the ladder. She demonstrated how they'd implemented the change in her department alone, and the figures she quoted showed the significant savings this had brought—not to mention the diminished waste footprint left on the environment.

"So you can imagine the long-term impact this will have on an entire floor, the entire head office and especially each and every HTT office around the globe."

There was a general murmur of assent from about seventy percent of the assembly. Sally took another breath and continued with her presentation.

"Small, consistent changes made on a wide scale is what we need. Can you imagine how something as simple as replacing the current management motor fleet with hybrid vehicles and installing solar panels on the rooftop of the HTT building to feed energy back into the grid would reduce the company's carbon footprint? And while there would be some initial costs, in the end all these steps would significantly reduce our overall expenses."

She was heading into the homestretch when a vicious wash of dizziness struck, and she faltered in her speech and put a hand out to steady herself. Kirk spoke from his position a couple of yards away from her.

"Sally? Everything okay?"

She pulled her lips into a smile and made her eyes flare open wide. Anything to stop the influx of black dots that now danced across her vision. She'd had her share of panicked reactions to public speaking, but this was new…and a little frightening. What was wrong with her? And would she be able to hide it until the presentation was complete?

"I'm fine," she said, but her voice was weak.

She looked at the people sitting there, all of them with eyes trained on her. Saw the smirk on Silas Rogers's face. And then she did the unthinkable. While she stared directly into Kirk's face, her tablet fell and bounced on the carpet, and she followed it down, sliding to the floor in an ignominious and unconscious heap.

Six

Kirk acted on instinct. He scooped Sally into his arms.

"Finish the presentation," he instructed the nearest member of her team as concerned murmurs swirled around them. "She's counting on you."

Then, without wasting another second, he stalked out of the room and down the corridor to Orson's office.

"What's wrong with Sally?" Marilyn asked, rising to her feet as he came into the executive suite.

"She collapsed."

"We have a nurse on duty for the staff here. I'll call her."

"Yes, do that, thanks."

He laid Sally down on a couch. Thankfully she was beginning to regain consciousness.

"Wha—?"

"You fainted," Kirk filled in as she looked around her. "At least I think you fainted. I want you to go to the hospital for tests to make sure it's not anything serious."

Sally tried to struggle to an upright position. "Go to the hospital? Don't be ridiculous. I'll be fine. I need to get back in there. I have to finish what I started."

He could understand why she felt that way. A little research had revealed that Sally's fear of public speaking had held her back from advancing within the company, purely because she'd been unable to speak to any size group in a situation like the one today. That she'd done as well as she had this morning had surprised him. Even more surprising was how proud of her he'd felt while she was doing it.

If he hadn't been so focused on getting her out of the conference room, he would have stopped to wipe that ridiculous expression off Rogers's face. He made a mental note to have a word with the man about the aside he'd heard him make about Sally riding on others' coattails, implying that she was incapable of completing anything on her own. There was so much more to her than that narrow-minded stuffed shirt realized...so many depths to Sally Harrison that Kirk, in spite of himself, wanted to explore.

Over the past five weeks, he'd tried to tell himself that the crazy attraction between them was just that. A moment of craziness and nothing more. But seeing her this morning had brought his attraction to her back to the fore again. He'd resented having to turn and say hello to that pompous idiot Rogers when he'd finally gotten the chance to see her face-to-face again. Add to that the sheer panic that flew through him as she lost consciousness and hit the carpeted floor of the conference room, swiftly followed by the instinctive need to protect her, and he knew that the way he felt about Sally Harrison was more than crazy. It was downright certifiable.

A movement at the door alerted him to the arrival of the staff nurse, with Marilyn close on her heels.

"I have some water for her," Marilyn said, putting a fresh pitcher and a glass on the side table.

"Nothing by mouth until we know what we're dealing with," said the nurse firmly but with a friendly smile. "Now, Ms. Harrison, how about you tell me what happened?"

The woman efficiently unpacked the small bag she'd brought with her and put a blood pressure cuff on Sally's arm while taking her temperature with a digital ear thermometer. Sally briefly outlined how she'd felt in the moments before she fainted. Kirk could see she was embarrassed, but he wasn't taking any risks by letting her brush this off. A suspicion began to form in his mind.

"Blood pressure is a little low. Temperature is normal. So you say you felt some nausea before you collapsed?"

Sally flicked her eyes to Kirk and then back to the nurse. "Yes, just a little. It's not unusual for me to feel that way, especially when talking to a large group. I'm okay with my team, but this was an important presentation and, I guess, I may have let that get to me."

"You've fainted before while speaking?" Kirk asked before the nurse could ask the same question.

"Not exactly. Usually I just feel sick and freeze. Today was different. But then again, today I actually got through a lot of my presentation. I was doing okay up until that dizzy spell hit."

"You were doing great," Kirk reassured her. "And your team is well trained and will do a fabulous job going through the rest of it in your absence. Don't worry about it."

"But—" she began in protest.

"Sally, I know you want to blame this on your difficulties with speaking in public, but given the situation with your father's health I'm going to insist you still go to the hospital to rule anything else out. HTT cannot sustain any weakness in any department right now."

His voice was sharper than he'd intended, and he forced a smile to his lips to soften his words. Thing was, his statement was truer than she probably realized. HTT was vulnerable right now, in more ways than one. He'd received news today that another major contract had been lost to their main rival. It made him all the more determined to find the wretched mole who continued to undermine HTT's every potential new success.

Sally looked at him, and he watched as the light of defiance left her soft blue eyes. "Fine," she said through gritted teeth. "But I don't want to go to hospital. It'll take far too long. I agree to going to either an urgent care clinic or my own doctor and I'm coming back to work straight afterward."

"That will depend entirely on the outcome of your examination," he replied firmly.

She rolled her eyes at him, but he wasn't about to be swayed. If what he suspected was confirmed...? No, she'd said she'd taken a test. Said the results were negative. But home testing wasn't always a hundred percent accurate, was it?

He couldn't jump the gun. They'd wait until she'd seen a doctor, had some tests, then they'd deal with what came next.

The nurse agreed with Sally that a hospital visit wasn't necessary and, after a quick discussion, agreed Kirk should transport her to the nearest clinic. After their arrival there, nothing could dislodge Kirk from her side, and in the end it had been easier to simply allow him to be there in the treatment room with her, especially since she suspected he wouldn't trust her to deliver the results in full when she got them. That said, when the doctor returned after what felt like an interminable wait, to deliver the results of the first run of tests, she felt strangely relieved to have Kirk by her side.

"Okay, Ms. Harrison, you're a little anemic, but that's not unusual in your case. Overall you're in excellent health, and I'm going to discharge you. It's going to be important that you not skip meals and that you take some supplements to counter the anemia, and I want you to make sure that you get plenty of rest and fluids."

"Hold on," Sally said, putting up a hand. "Not unusual in my case? Why? I've never been anemic before. Yes, I've been busy lately and under a bit of stress, but why would that lead to anemia?"

"Did the nurse not let you know?"

"She hasn't been back. Let me know what?" Sally's voice rose in frustration, but Kirk had a feeling he knew exactly what the doctor was going to say.

"You're pregnant," the doctor said without preamble. *Bingo.*

Kirk listened while Sally argued with the doctor, insisting that it couldn't be true, but apparently the proof was right there in the test results. Kirk said nothing, just let the news sink in. He'd been relieved when Sally had told him the home test had been negative. Hugely relieved. His life plan had been in the making from when he was in his early teens, and he'd seen no reason to ever veer from that. Marriage and children were far down the line in his ten-year plan. And yet...

He was going to be a daddy. The words resonated through his mind over and over. Together with the woman on the hospital bed, a woman he'd been completely unable to resist the night they'd met, he was going to be a parent. Sally, it seemed, was having an even harder time than him in accepting the news.

"I can't be pregnant," Sally said again, this time more adamantly than before. "It was only that one time."

"That's all it takes sometimes, I'm afraid. Perhaps I could refer you for some counseling?" the doctor said.

"I don't need counseling. I just don't see how this could have happened."

"Look, we'll deal with it together," Kirk hastened to reassure her.

"I guess we'll have to," she replied bitterly. "I didn't want this."

"I didn't plan for it, either," he agreed. "But now that we're faced with it, we can make plans."

And they *would* make plans. There was no way he was missing out on his child's life the way his father had missed out on his. His father's descent into drug addiction had seen him not only lose his position as the development manager for Harrison IT in its earliest incarnation, it had also resulted in Frank Tanner's death by suicide several years later—leaving his twelve-year-old son and his wife with more questions than answers and very little money to make ends meet. If it hadn't been for Orson Harrison's assistance, who knew where they'd have ended up?

No, his child would not go without—neither emotionally nor materially.

"Can I go back to work now?" Sally asked the doctor, interrupting Kirk's train of thought.

"Of course. Pregnancy isn't an illness, but I'd like you to reduce stress and get into a good routine ensuring you eat properly and regularly, take prenatal vitamins, and fit a little exercise into each day if you don't already."

"Surely you don't want to go back to work today," Kirk stepped in before Sally could respond. "Your body has had a shock. Take the day to recover fully."

She gave him a scathing look. "You heard the doctor. I'm pregnant, not sick. Besides, I need to get back to my team and find out the result of the Q and A after the presentation."

Kirk knew when to pick his battles, and this definitely wasn't one he'd be able to win. Better to give in gracefully rather than cause a scene in front of the medical center staff.

"Fine, we'll head back."

"Thank you."

Although she'd said the words with every nuance of good manners, he could sense the sarcasm beneath them. She was used to making her own decisions, and she wasn't going to accept him telling her what to do. He was going to have to become inventive if he was going to achieve his objectives with respect to being there for her and their baby. That was fine. He was nothing if not inventive.

They took a cab back to the office, barely speaking. Clearly Sally was still digesting the news about the baby, but this would be the last time she'd be doing any of it on her own—he'd make certain of that. Still, it wasn't the kind of discussion he wanted to have in the back of a cab, so he'd have to shelve it until they could be alone together again.

While he took care of paying the cab driver, Sally made her way into the building, and he managed to catch up with her by the elevators.

"In such a hurry to get back to work?"

"This is important to me, Kirk. It might have escaped your notice, but I'm the boss's daughter. As such, people either treat me as if I'm their best friend because they think being nice to me will advance their career, or I'm their archenemy because they think I'll run back to Dad and narc on them for any minor transgression—or you, now, since Dad's still recuperating. Many think I shouldn't be here at all. I have to work twice as hard and twice as long as anyone here for people to take me seriously, and all my hard work is probably ruined now thanks to fainting during the presentation today."

"I'm sure you're exaggerating."

"You think? Aside from my team and Marilyn, there are very few people here who believe I'm capable of doing the job I was hired to do. Yes, *hired*. I applied for that position just like anyone else, and that was after interning here during my summer and semester breaks as often as my father would let me."

"If it's all so hard, why bother? Why not go elsewhere? You are eminently employable. You have a sharp mind and great ideas. Any company would be lucky to have you," Kirk hastened to assure her.

He already knew a lot of what she'd just told him about her credentials and experience, but he'd had no idea that she was a pariah to so many, as well.

"Because my father started this business. It's in my blood, and as such I feel invested in it, too. And while I'll probably never be good enough to take over the company when he's ready to retire, like I always dreamed of when I was younger, the company and my father deserve my best—not some other nameless, faceless corporation."

The elevator doors opened onto Sally's floor, and she stepped out.

"Sally, wait. We need to talk about this."

"Thank you for your help today," she said, holding the elevator door open. "Call me and make an appointment if you want to talk. Right now it's—"

Her voice broke off, as if she couldn't even bring herself to discuss the child now growing in her belly.

"It's just too complicated," she continued, her cheeks flushing.

With that, she let the door close, and he caught a last glimpse of her walking away. Kirk wanted to refute her statement. It wasn't complicated as far as he was concerned. She was pregnant with his baby, and that meant they had a future together whether she realized it or not.

With the chemistry they shared, being together would be no hardship. But it seemed he had to convince her of that. He'd let her think she'd had the last word on the subject, that she had the upper hand. And then he'd try to change her mind.

Sally fielded the multitude of queries about her health in a convincing facade of good humor as her team gathered around her.

"I'm fine. I'd just been burning the candle at both ends and skipping a few too many meals. You know how important this project was to all of us. Everything else went on the back burner for me when it came to this. So, Nick, how did it go?"

"The presentation went really well. I'd say the majority of the managers there seemed very interested in exploring the concept further and starting to implement the changes. Everyone could see that it was a time-and-money-saver in the long-term, even though initial outlay in replacing what we're already using, especially the motor fleet, will be costly."

There was something in Nick's tone that made Sally's stomach clench.

"And did they vote on implementation?"

Nick fell silent, and one of the other members of Sally's team filled the silence.

"Before they could vote, Mr. Rogers spoke up."

"I see." A ripple of frustration cascaded through her mind, but she couldn't let her people know how the news upset her. "I take it he's not a fan of the suggested changes, then?"

Her staff looked at her with the same disappointed expression she was certain was on her own face and, as a group, shook their heads. Some things just didn't bear saying out loud.

"So we need to work harder, then. Tackle this from another perspective."

"That won't be necessary."

Sally wheeled around to find Kirk standing behind her, fistfuls of takeout bags clutched in his hands. Couldn't he leave her alone for a second?

"And why not?" she challenged, ready to do battle.

"Because there's nothing wrong with the perspective you presented. Here," he said, putting the takeout bags on the meeting table in front of them. "I heard you guys haven't had a break for lunch yet, so it's on me. From what I saw you've put a great deal of planning into this project, and I'd like to see it developed further."

"And Silas Rogers?"

"Is not the chairman of HTT, nor is he interim chairman of HTT."

"He's still the CEO, and what he says carries weight," Sally argued.

"That's true," Kirk admitted and pulled up a chair to sit beside her. He ripped open a takeout bag and passed her a sub filled with salad fixings and well-done hot roast beef. "Eat, then we'll discuss this some more."

Sally bristled at his high-handedness, but her mouth began to water at the smell of the sub, and hunger won the war over pride. She reluctantly took it from him and sank her teeth into the fresh bread, groaning in appreciation as the flavors of the fillings burst on her tongue. She hadn't realized she was quite so hungry.

Next to her, she felt Kirk stiffen and shift in his chair. He tugged at the front of his trousers and pulled a napkin across his lap, but not before she saw evidence of a hint of arousal pressing against the fine Italian wool of his suit. Shock rippled through her, accompanied by a powerful wave of something else—desire. No, no, no. She wasn't going to go there again. No way. Never.

Even though she scolded herself soundly, she couldn't help the prickle of heat that crept through her, couldn't prevent the surge of sheer lust that forced her inner muscles to clench involuntarily. It was a turn-on to know that she was capable of arousing an attractive man without even trying. And while she had a whole list of problems with this particular man, there was no denying he was gorgeous—he had a body like a Greek god and he knew exactly how to use it. All of it. His mouth, his tongue, those hands and especially—

No! She squirmed in her seat.

"Is your lunch okay?" Kirk asked with a curious expression on his face.

"Great," she said, taking another bite, this time with less audible enthusiasm.

She'd have to eat more carefully in the future, she decided, if enjoying her sub had this effect on him. And if his reaction had the same domino effect on her. So she'd have to remember to control herself. That couldn't be too hard, could it? She had no plans to eat with him again after this, did she? In fact, she had no plans to spend any more time with him than their jobs absolutely required.

For some stupid reason, that thought caused a pang of something deep inside—something she didn't quite want to define. *He lied to you*, she reminded herself. By omission, yes, but keeping his true identity from her that night had been deliberate, and she still had no idea why he'd done it or what he'd hoped to gain by it. *So ask him*, the little voice at the back of her mind said pragmatically.

Maybe she would. But that would mean spending more time together, wouldn't it? Besides, referring to that night would bring back the memories of how she'd behaved so uncharacteristically. Of what they'd done—and of how it had made her feel.

Darn it! Maybe it was hormones, she thought. She'd never been the type to play sex kitten. In fact, she'd always been slightly embarrassed and a little uncomfortable when the girls around her in college, and even sometimes here in the office, ever discussed their sexual activities. But there was something about this guy that opened sensual floodgates she hadn't known existed. She'd always thought that maybe she was just slightly different from the other women she knew—less passionate, less sensual. But maybe she'd just been waiting for the right man to come along.

Except he wasn't the right man, was he? He was her boss. He was a sneak. And yet he was the best lover she was ever likely to have in her lifetime.

She sighed and put down her now empty wrapper. She'd been so caught up in her thoughts that she hadn't even realized she'd finished the sub.

For the next several hours, Kirk chaired a discussion between Sally and her team on the best way to begin implementing the proposal. By the end of the workday, she didn't know if she was energized because she was so excited about seeing her spark of an idea being set on the road to fruition or exhausted at the thought of all the work ahead. She did feel a deep sense of satisfaction, though, and she'd begun to see Kirk in a new light.

He had that rare talent of listening—and listening well—to what her team had to say. And when he injected his own thoughts and ideas, he was gracious about accepting criticism if those ideas were challenged. A part of her wished she'd never met him that night, that instead she'd had the chance of meeting him in the normal course of work and of seeing whether the attraction that crackled between them like static electricity might have grown naturally over time rather than exploding all at once in the accelerated fling they'd had.

But now they were linked by a baby. Her mouth turned dry as sawdust. While she wanted to have as little to do with Kirk as possible, she would never deny her child access to their father. The very thought was impossible to her, especially when her own relationship with her dad was such an integral part of who she was. But how could they coparent a child when there was still so much tension between them?

Maybe she was getting ahead of herself. She had plenty of time to think about all that. Plenty of time to work out adequate coping strategies and discuss this situation they had found themselves in like rational adults. People did that all the time, didn't they?

But did they spend half their time fighting a magnetic pull so strong she felt like a helpless tide being influenced by a supermoon? She didn't want to think about that right now. She'd have to put it on the back burner for as long as she could. But, judging by the quick glances flung her way by the man sitting next to her, that wouldn't be very long at all.

Seven

The meeting finished and Kirk hung back, talking to Nick, as Sally gathered her things together and stopped to give instructions to a handful of people. He liked watching her in action. Hell, he liked watching her, period. As if she sensed his perusal, she looked up and caught his eye. And, yes, there was that telltale flush of color on her cheeks. He was finding it more and more endearing each time he saw it.

Finally she was ready to leave, and he fell into step with her as she headed to the elevators.

"Feeling okay?"

She rolled her eyes. "I'm fine, seriously. There's nothing wrong with me."

"You're carrying my baby," he murmured close to her ear. "I think I'm entitled to be concerned."

She stiffened at his words. "So, what? You want to monitor me twenty-four-seven? Is that what it is?"

The idea had merit.

Sally huffed an impatient sigh. "Look, it's still early, and I can assure you I will do whatever is in my power to stay healthy and to ensure that everything goes as it should."

Somehow that didn't satisfy him. For reasons even he didn't understand, it just didn't go far enough.

"I'm sure you will," he agreed. "But you have to admit, sharing that responsibility has its advantages, too."

"What do you mean?" she asked as they stepped into the empty elevator.

"I don't know if you've been sick yet, but what if nausea does occur?"

"Then I'll deal with it," she said grimly and crossed her arms over her body. "I'm a big girl, Kirk. I've been looking after myself for a good many years now. I think I can cope with a pregnancy."

"I've no doubt. But I'd really like to be a part of things. I know this news has come as a shock to both of us, but I'd like to think that together we can get through it. Look, can I see you home so we can talk about this in a more private setting?"

Sally rolled her eyes at him. "You're not going to leave me alone until I agree, are you?"

He didn't want to leave her alone at all. The thought came as a shock, but it felt right at the same time.

"I like to get my way," he conceded. "But I'd feel happier if you conceded that this is something we should iron out sooner rather than later."

"Oh, of course, your being happy is so very important," she said with a touch of bitterness. "Okay, then. You can take me home. Benton will be waiting downstairs for me. I'll have to let him know."

It was a small victory, but Kirk was happy to take it.

Benton was waiting in the elevator lobby of the parking garage, and Kirk stepped forward to introduce himself. The man looked him over as if he was a potential threat before relaxing an increment when Sally stepped forward with an apologetic smile.

"I'm sorry I couldn't give you notice of this, Benton. Mr. Tanner and I need to extend our discussions, so he'll be taking me home this evening."

"Whatever you want, Ms. Harrison. I'll see you in the morning, then?"

"Yes, thank you."

Kirk walked Sally over to his SUV and helped her in.

When they arrived at her apartment building a few minutes later, he pulled into the parking space she indicated. They rode the elevator to the top floor, and he followed her into an elegant and well-proportioned apartment. While it was mostly decorated in neutral tones, an occasional pop of color drew his eye—a cushion here, a throw rug there. But overall there was very little to tell him about the woman who intrigued him far more than he wanted to admit.

He moved to the large windows that looked out in the direction of Lake Washington. It was growing dark, and across the lake he could make out the twinkle of lights around its rim. A sound from behind him made him turn. Sally had pulled the band from her hair and was tousling her fingers through the mass of spun gold. He liked this more relaxed version of her more than the buttoned-down woman who headed her social engineering department. On second thought, he liked the naked, warm and willing version from just over a month ago the best, but she'd made it quite clear they weren't going to go there again.

But it was oh so satisfying, he reminded himself. *And yet look at the trouble it has put us in*, he countered. Kirk

slammed the door closed on his thoughts and looked at
Sally more closely. Beneath her makeup he could still see
the telltale signs of the stress she'd been under today. She
had to be exhausted.

"Look, I won't take up a lot of your time. I know you
need to get something to eat and then probably have an
early night."

She barked a cynical laugh. "Are you my mother
now?"

He gave her a half smile of apology. "I'm sorry, I guess
I'm overcompensating."

"You think?" She moved toward the kitchen. "Did
you want something to drink? I have beer, water, wine."

"A beer, thanks."

He watched as she poured the beer into a tall glass
then opened a small bottle of sparkling water for herself.
Of course she wouldn't be drinking alcohol. The realization hit him hard. She was going to have to make so many
changes. So many adjustments. It was hardly fair, was it?

"Take a seat," she said, bringing their drinks through
to the small sitting room.

Kirk sat at one end of the sofa, and Sally took the other
end. Awkward silence stretched between them.

"You wanted to talk, didn't you? What about, exactly?" Sally asked.

"The baby, for a start. How do you feel about it?"

"Shocked, surprised. Scared."

"Yeah, me too. I hadn't planned on this at this stage
of my life."

Sally sat a little more upright. "And just when had
you planned it for?"

He couldn't tell if she was sniping at him or genuinely
curious. He decided that honesty was probably the best
policy right now.

"To be honest, I had hoped to start looking for a wife about five years from now and hopefully start a family a few years after that."

"Just like that?"

"Look, I know it sounds clinical, but I grew up with a lot of instability. Being able to make a plan and stick to it kept me anchored when things were tough at home, even when my dad was still alive." He didn't want to admit his father's weakness to her. He'd spent his entire adult life working hard to erase those memories, to overcome the hardships he and his mother had endured—and he'd succeeded. He wasn't about to be made to feel ashamed of that. Not by anyone.

Sally shrugged and took a sip of her water. "That makes sense, I guess. I'm sorry things were so hard for you."

"You know that saying about gaining strength through adversity? Well, I decided to adopt that a long time ago. And I've managed to achieve a lot of success by staying strong and keeping my focus on my goals. But now I need to reevaluate. This child we're having, I very much want to be a part of its life, Sally. I don't want to be a weekend father or an absentee parent. I want to be there, for everything."

"That could be difficult, considering we're not even a couple."

"But we could be. We already know we're compatible in the bedroom."

"Too compatible, it seems," she commented acerbically.

"Look, I never considered having a committed relationship or starting a family until I'd achieved my career goal targets because I never wanted a child of mine to miss out on anything—whether it be financially or emotionally. You want the same thing, right? For our child to have everything he or she needs to be happy, healthy and safe? Loving parents are part of that package. Perhaps we ought to consider being a couple."

"What, go steady, you mean?" she said with a gurgle of laughter.

"More than that. We should get married. Think about it—it makes perfect sense. This is only a one-bedroom apartment, right? Where would you put the baby when it's born? Have you even thought about that? And what about work? Do you plan to be a stay-at-home mom or continue with your career?"

Sally put her glass down very slowly. "Kirk, we only just found out about this pregnancy today. We have plenty of time ahead of us for decision making. Let's not be rash."

"Rash? I don't think so. It's logical."

"I'm sorry, but it isn't logical to me in the least. We hardly know each other, and I'm not sure that I want to be married to you. I'm certainly not going to make a decision like that on such short acquaintance."

Kirk fought back the arguments that sprang to the tip of his tongue. It was clear she was feeling more than a little overwhelmed by his suggestion, which was entirely understandable. She needed time to think, and so did he. If he was going to campaign successfully to win Sally's hand, he would have to go about it carefully.

"At least think about it," he urged. "And talk to me— seriously, anything. Any questions, any problems, bring them to me and we'll solve them together."

"Oh, I'll be thinking about it," she admitted with a rueful shake of her head. "I imagine I'll be thinking about little else. By the way, I don't want anyone else to know about this just yet."

He nodded. The only person he would have shared the news with would have been his mother, and with her gone he had no one else. No one else except the child now nestled inside the woman sitting opposite him. A feeling bloomed within his chest—pride tinged with a liberal dose of an emotion he'd had little enough experience with. Love. It was odd to think that he could love another being before it truly came into existence in the world, but he knew, without doubt, that he loved his child, and the intensity of the emotion shook him to his core.

Sally wasn't sure what was going through Kirk's mind, but if the determined look on his face was anything to go by, she was going to have some battles on her hands over the next few months. Probably over the next few years, she amended. He was a man used to having his way— it was inevitable that they were going to bump heads from time to time when it came to deciding what was best for the baby.

Her head swam. Discovering she was pregnant was shocking enough. Dealing with Kirk as her baby's father was another matter entirely—especially now that he seemed to believe they should get married.

Over the past couple of years, life had shown her that you had to reach for the things that mattered most to you. Had to fight for them. Her best friend from college, Angel, who'd turned out to be a secret European princess, had shown her how important it was to follow and fight for your dream.

Dissatisfied with a politically arranged betrothal based only on expedience with no affection attached, Angel— or, Princess Mila, as she'd been officially known—had broken with tradition and done everything in her power to ensure she won her betrothed's heart, even at the risk of losing him altogether.

Just weeks ago, they'd celebrated the christening of their first child, a little boy who would become crown prince of Sylvain—and to Sally's eyes, when she'd visited to attend the ceremony, neither Angel nor King Thierry had ever looked happier or more fulfilled.

She wanted that. She wanted a man who would look at her the way King Thierry looked at Angel. There was no doubt in the world that Angel was his queen in every sense of the word. While Sally had always hoped to be a mother someday, she'd intended to start that stage of her life by finding the right man to be a husband and father first. Had planned to bring her child into a home already filled with love and trust. How could she have any of that with Kirk? She didn't love him—she barely knew him. And trust? Not a chance. The only positive traits she could assign to him were his appearance, his bedroom skills and the fact that he seemed to be a very capable boss. *Her* boss, in fact. And that added another layer of complication.

Sally wanted a life that was lived with purpose. One that yielded great results for others as well as for herself. She wanted to make a difference, and she ached to fulfill her potential. It's what she'd spent at least eight years of her life studying for and even more time interning at Harrison IT for. And yet despite her dreams, she continued to remain in the background. Knowing she was being held back by her phobia was one thing, but having a baby added a whole other layer to things.

Kirk had spoken of his career plans, but what would this do to her long-term goals? No matter what anyone said, life was very different for a woman in the workplace. That glass ceiling was still well and truly in place, and there were few women in the upper echelons of management. She'd hoped that one day, if she could overcome her phobia, she might earn a position up there. That the people she worked with would respect that she'd climbed her way up that corporate ladder, striving as hard as the rest of them.

No one would take her seriously if she was married to the vice president. Any advancement in her career would be looked upon as being won because of who she was, not what she brought to the role.

"Look," she started. "I've got a lot to think about, and you're right—I'm tired and I need an early night. Would you go, please?"

"You promise me you'll have something to eat?"

She gave him an are-you-serious look.

"Okay, okay," he said, holding up one hand. "Don't shoot me for caring. You have no idea what it was like to watch you crumple like that this morning."

He made it sound like he actually cared.

"I will have something to eat."

"I cook a mean omelet. If you have eggs, I could make it for you."

Her mouth watered. "Fine," she said, making a sudden decision. "I'm going to grab a shower. I'm not sure what's in the fridge, but go knock yourself out."

Maybe once he fed her, he'd stop hovering over her like some overprotective parent. She stopped in her tracks. But that's exactly what he was—a parent—and so was she. She shook her head, went through to her bathroom and quickly stripped off her work clothes. She looked at herself in the mirror.

"Nothing to see here," she murmured out loud.

But her hand settled on her lower belly, and for a moment she stopped to think about the changes that were happening inside. Changes that would force her to make monumental adjustments in her life. For a moment it all seemed too much and far too hard. But she reminded herself of what Kirk had said about wanting to be there every step of the way. She wasn't in this alone. Not by any means.

Did she have the strength to embark on this journey with him?

By the time she stepped out of the shower and dressed in a pair of yoga pants and a long-sleeved T-shirt, she was no closer to reaching a decision. A delicious aroma wafted from her kitchen, and she followed the scent to see what Kirk was up to.

"Perfect timing," he said, folding an omelet in the pan and sliding it onto a plate that already had a generous helping of diced fried potatoes, bacon bits and onions on one side.

"I had all these ingredients?" she asked, sliding into a chair at the breakfast bar.

"You can do a lot with just a few key things. When I was growing up, I often helped my mom in the kitchen. She taught me a lot."

Sally felt a pang for the boy he must have been. Her own upbringing had been so vastly different. They'd always had staff, including a cook, and as far as Sally could recall, her mother had never so much as baked a cookie her entire privileged life.

Kirk reached for a jar of salsa and ladled a little across her omelet before putting her plate down in front of her with a flourish. "There, now eat up before it gets cold."

She forked up a bit of omelet and closed her eyes in bliss as delicate flavors of herbs and cheese burst on her tongue.

"This is so good," she said. "Thank you. I hope you made one for yourself, too."

"I can get something later."

"Oh, please, you've given me far more than I can eat. At least help me with what I have here."

"How about I whip up another omelet and you can give me some of your potatoes."

"That sounds like a good idea."

It felt oddly normal to watch Kirk working in her kitchen. He moved with an elegant grace and confidence that she found all too appealing. *He withheld his true identity*, she reminded herself. *And he slept with you knowing exactly who you were.*

And now they had made a baby.

She was going to have to press him for an explanation about that night, especially if they were going to move forward together and most especially if she was even going to begin to seriously consider his proposal. But not now. Not tonight. Right at this moment she was struggling to make sense of what her next step would be and how on earth she was ever going to be able to tell her father that she was expecting Kirk's child.

Kirk took over cleanup duties when they'd finished their impromptu meal. Sally was too tired to argue the point by then. The food had given her a boost, but right now her bed was calling. Once he'd finished, she walked Kirk to the door.

"Thank you for dinner," she said softly.

"I enjoyed it. I…" He paused a moment as if debating whether or not to say what was on the tip of his tongue. "I enjoy being with you."

Sally didn't quite know how to react. He was good company and she felt drawn to him in a variety of ways, but there was so much about him that she didn't know—

or trust. She reached for the door and opened it to let him out.

He was standing close, too close. The lure of his cologne mingled with the heat of his body and wrapped itself around her. She looked up at him and saw the way his pupils dilated as their gazes meshed. She wasn't sure who moved first, but one moment she was standing there with the door open, the next it was closed and her back was pressed against the wooden surface as his lips hungrily claimed hers.

Eight

She gave a small moan of surrender, and in the next moment he was lifting her as if she weighed nothing, the hard evidence of his arousal pressing against her sex, sending jolts of need through her body.

She wrapped her legs around his hips, pulling him tighter against her. His mouth was hungry and demanding, and she was equally voracious—meeting the questing probe of his tongue with her own, nipping at his lips. Through the cloud of need that gripped her, Sally became aware that she was no longer pressed against the door and Kirk was carrying her in the direction of her bedroom.

He lowered her to her bed and bent over her.

"I want to see you. All of you," he murmured even as he peppered small kisses along her jaw and down the column of her throat.

She was at a loss for words. One minute they'd been saying goodbye and the next, here they were, tugging each other's clothing off as if they couldn't bear to wait another second before they were skin to skin again. Right now, the only thing that mattered was losing herself in his touch, in the sensations that rippled through her body with his every caress.

"Your skin—it's as soft as I remember," he said reverently, stroking her underneath her top.

"You remember touching my skin?" she asked on a breathless laugh.

"Among other things."

"Tell me about those things," she implored him.

And he did, in clear and graphic detail. Following up every word with a stroke of his tongue on her heated flesh, with the heat of his mouth through her bra as he teased her tightly drawn nipples into aching buds of need, and with the tangle of his fingers as they stroked and coaxed the slick flesh at her core. Her first orgasm rocketed through her body, taking her completely by surprise, but he took his time over coaxing her body to her second.

She continued to shiver in aftershocks of delight beneath the onslaught of his mouth as he traced her every curve. And when his head settled between her thighs, she nearly lifted off the bed as he gently drew the swollen, sensitive bud of her clitoris against his tongue. Her second climax left her weak and trembling against the sheets, and when he shifted slightly to slide on a condom, she laughed.

"Locking the stable door after the horse has bolted?" she teased, reaching for him as he hovered over her again.

"You could say that. Maybe it's just taking longer for the news to sink in than I thought it would."

Whatever she'd been about to say in reply fled her mind as he nudged his blunt tip against her entrance and slid deep within her. She rocked against him, meet-

ing his movements—at first slow and languid and then
speeding up as demand rose within them both again. This
time, when she came, he tipped over the edge with her,
and she held his powerful body as paroxysms of pleasure
rocked them both.

Minutes later, exhausted, she slipped into sleep, un-
aware of the man who now cradled her sweetly in his
arms.

Kirk lay there waiting for his heart rate to resemble
something close to normal. If he didn't take care, *he'd*
be the one needing a bed in the cardiac care unit. The
dark humor sobered him up immediately. This was Orson
Harrison's daughter he was sleeping with. And while the
man was recovering nicely from his heart attack, he still
wasn't back at full strength. He still needed Kirk to carry
the load of the company for him. Finding out about the
baby had thrown Kirk for a loop, but he couldn't allow it
to make him forget all his other responsibilities.

He allowed his fingertips to trace small circles on
Sally's back as he listened to her deep gentle breathing.
Somehow he had to disentangle himself from her warm,
languid body and get dressed and get out of here. Put
some distance between them so he could clear his head
and do the job he was here to do.

While it was still possible that Sally was the leak that
was passing information on to HTT's biggest competitor,
he no longer wanted to believe that it could be her. Not the
mother of his child. Not the daughter of the man he held
in higher regard than any other man he'd ever known.

This pregnancy was a messy complication, but they'd
work through it. Sally shifted against him, and Kirk
found himself curving naturally to her. This wasn't the
action of a man about to leave the woman lying next to

him, he warned himself, and yet, try as he might, he couldn't find the impetus he needed to pull away. Perhaps just this once, he told himself, letting sleep tug him into its hold. It wasn't the cleverest thing in the world to remain in her bed, but for now it felt like the right thing.

It was still dark when he woke. Dawn wasn't far away. Beside him, Sally slept deeply, and he gently extricated himself from their intertwined limbs. His body protested, an early-morning erection telling him that leaving the bed was the last thing he should be thinking about. But he needed to get home to change before getting into the office for an early meeting. And he needed to examine his growing feelings for the woman still slumbering in the mussed-up sheets. He quickly and quietly dressed in his shirt and trousers and, carrying his jacket and shoes in one hand, he made to leave the room.

Something made him look back and take one more look at Sally as she lay there, the sheet halfway down and exposing her back and the curve of a perfectly formed breast. It took all his self-restraint not to drop his things where he stood and move to take her back in his arms.

Work, he told himself. *Think of work.* He wanted to be in full possession of all his faculties by the time he and Sally crossed paths in the office today. As he left her building and walked toward his car, he saw a town car creep into the visitor parking area. He recognized the man at the wheel as the bodyguard he'd met last night. It made him think. One of Sally's security team could just as likely be the leak he needed to find and eradicate from HTT. He knew how easy it was to conduct a business call in the back of a car without considering the ears of the person driving.

Benton got out of the vehicle and looked across to

where Kirk was parked. The man's eyes narrowed as he identified him. Taking the bull by the horns, Kirk walked toward him. He didn't want gossip about his relationship with Sally, such as it was, getting back to the office until she was ready for it to be made public.

"Good morning," he said to the bodyguard, extending a hand.

Benton's grasp was firm. Perhaps a little too firm, Kirk judged with an ironic lift of his brow.

"Morning, sir."

"I trust that Ms. Harrison's best interests are always at the forefront of your mind, Mr. Benton."

"Always, sir."

"Then I hope I can rely on you to keep the fact you saw me here this morning to yourself?"

The man hesitated a moment. "That depends, sir."

"On?"

"On whether or not *you* are in her best interests...sir."

Kirk nodded. "Fair comment. I will never do anything to hurt Ms. Harrison. You can rest assured on that score."

"Then we don't have anything to worry about, do we, sir?"

"No, we don't. Have a good day, Mr. Benton."

"Just Benton will do, sir."

Kirk nodded again and returned to his car. Somehow he didn't think that a bodyguard who took his duty to Sally so seriously could be a mole, but he'd have to check. Both Benton and whoever else ferried her about.

He looked up to Sally's apartment windows and saw the bedroom light come on. He needed to get going.

That evening, after work, Benton drew the car to a halt outside the front portico of her father's house. Sally thanked him and made her way to the door, where the housekeeper stood with a welcoming smile on her face.

"Good evening, Ms. Harrison. Mr. Harrison is in the library waiting for you."

"How is he today, Jennifer?"

"He's almost his old self, but we've had to remove all the saltshakers from the house."

Sally gave a rueful laugh. No matter what his cardiologist told him, her father still railed against his new dietary restrictions. "I'm so glad you have his best interests at heart. I don't know what we'd do without you all."

"It's our honor to work for Mr. Harrison. We're just glad he's recovering so well."

"Aren't we all?" Sally said with a heartfelt sigh.

She made her way to the library, where her father sat before an open fire nursing his one approved glass of red wine a day. He put down his drink when he saw her and rose to give her a welcoming hug. There was nothing quite like it in the world, Sally thought as she allowed her father's scents and strength to seep into her. And it still terrified her that she'd come so close to losing him.

"Hi, Dad. I hear you're giving the staff grief about your food again?" she said as they let each other go.

"Just keeping them on their toes," he said with a gruff laugh. "Can I pour you a glass of wine? This is a very nice pinot noir—you should try it."

"I—no, not today, thanks, Dad. I'll just stick with mineral water."

At some point she was going to have to tell her father why she wasn't drinking alcohol. She wasn't looking forward to the revelation, but she certainly wanted him to hear it from her before he had the chance to find out through anyone else. Especially after her fainting spell at work yesterday. Gosh, was it only yesterday? It already seemed a whole lot longer ago.

Her cheeks fired as she remembered exactly what had chased so much of yesterday's activity from her mind.

"Too hot in here?" her father asked, handing her a glass of water.

"No, no. It's fine. Lovely, in fact," she answered, flustered.

"Then what is it? What's bothering you?"

That was the trouble with being close to your parent, she admitted. They knew you too well and saw too much.

"A few things," she hedged.

"Is it work? I hear that Kirk has ruffled a few feathers. Glad to hear he's given your sustainability initiative the green light. It's about time we did more than just talk in circles about that."

He'd heard that already? Sally gave an internal groan. What else had he heard?

Knowing her father was expecting a reply, she managed to say, "Well, I always expected some pushback. You didn't seem so eager to embrace the idea, yourself."

"Couldn't be seen to be championing my own daughter, now could I. Had to make you work for what you wanted. I've always thought, if you're passionate enough about something, you'll make it work." Orson took a sip of his wine and put the glass back down beside him. "Now, tell me what you think about Kirk."

Sally felt the burn of embarrassment heat her from the inside out. Ah, yes, Kirk. That would be the man she'd slept with after turning down his proposal, after discovering she was pregnant with his baby. It sounded worse than the plot of a soap opera. She groaned to herself. Her father sat opposite her, clearly awaiting some kind of response from her.

"He seems to be very…focused."

Orson snorted. "He's good-looking, isn't he?"

"Dad!" she remonstrated.

"Focused." He snorted again. "The man looks as though he stepped off the front cover of *GQ* magazine, has a Mensa-rated IQ and you tell me he's *focused*. You're attracted to him, aren't you?"

"Dad, I don't think…" Sally let her voice trail off.

How did she tell him just how attractive she found Kirk? How he was so irresistible that the first night she saw him, she slept with him? That she'd done the same again last night?

Orson laughed. "I'm sorry, honey, can't help but tease you a little. You're so buttoned up these days. You can't blame your father for giving you a little prod. Besides, you can't argue the truth, can you?"

Sally chose to ignore his question and turned the conversation in another direction.

"Actually, now that you're better, could you please explain to me just why you brought him into Harrison IT? We were doing okay. We certainly didn't need to merge with anyone else, did we?"

And she certainly hadn't needed to *merge* with Kirk Tanner, but that hadn't stopped her from doing it again, that pesky little voice inconveniently reminded her.

Orson picked up his wineglass and swirled the ruby-colored liquid around the bowl, staring at it for a while before putting it back down.

"I guess, in part, you could call it guilt. Kirk's father, Frank, was my best friend in college. We started in business together. But what I didn't notice was that the man whose partying seemed harmless in college got in over his head when he partied hard in the real world, too. It got to the point where it took a lot of chemical help for him to get through the day. I didn't realize he was a drug addict until it was too late. By then he had a wife and son, and he was pretty resistant to help. Eventually he agreed to go to rehab, but he never got there. Instead he loaded up on drugs and took a dive off Deception Bridge."

He fell silent for a while, obviously lost in the pain of his memories. Eventually he drew in a deep breath and huffed it out again.

"I felt responsible. I should have been able to see the problem sooner, step in earlier, help him more."

"Dad, not everyone wants to be helped."

"I know that now, but back then I felt like it was all my fault. I did what I could to assist Sandy and Kirk when they relocated to California, and I set up a college fund for the boy. I've kept an eye on him. What he's done pleases me. I guess, in the grand scheme of things, you could say he's where he'd have been all along if things had gone differently with his father. Merging with Tanner Enterprises was a logical move—gives us both more strength in an ever more competitive market."

Even though he'd given her a backstory of sorts, Sally had a feeling he was still holding something back. As it was, she was still hurt he'd had such an influence in Kirk's life and yet never shared any of that information with her.

"Marilyn called me just before you arrived. She tells me that Kirk took you to the doctor yesterday, that you collapsed or something during your presentation. Honey, you have to stop pushing yourself. You may never get over that public speaking thing, and if so, that's fine. But, that aside, tell me—you're all right?"

His pale blue eyes, the mirror of her own, looked concerned. While he might not see fit to include her in his business plans, he was still and always would be her dad, and she knew he loved and cared for her.

"Everything's fine, Dad. Nothing to worry about."

He looked at her with a piercing gaze. "What are you not telling me?"

She gave a gentle laugh. "I could ask you the same thing. Like why had I never heard of Kirk before the merger announcement. Don't you think that's something you might have shared with me at some stage? You've treated him like an absentee son."

An awful thought occurred to her. Could Kirk be his son? But her father's perspicacity showed true to form.

"Don't be silly. You can turn that overactive imagination of yours off right now. There's no reason for the secrecy other than the fact that his mother wanted no reminders of her late husband or her life in Seattle in any way. While she reluctantly accepted financial help, that was where she drew the line. I had very little direct interaction with her or with Kirk. Your mother and I were friends with Sandy and Frank. We would have supported Sandy here, too, if she'd have let us."

Sally felt all the tension drain out of her in a sudden rush. Jennifer chose that minute to return to the library.

"Dinner is served in the small dining room, if you'd like to come through now."

Sally got up and tucked her arm in the crook of her dad's elbow, and together they walked to dinner.

"Dad, this place really is too big just for you. Have you ever thought of downsizing?"

"Why would I do that, honey? This house was your mother's pride and joy, and she loved every inch of it. She might not still be with us, but I feel her in every nook and cranny of the house and see her touch in every piece of furniture and art. Besides, I'd like to think that one day you might move back home and build your own family here."

Sally felt a clench in her chest. She should tell her dad about the baby, but how to bring it up? There was no way to dress up the fact that this child was the product of an unfortunate accident during a one-night stand. Granted, the man in question was already held in high regard by her father, but didn't that just complicate matters more?

Her father seated her at the table before taking his own place. Jennifer brought in the first course—smoked salmon fillets on a bed of lettuce and sliced avocado. Sally eyed the plate warily. She didn't know much yet about how to weather this pregnancy but she'd done a little research on foods she could and couldn't eat, and she knew that smoked or pickled fish was on the horribly extensive no list.

Orson noticed immediately that Sally only picked at the lettuce and avocado, pushing the salmon to the side of her plate.

"You're not going to eat that? I thought it was one of your favorites. You're not on some weird diet, or something, are you?"

She sighed. He was going to have to know sooner or later. "No, Dad. Not a diet. Actually, I have a bit of news for you."

"What's that? You're not going to tell me you're pregnant, are you?" He said it jokingly, but his face sobered when he saw Sally's expression.

"Well, that rather takes the wind out of my sails," she said softly.

"Really? You're making me a grandpa?" Orson's face lit up.

It wasn't the reaction she'd expected. After all, as far

as he knew, she wasn't even in a relationship with anyone, and he'd always made his thoughts on the challenges of sole parenthood quite clear. It was probably another reason why he'd supported Sandy Tanner and Kirk the way he had.

"Apparently," she admitted ruefully.

"Was that the reason for your fainting spell at work yesterday?"

She nodded.

"So you managed the speaking part okay?"

What was wrong with him? Why wasn't he demanding to know who the father of his grandchild was? She nodded again.

"That's great news, honey! And a baby, too."

He leaned back in his chair and smiled beatifically.

"You're not bothered by that, Dad?" Sally had to ask because his lack of questions was driving her crazy. She'd expected a full inquisition. Had mentally prepared for one all day, knowing she wouldn't keep this secret from her father for long.

"Bothered by the baby? No, why should I be?"

"But don't you want to know—"

Her father leaned toward her and patted her on the hand. "It's okay, honey, I know where babies come from these days. I expect you got tired of waiting for Mr. Right and decided to go with one of those designer baby outfits. Of course, I'm sorry you didn't feel as though you could discuss it with me first but—"

Sally had been in the process of taking a drink of water and all but snorted it out her nose.

"Dad!"

"Well, it's not as if you have a regular guy, is it? I'd hoped you might meet someone special when you were at college, like I did with your mom, but that's neither here nor there. Looks like you'll be moving home sooner rather than later, huh?" He rubbed his hands with glee.

"Why would I do that?"

"Well, you don't have room in that cute little apartment of yours, do you?"

Sally rolled her eyes. What was it with everyone lately that they wanted to make all her decisions for her? First Kirk, now her dad—didn't anyone think she was capable of looking after herself?

"There's plenty of time to think about that, Dad. Besides, I can always get a bigger place of my own."

"But why on earth would you need to when we have all the room in the world here?"

It was about then that Sally noticed another place setting at the table.

"Were you expecting someone else?" she asked.

Just then, the chime of the front door echoed through the house.

"He's late, but he called ahead and said not to hold dinner."

"He?"

She didn't have to wait long to find out who *he* was. Within about thirty seconds of the door chime sounding, Jennifer showed Kirk into the dining room. Great, just what she needed.

"Good to see you, Kirk!" Orson said effusively, standing to shake Kirk's hand. "About time there was someone here who can share a celebratory champagne toast with me. I'm going to be a grandpa! Isn't that great news?"

Kirk looked at Sally, and she suddenly understood the expression "deer caught in the headlights."

"Dad, you know you shouldn't have more than your one glass of red wine a day. Doctor's orders, remember?" she cautioned, desperate to shift focus to something other than her pregnancy, especially since she and Kirk had agreed to keep it quiet for now.

"Just a half a glass isn't going to kill me. This is cause for celebration, whether you know who the daddy is or not."

"Know who the father is?" Kirk asked with a pointed look in her direction.

"I know exactly who the father is," Sally felt compelled to say.

"You do? Is it someone I know?" Orson asked, looking from Sally to Kirk and back again as he began to sense the tension between them.

"It is," Kirk said firmly and straightened his shoulders. "It's me. I'm the father."

Nine

"I didn't even realize you two knew each other that well," Orson said, sinking back into his chair.

"We don't," Sally said bluntly.

Kirk wasn't too pleased about the older man's color. Obviously hearing that his new business partner was the father of his impending grandchild had come as something of a shock. Just then, Jennifer came bustling through the door, bringing a serving of the appetizer for Kirk. He took a seat at the empty place setting and waited as the silence lengthened in the room. A silence Orson eventually broke.

"So what now?" he asked, reaching for his glass of water. "Are you going to marry the girl?"

"I have asked her to marry me."

"And?" Orson demanded, color slowly returning to his cheeks.

"The girl said no," Sally said, her tone revealing her

annoyance at being discussed as if she was an accessory to the conversation.

"Why on earth did you say that?" Orson asked incredulously.

"It's still early," Kirk said smoothly. "We don't know each other that well yct, but I'd like to think that by the time the baby comes we'll be a great deal closer."

"You're obviously close enough to—"

"Dad—please! Can we not discuss this right now? We only found out yesterday ourselves, and we'd agreed to keep it quiet. I only told you because, well, you'd pretty much guessed already and I hate having secrets between us."

Kirk wasn't oblivious to Sally's silent censure toward her father. Those secrets included him, he had no doubt.

"It's only right that you told Orson," Kirk added.

"I don't need your approval, either," Sally said tightly.

"Now, honey, there's no need to be unpleasant," Orson interjected. "While I'm shocked, I have to admit that I'm relieved you have someone else in your corner. Becoming a parent is a big enough change in anyone's life. Doing it alone just makes things a whole lot harder than they need to be. What you need to realize is that you're more vulnerable now than you've probably ever been, and you have to make choices that are best for the baby, not just for yourself."

"I'm aware of that."

Kirk could see Sally didn't appreciate being talked down to. Orson apparently realized it, too.

"And now you're mad at me."

"Dad, I just wish you would let me be me sometimes. I'm a grown-up. I am capable of making decisions for myself."

Kirk had no doubt that last bit was directed at him, as well.

"Well, honey, I want you to think long and hard about the decisions you make now. I know your work is important to you. Mine always was to me, and over the years, I usually put it first. I have my regrets about that now."

"Regrets?" Sally asked, giving up all semblance of eating and pushing her plate to one side.

"Yes, I wasn't available enough to you while you were growing up, especially after your mother passed. I grew my business at the expense of my family, and while I can't turn back the clock on that, I can be there for you now. I hope you'll let me support you where I can."

Tears sprang to Sally's eyes, and Kirk felt something twist in his chest at being witness to this exchange between father and daughter. Far from offering his son this kind of support, Kirk's father hadn't even been able to hold himself together, gradually falling deeper and deeper into addiction. The memory and the scene before him only served to firm his resolve to be an active part of his child's life. No matter what transpired between him and Sally, he would be there for his son or daughter.

He hadn't managed to catch up with Sally in the office today. After returning to his new home before dawn and getting ready for work, he'd been caught up in meetings all day. One in particular had been distinctly disturbing, and it was part of the reason he'd agreed to come to dinner with Orson tonight.

It seemed Sally's project had been leaked to their main rival, who'd taken to the media already to advertise their willingness to implement sustainable workplaces throughout all DuBecTec offices, taking the thunder out of any similar announcements HTT might make in

the future. Kirk's initial reaction had been to lay blame
squarely with someone like Silas Rogers, who seemed to
have some sort of grudge against Sally and might have
taken action to keep her from getting credit for her ideas.
But Kirk had enlisted the help of a forensic IT specialist,
and it appeared that the information had been sent from
Sally's own laptop.

The knowledge made him sick to his stomach. Not
only because he'd spent last night with her, allowing his
passion for her to overcome any sense of reason, but also
because he realized he'd begun to develop feelings for
Sally that went beyond the fact that he couldn't even be
in the same room as her without wanting to touch her.
Feelings that were now inextricably linked to the fact
she was carrying his child—another complication he
couldn't ignore.

His disappointment in discovering this proof that she'd
been their leak all along was immeasurable. And, once
the forensic specialist had found that link, it hadn't taken
long for him to discover the others. All information going
out had gone through Sally's device.

But mingled with his own feelings about the situation was the sadness of knowing Orson would be devas-
tated. His own daughter behind the potential downfall of
his pride and joy? They had to work fast to immobilize
Sally and prevent her from doing any further damage.
The fallout among her team would be another blow to
the company. Those men and women would feel utterly
cheated after all their hard work. Of course, HTT would
carry on with implementing the plan—it made sense on
so many levels Kirk was surprised it had taken this long.
But they wouldn't be viewed as the leaders in their industry—they'd be the copycats. And that stuck in his craw
like a particularly sharp fish bone.

He went through the motions with Orson, accepting a glass of champagne to toast the news of the baby, but his heart wasn't in the celebration and he could see Sally couldn't wait to be away from it, too. Dinner passed quickly, and Sally asked to be excused from sharing the dessert the housekeeper brought to the table—pleading weariness and the desire for an early night.

She'd blushed when she'd made her apologies. He knew exactly why she was so tired, but thankfully her father simply accepted her words at face value and, after exhorting Kirk to remain at the table, Orson saw his daughter to the front door, where her driver was waiting for her.

Kirk felt his stomach tie in knots as he considered what he was about to tell the older man on his return. There were many things the man needed to know—even if he wouldn't enjoy hearing any of them. Orson would be none too pleased to know that Kirk had deliberately hidden his identity from Sally that first night he'd met her, but Kirk knew he had to come clean and lay everything on the table—including the new evidence that had arisen today.

Last night had been one of the worst things he'd ever had to do in business. Seeing the devastation roll over Orson's face and knowing that he was the messenger responsible for putting it there hurt Kirk in ways he wouldn't have believed possible a few short years ago. But worse was yet to come. In light of the evidence, another special meeting of the board had been called this morning, and Orson had insisted on being in attendance.

Orson sat now at his desk and nodded to Kirk to make the phone call he was dreading.

He picked up the receiver and listened to the sound as

Sally's office phone rang at the other end. The moment she answered, he spoke.

"Sally, would you be so good as to come to the board-room at ten this morning? And I think it would be best if you brought a support person with you."

"A support person?" she repeated down the line. "What on earth for?"

"Please, I'll explain everything when you get there but you will need an advocate."

"Kirk, I don't like the sound of this," she insisted. "What's going on?"

"You'll get everything laid out at 10:00 a.m. Please be prompt."

He hung up before she could say anything else. Across the desk, Orson looked deeply unhappy.

"I'd never have believed she could do something like this to me, or to the company. Why? Why would she do it?"

That was the big question plaguing Kirk, too. Sally stood to gain little from the internal sabotage that had taken place. If her goal was to cause the company to fail, then she hadn't been very successful. While the firm had taken a hit in terms of new client work, they contin-ued to operate strongly with their existing clientele. But growth was key to any firm's success, and she'd stymied that with her interference. The subsequent weakness now made them a prime candidate for a takeover bid. Had she been bribed or blackmailed by one of their competitors? What was really going on here?

He and Orson assembled with the board in the meet-ing room at nine thirty, and Orson quickly acquainted the board with the information about the leaks he'd gathered in the lead-up to the merger. Kirk then went on to explain the investigation he'd undertaken and the evidence the IT specialist had uncovered—in the briefest and most succinct terms possible. No one looked happy at the outcome, and all concurred with Kirk's suggestion of dealing with the perpetrator pending a fuller investigation. When the knock came at the door to announce Sally's arrival, there was a collective shuffling of papers and clearing of throats.

She looked shocked as she saw the full board assembled there, her face paling and reminding Kirk all too well of how she'd reacted during the video conference the morning after Orson's heart attack.

"Dad? What are you doing here?" she said. "What's this all about?"

"Take a seat, Sally," Orson answered with a voice heavy with gravitas.

Kirk noted Orson's PA, Marilyn Boswell, come in behind Sally and gestured to the two women to take a seat at the table. He saw Sally's hand shake as she reached for the glass of water in front of her and forced himself to quash the compassion that rose within him. He'd slept with this woman. Celebrated intimacies with her. Made a baby with her. And now she was the enemy. You'd have thought his experiences with his father would have taught him how to handle this feeling of betrayal.

"Thank you for coming this morning, Ms. Harrison, Ms. Boswell," he said in welcome.

Marilyn stared back at him fiercely before flicking her gaze to Orson. Her expression softened immeasurably. "What's this all about, Orson? We weren't expecting you back yet. What's going on?"

Orson looked across the table at his daughter, a wealth of sadness in his eyes. Kirk wished it could have been anyone else but Sally doing this to him. The betrayal that one of his own staff had sold out to the opposition was bad enough, but that it was his daughter?

* * *

Sally clenched her hands together in her lap to stop them from shaking. She felt as though something truly dreadful was about to happen. Her father hadn't mentioned anything about this meeting last night, but then again, he had been a little distracted by her news. When Kirk had told her to come to a meeting this morning and bring an advocate, to say she'd been stunned would be an understatement. This was their usual protocol when someone was being brought into a disciplinary discussion or, worse, being notified of redundancy. Why would either of those situations apply to her?

What if she actually had to speak in front of these people? Already she could feel her throat closing up and the trickle of perspiration that ran down her spine. Next to her, Marilyn reached over and placed her hand over Sally's.

"Everything will be okay, don't you worry. Your father won't let anything happen to you," the older woman whispered reassuringly.

Sally couldn't respond. Already her mouth had dried and her throat choked. Kirk rose to his feet and began to speak. He was a commanding presence in the room and everyone gave him their full attention. Or maybe it was that none of them wanted to make eye contact with her. Not even her father. The remains of the breakfast she'd eaten so hastily at her desk this morning, in deference to the growing child inside her, threatened to make a comeback.

The only one paying attention to her was Kirk, who seemed to be addressing her directly as he gave what he described as a summary of the information he'd shared with the board before her arrival. She listened with half an ear as Kirk listed a series of HIT initiatives that had been leaked to another company before the merger with Tanner Enterprises and explained the assignment that Orson had given him when he'd agreed to the merger. The lost contracts weren't news to her. After all, she'd also been shocked at how they had happened.

"The only logical conclusion we could come to is that there was someone internally working against the company. After an investigation, we believe we know exactly who that person is."

Sally looked around the room. All eyes were on her now. Realization dawned. They thought she was the leak?

No!

Ten

"Are you suggesting it's me? That I'm behind all this?" The words felt like cotton wool in her mouth.

"Based on the evidence presented to us, yes. Would you like to respond to the allegation?" Kirk asked.

"Damn straight I would!" Anger seemed to overcome her fear of speaking in a group like this, and she shot to her feet. "How dare you accuse me of this? Dad? How could you believe him?"

"I'm sorry, honey. I didn't *want* to believe it, but the facts are all there. The information came from your laptop."

Sally felt the world tilt. Her laptop? The one she carried with her everywhere? The one with double password protection? She slowly sat back down, shaking her head.

"It wasn't me. Someone else must have accessed it."

"Are you saying you shared your passwords with someone else?" Kirk pressed.

"Of course I didn't. That's against company policy."

Giving access to her computer was almost as serious an offense as what they were accusing her of.

"I need a lawyer," she said, her voice starting to shake again as her rush of anger faded as quickly as it had happened and reality began to dawn. Whoever had framed her had done a thorough job. There was no way out of this without serious consequences.

"Yes, I believe you do," Kirk said firmly. "In the meantime, you will stand down from all duties and will forfeit all company property and passwords pending a full, externally run investigation."

"Stand down?"

"Standard operating procedure in a case like this," Marilyn said. "But don't worry. I'm sure everything will be just fine."

Sally begged to differ. Right now it seemed as though every facet of her life was in turmoil, and all of it tied back to the moment she'd met Kirk Tanner. Oh, yes, it was all too convenient, wasn't it? She remained seated at the table as one by one, the board members and her father and Marilyn left the room, leaving her alone with Kirk.

"This is all very convenient for you, isn't it?" she said bitterly when the last person closed the door behind them.

"Convenient?" He shook his head. "It's anything but."

"Tell me, then. When you met me that night at the club, did you already suspect me of this?"

She had to know, even though hearing the truth from his lips would cause no end of hurt.

"Everyone was under suspicion. But—"

"But nothing. I was under suspicion, and you seduced me, knowing who I was. Did you think I'd let something slip in the heat of the moment? If so, you were wasting your time. I'm innocent. Someone, or several someones, have set me up. I already told you that it was hard for me to prove myself here. Obviously that goes deeper than I thought if an employee is prepared to go to these lengths to discredit me."

"And if that is the case, the investigation will show it and you'll be reinstated. In the interim, there'll be an announcement that you're taking a short medical leave."

Sally barked a humorless laugh. "And doesn't that fall right into your hands."

"What do you mean?" Kirk paused in collecting the papers that had been in front of him on the table.

"You already made it clear you want to take care of me and support me while I'm carrying your baby, and I refused you. Is this your way of ensuring you get your way? You're already proving yourself to be the son my father never had. How much more are you going to strip from me before you're done?" She wished she could unsay the words she'd uttered, but maybe now that they were out, she could face the truth of them. The truth that she'd never been good enough, articulate enough, strong enough to be the person her father had truly needed.

To her horror, she burst into tears. Kirk rushed to her side, and she shoved him away from her.

"Don't touch me. Don't. Ever. Touch. Me. Again."

She clumsily swiped at the tears on her cheeks. Kirk withdrew, but she could see the concern painted clearly on his face.

"You didn't answer my question," she said, her voice shaking with the effort it took to bring herself under control. "You already admitted you slept with me that first time, knowing who I was. Did you think it was me from the start? Was that why you didn't disclose who you were when you first met me? Because you suspected me of being the person responsible for undermining HIT— was that why you slept with me?"

He didn't say anything, and she could see her words had found their mark. It was a cruel reality to have to face that she'd been a target all along. For information and nothing else.

A shudder racked her body. And to think she'd even begun to consider what it would be like to be married to him. To build a family home together. What kind of a fool was she?

One who learned from the past, that's who.

"Sally, that night wasn't what I expected—hell, *you* weren't what I expected—"

"No. Stop." She held up her hand. "Don't bother. I get it. If you hadn't wanted information out of me, we'd never have met until the merger announcement."

"I didn't fake my attraction to you, Sally. From the minute you walked in that bar, you had my attention. But, yes, I realized that I'd seen you before, and it didn't take me long to figure out it was from the files your father had supplied me. I'd been going through all the staff profiles, trying to get a sense of the people I would be dealing with and, to be honest, trying to see who might have the means and a reason to be supplying our rival with sensitive information."

"Did my father suspect me?"

"No, he didn't, but he had to include you in the profiles because not to do so would be seen as showing bias. You understand that, don't you?"

She sighed heavily. "And now you think I'm it. So what now? You get security to escort me to my office to empty my drawers and then march me out of the building?"

"That won't be necessary."

She felt a glimmer of hope that she wasn't to be treated like a criminal, but then he continued.

"Marilyn will be instructed to remove your personal items from your office. As to the rest, including all your electronics and your cell phone, they'll be retained as part of the investigation."

Even though she knew she was innocent, the very thought of what was happening made her feel dirty somehow. Tainted. Would she ever be able to return and hold her head up high? Would her colleagues be able to look at her the same way? Trust her? Oh, sure. She knew that they were being told she was going on medical leave, but they were clever people. Her taking time off hard on the heels of the announcement by a competitor of an identical project to the one they'd touted to the senior management only two days ago? They'd put two and two together and links would be made.

She was ruined. Everything she'd yearned for, trained for and dreamed of had been torn from her by a traitor in this very building. She had to find some way to prove her innocence. Maybe then she could redeem herself in her father's eyes and in those of her peers.

"I see," she said with all the dignity she could muster. "Tell me, Kirk. Was I worth it?"

"Worth it?"

"The sacrifice of sleeping with me? Taking one for the team."

Before he could answer, she slammed her cell phone on the table in front of her, swept out of the boardroom and headed for the elevators. She pressed the down button and prayed for the swift arrival of a car to get her out of here. All her life she'd wanted to prove herself here—to be a valued member of the team—and now she was a pariah. She couldn't even begin to parse through her grief. And her dad? She'd seen the look on his face, seen the disappointment, the accusations, the questions. She hoped he would believe in her innocence once they'd had a chance to talk, but since Kirk so obviously already had her father's ear, what hope did she have of him believing her over Kirk?

The elevator in front of her pinged open, and she stepped into the car and hit the button for the lobby level. The doors began to slide closed but jerked back as a suited arm stopped them from closing. Kirk, of course.

"What? Did you forget to frisk me before I leave the building?" she baited him as he faced her and the doors closed behind him.

"Don't take this out on me, Sally. You know everything we've asked of you is standard practice while the investigation is being conducted."

"Don't be so pompous. You've lied to me from the moment you met me. Why not try being honest for a change?"

"You want honest?" he said tightly. "I'll give you honest. You caught my eye the second you arrived in the bar that night. I didn't recognize you immediately, but I couldn't take my eyes off you."

She snorted inelegantly. "I may be a little naive from time to time, but don't expect me to believe you on that one. There were any number of women, far more beautiful than me, in the bar that night."

"And yet I only had eyes for you."

The look she gave him was skeptical. "A little clichéd, wouldn't you say?"

"Sally, stop trying to put up walls between us."

"Me?" She was incredulous now. "You're the one accusing me of corporate espionage!"

"Look, I feel sick to my stomach about this entire situation. We have to investigate further and we have to be seen to be dealing with this in the correct manner. I don't want to believe you're the culprit, but the evidence is too strong to suggest otherwise."

"How sweet of you to say so," she replied in a tone that made it quite clear she thought it anything but.

Sally held herself rigid as the doors opened to reveal the lobby. She had to get out of here. Out of the elevator, out of the building and out of Kirk's sphere. She started to walk, barely conscious of Kirk walking beside her.

"Sally!" he called as she strode out the front doors and onto the sidewalk.

She stopped and turned around. "You have no power over me out here. I'm just a regular person on the street right now. Remember? I don't answer to you or to anyone else."

"Where's Benton?"

"Right now, I don't know and I don't care. Maybe the decision has been made that I don't need a bodyguard anymore. I'd say my commercial value has dropped given this morning's revelations, wouldn't you? Don't worry your handsome little head about it."

Kirk took a step forward and took her by the arm. "You're still carrying my baby," he said coldly. "I have a duty to care for my child."

She closed her eyes briefly. Of course. The baby. There was always something or someone else that would take precedence over her, wasn't there. She opened her eyes and stared at his hand on her arm then up at his face. He wasn't holding her firmly, but he wasn't letting go, either. It drove it home to her that the life she thought she'd had was not her own. Never had been and likely now never would be.

Sally looked very deliberately down at his hand and then up to his face. He let her go. Turning on her heel, she walked briskly away from him and headed for home.

* * *

She'd been stuck at home for a week. The weather, in true Seattle fashion, had been gloomy and cold. Thanksgiving was only a week away, and Sally was finding it darn hard to be thankful for anything right now. The lawyer she'd spoken to had told her there was little they could do until charges were officially brought against her, if that indeed happened. In the meantime, she'd had dinner with her father a couple of times but the atmosphere between them was strained, to say the least. The good news was that he'd recovered enough to begin working again. He was doing half days at the office three times a week, and she had a suspicion he was also working a little from home. Not surprising, since his work had been his key focus all his life.

Medically he was hitting all his markers, and his cardiologist was pleased with his recovery. For that, at least, she was grateful.

Sally had caught up with her leisure reading and, wrapped up warm, had gone for several walks in the park over the past few days, but she itched to be able to use her mind to do more. Being inactive didn't suit her at all. And, all the time, it bugged her that whoever was truly behind the leaks from the office continued to work there. Obviously lying low for now.

She had spent a lot of her walking time thinking about the situation and what she could do to prove her innocence. Since her own access to the internet had been restricted by the confiscation of her equipment, she decided that she would have to use public means to conduct her own investigation. And that investigation would start with Kirk Tanner.

Last night she'd booked time for a computer at the Bellevue Library and when the cab dropped her off at the building this morning, she felt a frisson of excitement for the first time in days. She had a maximum session length of only two hours. She'd have to work fast.

Sally had always loved research and delving deeper into problems. Now she had something she really needed to get her teeth into. She started with Kirk. After all, wasn't he the epicenter of the quake that had shaken her life off its foundations?

It didn't take too much digging before she began to bring up information that related to Kirk's family. Thanks to the digitization of the local papers, there was plenty of information readily available about Frank Tanner, starting with a photo and article of him and her dad excitedly announcing their start-up IT company.

She stared at the photo of the younger version of her dad and a man who looked a lot like Kirk. The men's pride in their achievement was almost palpable. Sally sent the article to the printer and moved on to the next news story. This one was a lot less joyful. It described the arrest of a man under the influence of substances after police had been called to a domestic violence incident. The man was Frank Tanner.

A chill shivered down her spine as she read the brief report of his court appearance. A few years later there was another report—again with substance abuse, again with domestic violence. And then, finally, a brief report of Frank Tanner's death from a fall from Deception Bridge. The autopsy had reported that he had enough drugs in his system to cause multiple organ failure, even if the fall hadn't killed him.

Sally looked at the first picture she'd printed. Frank and her father had been so young then, so full of hopes and dreams for their future. Sally felt a pang of sympathy for Kirk, wondering what it must have been like for him to watch his home disintegrate, and at the same time grateful that she'd never have to truly know. Her father might have been focused on business, but at least he never raised a hand to anyone or ever let his family go without.

Discovering more details about Kirk's father's past went a long way toward explaining why his mother had been so determined to leave the area and make a new life for herself and her son in California. Sally could understand why Kirk was so driven, why he had a plan that he lived and worked by. His youth must have been so unsettled.

Her time was running out on the computer, so she quickly collated her printed pages and shoved them in her tote to read further at home. She knew her father had provided financial help to the Tanner family, including the fund that had seen Kirk through college. But was there more? Had Kirk somehow believed he had a rightful place at HIT? Had it been him who approached her father about merging their two companies? Had he possibly engineered a risk of potential takeover of her father's company to create an opening for himself where he felt he should have been all along?

Sally called her father that night and asked if she could come and visit with him over the weekend. When she arrived, he was still a little reserved with her, but as they sat together in front of the fireplace in his library, she decided to go at this situation head-on.

"Dad, do you really believe I'm responsible for the leaks at HTT?"

He looked at her as if he was shocked she would ask him such a thing. "I'd like to think not, honey. After all, why would you do such a thing? But Marilyn said you were frustrated at work, even though I never saw any evidence to support that. I always thought you'd bring any problems to me if you had them. It leaves me asking myself what you would hope to gain from such a thing."

Sally was a little taken aback. Marilyn had been telling her dad she wasn't happy at work? Sure, she'd often told the PA that she wanted to climb further up the corporate ladder, that it had been her goal to support her father in any way that she could. But she'd never expressed dissatisfaction to the extent that anyone could say she wasn't happy.

"Obviously I have nothing to gain," she said. "It wasn't me. I want you to believe that."

"And I want to believe it, too. However, what I think isn't the key here. We have to prove, beyond a shadow of a doubt, that it isn't you, don't we?"

She was heartened by his use of the term *we*, rather than the singular *you*.

"Tell me about the early days, Dad. About when you and Frank Tanner set HIT up. They must have been exciting times, yes?"

A gentle smile curved her father's lips. "They were very exciting times. The beginning of the boom times in information technology, and we were full of ideas and passion. Those were good years—challenging and exciting, difficult at times, but good nonetheless."

He fell silent and she knew he was thinking about his business partner's death.

"I learned a bit more about Frank Tanner's addiction, Dad. Why do you think he fell victim to it?"

Her father knotted his hands together and sighed heavily. "I don't really know. In college he was always the party guy, but he was so brilliant that it didn't hold him back. He never struggled to keep his grades up and always skated through exams without needing to crack open a reference book. I envied that about him. Everything I did, I did through sheer hard work."

Sally nodded. She was much the same.

Her father continued, "I guess he always put more pressure on himself to be more and do more than any other person. It was as if he was constantly trying to prove himself. Constantly striving for more and better than he'd done before. Money was tight for all of us when we started up, and we worked long hours. Frank even more than me. I guess he started depending on the drugs to keep himself sharp through the all-nighters. I could never figure out how he did it, but when I stop and look back, I realize he had to have been using something to boost himself.

"Anyway, by the time I realized he was dangerously hooked on drugs, it was too late. Not long after that, he was dead. As his friend I should have seen it, should have questioned him more closely. I should have recognized that he needed help, especially when things at home weren't so good between him and his wife."

"She always dropped the abuse charges, didn't she? Maybe, deep down, she still loved him and still hoped that he could change."

Orson looked at her. "I might have known you'd find that horrible history out."

"What can I say? I'm methodical, like my dad."

He gave her a smile, and he looked at her warmly. She'd missed this expression in his eyes since Kirk's accusations.

"What happened to Frank wasn't your fault, Dad," she said with deep conviction. "He was on a road to self-destruction long before you guys set up in business together. Even if you'd have noticed back then, do you honestly think you could have made a big difference? He had to want to change. If he couldn't do that for his family, he wouldn't have done it for you."

Her words were blunt, but they had the weight of truth behind them. She hoped her father would see that.

"I guess I know that deep down, but I still feel the loss of his friendship. When he died I had to help Sandy. She was a wreck, though she tried to hold it together for Kirk's sake. He was twelve when his dad died, a difficult age for a boy even without the additional test of having an addicted parent. I discussed it with your mother, who agreed we had to do whatever we could to help Sandy and Kirk start fresh. So we did."

Sally looked at her father. Going over the past like this obviously caused him pain, but she wasn't sorry she'd asked. She needed to understand the whole situation. She'd also hoped that perhaps learning more about the history of HIT might give her more insight into who was trying to hurt the company now. It distressed her that her father may still consider that she might be responsible for the leaks from HTT. Until she could remove every element of doubt, there would always be a question in his eyes whenever he looked at her. She couldn't live with that for the rest of her life.

"Dad, when did you begin to suspect there was a problem with information security at work?"

Orson looked a little uncomfortable and shifted in his chair. "It's been happening for about a year," he finally admitted.

Sally looked up in shock. About a year? That coincided with her appointment as head of her department.

Her father continued. "I did what I could but kept hitting blank walls when it came to trying to figure out who was behind it. That's when I turned to Kirk."

"Why him?" *Why not share your worries with me?* The silent plea echoed in her mind.

"I guess you're upset I never mentioned anything about him to you before," Orson commented with his usual acuity.

"Of course I am. I won't lie to you, Dad. It really hurt to discover him behind your desk the morning after your heart attack, especially after you'd presented me with the done deal at dinner the night before with no warning or prior notice."

"Well, in my defense, I did plan to be there with him. I didn't plan for my ticker to act up the way it did."

Sally got up from her chair and walked over to the fire, putting her hands out in front of her and letting the heat of the flames warm her skin.

"Why did you never tell me about your involvement with Kirk and his mom?"

"It wasn't something you needed to know," he said bluntly.

She thought about it awhile and was forced to concede he was probably right, except for one small fact—that he'd decided to bring Kirk in as his equal the moment the firm had been weakened. She decided to take a different tack with her questioning.

"Why do you think that someone has been sharing our details?"

Her father's response was heated. "Why does anyone do it? For money, of course. Why else would anyone betray the firm they work for? Someone has put their personal greed ahead of the needs of the company. Corporate espionage is a dreadful thing, and it creates weaknesses that allow others to gain leverage when it comes to hostile takeovers."

"Is that what was happening to us?"

Orson looked nonplussed for a moment, as if he'd let out more than he ought to have. Eventually he nodded.

"So there's been a threat of takeover," Sally mused out loud. "How do you know it wasn't Kirk behind it all along? Maybe he set it all up so he could come in as a white knight and suggest a merger."

"Kirk?" Her father sounded incredulous. "No. He'd never stoop that low. He's the kind of man who would come at a thing head-on. No subterfuge about that guy."

Wasn't there? Hadn't he withheld his identity from her the night they'd first met? It hurt and angered Sally, too, to realize that while her father refused to consider Kirk a suspect, he'd had no trouble believing it could be her.

"Besides, it was me that approached him from the get-go. I've kept an eye on him and his achievements ever since he and his mother left Seattle. I may have put him through college, but it's because of his own abilities that he's been able to really do something with his life. From the outset it was clear that he had his father's brilliance, but beyond that he had the sense to apply it where it would do him the most good. He had all of his father's best attributes, and none of the bad.

"To be totally honest with you, Sally, HIT needed Tanner Enterprises far more than the other way around. I was up front with him from the start. It was a risky move for Kirk to agree to the merger, but I needed him."

Sally could hear the honesty in her father's words, but that didn't stop the emptiness that echoed behind her breastbone that told her that no matter how bold she thought she could be, she would never be the kind of person who had the drive and hunger for success that Kirk so obviously had. If she had, wouldn't she have found a way to push past her phobia instead of hiding behind it?

She couldn't hold herself back any longer. She had to prove her innocence of the accusations leveled against her. And soon.

Eleven

Over the next couple of days, Sally spent hours trying to figure out who could be responsible for the leak. She covered her dining table with sheet after sheet of paper, many of them taped together with lines drawn between names and dates and points of data. On another sheet she wrote the lists of names and what people might stand to gain by such a thing.

After all her years at HIT, from intern to paid employee, she had gotten to know a great many of the staff within the various departments. She knew that because of the positive working environment and the benefits offered by the firm, staff retention was very high. She could understand the idea of a disgruntled employee wanting to punish their employer, but how could that apply here? Despite all the time she spent poring over everything, she still couldn't reach a solid conclusion.

Her days began to stretch out before her with boring

regularity, and even a visit to her ob-gyn couldn't give her the lift she needed. Kirk had accompanied her, and the atmosphere between them had been strained. His presence at the appointment was just another confirmation of her links to a man who neither trusted her nor could be trusted. And yet, every time she thought of him, she still felt that tingle of desire ripple through her body.

A week after Thanksgiving, which she'd spent with her dad and Marilyn, she was struggling with a knitting pattern she'd decided to teach herself when the intercom from downstairs buzzed. She looked up in surprise, dropping yet another darn stitch from the apparently easy baby blanket she was attempting, at the sound. She certainly hadn't been expecting anyone, and when she heard Kirk's voice on the speaker she was unable to stop the rush of heat that flooded her body. Flustered and certainly not dressed for any kind of company, an imp of perversity wanted her to tell him to leave without hearing what he had to say, but she sucked in a deep breath and told him to come on up.

In the seconds she had to spare before he arrived, she dashed into the bathroom and quickly brushed her hair, tied it back into a ponytail and smoothed a little tinted moisturizer onto her face.

"There, that's better than a moment ago," she told her reflection. "Shame you don't have time to do anything about the clothes."

Still, what was she worried about? This couldn't be a social call. A dread sense of foreboding in the pit of her stomach told her that this had to relate to her suspension.

Despite the fact she was expecting him, his sharp knock at her door made her jump.

"Just breathe," she admonished herself as she went to let him in.

She hadn't been prepared for the visceral shock of actually seeing him again. Dressed in sartorial corporate elegance, he filled the doorway with his presence, making her all too aware of the yoga pants, sweatshirt and slippers that had virtually become her uniform over the past couple of weeks. But it wasn't so much the way he was dressed that struck her—it was the hungry expression in his eyes as they roamed her from head to foot before coming back to settle on her face again.

"Hello," she said, annoyed to hear her voice break on the simple two-syllable word.

"You're looking well," Kirk replied. "May I come in?"

"Oh, of course," she answered, stepping aside to let him in the apartment.

As he moved past her, she tried to hold her breath. Tried not to inhale the scent that was so fundamentally his. Tried and failed miserably. Whatever cologne it was that he wore, it had to be heavily laden with pheromones, she decided as she closed the door and fought to bring herself under some semblance of control. Either that or she was simply helplessly, hopelessly, under his spell.

Maybe it was the latter, she pondered glumly as she offered him something to drink. Wouldn't that be just her luck.

"Coffee would be great, thanks."

"Take a seat. I'll only be a minute."

He sat down on the sofa where she'd been attempting to knit just a few minutes ago, and she saw him lean forward to pick up the printed pattern for the baby blanket.

"Nesting?" he commented, sounding amused as he picked up her knitting and tried to make sense of the jumble of yarn, comparing it to the picture in his other hand.

"Something like that. I needed to do something to

keep me busy," she said a little defensively. "It's my first attempt."

It wasn't, in truth her first attempt at this blanket. In fact it was about her twelfth, but the project was very much her first foray into the craft of knitting, and as she ripped her successive attempts out yet again and rewound the yarn, she found herself missing her mother more and more. Her mom had loved to knit.

"You're braver than me," he said simply as he put everything back on the coffee table.

Sally made herself a cup of herbal tea and brought it through to the living room with Kirk's coffee. She put the mug down on a coaster in front of him then took a seat opposite, not trusting herself to sit too near. Maybe with a little distance between them she could ignore the way her body reacted to his presence and maybe her nostrils could take a break from wanting to drown in that scent that was so specifically him.

"Why are you here?" she asked bluntly, cupping her mug between her hands.

"I wanted to deliver you the news myself," Kirk said, giving her a penetrating look.

"News?"

"You've been exonerated of any wrongdoing."

Even though she knew all along that she was innocent, Sally couldn't hold back the tidal wave of relief that now threatened to swamp her. Her hands shook and hot tea spilled over her fingers as she leaned forward to put her mug on the table. Kirk jumped straight to his feet, a pristine white handkerchief in his hand, and he moved swiftly to mop her fingers dry.

She thrilled to his touch but fought back the sensation that unfurled through her as his strong, warm hands cupped hers. She tugged her hands free and swiftly stood, walking away to create some distance between them.

"I can't say I'm surprised," she said, fighting to make her voice sound firm when she was feeling anything but. "I told you it wasn't me."

"Your father told me the same thing," he said smoothly.

Sally briefly savored the evidence that her father had supported her in this after all. "But you still felt there was room for doubt?"

Kirk ignored her question. "The forensic investigation of your devices showed that a false trail had been set up to look as though the data had been sent from your computer. At this stage, they still haven't been able to ascertain exactly who created that path. Obviously it was someone with a very strong knowledge of computer technology."

"Which, considering we're an information technology company, narrows it down to maybe ninety percent of the workforce at HTT," she said in a withering tone. "Do you plan to suspend everyone until you've figured out who it is?"

"That would be counterproductive," Kirk responded with a wry grin. "As I'm sure you know."

She looked at him, wishing that seeing him again didn't make her feel this way. Wishing even harder that none of this awfulness of suspicion and doubt lay between them and they could actually explore what it would be like to be a couple without any of the stigma that the investigation had left hanging like a dark cloud around her.

"I'm free to return to my work?" she asked.

"Tomorrow, if that's what you want."

"Of course that's what I want. I have a lot to catch up on."

"I thought you might say that." He reached into the

laptop bag he'd brought and fished out her computer, her tablet and her smartphone. "Here, you'll need these."

She all but dived in to take them from him. She flicked on her phone and groaned out loud at the number of missed calls and the notification that her voice mail was full. It was going to take her hours to sift through everything. Still, at least she had her devices back.

She put her things on the table and looked Kirk in the eye. "Are you satisfied with the outcome? With my being cleared of involvement?"

He sighed deeply. "More than you probably realize, yes."

"I'm glad. I would hate to think you still suspected me."

He looked at her again. "Why is that, Sally?"

"Because, despite everything, we still are going to have to raise a child together."

Was it her imagination, or was there a shaft of disappointment visible in his aqua-colored gaze?

"I would like to think that we can handle this thing between us with civility, if nothing else," she continued.

"Civility." He nodded. "When I look at you, civility is the farthest thing from my mind."

His voice dropped a level, and Sally felt the intensity of his words as if they were a physical touch. She fought for control again, determined not to allow herself to fall victim to her confused feelings for this man.

"My father told me about your dad and why he asked you to join forces with him. What he couldn't tell me is why you agreed."

Here it was, his opportunity to begin to mend fences with Sally. It had been such a relief when she'd been cleared of wrongdoing that he had come straight here tonight instead of calling her into the office in the morning. His motives hadn't been entirely altruistic. He'd missed her and ached to see her again. He'd spent every day wondering what she'd be doing, how she was feeling and hoping like hell she was looking after herself properly.

She deserved his honesty now more than ever before.

"I had several reasons," he said carefully, looking directly into Sally's eyes. "One of which was the fact that I had always held your father in very high esteem. He owed my mother and me nothing, but when my dad died your father helped Mom and me get a fresh start—away from the memories that made my mom so miserable, away from the shame that she carried in her heart that she couldn't help her husband or prevent him from killing himself."

He looked at Sally, searching for recrimination or disgust in her eyes. Instead he only saw compassion. It gave him a ridiculous sense of hope. He took another deep breath.

"That sense of helplessness was one I struggled with, too. You see, the whole time I'd been growing up, it was with a kind of barter system where I'd convince myself that if I kept my room clean and tidy, my mom wouldn't cry that day or my dad wouldn't fly off into one of his temper rants. Or I'd convince myself that if I did well at school and got good grades, my dad would smile and play ball outside with me rather than lie on his bed shaking.

"It became vital to me to control everything around me, to do whatever it took to coax a smile from my mother's face, to keep my father calm when he was at home, to deflect the attention of the neighbors on the nights when everything turned to shit. And then to act like nothing had happened each time the police came and took Dad away. I learned that if you wanted things a particular way, you had to do certain things in repayment—that you had to earn any good thing that you wanted in your life. And yet, with your father, he didn't expect anything in return for aiding my mother and me. He just wanted to help."

Kirk looked at Sally, wondering if she could even begin to understand the depth of his gratitude to Orson for all he'd done.

"Dad has always had a compassionate heart," she replied. "I think it's helped him do so well, but he tempers it with drive and determination. He doesn't suffer fools gladly, and he won't tolerate injustice or laziness."

"Exactly. I actually used HIT as my business study in college—I guess you could say my family connection led me to being a little obsessed with understanding everything my father had been a part of before it all went so wrong. Through that, I grew even more respect for your father. In fact, I modeled my own business structure on what he'd done—and I modeled myself on how he's lived. When he approached me and asked me if I'd consider merging Tanner Enterprises with HIT, I could see more than one benefit for both of us. Structurally, it was a solid, sensible decision that would benefit both companies. But personally…he said he needed me, and I finally had a way to pay him back for all the good he'd done for Mom and me over the years."

Sally looked at him, her eyes glistening with emotion. "Kirk, I'm so sorry your childhood was so awful. I wish it could have been different for you."

"I don't. Not anymore. It helped to shape me into the man I am now—it helped me know exactly what I want from life and where I want to be."

"Ah, yes," she said with a soft smile. "Your plan."

"Hey, don't laugh. Everyone needs a plan, right?"

Sharing this with Sally felt right. He felt as if a weight had lifted from him.

"So, what happens to HTT from here?" she asked. "Now that you know I'm not the leak?"

"We keep investigating," he answered in a matter-of-fact tone. "And we will find the perpetrator. It's a deliberate criminal act, and they must be held to account."

"And what happens now with *us*?" she asked unsteadily.

"What do you want to happen?"

"Kirk, I don't know how to cope with this. I don't know who I am with you." She felt lost, afraid to speak of her feelings, but she forced the words out. "You made me believe things about myself that first night we were together that gave me confidence and strength. When I found out who you were, all that confidence in myself shattered and made me doubt my attractiveness and appeal all over again.

"You see, I may have grown up with more than you did, and certainly without the uncertainty you had when your father was alive, but because of who I am and who my father is, there have always been expectations on me. Expectations I haven't always been able to fulfill. You've seen the worst of it, the fear of public speaking—"

"But you've made inroads on that, Sally. I saw you at that sustainability presentation. You were totally in control."

She smiled. "Well, not *totally* in control, but better than in the past, I'll accept that. Until I fainted, anyway."

"But even that wasn't you. It was your pregnancy, not your fear."

She nodded again. "Even so, I ended up delivering what everyone there expected me to deliver. Failure. It's something I've made rather a fine art of since my mother's funeral. I had written a poem for her. All I had to do was read it, but I couldn't. I choked. I couldn't even tell my mom goodbye the way I wanted to. Now, whenever I get up to speak to a group of more than two or three people, I'm back there in the chapel, standing there in front of all those expectant faces—disappointing all those people and failing my mother's memory."

Her voice choked up, and tears spilled on her cheeks. "Even remembering it—" She shook her head helplessly. "It feels like it was yesterday. It never goes away."

Kirk was at a loss. He knew from Orson that Sally had had professional counseling to help her deal with her phobia—and that it had been unsuccessful. He reached for her hands, holding them firmly in his and drawing her to him until she was nestled against his chest. He felt her body shudder as a sob escaped from her rigid frame. He put his arms around her and stroked her back slowly, offering her comfort when words failed him. He felt her draw in a deep breath and then another.

"I've failed my dad, too. And that's the worst of it. I wanted to be his trusted, dependable right-hand man more than anything in my life. I pushed myself in college, I interned at HIT—I did everything I could to be an asset to him, rather than another disappointment. Oh, don't get me wrong, he's never made me feel as if I've let him down. In fact, I don't think he ever expected me to join him in the upper echelon at HIT. Sometimes I think nothing would have made him happier than if I'd just stayed at home and taken on my mother's old positions on the boards of the charities she supported. He's always told me he will support me in whatever I decide to do. But I wanted to support him, too."

"He values your input, Sally. Never think for a minute that he doesn't."

"But he doesn't turn to me. I'm not there for him the way I should be. At least not in his mind. When push came to shove and the company needed help, he turned to you."

Again, Kirk was lost for words. There really was nothing he could say in response to what was an absolute truth. Sally's father loved her. But he didn't see her as the strong, capable woman she truly was—the woman hidden behind her fears and insecurities. Somehow, he had to help Sally fight past her demons, to achieve the goals she'd set herself. He, more than anyone, understood how important those personal goals were.

Sally tried to pull away, and he reluctantly let her go. She sat up and dashed her hands over her cheeks, wiping away the remnants of her tears and visibly pulling herself together the way he had no doubt she'd done many times before.

"Listen to me blubbering on. It must be pregnancy hormones," she justified with a weak smile. "I hear they wreak havoc on a woman."

"Hey, you can blubber on me any time you need to," he said. "Sally, I don't want you to ever feel you're alone in any of this."

"This? The pregnancy or the fact that you suspected me of being the company mole?"

She said the words with flippancy, but he clearly heard the hurt beneath them.

"It's little excuse, but I had to follow procedure when the evidence pointed to you. I already knew you couldn't possibly be the leak."

"Well, it certainly didn't feel like you were sure I was innocent at the time."

"I'm sorry," he said frankly. "I'm sorry I wasn't honest with you when we met, and I'm sorry I put you through these past few weeks alone. I know it's little consolation, but I was massively relieved when it was proven, without doubt, that you were in the clear. It was also vital to the integrity of the investigation that we be seen to follow all the right procedures."

He winced. The words coming from his mouth were so formal, so precise and correct. They weren't the words he wanted to say at all. He wanted to tell her how much he'd missed her, ached for her—how much he wanted to hold her and show her how he felt about her.

"You're right, it is little consolation, but I'll take it. Which brings me back to my earlier question—where do we go from here?"

He knew exactly where he wanted to go. Right into her arms. For now, he hoped actions would speak louder than words. He reached a finger to her cheek and traced the curve of it.

"I know where I'd like us to go," he said softly.

Her pupils dilated. He leaned forward. Her lips parted, and her eyelids fluttered closed as he sought her mouth with his own. When their lips connected, he felt his body clench on a wave of need so strong it made him groan out loud. Sally's hands were at his shoulders, then her fingers were in his hair, holding him close as he deepened their kiss—as his tongue swept across her lips and he tasted her. Every nerve, every cell in his body leaped to demanding life, and he swept his hands beneath her sweatshirt, skimming over her smooth skin, relishing the feel of her. Wanting more, wanting her.

She arched toward him, and he tore his lips from hers to trace the line of her jaw with small kisses, then down the cord of her throat. He felt her shiver in response, felt her fingers tighten. He pushed the fabric of her top up, exposing her lace-clad breasts to his gaze. With one hand, he slipped one breast from its restraint. Her nipple was already a taut pink peak. He bent his head and caught the sensitive flesh between his lips, flicking the underside with his tongue and coaxing sweet sounds from her that drove him mad with need.

Kirk scooped her up into his arms and walked with her to the bedroom. After that, time blurred but sensation didn't as they rediscovered the physical joy they promised each other, and when pleasure peaked, it was the most natural thing in the world to fall asleep locked in each other's arms.

"Marry me."

Sally barely had her eyes open, and those two little words were echoing in her head.

"What?" Her voice was still thick with sleep.

"Marry me."

"Good morning to you, too," she said, rolling out of the bed and grabbing her robe from the back of a chair.

"I mean it, Sally. You can move in with me now— my house is huge and designed for a family. If you don't like it, I'll buy something else. We can create the nursery together. Plan for the future together. Travel to work together. It makes perfect sense."

Did it? Shouldn't a declaration of love come with a proposal of marriage? Shouldn't it sound better than being just the right thing to do?

"I'll think about it. I…I'm not sure I'm ready for marriage."

"Hey," he said, pushing up to a sitting position—and Sally had to avoid looking at him as the sheet dropped to just below his waist. "I didn't think I was ready, either, but we can make it work. We have a lot going for us."

"In bed, maybe," she admitted, tying the belt on her robe tightly at her waist. "But we still hardly know each other."

"We can learn about one another better if we're living together."

"You're persistent, aren't you," she said with an evasive laugh. "I need time. We don't have to rush. I said I'd think about it, and I will."

Kirk rose from the bed, the sheet falling away to expose his nakedness as he walked toward her and lifted her chin with one finger. His lips were persuasive as he kissed her, coaxing hers to open so he could explore her mouth more intimately.

"I'll be waiting for your answer," he said, his voice—and a very specific part of his anatomy—heavy with desire. "Shall I wash your back in the shower?"

And just like that she was putty in his hands. Hands that were already at the sash of her robe, undoing the knot and pushing the silk from her shoulders. Hands that roamed her body, cupping her breasts and tweaking at her nipples until they were tight points that sent shivers through her body as his palms skimmed their hardness. Hands that moved lower and pressed against the other nub of sensitive flesh at the apex of her thighs until she was quivering with need.

Needless to say, they barely made it into work on time. Even though her hair was pulled back into its usual ponytail, it was still damp. Sally hoped no one would notice and jump to the right conclusion, especially as she and Kirk had been seen together.

As she walked through her floor, she was welcomed back by several members of her team, who appeared genuinely concerned for her. It was gratifying. She was a part of this, a part of these people and what they did here. But she wanted more than that. She wanted more, period. She wanted a sense of certainty that she was working to her full potential, that she was achieving something worthwhile for herself, on her own merits.

If she agreed to marry Kirk, wouldn't she simply be absorbed into the life he'd created for himself? How would she maintain her hard fought for identity? How could she expect her colleagues to treat her as an equal rather than as someone they had to watch themselves around? And then there was her goal of moving up the professional ladder. Who would believe she earned a promotion when she had things nicely sewn up between her father and Kirk?

On a more personal level, Kirk had admitted modeling himself on her father, both professionally and personally. She already had one overprotective father in her life— she didn't need another person sheltering her constantly. When—if, she corrected herself firmly—she married, she wanted to be treated as an equal by her partner.

Kirk had already made it more than clear that he wanted to be her protector and provider. That sounded to her as if what she brought into a marriage didn't even rate a consideration on his revised grand plan. And, when it came to working together, based on Kirk's standing within HTT and his grasp of what the company offered and how they could remain current and relevant into the future, his knowledge and experience far exceeded her own.

Doubts flew at her from all directions. Maybe she never really would be any better than who she'd always been—the woman on the eighth floor who stayed in the background and allowed others to get the credit for her ideas.

Over the course of the day, as she caught herself back up on her projects, she found her mind wandering backward and forward until she was almost dizzy with it all.

As she sat down in her office to the lunch Kirk had packed for her before they'd hurriedly left her apartment, she forced herself to reevaluate her goals. After a great deal of deliberation, she had to recognize that, no matter what, she wanted to be a part of Harrison Tanner Tech now and in the future.

When Benton took her home that Friday evening, she was still in turmoil. Over the weekend, she spent time making a list of all the reasons why it would be good to marry Kirk Then, she made a list of why it wouldn't work.

"No matter which way you look at it, great sex does not equate to a great marriage," she said out loud once she was done. "And great sex does not equate to lifelong happiness, either."

By the time she went to bed on Sunday evening, she felt sure she'd reached her decision. Now it was just a matter of telling Kirk.

Twelve

Kirk had been in the office since five this morning. Staying one step ahead of the mole was a challenge he enjoyed getting his teeth into. The only thing he'd enjoy more would be unmasking the traitor and seeing them punished to the fullest extent of the law.

In the meantime, the company was running smoothly and the merger activities were fully on track. This week was shaping up well, and he was relieved that Orson would be back in the office full-time starting today. The man's recovery had been steady, and he'd been itching to get back to his desk full-time.

Kirk paused for a moment and considered the talk he'd had with Orson last night. Orson had continued to express his approval of Kirk marrying Sally. He was old-fashioned enough to want to see his grandchild born in wedlock, but he'd cautioned Kirk that while Sally appeared to be soft and gentle, she had a core of steel and a determined independence that didn't waver once she had her mind made up on anything.

He was heartened her father saw that in her but wondered if Orson had ever expressed any admiration for those traits to Sally's face. It might have gone some way toward helping her beyond her phobia if she realized that her father wasn't waiting for her to fail in everything she did—he was actually waiting for her to succeed. Of course, maybe she knew that all along. Maybe that was, in itself, as much of a yoke around her slender shoulders as anything else.

He felt a buzz of excitement at the idea of being married to Sally, of being a couple. Of waking to her each morning, of spending free time together and looking forward to the birth of their child. His son or daughter's life would be so vastly different from his own. And his wife wouldn't experience any of the suffering his father had put his mother through. Sally would never have to fear a fist raised against her in frustration or anger, and his child would grow up secure in the knowledge that their father was there for them every step of the way. There'd be no trade-off. No coercion. There would be love and stability and all the things Kirk had dreamed of as he'd made his plans for his future all those years ago.

A sound at his door made him look up. As if thinking about Sally had caused her to materialize, there she was. Kirk felt a now-familiar buzz of excitement as he saw her standing there. He'd seen Sally wear many different faces and in today's choice of a black tailored pantsuit with a pale gray patterned blouse underneath, she looked very serious indeed. As he rose and walked around his desk to greet her, he wondered if she wore one of those slinky camisoles beneath the blouse. His hands itched to find out.

"Good morning," he said, bending to kiss her.

She accepted his greeting but withdrew from his embrace quickly.

"Kirk, have you got some time to talk?" she said without preamble.

"Sure, for you, always."

He gestured for her to take a seat and he took the guest chair angled next to hers. As he did so, he studied her face carefully—searching for any telltale signs of tiredness or strain. She was a hard worker, harder than many here, and she needed reminders every now and then to put her needs before the needs of the company.

"I missed you over the weekend," he said.

She'd made it clear to him on Friday that she'd wanted space—time to think about them—so he'd given it to her. Now he wondered if that had been the right move. Her expression was hard to read as she looked up at him, the pupils in her eyes flaring briefly at his words. Did her body clench on a tug of desire the way his did right now? Had she spent the weekend reliving their lovemaking on Thursday night? She averted her gaze and shifted in her seat.

"What did you need to talk about?" he coaxed.

"I've reached a decision about your proposal."

He felt a burst of anticipation. "When can we start making plans?"

"I don't want to marry you."

What? "I see," he said slowly.

But he didn't see at all. When they'd come to the office together on Friday morning, it had felt so right, so natural. As if they'd been together forever and would be in the future, too. He searched her face for some indication of what she was thinking and watched as she moistened her lips and swallowed a couple of times, as if her mouth was suddenly dry. He got up and poured a glass of water from the decanter on his desk and passed it to her.

"Thank you," she said, taking a brief sip and putting the glass back down on his desk. "I didn't see the point in keeping you waiting on my answer. So, if there's nothing else we need to discuss, I'll get to work."

She got up from the chair and started for the door.

"Hold on a minute."

She froze midturn. "Yes?"

"I thought we were a little closer than that. Can you at least tell me why? Are you sure you've thought this through?"

"Since the first time you asked me, I've thought of little else. We don't live in the Dark Ages. Having a baby together is not enough reason to marry. We can coparent just as effectively while living our separate lives. I don't see why this—" her hand settled briefly on her lower belly "—should change anything."

Her voice grew tighter with each word. If he didn't know better, he'd have thought she was on the verge of a full-blown panic attack. But didn't that only happen when she had to speak to a group? Unless, of course, she was so emotionally wrought by the idea of turning him down that she was working herself up.

"Take a breath, Sally," he urged her.

"I'm fine," she said testily. "I'm perfectly capable of looking after myself. Look, I knew it wouldn't be easy to tell you my decision, and I suspected you wouldn't be happy about it. I just would like you to respect my choice and let us move on."

"You're right, I'm not happy about it," he said, trying to rein in his frustration and disappointment. "I didn't just ask you to marry me for convenience's sake, or because of how things look. I want to be a daily, active part of my son or daughter's life. I want to ensure that he or she doesn't miss out on the bond between father and child the way I missed out with my own father."

She closed her eyes briefly, and he saw her chest rise and fall on a deep breath. When she spoke, she sounded calm, but he could see the tension in her eyes and etched around her mouth.

"We can work to make sure that our kid knows we're always going to both be there for them. But that doesn't mean we have to get married or even live together—a shared custody arrangement will work perfectly well in our situation, just as it does for people all over the world. Seriously, Kirk, being married is no guarantee of a happy home when the two people involved don't love one another—it isn't even a guarantee when they do!"

Her voice rose on the last sentence, and he watched as she visibly paused to drag in a breath and assume a calmer attitude. "Look, I understand how you feel, but remember, you are not your father. You're not a drug addict. You're not going to let down this child, or any other child you might have in the future. It's not in your nature. I believe you'll be a good father, and I'm happy for you to be fully involved in your child's life. I just don't want to marry you. Please, will you respect my decision?"

There was a quiver in her voice that betrayed her rigid posture. If he was a lesser type of man, he'd push her now, try to persuade her otherwise. Use all the ammunition he could think of to try to get her to change her mind. But despite the desire to do so, he realized that if he pushed her too hard, he'd probably only succeed in pushing her away for good. He clenched his hands and then forced himself to relax, unfurling his fingers one by one. Decent men didn't give in to emotion like this. Decent men didn't bully or threaten so they could get their way.

"I do respect your decision," Kirk said heavily. "But I would beg you not to close the door on the idea entirely. Please allow me the opportunity to try to get you to change your mind."

"No. Please don't." Her voice was firm again and she was very much back in control. "In fact, I think it would be best if we confine our interactions to work-related matters only."

"You can't be serious. What about the baby?"

He couldn't help himself. The words just escaped. Was she truly closing the door on everything between them? Everything they'd shared?

"I will keep you apprised of my ob-gyn appointments and of course you can come along with me to those, but everything else—" she waved her hands in front of her "—stops now."

Kirk felt a muscle working at the side of his jaw, and he slowly counted to ten, forcing himself to relax. Then he nodded.

"If that's what you want."

"It is. Thank you."

He stood there, overwhelmed by disappointment and frustration as she walked away. This wasn't how he'd imagined this panning out at all. Sometimes, it seemed that no matter how well you planned things, it all just fell apart anyway.

By the time she got home, Sally couldn't remember how she'd gotten through her workday. From the moment she'd left Kirk's office, it seemed that everyone had wanted a piece of her and her time. The first of the new hybrid cars for the fleet were ready for pickup, and she'd had to coordinate the coverage with the managers involved and the PR team so when the next company newsletter went out it did so with the appropriate fanfare. There had been no point in making a media announcement. Not when DuBecTec had already stolen the wind from their sails.

Sally slumped down on her sofa, weariness pulling at every part of her body. All she wanted to do right now was take a nap. In fact, a nap sounded like a great idea, she decided as she swung her feet up onto the sofa and leaned back against the pillows she had stacked at one end. She'd no sooner closed her eyes than her cell phone rang. With a groan she struggled upright and dug her phone out of her handbag.

Kirk's number showed across her screen. She debated rejecting the call but then sighed and accepted it.

"Hello?"

"I just wanted to give you a heads-up. The media have gotten wind of the fact that you're pregnant, and that it's my baby."

All weariness fled in an instant. "What? How? Who?"

"That's what I'm going to find out," he said grimly. "But I wanted you to be prepared."

"But we agreed not to tell anyone. I'm not even showing yet. How could something like this have happened?"

Was this some ploy of Kirk's to try to get her to agree to marry him after all?

"The only other person we told is your father and I doubt he's responsible, but you can rest assured that I will be asking him."

With a promise to get back to her the moment he had any further news, and an admonition to screen her phone calls to avoid being badgered by the tabloid press, he severed the call.

Sally stood where she was, trapped in her worst nightmare. Now it didn't matter what she did anymore. Everyone at work would know. There'd be sly looks and innuendo and, no doubt, outright questions, as well. She'd hoped to have time to manage the situation. After all, she was still getting used to the whole idea herself.

Over the last few weeks, whoever it was that had been leaking information had held back. Oh, sure, the company had still faced some media criticism. There'd been the occasional aspersion about her father's illness in the media—the rhetorical questions about whether or not HTT's dynamic leader would remain as much of a power broker as he'd been in the past—but with Kirk's strong hand at the tiller and his no-nonsense leadership style while her father returned to full strength, those questions had faded as quickly as they'd arisen. But this was a personal attack against her and against her right to privacy. She felt violated and sick to her stomach.

She had to do something. But what? Attempting to discover who their problem was by using logic hadn't worked. So what did that leave? Her mind reached for something that she felt she should know, but everything came up blank.

Her landline began to ring. No one she knew actually used it. Even her dad used her cell number. She took a look at the caller ID but didn't recognize the number and switched the phone through to her voice mail.

Sally went to take a shower and change for an early night. She was no sooner out of the bathroom than the doorman buzzed from downstairs. Apparently there was a TV crew from a local morning show wanting to speak to her. Sally shook her head in disbelief. Aside from the time when she'd almost been kidnapped as a child, she'd only rarely been deemed newsworthy. After all, it was hardly as if she held the same kind of profile as her friend Angel, and Orson had actively avoided letting his family be exposed to the limelight of what he called pseudo celebrity. "I'd rather our family be judged on our achievements and what we do for others than by whose clothes we wear or what we were seen doing," he always said.

With a few tersely chosen words, Sally asked the doorman to ensure that she wasn't disturbed by the TV team or by anyone else not on her visitor list. She walked over to her windows and looked down at the parking lot. A second TV crew pulled into the lot. The onslaught had begun.

Thirteen

Thankfully, by the next morning, the gossip news focus had moved to the latest public celebrity meltdown and Sally's pregnancy had been relegated to a footnote. That said, when she was ready to leave her apartment for work, she discovered there were two bodyguards assigned to her—one to remain with the car at all times, the other to escort her inside and ensure she wasn't harassed by anyone. She was surprised to learn that the additional man had been ordered by Kirk, but she wasn't about to complain. She had no wish to discover that her car had been bugged or to be ambushed by anyone with a microphone.

She had planned to have lunch with Marilyn today and was looking forward to catching up with her. Everyone had been working so hard lately that it felt like forever since they'd had a good talk. The morning went by quickly, and the photo shoot for the new cars and their assigned drivers went according to plan. Sally was beginning to feel like she had a handle on things. At one o'clock she went down to the lobby to wait for Marilyn, who was just a few minutes late.

Sally kissed the older woman on the cheek and gave her a warm smile when she arrived. Shadowed by Sally's bodyguard, they walked a block to their favorite Italian restaurant for lunch and were shown to their regular table.

"So, tell me," Sally asked after the waiter had poured their water and given them menus to peruse. "How are things in the ivory tower?"

Marilyn smiled a little at the moniker given to the executive floor at the top of the building. "Busy. Mr. Tanner has yet to appoint a PA of his own, which doubles my workload."

"Have you asked for an assistant? I'm sure Dad—"

"Oh, I don't want to worry your father about something as ridiculous as that. I do work a few extra hours now, but it's nothing I can't handle. I guess I should consider myself lucky. At an age when most of my peers are settling down and enjoying their grandchildren, at least I still have a rewarding career."

Did Sally imagine it, but was there a tinge of regret, or possibly even envy, in Marilyn's tone?

"I'm sure Dad wouldn't see it as a worry, Marilyn—you know you can talk to him about anything. After all, you've worked for him for how long now?"

Marilyn's face softened. "Thirty years next week."

"Wow, that's got to be some kind of record."

"Your father and I are the only original staff left. I keep telling him it's time to pass the reins on to someone else. For him to slow down and actually enjoy the rest of his life. For us both to retire." Her mouth firmed into a straight line, and her eyes grew hard. "But you know your father—work comes first, last and always with him. I would have thought with this latest business with the leaks to competitors, and then with his heart attack, that he would have learned his lesson about slowing down— but oh, no. Not him."

It was the first time Sally had heard bitterness in the other woman's voice when talking about Orson, and it came as surprise. Normally Marilyn would stand no criticism of her boss from anyone. To hear it from her own lips was definitely something new. Maybe it was just the extra workload she had now, supporting two senior managers, that had put Marilyn in a sour mood. Even so, Sally felt she needed to defend her father.

"He's always tried to make time for family—and HIT has always been his other baby. I don't think you should be too harsh on him."

"You know I care about your father. I only want what's best for him. It would be nice if he'd just stop focusing on work with that tunnel vision of his and look around him once in a while. Anyway, that brings me to something that's been bothering me awhile. When were you going to tell me about the baby, Sally?"

Sally swallowed uncomfortably. "I didn't want to make a fuss at work, Marilyn. I'm sure you understand why, especially given how hard I've had to work to earn any respect there."

"But I'm not just *anyone*, am I? I thought we were closer than that."

"And we are," Sally hastened to reassure her. Marilyn looked truly upset that she hadn't been told, and, in hindsight, perhaps Sally should have included her in the news, but she'd had her reasons for wanting privacy, and they hadn't changed. "I'm really sorry, Marilyn. I don't know what else to say."

The older woman sniffed and reached in her handbag for a tissue and dabbed at her nose. "Apology accepted.

Now, what are you having today? Your usual chicken fettuccine?"

Sally hesitated before closing her menu. "Yes, I think so."

Marilyn placed their orders and the food was delivered soon after, but Sally found herself just toying with her fork and pushing pasta from one side of her plate to the other. It wasn't that she wasn't hungry, but she was still unsettled by how Marilyn had spoken about Orson. She'd never heard the other woman make a criticism of her father before. Ever. To hear it now had struck a discordant note, and it got her to wondering.

Marilyn was privy to pretty much everything that went over Orson's desk. Given her current disenchantment, could she be the leak Kirk and Orson were looking for? She was the last person anyone would suspect, given her long service and well-documented loyalty to Orson. Was it even possible that she'd do something so potentially damaging to the company? How on earth would she benefit from something like that?

The questions continued to play in the back of Sally's mind over the next day and a half until she couldn't keep her concerns to herself any longer. She had to talk to someone about it. She called her dad at home and asked if she could come over.

Jennifer let her in the door as she arrived.

"Dad in the library?" Sally asked as she stepped inside.

"Where else is he at this time of evening?" the housekeeper answered with a smile. "Mr. Tanner is with him."

Sally hesitated midstep. Her dad hadn't mentioned anything about Kirk being over when she'd called. Maybe he hadn't wanted to put her off coming. She'd already told him that she wasn't planning to see any more of Kirk outside the office and that she'd turned down his proposal. Her father had expressed his disappointment, stating that he firmly believed a child's parents ought to be married. Without pointing out the obvious—that his stance on the matter was archaic at best—Sally had made her feelings on the subject completely clear, and he'd eventually agreed to abide by her wishes.

She'd barely seen Kirk in the office over the past few days. And she'd kept telling herself that was just the way she liked it. Regrettably, her self begged to differ. The thought of seeing him now made her pulse flutter and her skin feel hypersensitive beneath her clothes. *You can do this*, she told herself. She could talk to him and her father in a perfectly rational and businesslike manner without allowing her body's urges to overtake her reason.

"Thanks," she said to the housekeeper. "I'll let myself in."

"Can I get you something?"

"No, I'll be fine, thank you."

The idea of eating held no appeal. She already felt sick to her stomach over what she suspected. Maybe she was completely off track with it, but what if she wasn't? It would be good to have the benefit of someone else's opinion.

Her father and Kirk rose from the wing chairs by the fireplace as she entered the library. She crossed the room and kissed her father, nodding only briefly to Kirk.

"It was an unexpected, but lovely surprise to get your call this evening," Orson said when they'd all settled down again.

"It may not be so lovely when you hear what I came to say," Sally replied, smoothing her skirt over her thighs.

She stopped the instant she realized that the movement had attracted Kirk's attention. Her gaze flicked up to his face, and she saw the flare of lust in his eyes be-

fore he masked it. Lust was all very well and good, she
told herself, but it wasn't love, and unless he could offer
her that as well, she had to hold firm.

"That sounds ominous," Kirk observed.

"I could be completely wrong, but I think I might have
uncovered the leak."

Both men sat upright, all semblance of relaxation gone
in an instant.

"Who?"

"You have?"

Their responses tumbled over each other, and Sally
put her hand up and looked directly at her father.

"Dad, you're not going to want to believe this, but I
think Marilyn is behind it all."

"Marilyn? What? She's worked for me since before
you were born. Heck, I've known her longer than I even
knew your mother."

A shaft of understanding pierced Sally's mind. Was
that an explanation for Marilyn's behavior? She'd said
she cared for him, but was she in love with Orson? Had
she been all along? Was that why she wanted him to
slow down?

"Think about it, Dad. Who else had access to the information that's been spread? Even the news of the baby.
No one else aside from the three of us knew at HTT. Unless you told Marilyn."

Orson shifted uncomfortably in his chair and puffed
out his cheeks. "Well, I might have told her that I was
looking forward to being a grandfather. She may have
put two and two together from that. And as for linking
you and Kirk together, she's very astute, and someone
would have to be deaf, dumb and blind not to see the way
you two look at each other."

Sally stiffened in shock. They would? She looked over

to Kirk, who appeared equally shocked. He rubbed a hand over his face and leaned forward, elbows on knees.

"Sally, what brought you to this conclusion?"

Of course he wanted proof. As would she in the same position, but somehow it rankled that he was the one asking her, not her father.

"It was a few of the things she said to me over lunch the other day." Sally repeated them for the men. "There was a tone to her voice, a hardness that I hadn't heard in her before. She sounded really fed up. Bitter. Angry. Plus, she was the one to cast doubt on me, telling Dad that I told her I was frustrated with my job—which is not true."

"We'll have to interview her," Kirk said to Orson. "Test the waters without making an outright accusation. We'll need to be careful. We don't want her suing us for defamation."

"Oh, Marilyn wouldn't do that," Orson protested.

"If she's behind the leak of information, then she's already shown she's willing to hurt the company. I tell you what. I'll do a little investigating of my own. Have my forensic specialist delve a little deeper. If she is responsible, she's very, very good at hiding it. It might not be so easy to prove."

Sally fidgeted in her chair. She felt terrible for believing that the culprit could be Marilyn, but if she was their leak, she had to be stopped before she did irreparable damage to the company. Each information release had undermined HTT's integrity just that little bit more. The loss of new business had been felt, and if existing clients began to doubt the safety of their information and started to withdraw from HTT, it wouldn't take long before the company truly began to crumble.

"Should I tell her to take some days off?" Orson asked

Kirk. "She's due for some time, and she's been working long hours lately."

"No, I think that would tip her off that we suspect her. Better to just keep things going as normal."

After a brief discussion about their plan of attack, Sally stood to leave.

"It's late and I'm tired. I'll be heading home unless there's anything else you need me for?"

Kirk stood, too. "I'll take you home. It's time I headed off, too."

"That's not necessary. I have my driver and my guard."

"Please, I'd like to talk."

"I'll tell Jennifer to let your men go," Orson said, getting up and going to the door. "And I'll see you two at work."

He was gone, leaving them alone together. Sally bristled at Kirk's nearness. She grabbed her handbag and headed toward the door, but Kirk beat her to it, holding the door open for her as she went through.

The scent of him tantalized and teased her. Reminding her of what she was missing out on, of what was right there, hers for the taking if she wanted it.

And she did want him. But what she really wanted was more than he seemed willing to give. Love, forever, the whole bundle. And he hadn't offered her that.

"Sally, slow down a sec," Kirk called as she strode out down the corridor to the front door.

He drew level with her, and she gave him a querying look.

"In such a hurry?" he teased, taking her by the arm and making her slow to his more leisurely step.

"I am, actually. I wasn't lying when I said I was tired. I really need to get home."

Kirk looked at her more carefully. In the subdued lighting in the library he'd only seen how beautiful she was, but here, in the main entrance, he became aware of the shadows under her eyes and the strain around her mouth. It brought his protective instincts to the fore and made his gut clench in concern.

"Is everything okay with you, the baby?" he asked.

He'd been so frustrated by her refusal to consider their marriage that in all honesty he'd been avoiding her these past couple of days. Part of him hoped that absence might make her more willing to reconsider his proposal, while another, less calculating part was learning to deal with not getting his own way. It wasn't something he'd had to do often in adulthood, and he found he didn't like it now any more than he had back when he was a powerless child. But he couldn't force Sally to accede to his suggestion, and she had made it very clear that she wouldn't be coaxed, either. Which was all the more frustrating.

Kirk escorted her down the front stairs of the house and held the door to his car open for her. She stopped in her tracks.

"This isn't your usual SUV, is it?"

"Nope. This one's a hybrid."

She turned and looked at him. "Really?"

"How can I expect everyone else to follow your sustainability proposal if I'm not doing it myself?"

He closed the door as she settled in her seat and resisted the urge to punch the air in triumph—he definitely hadn't missed that look of approval on her face. Score one for him, he thought with a private smile as he walked around the back of the vehicle and to his door. As he got in and secured his seat belt, Sally spoke again.

"And the other managers?"

"As their leases come due on their existing vehicles, even good old Silas will be going hybrid or full electric."

"Seriously?"

"No point in being halfhearted about it, is there?"

"And you approach everything in your life full-out like that?"

He caught her eye and hesitated a few seconds before answering. "When I'm permitted."

She looked away.

"Are you sure you're okay? Not overdoing things?" he asked.

"I'm fine. Did you get my schedule of prenatal visits?"

He nodded. He hated this skirting around the subject he really wanted to discuss, so he took the bull by the horns.

"Sally, I wish you'd change your mind about us marrying. I can promise you my full commitment to making it work. To being a good husband and father."

She shook her head slightly. "I thought we agreed to leave this subject where we finished it."

"Actually, no. *You* said the subject was closed. But *I'm* still very open to negotiation." He started the car and put it in gear, driving smoothly up the driveway and through the automatic gates that swung open as he approached. "I miss what we had."

She stiffened beside him. "What we had was a few brief and highly charged sexual encounters. Nothing more than that."

"Really? Is that how you see it? You know more about my background than any other woman I ever dated."

She snorted. "If they know less than me, then I'm sorry for them. I don't even know what your favorite color is. What kind of food you like. Your favorite drink. Your favorite author. We don't know one another at all."

"Blue, Italian, beer and J. K. Rowling."

"Kirk, it's not enough. And not knowing you isn't the only thing. I don't want to marry you. Please respect that."

Silence fell between them. And then Sally giggled.

"What?" he asked, not feeling at all like laughing given her very solid rejection.

"J. K. Rowling? Really?"

He shrugged. "What's wrong with a little fantasy in a man's life? I've done reality every day for thirty-four years. When I read I like to escape into someone else's world."

Sally fell silent again. When he pulled into the parking area at her apartment, she sighed heavily.

"I apologize for laughing. I didn't mean to poke fun at you—it just seems so incongruous. You strike me as more the type to enjoy self-help books, or male action adventure."

"I read those, too. You asked for my favorite author." He shrugged. "I told you."

He got down from the car and opened her door for her before escorting her up to her apartment. She opened the door and turned to him.

"Thank you for driving me home. I'm sorry if I disappointed you again. Good night."

And before he could reply, she was inside her apartment and the door was firmly closed behind her.

Kirk stood there a full minute before spinning on his heel and heading for the elevator. She might think she'd had the last word on the subject of their marriage, but one thing she hadn't yet learned was that, for him, disappointment only served to whet his determination and appetite for success. One way or another, he'd figure out how to break her walls down. He had to, because somewhere along the line she'd become less of a challenge and more of a necessity in his life.

Fourteen

Sally tried to give Marilyn a breezy smile as she arrived at her father's office. She'd never make it as a spy, she told herself. It was all she could do not to break down and beg Marilyn to explain why she'd done it. It had taken a week, but Kirk's specialists had found a trail, well hidden, of the information Marilyn had misused. She and Marilyn had been called to a meeting with Orson and Kirk to discuss what was going to happen next. Sally knew Kirk wanted to press criminal charges, and he had every right to, but she honestly hoped it wouldn't go that far.

"I don't know what this is about, do you?" Marilyn asked her as she quickly smoothed her always immaculate hair and reapplied her lipstick.

"No," Sally lied, not very convincingly. "Have you heard anything?"

"Not me," Marilyn said with pursed lips and a shake of her head. "But then, since Kirk Tanner has come on the scene, I'm the last to find out about anything, even your pregnancy."

Sally stiffened at the veiled snipe and watched as Marilyn fussed and primped in preparation for the meeting. She wondered again how it had come to this. The woman had been a maternal figure to her for as long as she could remember. It was one thing to betray the company, but the betrayal of Orson and his family went far deeper than that. What on earth had driven her from faithful employee to vindictive one?

Marilyn snapped her compact closed and returned it to her handbag, which she locked in the bottom drawer of her desk.

"Right, we'd better go in, then," she said, standing and squaring her shoulders as if she was preparing to face a firing squad. "Ironic, isn't it? That I was your support person not so long ago and now you're mine?"

Sally could only nod and follow Marilyn into her dad's office. Her eyes went first to Kirk, who wore an expression she'd never seen on his face before and, to be honest, hoped never to see again. Anger simmered behind his startling blue eyes, and his lips were drawn in a thin, straight line of disapproval. Orson, too, looked anything but his usual self. The second she saw him, Marilyn rushed forward.

"Orson, are you all right? You look unwell. Are you sure you should be here today? I told you you've come back to work too soon."

Orson stepped back from her. "Marilyn, please. Don't fuss—I'm absolutely fine. Take a seat."

"But surely we can put this off until some other time. You probably should be resting."

"Please, sit!" he said bluntly.

Marilyn looked affronted at his tone, her gaze sliding

from Orson to Kirk and back again before she sniffed to show her disapproval and finally did as Orson had asked. Sally sat in a chair next to her, perched on the edge of her seat. She knotted her fingers together in her lap and kept her gaze fixed on the floor. Orson resumed his position behind his desk and Kirk drew up another chair next to Marilyn and turned slightly to face her.

Once everyone was settled, Orson began.

"We have had some…difficulties…in the past year with losing business to DuBecTec. At first I thought it was just their good luck, especially with their strengths in networking systems, but as it happened more often, I began to suspect that we had a traitor in our midst here who was feeding information about our prospective clients to our competition."

Sally flicked a look at Marilyn, who shifted in her seat but kept her silence. The tension became so thick you could cut it with a knife.

"And it seems that the traitor was quite happy to set Sally up to take the fall for their insidious and, quite frankly, illegal behavior. I could have forgiven a lot, but I cannot, ever, forgive that."

Sally was shocked to hear the break in her father's voice. She hadn't expected him to bring the suspicions of her own conduct into the equation, but to hear him stand up for her like that came as something of a surprise. He'd barely mentioned the accusations against her when she'd returned to work, but now she could see a cold fury simmering beneath his professional facade. She began to feel some sympathy for Marilyn, but that was soon dashed as the older woman began to speak.

"But Sally was cleared, wasn't she? Of course she was. She had nothing to do with it, I knew that all along and so should you!" Marilyn protested.

"That's right, she had nothing to do with it," Kirk said, rising from his chair and moving to stand beside Orson's desk. "But the strain *you* put her under by planting evidence against her was inexcusable."

"What? Wait. Me?" Marilyn's voice rose in incredulity.

"We have proof, Marilyn. We know who our culprit is," Orson said heavily. "What we don't know is…why?"

"I don't know what you're talking about," Marilyn insisted, but her face had paled and small beads of perspiration had formed on her upper lip. She looked toward Sally. "Tell them, my dear. Tell them I could never be involved in something like that. I love this company and I love your fa—"

Her voice cut off before she finished her sentence, as if she'd suddenly realized she'd revealed too much. She slumped back in her chair, her gaze shifting from Orson to Kirk and then Sally before settling back on Orson.

"I have loved you for thirty years, Orson Harrison. And this is how you treat me?"

Orson, too, had paled. "This is about your behavior— not mine," he said gruffly. "And you know there has only ever been one woman for me."

Marilyn laughed, a brittle, bitter sound. "Well, I was good enough for you once, wasn't I?"

"I told you then and I'll tell you now, it was a wretched mistake. I was a grieving man reaching out for comfort, and I never should have put you in that position."

Sally looked at her father in shock. He'd had an affair with Marilyn after her mother's death? How on earth had they continued to work together for so long after that? Had Marilyn's unrequited love been what kept her, day in and day out, at her desk in the hope that one day

Orson Harrison would change his mind? Sally swallowed against the lump that had solidified in her throat.

All her life Marilyn had been there. With no mother to turn to, Marilyn had been the one to explain about the things girls needed to know about their bodies, to talk about what was right and wrong when it came to boys, to take her shopping for her first bra. To dry her tears when her best friend from elementary school moved away or when a high school crush broke her heart.

At every major turning point in her life, Marilyn had been the female perspective she'd needed. Now she was learning that Marilyn had loved Orson for all those years. And yet, despite all of that, despite all those years, she'd been quite happy to let Sally take blame for something she herself had done—even knowing how much that stigma would hurt Sally and Orson.

"I can't believe you were going to let me take the fall for this, Marilyn."

"Oh, please. As if it would have been an issue for you. Your father would never press charges against you. And besides, it's not as if you need the work. You were born with a silver spoon in your mouth. No, it would all have been neatly swept under the carpet and maybe, just maybe, the shock would have been enough for Orson to finally see *me* again. Do you know why he never took our affair any further? Because of you. Because he didn't want you to feel he was replacing your mother. After you freaked out at the funeral, he realized how weak you were. How needy you'd become. So he put me on the back burner."

Orson rose to his feet. "That's not true!"

Marilyn also stood. "Isn't it? It certainly felt like that to me. Do you realize what I've given up for you? Everything, that's what. My youth. My hopes. My dreams for a family of my own. But you didn't care. And when I thought you might finally be coming around, that with the right encouragement you might step away from the business and maybe actually look at retirement with me still there by your side, what do you do? You merge with *him*! The son of the man who almost destroyed this company just as it was getting off the ground!"

She pointed a finger sharply in the air in Kirk's direction. "Even after your heart attack you kept working, when a rational man would have given up. Don't you see? I did all that for you, for us! Can't you understand what it was like for me? How I was looking down the barrel of retirement alone? I gave my life for you, Orson. And in return you gave me nothing."

Kirk stepped forward. "I think you've said enough, Marilyn. You are hereby relieved of your duties at Harrison Tanner Tech. I'm calling security to come and hold you until the police can be called so we can press charges."

"No, wait," Orson said, looking a lot older than he had only short moments ago. "This is my fault."

"Dad, no. It's not," Sally cried, pushing upright out of her chair.

"Honey, I'm man enough to admit my mistakes. I shouldn't have turned to Marilyn for comfort, but I made a much bigger error when I expected there not to be any repercussions. Marilyn, I'm sorry. I should have taken better care of you at the time. I should have found you employment elsewhere instead of continuing to take your loyalty to me for granted."

"Orson, she betrayed everyone here with her actions. She could have destroyed everything," Kirk argued, his hands clenched futilely at his sides.

"But we stopped her in time, didn't we? I don't want

to press charges." Marilyn gasped in shock, and Orson fixed his gaze on her. "Even though they are warranted. What you did threatened not only my family but the families of all the staff here. It was unforgivable."

"I did it for you," Marilyn repeated brokenly.

"No." He shook his head sadly. "You did it for you. But I will right my wrong." He mentioned a sum of money that made even Sally's eyebrows rise a little. "I will offer you that severance on the condition that you leave Washington, never come back and never contact me again. The legal department will draw up a nondisclosure agreement. Upon signing, you will agree to say absolutely nothing about what transpired during any of your time working here. You will never share information about the company, me or my family ever again. Do you understand me?"

Marilyn sank back in her chair and nodded weakly. "You're sending me away?"

"I'm giving you a chance to make a new life, Marilyn. The choice is yours. Take it and rebuild, or stay and face the consequences of what you've done."

Not surprisingly, Marilyn accepted his offer with the scrap of dignity she had left. As she turned to leave the room, she looked at Sally.

"You think it's all about work and making a name for yourself here, but it's not. One day you'll be just like me. Alone."

Sally stood to face her. "No, I won't be like you, Marilyn, because I could never do what you've done to hurt the people who've always supported you."

Kirk escorted Marilyn from the office and requested security to accompany her from the building once she'd removed her personal effects. Anger still roiled through him, unresolved. He didn't agree with Orson's offer, didn't trust Marilyn as far as he could kick her, but he had to abide by the older man's dictates.

Marilyn looked broken as she moved about the outer office, packing her personal mementos. All the fight and fire gone, every one of her years etched deeply into the lines on her face.

So much damage, so much risk—and all for unrequited love? It wasn't as if she'd even done it out of spite or greed. She'd done it to try to force the man she loved to notice her—to stop being the work-driven tycoon he'd always been.

And wasn't he just like that, too? Hadn't he modeled himself on Orson Harrison his whole adult life? Didn't he aspire to enjoy the same success Orson had? But at what cost? After Marilyn had been escorted away, Kirk sighed heavily and returned to Orson's office, his thoughts still whirling. He'd asked Sally to marry him, more than once, without stopping to consider what he was offering her. Oh, sure, he said he wanted to be a hands-on parent—there for his child every step of the way. But had he even once stopped to consider Sally's feelings?

What about *her* needs, her dreams for the future? Had he ever asked her about what she wanted? No, it had all been about him. Him and his desire to be everything his father wasn't. The realization was an unpleasant one.

He'd never considered himself a selfish man—he'd always bestowed that honor on his father, who always put his needs and addictions first. But looking at himself right now, Kirk found his actions wanting. He needed to change. He needed to be a man worthy of a woman like Sally Harrison if he was ever going to win her.

Kirk closed Orson's office door behind him and sat heavily in the chair Marilyn had vacated.

"She's gone?" Orson asked.

He still looked drawn, but beneath his pallor Kirk detected the steely determination that had made Orson the successful man he was. On the other side of the desk, Sally looked shaken, as well, but he saw the same strength in her. He wondered if either father or daughter realized how alike they truly were.

"Yes," Kirk answered. "The legal department is standing by for your instructions."

"Good, good. I'll get to that next. Have you two got a few minutes? We need to talk."

"I'm okay for a while," Sally said. "But if you'd rather, Dad, we can do this later. I know you're upset. I'm pretty stunned myself. I trusted her all my life."

"And I trusted her with mine. It's taught me a painful but valuable lesson. My own lapse in judgment in having that brief affair with Marilyn led her to nurse false hopes that there could one day be more between us. For myself, all I ever felt after that encounter was guilt and disappointment in myself. I guess that's one of the reasons I kept her on here. I felt I needed to make it up to her that I couldn't offer her more." He sighed and shifted a set of papers on the desk in front of him.

"Looking back won't change anything, but we can look forward, and my heart attack was a long overdue wake-up call. I've been reevaluating things, and I believe I am ready to step back and relinquish many of my responsibilities here. I want to be able to enjoy the rest of my life, enjoy my grandchild when he or she comes along. I want to take time to focus on what really matters before it's all taken from me."

"Dad, are you sure? Medically there's no reason—"

"No, medically there is no reason for me not to stay in this saddle for a good many more years yet. The thing is,

I don't want to anymore. And I'm starting to think I don't need to. The company will be in fine hands even if I step back, and you...I suppose part of the reason I stayed was because I felt the need to look out for you. I turned to Marilyn for advice about you once your mother passed away, especially when it became apparent that you were struggling with your phobia. When Marilyn told me not to push you, I didn't. In fact, I didn't ever encourage you to reach your full potential, did I? I could have done a better job in teaching you to reach past your fears, but I deferred to what I believed was her better judgment instead of listening to my own heart as your father. And despite all that, you strove for excellence anyway. Look at you now—head of your own department here and motivating the entire firm to embrace sustainability. You've achieved that by your own hard work, not from any handout from me.

"I know it hasn't been easy for you here. I've heard the rumors that you only got your position because you're my daughter. Despite—or maybe because of—my doing my best to protect you, there are others who've made things difficult for you. And still, you've never quit, never given up."

"I get that from you, Dad. When it comes to tenacity, you're king, right?" Sally smiled, and Kirk felt his gut twist at the bittersweet expression on her face.

Sally's father's words echoed in his head. He'd been just the same, just as determined to try to shelter and protect Sally—to make her decisions for her rather than trust her to make her own. To be her own person.

"I'm very proud of you, Sally, I want you to know that. I'm not just proud of you, the woman, I'm incredibly proud of what you have achieved here. If you were anyone else, I would have been fast-tracking you on a devel-

opment program—pushing you up through the ranks to
senior management. But I obviously had my own preju-
dices when it came to my daughter in the workplace. So,
I want to ask you a question. Do you want to take on the
additional training and responsibilities that come with
escalating your seniority in the company?"

"It's what I've always wanted," Sally said in a strong
voice.

Her blue eyes glowed with excitement, and Kirk began
to see the woman she truly was. Not just the beautiful
blonde who'd turned his head in a bar one night. Not just
the lover who'd tipped his world upside down. And not
the woman who now carried his child. Instead he saw
who she should have been all along. A strong, intelligent
individual who deserved to shine.

"But what about my phobia?" she asked. "Won't that
be a problem?"

"We will find a way to work around it. You're getting better—I'm told your sustainability presentation
was going very well until you fainted." Orson's tone was
teasing and indulgent. "Right, that's decided then. Kirk,
she's going to need support from you in this. Can I rely
on you to be there for her?"

"If it's what Sally wants, then I will be there for her
every way she needs me," Kirk said in a steady voice.

"Good," Orson replied. "Now, if you'd give Sally and
me a moment or two alone? Then perhaps you and I can
meet over lunch to iron out a few changes."

"Sure." Kirk got up to leave and paused at Sally's
side. He resisted the urge to lay a hand on her shoulder.
It wasn't what he'd do with any other colleague, and his
desire to touch her would have to be firmly kept in rein
from now on. "I'll call you this afternoon to schedule
some time to discuss your plan going forward, okay?"

"Thank you," she said with an inclination of her head. "I'll look forward to it."

And yet, as Kirk left the office, he had the distinct impression she looked forward to anything but.

He'd created that resistance between them with his behavior from the very first moment he'd met her. He had a lot of work to do if he hoped to build their relationship to any kind of level where she would let him back in again.

Fifteen

Sally watched her father reorder the papers on his desk again. Clearly, he was uncomfortable with what he was about to say to her. Never hugely demonstrative, to hear him offer the words of pride he'd given her today had been a golden moment for her. For the first time since that awful moment at her mother's funeral when she'd frozen in front of all the mourners, she felt as though she had his attention for all the right reasons.

Orson cleared his throat. "Sally, are you sure you want to follow this leadership track?"

"As I said, Dad, it's what I've always wanted. I just never thought you believed in me enough to suggest it, to be honest."

Sally cringed inwardly at her words. She'd never had this kind of discussion with her father before, but obviously the time for openness between them was long overdue. They'd each always done what was expected of them, without a thought for what either of them really wanted. Orson was right—it was time for change.

"Hmm." Her father nodded, then looked up and pinned her with a look. "What are you going to do about your feelings for Kirk?"

"My what?"

"Don't play coy with me, my girl. It's no use denying it. I might not have been the best father in the world, but I know my daughter. You love him, don't you?"

Sally sat frozen in her chair. She'd pigeonholed her feelings for Kirk as inconvenient at best, especially when it was clear he didn't love her. But had her developing love for Kirk been so painfully obvious? Her father continued.

"I guess what I really want to know is, are you going to act on those feelings, or are you going to let the opportunity for a long and happy married life slide by you because you're too afraid to speak up for what you really want?"

"I'm not afraid. I know what I want, and it begins and ends with this company," she said bravely.

"Are you sure about that? Your mother and I didn't have long enough together. There isn't a day that goes by that I don't think of her and miss her with an ache that never fades. Work gives me something to do—but it's no substitute for her. Don't be like me, honey. Please. You and my grandbaby deserve more than that."

Sally looked at her father in surprise. Were those tears shimmering in his eyes? Surely not. But then, he'd changed since his heart attack. He'd obviously spent time reevaluating his life and found it wanting. He was right, though. She had to give her own and the baby's future careful thought. Obviously she wouldn't block Kirk's access to his child, but marriage? She still wanted to hold out for what she believed marriage to be—a deep commitment to blend the lives of two people who would love each other until their dying breath, and beyond.

She chose her words very carefully. "I have given it a lot of thought, and I reached my decision. I would ask that you respect my choice. I want more than just a marriage and security. Between the trust fund Mom left me and my salary, I'm in the fortunate enough position that I certainly don't need a partner for financial security—even with the baby. But if I'm to consider marrying anyone, I need to be certain that they can provide what I need on an emotional level, and right now I don't think he can."

Orson slumped in his chair, disappointment and acceptance chasing across his features.

"Thank you for being honest with me about how you feel, Dad," Sally continued. "It means more to me than you probably realize to know you care. And I'm sorry it isn't what you wanted to hear, but this is my life and I have to take care of me, too, not just the baby."

She rose and went around to him and wrapped her arms about his shoulders. "I love you, Dad."

"I love you, too, honey."

Sally went back downstairs to her department and shut herself in her office, but she couldn't concentrate on the work in front of her. Her mind was whirling with everything that had happened today. So much to take in. But if her father and Marilyn's example had taught her anything, it was that she shouldn't settle for a relationship that was anything less than what she truly wanted.

She wanted more than just to settle for the sensible option. More for her baby, more for herself. And one day maybe she could have that. Working her way up the ladder, taking more responsibility here at work was all she'd ever wanted careerwise, and now, finally, she was on track to attain that. If she found a truly fulfilling love, then she'd embrace it. If not, she'd be fine without it. She didn't doubt for a minute that she'd be able to balance motherhood and work. Of course it wouldn't be easy, but women around the world combined successful, high-octane careers with parenting. She would make adjustments and she'd cope.

And, with that, Sally was finally completely satisfied with her decision. She would not compromise. She would not marry without a reciprocated love. Despite their chemistry, she and Kirk both deserved more out of a relationship than that. They would successfully co-parent, the way countless others had before them. And even if seeing him every day—being mentored by him—would likely be absolute physical and emotional torture, she would do it rather than compromise on her values.

You couldn't make someone love you—Marilyn was proof of that. All the wishing, hoping or pushing couldn't do it. And living with unrequited love was equivalent to a lifelong sentence of unhappiness.

If she was certain of anything, it was that she deserved so much more than that.

Kirk kept his distance from Sally even though it killed him. Orson had cut his hours back to two and a half days a week, which put a great deal more responsibility on Kirk's plate. Thankfully, he'd been able to hire a new PA, and the woman was a marvel at organization. She also had the uncanny ability to anticipate his needs, which made his life roll a great deal more smoothly.

Without being obvious, Kirk kept a close eye on Sally. She'd quickly settled into a pattern, attending the leadership program mentoring sessions with regularity. Judging by the standard of work she was returning to him, she was spending a lot of hours outside the office on the tasks assigned to her. He was surprised at her tenacity, but then again, didn't her résumé reflect that she'd been tenacious all her life?

She was doing excellent work with the sustainability rollout. It was also being implemented in the other branches of HTT, which meant some travel time for her, both by air and road. He'd heard she was slowly overcoming her speaking issues, too. Granted, the groups she was dealing with were all smaller than here at the head office, but Nick had reported back regularly that she was doing better with each presentation.

He hated it when she was away and had recruited Nick to ensure that she ate regularly and well. The other man had been surprised but had taken it in stride. It meant that when Kirk made his nightly calls to her while Sally traveled, he didn't have to come across like a drill sergeant checking she was taking her vitamins and supplements and getting enough sleep.

Christmas had come and gone. Sally was sixteen weeks pregnant now and had the cutest baby bump. Kirk had bookmarked a website on his laptop that showed him the stages of pregnancy, and he marveled every day at the changes that were happening in Sally's body. The realization that it was his child growing inside her still took his breath away. Their latest prenatal appointment, where they'd heard the baby's heartbeat, had made the pregnancy overwhelmingly and incredibly real and had left him feeling oddly emotional.

He looked at his watch. She should be back home from her New York presentation by now. Her flight had been due in about ninety minutes ago. Would she object to him making a check-in call? Too bad if she did. Suddenly he had the overwhelming urge to hear her voice.

Except when he dialed her apartment, there was no reply. That was odd. He called her cell phone and got an automated message saying her phone was off or out of range. A sick feeling crept through him. He wasn't one to jump to conclusions, but something didn't feel right.

Kirk was just about to call Nick's cell phone when his screen lit up with an incoming call. It was Orson.

"Kirk, it's Sally. She's been taken to the hospital."

A shaft of dread sliced through him, stealing his breath and making his heart hammer in his chest.

"What is it, what's wrong? Is it the baby?"

"I'm not sure, and she's not answering her phone. I just got out of a meeting to find that she'd left me a message saying she'd landed but that her leg was sore and swollen and that Benton was taking her to the hospital to be checked out. A swollen leg after flying, that's not good, is it?"

It wasn't good, not under any circumstances. Along with learning about the growth of the baby, Kirk had been driving himself crazy reading about risks in pregnancy, and he knew that a swollen leg could be indicative of a blood clot.

"Where do they have her?"

"She didn't say. She told me not to worry, but it's kind of difficult not to when you love someone, right?"

Orson's question reverberated through Kirk's mind. Was that what this sudden abject fear was? Love?

"Leave it with me, Orson. I'll see what I can find out and let you know the minute I hear anything."

"Good, thanks. And if she calls me, I'll be sure to tell you."

Kirk called Nick's phone and finally got hold of him, except the man could offer him no help. Sally had apparently been fine when he'd left her at the airport with

Benton. Kirk hung up as quickly as he could and called
the bodyguard, who was in the ER waiting room at the
hospital. The moment Kirk had the details and had shared
them with Orson, he was in his car and on his way to
the hospital.

He released Benton to go home as soon as he arrived,
promising to let the man know Sally's prognosis the moment he heard anything. Then began the struggle to get
some information on Sally's condition. But it appeared
that no amount of coercion, charm or outright badger-
ing would budge the staff. And so began the longest two
hours of his life.

This was far worse than when his mother had died. By
the time her cancer had been diagnosed, it had been too
late for treatment and they'd had a few months to come
to terms with things—as much as anyone came to terms
with impending death. But he'd known and understood
every step of her journey. Had made it his business to.
This, though—it was out of his control, and he found he
didn't like it one bit.

Fear for the baby was one thing, but a possible blood
clot was a serious business and could potentially put Sally's life at risk. The very idea of losing her terrified him.
He'd agreed to abide by her wish not to marry, as much as
he'd hated it, but right now he wished he had pushed her
harder to accept him. Then he'd have the right to know
what was happening, how she was.

He got up and began to pace, but the ER was a busy
place and there was hardly enough room for anything, so
he found a spot against the wall and stared at the double
doors leading to the treatment area and waited. And, as
the hands on the clock on the wall ticked interminably
by, he couldn't help remembering what Orson had said.

She told me not to worry, but it's kind of difficult not to when you love someone, right?

Love. He'd never imagined he'd ever know what true, romantic love was. He'd seen what love had done for his mother and how her affection for his father had slowly been crushed out of her until all that was left was sadness and despair. When he'd created his life plan, he'd known he was prepared to settle for respect and affection in marriage without the soaring highs or devastating lows that so many people experienced on the road to happily-ever-after. He didn't have time for that, didn't need it, didn't want it.

And yet, he wanted Sally. Wanted everything to do with her—to be by her side, to guide her and see her reach her career goals, to watch her become a mother and to traverse the minefields of parenthood together. But most of all, he finally realized, he wanted to love her. He wanted the right to be the one she turned to in times of trouble or in times of joy. He wanted to be the one to fill her heart with happiness, to take her problems and make them go away. He wanted to laugh with her, live with her and love her forever.

Kirk realized he was shaking. The yearning inside him had grown so strong, so overwhelming that tears now pricked at the back of his eyes. He hadn't cried since his mother passed, and then only in the privacy of his own home. But this—it was raw, it was real and he'd never felt so damned helpless in his entire life.

A movement behind the doors caught his attention and he saw Sally being wheeled out by an orderly—a fistful of papers in her hand and a tired smile on her face. A smile that faded away in surprise when she saw him striding toward her.

"Kirk? What are you doing here?"

"I'm here for *you*, Sally," he said, and he'd never meant anything more seriously in his life.

Unfortunately the ER waiting room was not the place for the discussion they desperately needed to have.

She looked a little disconcerted but then nodded. "I'm fine—honestly. I've been cleared to go home."

"Everything's okay?"

"Yes. It was just an overreaction on Benton's part. I mentioned my leg was a bit achy and swollen when he met me at SeaTac, and he insisted on bringing me straight here."

"I'm giving him a bonus. That's exactly what he should have done. You didn't give him grief about that, did you?" he asked as they walked toward the exit.

"I was going to, but then I thought about the traveling I've been doing lately and, to be totally honest, I got scared about what it could have been and was only too happy for someone else to make the decisions for me. But why are you here?"

"Orson called me. He got your message, which was pretty scant on details and left us both worried."

"I should call him," she answered, reaching in her bag for her phone, which she turned on. "Oh, I've got missed calls. Dad—" she scrolled through the list "—and you."

"We were concerned."

Those three words didn't even go halfway to explaining how worried he'd been. They reached the parking area and Kirk helped her into the car and waited, not bothering to start the car yet, as she called her dad to reassure him that everything was okay.

"No, no, I'm fine. I don't need to come to your place. Everything checked out normal—just a bit of fluid retention. No, Dad, it's really nothing to worry about. They did scans and everything."

Eventually she hung up and sighed heavily.

"Tired?" Kirk asked.

"Worn-out."

"Let me take you home. You're sure you don't want to go to your father's? Or my place?"

"What part of 'I'm fine' don't you men seem to understand? Look—" she yanked her discharge papers from her bag and shook them at him "—everything is normal."

But there was a wobble to her voice that struck Kirk straight to his heart. She'd been afraid and alone. He didn't stop to think twice. He simply reached out his arms and closed them around her, pulling her toward him. In the confines of the car it was a challenge to offer her the comfort he knew she needed, but he did his best.

At first she stiffened and began to pull away, but then she sagged into him and he felt her arms reach around his waist.

"I'm so glad you're okay, Sally. Quite frankly, I was terrified for you. I never want to feel that afraid again."

She sniffed, and he loosened his hold so he could grab a bunch of tissues from the glove box. She took them from him and wiped her eyes and blew her nose.

"Thanks. Can we go home now?"

"Sure."

He waited for her to buckle her seat belt before doing the same, and then he drove to her apartment. Once there, he followed her inside.

"Sit down," he instructed. "I'll make you a hot drink."

It was a measure of how tired she was that she didn't protest, just merely offered her thanks. Kirk quickly brewed a cup of chamomile tea and brought it to her. The china cup and saucer felt incongruously delicate in his large hand, a simile for the delicacy of their relationship and how he could all too easily damage it if he didn't use care, he realized.

He sat down with her as she sipped her tea, and when she was finished he put an arm around her, encouraging her to snuggle against him and relax. She felt so right in his arms. Sexual attraction aside, there was something incredibly satisfying about just being with her. And that was a crucial part of getting to know one another that they'd skipped. Maybe if he'd been more restrained, had shown more of his interest in getting to know all of her and not just her body, they'd have stood a better chance.

But now he had something to fight for. He knew, without any doubt, that he'd fallen crazy in love with this incredible, strong woman. He just hadn't let himself see that his feelings went deeper than physical appeal. Hadn't wanted the mess and the clutter in his emotional life that he knew being in love could bring. Today had taught him that he'd been so very wrong.

"Sally?" he asked, wondering if she'd fallen asleep.

"Hmm?" she answered.

"Could I stay tonight?"

She shuffled away from him, and he felt the loss as if a piece of him had been sliced away.

"Stay? Here?"

"I can sleep on the couch. I don't expect…I just need to know you're going to be okay and to be on hand to get you anything you need."

When she started to protest, he put up a hand.

"Seriously, I know you're worn-out with the visit to New York and flying home and having been to the hospital. And if I left you here alone, I wouldn't sleep a wink—I'd be up all night, worrying about you. Let me help you, for both our sakes, okay?"

She stared at him, her blue eyes underlined by shadows of weariness that made him want to do nothing more than swoop her up into his arms and take her to her bed and insist she stay there for the next week. But he didn't even have the right to suggest it.

"Okay, if that's what you want."

"Thank you."

"But why, Kirk? You know I'm okay, don't you? I don't need to be monitored or anything."

"I know. *I* just need to be sure. Today scared me more than I thought it was possible to be. It brought a few truths home to roost."

Sally raised her brows. "Oh?"

"It made me take a good long hard look at myself. At what I want. I meant what I said at the hospital. I'm here for you. And I really wish I had the right to be here for you on a permanent basis."

She sighed and looked away. "Kirk, we've discussed this. I told you I don't want to marry you."

"I know. I've been an idiot. You were right to turn down what I was offering. I thought that all it would take was for us to agree to be a couple, but today taught me that there's so much more than that. Yes, I wanted the dream—the beautiful wife, the perfect child, the career every man envies. But I wasn't prepared to work hard enough for any of that. I wasn't prepared to make myself vulnerable or even admit that I needed anyone else to achieve my goals. To be totally honest, I was prepared to accept something that would look more like a business partnership than a marriage, and it absolutely shames me to admit it."

Sally frowned, looking uncertain. "What are you saying?"

"I'm saying that I didn't believe you needed love, real love, to make a successful marriage. But now I know that for a marriage to really mean something, the people have to truly mean something to each other."

She nodded slowly. "That's my understanding of it, too. I won't settle for less."

"Me either. Standing there in that ER waiting room, knowing I had no right to be there with you, no right to support you the way you deserve to be supported—" His voice cracked, and he rubbed a hand across his face. "Sally, it was the toughest thing I've ever done in my life, and it made me realize something very important."

"And that is?"

"That I love you. I'm not a man who is big on expressing my feelings, but please believe me when I say that today was hell on earth for me. You mean more to me than any person I've ever known. I want to spend the rest of my life proving that to you, if you'll let me."

"And the baby?"

"And the baby, too, of course. But no matter what, I love you—and whether you agree to marry me or not, I always will."

Sally's eyes washed with tears and she looked away. For a moment he thought she was going to turn him down, but then she looked back at him and a tentative smile began to pull at her lips.

"Always?" she asked, her smile broadening.

"Forever. I mean it."

"And I'll continue in the leadership program at work?"

"Of course. You're a valuable member of the team, why wouldn't I want you there?"

"Forever, you say?"

He nodded, holding his breath.

"I couldn't accept your proposal without love, Kirk. My parents had a short but loving marriage. No one deserves less than that. Even you."

He looked at her in confusion. Was she turning him down again? Was she saying she couldn't love him? It would kill a piece of him to accept her decision, but he'd do it if that was what made her happy.

Sally reached out and took his hands in hers. "Thank you for opening up your heart to me tonight. I needed to hear it—needed to know that you had it in you to feel as deeply for me as I feel for you, because I love you, too."

Kirk sucked air into his lungs, barely able to believe the words she'd just said.

"Thank you," he said on a whoosh of air. "You have no idea how happy that makes me."

She nodded and leaned in until her lips were just a whisper away from his. "Me too," she answered before kissing him. She drew away far too quickly and smiled. "There's just one thing I need to ask of you."

"Anything," he hastened to say. "Name it and I'll move heaven and earth to make sure it's yours."

She shrugged and gave him another of those beautiful sweet smiles. "You probably don't have to go that far," she teased.

"What do you want from me?" he asked.

"Will you marry me?"

"I absolutely will," he said and bent to kiss her again.

When they drew apart, Kirk looked at Sally, stunned by the gift she'd bestowed on him. "You won't regret it. I promise to spend the rest of my life making sure you don't."

"As I will, too," she answered solemnly.

For a moment they simply sat there and drank in each other's presence, but then Kirk looked around them. "So, about me sleeping on the couch…"

Sally laughed out loud, a full-throttle belly laugh that immediately had Kirk responding in kind.

"I think we can forget the couch tonight, don't you?" she said, getting to her feet and offering him her hand.

And, as Kirk walked with Sally into her bedroom, he knew that he was the luckiest man on earth. Lucky to have learned the truth about love before it was too late. Lucky to have a child on the way. And most of all, lucky to have this woman in his life.

* * * * *

If you liked this story of pregnancy and passion,
pick up these other novels from
USA TODAY bestselling author
Yvonne Lindsay!

THE CHILD THEY DIDN'T EXPECT
ONE HEIR... OR TWO?
A FATHER'S SECRET
WANTING WHAT SHE CAN'T HAVE

Available now from Mills & Boon Desire!

* * *

And don't miss the next Little Secrets story,
LITTLE SECRETS: SECRETLY PREGNANT,
by Andrea Laurence.
Available October 2017!

MILLS & BOON®

Desire™

PASSIONATE AND DRAMATIC LOVE STORIES